BLUE DEVIL ISLAND

BLUE DEVIL ISLAND

STEPHEN MARK RAINEY

FIVE STAR

An imprint of Thomson Gale, a part of The Thomson Corporation

Detroit • New York • San Francisco • New Haven, Conn. • Waterville, Maine • London

LIBRARY OF CONGRESS CATALOGING-IN-PUBLICATION DATA

Rainey, Stephen Mark.
　　Blue Devil island / Stephen Mark Rainey. — 1st ed.
　　　　p. cm.
　　ISBN-13: 978-1-59414-442-4 (alk. paper)
　　ISBN-10: 1-59414-442-7
　　　1. World War, 1939–1945—Campaigns—Solomon Islands—Fiction. 2.
United States. Navy. Pacific Fleet. Air Force—Fiction. I. Title.
PS3618.A394B58 2007
813'.6—dc22　　　　　　　　　　　　　　　　　　　2006008411

First Edition. First Printing: January 2007.

Published in 2007 in conjunction with Tekno Books and Ed Gorman.

Printed in the United States of America on permanent paper
10 9 8 7 6 5 4 3 2

To all who have sacrificed themselves for this country
and for their brothers.
And to my family, without whom I would be lost.

THE BLUE DEVILS

VF-39 Roster

Pilot Name	Rank	Nickname
Albanese, Michael R.	LT	Mike
Arsenault, Jasper J.	LCDR	Aramis
Asberry, Timothy A.	ENS	Timmy
Bartholomay, Richard M.	ENS	Dick
Bellero, Richard C.	ENS	Rick
Collins, Maximilian T.	LT (JG)	Max
Comeaux, W. Davis	LCDR [XO]	Porthos
Cox, Roger F.	LT (JG)	Rufus
Dillon, Michael R.	ENS	Mike
Gilliam, Edwin S.	ENS	Gummy
Grogan, Daniel B.	ENS	Danny-Boy
Hart, Lewis S.	ENS	Lew
Hazelhurst, Lawrence T.	LT	Lefty
Hedgman, Armfield C.	ENS	Hoagie
Hensley, Emmett R.	ENS	Smitty
Hubbard, Henry G.	LT (JG)	Hank
Kinney, Elmer P.	ENS	Kinney
McCall, Robert G.	LT [Flt Surgeon]	Doc
McLachlan, Drew R.	LCDR [CO]	Athos
Penrow, James L.	LT	Jimmy
Rodriguez, José F.	LT (JG)	José
Staunton, T. Archer	ENS	Archie
Trimble, Charles N.	LT [ACIO]	Chuck
Vickers, William D.	LT (JG)	Willy
Wickliffe, Theodore S.	ENS	Tank
Willis, F. Todd	ENS	Tubby
Woodruff, Donald K.	ENS	Dusty

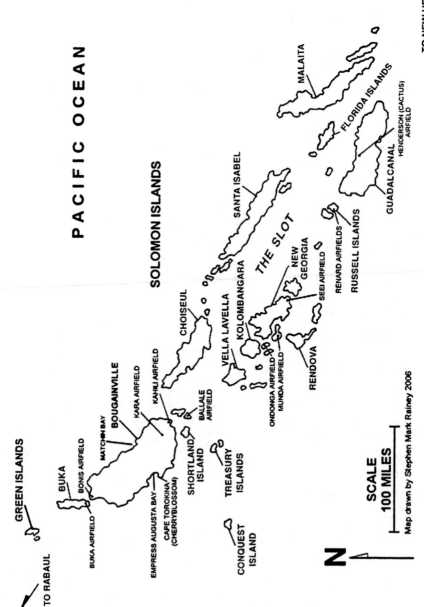

GREEN ISLANDS

TO RABAUL

PACIFIC OCEAN

SOLOMON ISLANDS

BUKA

BUKA AIRFIELD

BONIS AIRFIELD

MATCHIN BAY

BOUGAINVILLE

KARA AIRFIELD

KAHILI AIRFIELD

EMPRESS AUGUSTA BAY

CAPE TOROKINA (CHERRYBLOSSOM)

SHORTLAND ISLAND

BALLALE AIRFIELD

TREASURY ISLANDS

CONQUEST ISLAND

CHOISEUL

VELLA LAVELLA

KOLOMBANGARA

ONDONGA AIRFIELD
MUNDA AIRFIELD

NEW GEORGIA

SEGI AIRFIELD

RENDOVA

RENARD AIRFIELDS

RUSSELL ISLANDS

SANTA ISABEL

THE SLOT

MALAITA

FLORIDA ISLANDS

GUADALCANAL

HENDERSON (CACTUS) AIRFIELD

TO NEW HEBRIDES

N

SCALE
100 MILES

Map drawn by Stephen Mark Rainey 2006

INTRODUCTION

LIEUTENANT COMMANDER
DREW MCLACHLAN, USN

According to official U.S. Navy records, VF-39, or Fighting Squadron 39, was commissioned on March 15, 1945, equipped with Grumman F6F-5 Hellcat fighters, and stationed at Salome Island (now Delap) in the Marshalls until the end of World War II. On September 10, 1945, the squadron was decommissioned, and the VF-39 designation retired.

However, although unsubstantiated by most Navy sources, an earlier fighting squadron actually bore the VF-39 designation; formed in the spring of 1943 at Pensacola, Florida, it served a single, incomplete tour of duty, and was abruptly and quietly decommissioned in November of that same year. Equipped with the then-new F6F-3 Hellcat, the squadron deployed to a small island in the Solomons known only as Conquest, about 180 miles southwest of Bougainville. This region of the south Pacific saw some of the fiercest fighting of the entire war and produced some of history's most renowned fighting squadrons, such as the Jolly Rogers (VF-17), commanded by Tom Blackburn, and the Black Sheep (VMF-214), commanded by Greg "Pappy" Boyington, whose exploits are legendary even now, after more than half a century. Had VF-39's career not been ingloriously terminated—due to events that the Navy refuses to disclose—the Blue Devils, as the squadron came to be known, might have been ranked among the famous.

I was commanding officer of the Fighting 39 from the day I

oversaw its commission until its untimely disbanding, and I can state with the utmost objectivity that no other group of men could have been more professional or more spirited in their service to their country. Sadly, as is always the case in war, many wonderful young men lost their lives during that short but terrible period, and the tragedy is compounded by the fact that many of them died fighting not the Japanese, but an enemy far more insidious and unexpected. Of those who did survive, few have since spoken of those dark days even to each other, much less to the world at large. And as the years continue their inevitable march into the future, all too soon, there will be no one left who experienced what, to many, came to be known as the ultimate horror.

This is the story of a small, courageous group of men facing overwhelming odds, and their struggle with an unknown, unimaginable enemy, the likes of which—if we are fortunate—no human being will ever have to witness again.

CHAPTER 1

Latitude South, 8° 50' 03", Longitude West, 154° 38' 27"
Friday, October 29, 1943
1635 hours

I had never much craved a drink while piloting a fighter plane until the first time I saw the knobby, mist-wreathed crown of Conquest Island, some 10,000 feet below, protruding from the ocean like the bloated carcass of a gigantic, grotesquely deformed whale. My sudden passion for spirits might have stemmed from the realization that, for the next three months or so, I was destined to call this lonely, distant outpost home. Or it might have been the somewhat more sobering knowledge that I stood a better-than-average chance of being killed before shipping back to the States as a happy, retired veteran. Anyway, something about the dark, verdant hump swimming alone in the vast expanse of the south Pacific suggested that it was anything but a hospitable place. Its brilliant, lush vegetation, long sandy beaches, and crystal blue waters lent it a rare, mysterious beauty—the kind one associates with a lovely, poisonous flower.

No, not a whale, I thought. The island more closely resembled the half-submerged, smoking snout of a monstrous dragon lying furtively in wait for unsuspecting victims.

As I studied the area around the broad lagoon at the island's southeastern end, I finally made out the thin gray landing strip, foreshortened so that it resembled an arrow pointing to the island's heart. To my right, my wingman, Lieutenant (JG) Roger "Rufus" Cox, in the cockpit of his sea-blue Hellcat, swiveled his head constantly as his eyes scanned the sky for any sign of attackers. The chances of running into trouble out here were slim, but even a small enemy group with an altitude advantage could wipe us out on our landing approach, when we were at our most vulnerable. Throttling back, I gently pushed over into a 1,500-foot-per-minute descent, listening critically to the deepening thrum of the engine and glancing behind me to confirm that my twenty-three pilots were following me into the landing pattern.

We had maintained radio silence over the last 200 miles of the flight from Henderson Field, Guadalcanal, and would continue to do so all the way down to the runway. The Marine ground support unit, having picked us up on radar, would be ready to receive us, but only after they had confirmed the authenticity of our transmitted friend-or-foe identification signal and their spotters had visually ascertained that we were not a flight of Japs winging in for a surprise attack. As we passed directly over the field at 2,000 feet, I rocked my wings to make sure the antiaircraft gunners on the ground could see the stark white star and navy blue roundel on the underside of my right wing. At least I could credit their eyesight, for no tracers came blazing up to meet us as we set up our approach to the runway.

The R4D Gooney that transported our supplies, non-flying personnel, and several cases of medicinal alcohol went into the groove first. Since our fighters moved much faster than the slow, double-engine transport, we had flown a constant weaving pattern around it for most of the long journey, and my tailbone had gotten abominably sore from sitting on my parachute pack (a condition commonly known as "asserosis"). When the gooney set down safely on the runway, rolled to its end, and turned quickly onto the apron to make way for the rest of us to land, I felt a distinct and welcome sense of relief. My Hellcat, which I had dubbed "Old Grand-Dad" (in honor of the whiskey, yes), was by now desperately thirsty for fuel, and more than anything in the world, I just wanted to get my feet on solid ground, grab a cold beer, and light up a relaxing smoke.

But these little pleasures would have to wait. Once certain the runway was clear, I throttled back to 120 knots, dumped my flaps, cranked down the gear, and aimed my plane at the first 200 feet of runway to set down carrier-style—in other words fast, hard, and impressive. Below me, the ocean quickly gave way to coarse, dark sand and then to thick, spiky sawgrass as, to either side, the tops of tall, spindly coconut palms flashed past at eye level. Then I smoothly closed the throttle, raised the nose, and felt the plane rock gently as the wheels touched down on the ground. A sudden, loud clattering sound erupted from below, and my stomach lurched anxiously until I realized that my Cat was landing on Marston metal matting, which the Seabees had laid to prevent the rains that frequently soaked this region from turning the earthen runway into an unusable quagmire. Quickly recovering my wits, I held the stick steady as the plane slowed; then, when it was safe to use the brakes without risk of nosing over, I pressed the tops of the rudder pedals and rolled my Cat gratefully onto the right-hand apron.

I cut the engine and let go of the yoke, my palm tingling as if I were holding a fistful of bees; when I lifted my feet from the rudder pedals, my knees cracked with the sound of premature rigor mortis, so I grumbled "Brittle Bones" to myself. (Because I was thirty-three at the time—ancient compared to our youngest pilots—someone had coined the epithet for me, though most had the good sense to use it only behind my back. Those who preferred flying to being grounded called me "Skipper" or "Mr. McLachlan" to my face.) Cranking the canopy open, I leaned my aging face out into the brisk island breeze, which was ripe with the tang of salt spray, the sweet, citrus scent of tropical foliage, and the acrid bite of avgas. But before I could even take in my new surroundings, a hunched figure clambered noisily onto the left wing, and a pair of hands reached in to help me unfasten my harnesses.

"Welcome to Conquest, sir," said a youthful voice, and as I tossed aside my shoulder straps, a strong hand took hold of my arm and hoisted me out of my seat. The Marine plane captain wore grease-smudged khakis, thick, dark spectacles, and a broad, sincere-looking smile. He snapped a quick salute and then helped me onto the wing. I pulled off my sweat-soaked flight helmet, only to have my eardrums assailed by the deafening roar of a Pratt & Whitney R-2800 Double Wasp; turning, I saw Cox's Hellcat rolling up next to mine, its prop winding down with a shrill whine. Like all our Cats, Cox's engine cowling bore an evil-looking, devilish visage, painted in stark red, white, and blue—the Fighting 39's official insignia. After making sure my old legs would not collapse beneath me, I dropped onto the earthen apron and watched Lt. (JG) Willy Vickers's Cat touch down on the metal matting at the far end of the field. Behind him, Ensign Timmy Asberry's plane was less than a minute to touchdown. The southeastern sky, far beyond our formations, had begun to turn purple and black. In spring, in this part of the world, cumulus clouds often gathered for the better part of the day and then unleashed torrential rainstorms late in the afternoon. In an hour, this hard-packed apron would likely be an ocean of mud.

I was standing near the northwest end of the runway, facing south toward the lagoon, which hid behind several dense rows of coconut palms. To my left, just beyond the apron, a row of earthen revetments provided some protection for our planes should the enemy attempt to bomb us. Behind me, to the north, the shadowed mountainside loomed precipitously over the field, a natural barrier against enemy attack.

The base complex lay a quarter mile away, in the shadow of a steep, crescent-shaped ridge that grew out of the southern slope of the mountain. Amid thick clusters of trees, I could see the tops of a few tents, a good-sized Quonset hut, and a wood-framed tower with a camouflaged roof. The whole field looked to have been carved right out of the jungle, which minimized its exposure to prying enemy eyes; however, my stomach fluttered a bit at the idea of living with only a thin layer of canvas between me and the unknown denizens of what appeared to be a monumentally dense rain forest.

The Blue Devils were touching down with admirable precision, one every thirty seconds or so, and rolling onto the apron to park, where the plane captains immediately hurried out to attend to the pilots. The rumble of engines, swirling clouds of dust, and hordes of scurrying figures had transformed the silent, lonely-looking field into a noisy, bustling center of activity. From the direction of the revetments, a pair of flight-suited figures came sauntering my way; one of them took a pack of cigarettes from his upper pocket and offered one each to his partner and me. I took the smoke and lit it, savoring the sweet draft.

"Well, Athos," the big man said, pocketing the pack, "you got us here. I was beginning to think you were taking us straight to Japan."

Lieutenant Commander Davis Comeaux, my executive officer, was a broad-shouldered mountain with a jovial smile and the temper of a grizzly bear. We had been friends for over two years, since our early days in VF-3—the fighting squadron aboard the U.S.S. *Lexington*. He had a pair of kills—both Zeros—under his belt. "I'm surprised you were able to keep up, Porthos," I said. "Thought you might be nodding off back there."

"I had Aramis here praying for me." He clapped Jasper Arsenault on the shoulder hard enough to send the smaller man's cigarette flying from his lips. Arsenault rolled his eyes, picked up the butt, and leaned toward Comeaux to blow a cloud of smoke into his face.

"He's lying, Skipper," Arsenault said in his soft, clipped voice. "I only pray for sinners who have a hope of being saved."

"Speaking of hopeless," Comeaux said, pointing toward the next Hellcat coming in to land, "isn't that our new boy?"

I nodded, studying the Cat as it approached. Its pilot, Ensign Elmer Kinney, had only joined us the night before we left San Diego for our long haul across the Pacific—a replacement for Lieutenant Lawrence "Lefty" Hazelhurst, who had been stricken with appendicitis just before shipping out. Lefty had been an experienced flyer and accomplished marksman. Kinney was a scrawny, red-haired lad with a stutter, a faltering manner, and an almost effeminate air that drew more derision than I cared to see from the unit.

"He gets a chance like everyone else," I said. "He's a fair stick, judging by his scores."

"He didn't train with the rest of us," Arsenault said. "Something tells me he won't be able to keep up."

"It's up to you to see that he does. I'm assigning him to your division."

"No!"

"*Ja wohl.*"

Comeaux snorted and winked at Arsenault. "Well, aren't you the admirable Crichton."

An anemic horn honked behind me, and I turned to see a jeep approaching from the direction of the encampment. "Get everyone assembled," I said to Comeaux. "It's going to be dark in a while."

"Roger that," Comeaux said and produced a bosun's

whistle—a valuable antique he had "borrowed" from the CO of his first aviation training unit. He had the grace to employ it sparingly, but at times like this—when he deemed it appropriate—he blew the whistle with the gusto of a little boy hoping to shatter glass.

The jeep, which might have been muddier only if it had been driven through quicksand, pulled up next to my Hellcat with a harsh squealing of brakes. The passenger, a tall, lanky figure wearing a neatly pressed but sweat-stained khaki uniform, disembarked with a groan of effort, as if the heat had sapped most of his energy. His long, angular face bore a distinctly yellowish tint, which meant he had been taking Atabrine to ward off the symptoms of malaria—a trademark of the locale that everyone in the squadron would exhibit soon enough. He gave me a once-over with narrow, appraising eyes before snapping a perfunctory salute. "You must be the squadron CO," he said in a slow voice with a deep southern twang.

"Yes, sir," I said, returning the salute. "Lieutenant Commander Drew McLachlan. Fighting 39, reporting for duty."

He nodded and extended a hand. I took it, half-expecting a damp, clammy grip, but thankfully found it warm, strong, and dry. "Lieutenant Colonel Dan Rooker. Welcome to Conquest."

"Thank you, sir."

"Call me Rook. Everyone else does." He glanced toward the southeastern sky, where the last few planes were lining up to land. "Impressive formation. Many combat veterans in your group?"

"Very few, actually. But a lot of hours' flight time."

"What about you? I understand you were at Coral Sea."

"VF-3, aboard the *Lexington.*"

"Kills?"

"Four."

Rooker nodded. "I was at Henderson before this, with VMF-

121. Most of the personnel here served with the Cactus Air Force support teams."

"You were there in the dark days?" I asked, referring to the closing months of the previous year, when the Marines steadfastly kept the airfield on Guadalcanal (commonly known as "Cactus") operational even while ground forces from both sides waged an obscenely bloody battle all around them.

"That's right. Compared to that, this place is going to be a cakewalk."

"Let's hope so," I said with a chuckle, impressed by Rooker's claim. "But not so comfortable we don't see any action."

"You'll see action. This is a top-notch ground unit. These men maintained the Wildcats at Cactus, so they know the Grumman works inside and out. They'll do just as well with your Hellcats. Now, if your men can make do without you, I'll give you the grand tour."

I pointed to Comeaux, who had mustered the pilots into halfway orderly rows. "That's my XO. He's got everything well in hand."

"Hop in, then."

I climbed into the back of the jeep, nodding a greeting to the driver, a frighteningly young-looking corporal whose nameplate read "Gruber." Once Rooker had settled himself in the passenger seat, the jeep lurched into motion with a distressed groan, and I found myself fervently hoping that the mechanics would treat our planes with more respect than they apparently did the jeep. The harsh environment of a place like this played hell with anything mechanical, and our lives depended on every piece of hardware functioning at 100 percent.

"You from Georgia, Rook?" I asked as the jeep bounced down the rutted trail toward the camp.

"Obvious, is it?"

"My dad's family came from Hapeville. Spent some time there as a kid."

"I'm from Gainesville. Little town northeast of Atlanta."

I nodded. "I know of it."

"You don't sound like you come from anywhere. Where were you raised?"

"Absolutely everywhere," I said with a laugh. "My dad was stationed all over. Norfolk, Chicago, San Diego, Key West. I don't think I was ever in one place more than a year at a time."

"I count myself lucky for having had a stable environment as a child. Otherwise, who knows . . . I might have become a fighter pilot or something."

Rooker didn't crack a smile, but I found his dry manner engaging. Our jeep bounced along the rugged track, which had been cut right through the trees and undergrowth, and the high, leafy canopy all but obscured the late afternoon sun. We passed several rows of tents and a few ramshackle huts obviously built out of local timber and discarded scrap metal, all nestled in the shadows of the verdant rain forest. Understandably, comfort preceded decorum here, for I saw several men gathered near the tents, all wearing nothing but olive-drab shorts and boots, their bodies glistening with sweat and grease. The mechanics' lot, I thought, was not one to envy; they probably worked harder than anyone, without the benefit of glory, such as it was, or even recognition from anyone except the men whose machines they faithfully maintained.

Ahead, I saw the Quonset hut, which, according to Rook, contained his office, the pilots' ready room, a darkroom for developing gun camera films, and the communications center. Next to it, the field control tower, which had been constructed out of teak logs and planks, rose a dozen feet or so above the hut's roof. And just beyond the tower, at the edge of a sand dune that crept up to the treeline, the Stars and Stripes fluttered lazily atop a thirty-foot wooden pole that leaned slightly seaward, as if to ensure that any approaching visitors—whether friendly or unfriendly—couldn't miss seeing it.

"There's a wooden outbuilding behind the hut you can use for your office," Rook said as the jeep groaned to a stop next to the Quonset hut. "The generator's over there, so it might get a bit noisy, but I've got you a couple of fans so you can at least keep cool. And those fans help keep the bugs away. Some of the mosquitoes here are so big you need a howitzer to get rid of them."

I shook my head in distaste. Insects and I had never coexisted amicably at the best of times. Looking past the hut, I saw that the jeep track disappeared into the shadows of the nearby mountainside. Anticipating my question, Rook said, "Fuel depot. There's a large cavern back there. That's where we keep most of the avgas."

"I'd heard there were caves here."

Rook's face shadowed slightly. "I don't much care for them, myself. I'm a tad claustrophobic."

"I didn't think there were any claustrophobic Marines."

He smiled wanly, then pointed toward the southeastern sky, which had turned ominously black. "Don't much like thunderstorms, either. But they come in almost every day, late. Clear morning, cloudy midday, rainy afternoon. These are violent storms. You don't want to be flying when they hit."

"That's good to know."

"Well, come on inside, and I'll show you my place." He clapped the driver on the shoulder. "Get the other jeeps down to the flight line, Pete, so the pilots can ride back."

"Yes, sir," Gruber said, giving me a parting nod before shoving the jeep into gear and driving away, the engine wheezing like a grampus.

"We have five jeeps. They'll be at your disposal for getting back and forth to your planes. Cramped rides, but better than hoofing it." He jerked open the Quonset hut door and motioned for me to follow him in.

The odor of stale cigarette smoke immediately assailed my nostrils, but the interior was ten degrees cooler than the tropical furnace outside. At the moment, only dim daylight filtered in through four small, rectangular windows high in the arched walls. Several rows of uncomfortable-looking, metal folding chairs facing an ancient wooden lectern and a well-used chalkboard occupied the better part of the room. I made a mental note to bring a cushion with me any time I needed to spend more than a few minutes here.

Rook pointed to a door bearing the stenciled label "Communications." "In there's the radioteletype for secure communications with ComAirSols. And our radar monitor."

"Where's your antenna set up?"

"A couple of hundred yards east, on an outcropping off the ridge. Gives us good coverage of the area."

"What's your range?"

"Forty miles max."

"Not much warning time."

He shrugged. "Nope. But it's the best we can swing. We'd need a more powerful station to do any better. And out here, chances are we'll never see anything on it other than y'all."

It was true that the Japanese were not likely to devote any resources to attacking our outpost. From their point of view, we were too remote and strategically insignificant to risk an offensive—assuming they even learned of our presence here. Still, having learned early on to expect the worst, I could scarcely count on Conquest remaining beyond the enemy's scrutiny for long.

"Here's home," Rook said, ushering me through another door that led to his cluttered, cramped office. It had one window, open but screened, with a small rotating fan in front of it that stirred the humid air just enough to cool the sweat on the back of my neck. An oversized wooden desk had been either manhandled or assembled in here and shoved at an angle into one corner so that it faced the door. Stepping behind it, Rook opened a drawer and withdrew a bottle of scotch and two tumblers. "Want a belt?"

"I'd love a belt."

"I hoarded away a few cases when I came here," he said, opening the bottle and pouring the two tumblers impolitely full. "Just in case of emergency, you understand. Good drink is hard to come by out here."

I wasn't sure I should mention the beer we had brought with us. Thirsty Marines had a tendency to take what they wanted with the same devotion to purpose with which they engaged the enemy. The odds would not favor a bunch of Navy pilots if Rooker's men took to coveting our property. News of the goods would get around as soon as the first pilot produced a church key, so I said nothing and accepted the glass that Rook handed to me. The welcome burn of scotch on my tongue took my mind off the external heat almost at once.

"Hope you don't mind it straight up. Ice here is as rare as a blond bombshell."

"Thanks."

He nodded, then waved for me to follow him again. "Your office is over here. It's about the same size as mine, but you get hardwood floors." He led the way through the rear door and out to a wooden shack adjoining the hut. It was small, all right, but solidly built, with a thick post frame and a dense, thatched roof. A pair of coconut palms leaned protectively over it, their fronds waving slowly like fans wielded by lethargic court slaves. Beyond the small building, the rain forest rose like a towering monster, its impenetrable depths full of chattering, screeching sound. I again found myself somewhat unnerved by the prospect of occupying quarters so close to potentially hostile wildlife.

"You get used to it quickly," Rook said, his tone not altogether convincing. "But you don't want to go walking in the jungle alone. The critters tend to leave us be if we don't bother them. I don't recommend going looking to make their acquaintance."

"Not a problem," I said, gazing warily into the shadowy trees and at the steep, boulder-strewn ridge rising directly above us. Beyond the crest of the ridge, the mountaintop stared down at us broodingly. Its dark mass looked more oppressive than it had from the air—even menacing, as if it were aware of our presence and disapproved of it. Happy to escape its baleful glare, I followed Rook into the little wooden building, finding it almost pleasantly cool inside. Two small rotating fans kept the air constantly circulating, and I noted with both satisfaction and some trepidation that mosquito netting barricaded the windows.

"You'll want to keep your door closed all the time, or you'll be spending more time shooting down bugs than Japanese."

I chuckled, looking around at the pristine desk (much smaller than Rook's), shelves, and file cabinets that awaited the arrival of my effects. To my surprise, I found I had been provided with an old but apparently functional Brother typewriter—a commodity many a squadron CO would kill for, since it dramatically eased the burden of paperwork, which I despised almost as much as insects. Rook chuckled at my reaction.

"I wrangled a couple of these when we shipped out. General Moore owed me a favor. One day I'll remember what for."

I nodded in amusement. General Moore would have no idea where his typewriters had gone or who had absconded with them. Satisfied that my new space for doing business proved adequate, I downed the last of my drink and accompanied Rook back outside.

"My ACIO and I will be going over our mission orders

tonight," I said. "We'll be going up before dawn. I trust our planes will be gassed up and ready."

"I'd wager half of them are combat-ready as we speak. And the rest will be well before lights-out."

"Show-off."

"So, how did you come by the name Blue Devils? You're not from Duke."

"One of our guys, Lefty Hazelhurst. The one we just had to replace. Anyway, he's a naturalized Brit, and back in training, he always used to call us a bunch of 'bloody blue devils.' So the name stuck. And we have Lieutenant Rodriguez to thank for our nose art. He's an almost-reformed graffiti artist."

Rooker's lips tightened in a thin smile. "Well," he said, pointing to a long row of dull olive-colored tents just beyond the control tower, "those are your men's quarters. Three to a tent. You can bunk with them, or I can have a cot put in your office, if you prefer."

"No, I'll bunk with my XO and gunnery officer. We shared quarters on the *Lexington,* so we're used to each other."

Rook nodded. "Suit yourself. By the way—the tents are elevated on wooden tiers. Now and again, though, critters you won't like get up through the floor. Some of the guys put the legs of their cots in bowls of water to keep the bugs from climbing up for a visit. It's something to think about."

"I'll say," I said with a little shudder. The idea of sharing a bed with crawlies disturbed me far more than dogfighting an enemy ace. Making a mental note to remember to build moats at the first opportunity, I glanced at my watch to find that it was past 1730 hours. "So, is there a decent restaurant on this island? Most of us haven't eaten anything since this morning."

"Yeah, we're running a bit late on chow since your arrival. Should be ready in a half-hour or so. I gotta warn you, it won't be what you carrier guys are used to. Most of our grub's Navy surplus. But some of the more enterprising fellows gather fresh coconuts and papayas for variety. And we had some local saltwater croc a few nights ago. Clarence—he's our cook—knows a few tricks."

"There are crocodiles here?"

Rook pointed to the northeast, beyond the Quonset hut. "There's some marshland back over that way. Good many crocs in there. Big ones. That's an area to avoid unless you're specifically going hunting. And nobody goes there without at least one buddy. That's a standing order."

"No argument from me."

"There's also some jungle fowl that makes for fine eating if you can find it. Gallus gallus is reasonably tasty."

"What's that?"

"Wild chicken."

"Okay."

"You have to prepare your own, though. Clarence doesn't do special orders unless it's enough to feed everyone."

"Sound policy."

A new, gravelly voice said, "He thinks so."

I turned to see a stocky, muscular man with a long scar down the left side of his face grinning at me around a stubby cigar. He wore sweat-stained combat fatigues with major's clusters on the collars. Rooker said, "Lieutenant Commander McLachlan, meet Major Bernard Pearce, my XO. Mr. Pearce, Mr. McLachlan."

"Call me Bernie. Welcome, sir." He extended his hand and clasped mine in an iron grip.

I tried not to grimace. "Thanks."

I heard a distant, rough rumbling sound, and a few moments later, a couple of jeeps loaded with Blue Devils jolted up the road from the direction of the field. Ted "Tank" Wickliffe and Danny-Boy Grogan, riding in the first jeep, each had a case of beer slung beneath one arm. So much for secrets.

"Those gentlemen will be popular tonight," Pearce said. "You got any more of that?"

"A bit," I said with judicious terseness. "Something tells me it's not likely to last long."

Rooker smiled. "Well, apart from my scotch, we have a small supply of liquor—but only enough for special occasions. Now, speaking of which, here's what we propose to offer—in the name of goodwill to our buddies in the Navy. Any pilot that shoots down a Jap gets a bottle. He can keep it or share it, that's strictly up to him. Any man who makes ace gets two bottles."

"I like it."

"On the other hand, any man that cracks up a plane and lives to tell about it owes his plane captain half a case of your beer. It's only fair."

"Deal."

The rest of the jeeps came bouncing up the track with engines that sounded like drumsticks on metal. The pilots dismounted, and a moment later, Comeaux strode into view, still holding his bosun's whistle. Blowing a shrill blast, he herded the men into a pair of semi-neat rows in front of the Quonset hut, each pilot dumping whatever he was carrying at his feet. Arsenault drifted lazily up from the rear, puffing on a cigarette, looking dapper and authoritative, even in his rumpled flight suit. He settled himself at the far end of the first row and cocked his head with eyes half-closed and a blissful little smile on his lips, giving the impression he anticipated nothing less than a revelation from the Almighty Himself.

While no superior had ever accused me of being lax, I had never been a stickler for strict military discipline, especially in a frontline environment. But I did expect that, whenever I spoke, all ears would be attentive and that any order I gave would be followed to the letter. Almost to a man, the Blue Devils tended to be aggressive, impetuous, and sometimes outspoken; but to their credit, each of them always exhibited the courtesy and respect due a commanding officer. As I stepped in front of them and looked over their ranks, all mouths closed and eyes turned either impassively straight ahead or inquisitively to me.

"Gentlemen, welcome to Conquest Island. This is our home for the next few months, so let's do everything we can to impress upon our friends the Marines that Navy pilots are indeed the superior form of primate." Behind me, Rook and Pearce snickered in unison. "Now, as you can see, we will be not be living in the lap of luxury. There will be three men per tent; you're free to choose your own tentmates. We'll address any questions you have regarding living arrangements later.

"As you're all aware, we're here to fly combat missions. And we start tomorrow morning. Briefing will be at 0600. Lieutenant Trimble and I will draw up the roster tonight. I want everyone to get a good night's sleep, so we're going to square away our gear and hit the sack early. I know everybody's probably hungry. Chow is coming up in a few minutes. I'm told it's not gourmet cooking." A couple of exaggerated groans came from the ranks. "Now, the gentleman behind me is Lieutenant Colonel Rooker, USMC. He's the CO of our ground support unit. I've been assured we have the best mechanics in the Pacific looking after our planes. A lot of them, including Colonel Rooker himself, served at Guadalcanal during the dark days."

That was all I needed to make sure every ear was tuned in. An air of solemnity as thick as smoke settled over the men.

"Fellows, the one thing I've stressed to you over the last few months is teamwork. Each of you has the responsibility for not only getting your job done but for watching over your wingmates. I'd like to be able to tell you that every one of us is going to make ace and go home safe and sound after it's all over. You all know I can't do that. What I can tell you is that we've got the best training and the best machines possible for the job. I know I can count on each of you to give your utmost. I expect no less, and I know you all expect the same from each other.

"Now, I'm going to let Colonel Rooker say a few words and then we'll go claim our tents."

I stepped aside and Rook took my place, giving the men a long, thoughtful stare. "On behalf of VMF-264, I'll say welcome to you," he said in a voice barely loud enough for all to hear. "Most of you probably haven't lived under these conditions before. I've been here for about a month, and as Commander McLachlan said, I've had experience in these islands for some time, as have most of my men. We'll be ready to give you any and all assistance to get your job done. Rest assured that your planes are going have the best care they can get this side of the States. If you have questions about procedures or conditions here, please remember the chain of command, but by all means ask. There are hazards to be aware of quite apart from the threat of Nips. We'll cover some of these in detail before lights-out tonight.

"As for your accommodations, what you see is what you get. The nearest row of tents is for you pilots. The ones farther down, well, that's Marine City. Go there at your own risk. Now. Notice there's mosquito netting over everything. There's a good reason for this. You'll start taking Atabrine immediately in case you get malaria. It's going to be hot here, all the time, day and night. You'll be glad to know there's a waterfall right on the edge of the camp where you can get a freshwater shower. But don't go wandering beyond the watering hole. There's dangerous critters in the jungle, and we don't like to antagonize them needlessly.

"For field defense, we have radar and .50-caliber and 20-millimeter ack-acks around the perimeter. We don't anticipate air raids, but you'd be wise to dig yourself a foxhole close to your tent. I'm going to be mighty sore at any man who gets himself killed without good reason.

"Well, that's the main of it, for now. I'll give you back your CO. Chow's in fifteen."

I nodded my thanks to Rook and then said, "Any questions, gentlemen? No? All right then. Get your asses in gear and claim your quarters. Don't be late getting back here or you miss your vittles. Dismissed."

Just as the men began to disperse, a brilliant flash of electric light splashed across the sky, followed by a sharp crack that quickly lowered to a rolling boom: a heavy, thudding vibration that crawled like a horde of ants through my Brogan boots and up my shins. A distant patter of water on leaves began like the percussion of a Benny Goodman opus, and seconds later, raindrops the size of quarters began to pummel the encampment with the intensity of mortar fire. But the water was cold and, apart from the ferocious impact, felt like a welcome gift from the heavens. Looking up, I could see the remaining daylight disappearing behind huge, billowy clouds the color of India ink, the bases of which were low enough to smother the summit of the mountain. Somehow, the cloudburst seemed a dark omen, as if it portended a much bigger, more furious assault on us that would have devastating consequences.

A silly notion, I thought as I started toward the jeeps, which had arrived with our matériel from the transport gooney, and I dismissed the unseemly feeling as a product of anxiety. But a second later, a sudden tug on my sleeve startled me so that I spun around with fists balled and ready to swing.

To my surprise, I saw the diminutive, redheaded Ensign Elmer Kinney standing before me with a look of surprise on his round, chalk-hued face. I dropped my hands immediately and gave the young man a curious look. "What is it, Ensign?"

"Sorry, sir," he said in his reedlike voice. "You must not have heard me. I spoke to you twice."

"No, I didn't. I apologize."

"I didn't mean to startle you, sir."

"What is it?"

"I wanted to know if everyone has to bunk three men to a tent."

"That's the situation," I replied. "Space is at a premium here."

He looked crestfallen, but nodded. "I see. I figured, but I just wanted to ask."

"You have a problem with that, Mr. Kinney?"

He said quickly, "No, sir, not a problem. Most of the guys, well, I think they'd rather share tents with their regular buddies."

"Look, Kinney, I know you're new here, but you're going to have to depend on these men and they have to depend on you. It can't hurt you to bunk with a couple of them."

"I'll make do, sir."

"Tell you what. Go find Lieutenant Collins and tell him I said you're bunking with him."

"Yes, sir."

Kinney started to walk off, still looking not at all happy. I called after him, "Mr. Kinney."

"Sir?"

"For God's sake, stop calling me 'sir.' 'Skipper' will do just fine."

"Yes, sir—umm . . ."

And that was that. The young man went off to claim his bed. A few moments later, I saw Comeaux heading my way, offering me a broad, if somewhat forced grin. "Athos, you look edgy," he said.

"Ah, Porthos. This is an unusual place to call home."

His grin faded and his eyes took on an uncustomary grimness. "Not a hot spot for tourists, is it?"

"It certainly isn't."

"That boy is an odd one," he said, pointing after the small, retreating figure. "He gonna be all right?"

I shrugged. "He's got a lot of hours in the Cat, and he handled the formations fine. I reckon he'll do okay."

"You don't sound optimistic."

"Are you?"

Comeaux chuckled. "I'm the picture of optimism."

"That's because you're a moron."

"I can live with that."

I smiled in spite of myself, and for a few long, silent moments, we peered at the mountain as a bank of purple clouds rolled slowly across its face. A violent gust of wind swept over the mountainside, setting the treetops into rhythmic, undulating motion toward us. But by the time the current's leading edge reached us, the forest had broken it up, and the breeze brushed across our faces almost unnoticeably. A heavy raindrop slapped my cheek like a belligerent palm.

"It almost feels alive, don't it?" Comeaux said, surprisingly echoing my earlier sentiment, his eyes riveted on the mountainside. Then he glanced sharply at me. "This island is uninhabited, isn't it?"

"So they say. But I'll tell you something. The hills around the airfield at Espiritu Santo are full of headhunters," I said, referring to our main supply base for the southeastern Pacific. "Did you know that?"

"No, I didn't."

"It's true. So far, I don't think anyone's ended up in a stew, but it gives one pause to think."

"Thanks for that cheery thought."

"I might have more."

We started walking toward the jeeps, finally beginning to feel battered by the downpour. Several Marines were unloading duffel bags and crates from the jeeps, and I didn't relish the idea of having to search for mine among the lot, but then I saw a figure doggedly shambling our way under the weight of three heavy canvas bags.

"You heathens need to learn to travel light," Arsenault said as he dropped two of the bags at our feet. He straightened and haughtily turned his nose to the sky. "Now, take up your burdens and follow me. While you two were lounging around, I have claimed us a tent."

"Do you suppose there is anyone to whom Aramis doesn't consider himself morally superior?" Comeaux asked. "I bet he could find fault with the Pope."

"The Pope is God's infallible emissary," Arsenault said, his face solemn. "However, his barber does him little credit."

Suitably humbled, Comeaux and I fell in behind Arsenault, who led us through the trees to one of the tents nearest the Quonset hut.

"Looks like Tobacco Road," Comeaux said, nonplused.

"Well, we have number one," Arsenault replied.

Our bags were only marginally waterproof, so I expected that most of my clothes would be damp, if not waterlogged. Just as Arsenault pulled back the flap of our tent, the rain stopped as suddenly as it had begun and, above, the sun appeared amid the dark clouds and fought its way through the canopy. Somewhere nearby, a loud, shrill screech ripped through the jungle like a mortar shell—some variety of local fowl voicing its jubilation over the clearing of the weather.

I half expected to find the inside of the tent damp and steamy, but much to my relief, it was dry and no warmer than the air outside. Three narrow cots awaited us, one on each side of the tent, each with a sheet, blanket, and bundle of mosquito netting folded at one end. A wooden crate turned on one end in the center of the floor made for a usable table, and a single lantern hung from a canvas loop above it. In one corner, there was a chipboard armoire where we could hang our clothing. Like all military quarters, no matter the form they took, the tent smelled of mothballs. As Rook had indicated, the planked floor was raised several inches above the ground to keep the tent from flooding during heavy rains. However, this made for the strong probability of undesirables taking up residence beneath the floor, so I decided I'd better do some serious stomping whenever I came in to scare away potential squatters.

Fortunately, my clothes were only slightly soaked. The tent was certainly small and cramped, but not much worse than the quarters we had shared aboard the *Tarrytown*. My tentmates were old familiars, and so far, none of us had ever attempted homicide. Besides, I thought, if one or both of them became unbearable, I would take Rook's suggestion and move my bunk to my office next to the Quonset hut. And stick them with Ensign Kinney.

We unpacked in silence, for as our nervous energy from the flight abated, our minds turned to the profound gravity of the duty we were expected to carry out over the next few months. We were out here to kill or be killed. Immediately after chow, Comeaux and I would be meeting with Lieutenant Chuck Trimble—my Air Combat Intelligence Officer—to finalize the mission plan for the following day. Most of the men who would be taking off in their Hellcats tomorrow had never faced an enemy in combat and were even now likely to be contemplating their own mortality; even those of us who were already blooded could scarcely go up without wondering if this were to be the mission from which we would never return.

By far the heaviest weight upon me was the knowledge that, if we were successful in our efforts to engage the enemy, a certain number of us would never see our loved ones again, and would probably meet our Maker only after experiencing the most hideous suffering any human being could possibly imagine.

CHAPTER 2

Saturday, October 30, 1943
0600 hours
The Solomons can best be described as parallel chains of islands running roughly northwest/southeast, approximately a thousand miles from end to end, extending from New Ireland in the north almost to the New Hebrides in the south. The major islands in the southwestern chain include Bougainville (the largest of the group), Vella Lavella, Kolombangara, New Georgia, the Russells, Guadalcanal, and Rennell; the northeastern chain includes Choiseul, Santa Isabel, Tulagi, Malaita, and San Cristobal. The channel between the chains was adroitly named "The Slot," and the Japanese, undaunted by strong Allied resistance, still moved extensively up and down this passage by sea and air.

Two flights, or sixteen men and planes, were scheduled to fly our first mission, but I had ordered all twenty-four pilots to report to the first briefing. To a man, they arrived early at the ready room, each pilot eager to learn if he would be included in our first combat air patrol. As I watched them file in and anxiously scan the roster I had scribbled on the chalkboard, I could see the excitement and thinly disguised fear in the faces of those who would be going, and the disappointment and relief of those who would not. However, as they all knew, those who did not fly today would take part in tomorrow's mission.

The chalkboard displayed the following:

35

KAHILI CAP
10/30/43

Blue Flight:

01: McLachlan	22: Penrow
08: Cox	10: Gilliam
02: Vickers	15: Wickliffe
21: Rodriguez	18: Bellero

Red Flight:

03: Arsenault	09: Collins
23: Grogan	20: Dillon
13: Staunton	24: Hart
19: Hedgman	12: Kinney

Alternates: Hensley, Bartholomay, Willis, Asberry

Speed + Altitude = Life

On the wall next to the chalkboard, I had pinned a large map of the Solomons. Chuck Trimble came in carrying a cup of coffee and joined me at the lectern, facing the men. He was near my age, shorter but considerably huskier than I, with close-cropped hair already going gray and deep creases in his prodigious brow. His pale blue eyes peered out from a maze of tiny laugh lines, and one corner of his mouth was bent in a perpetual little smirk. He had never sat at the controls of a plane, but he could plot a course through blinding weather; estimate fuel consumption based on mileage, airspeed, and altitude down to a gallon; and calculate the duration of a flight over a given distance to the minute. In unfamiliar territory, a pilot needed the most accurate information possible, and Trimble could juggle variables like no one else I had ever met.

An almost funereal silence permeated the room as the men entered and took their seats. Each pilot was already wearing his flight suit and decked out with all his gear except his parachute. Training briefings routinely began with crude jokes and occasional horseplay, but there was none of that now. I was pleased to see Colonel Rooker and Major Pearce come through the door and take positions at the back of the room.

"Gentlemen," I began. "Three days ago, a brigade of the Third New Zealand Division landed on the Treasury Islands—here, about fifty miles south of Bougainville." I pointed to a tiny pair of islands on the map with a baton made from a reed I had pulled out of the jungle. "Resistance has been minimal, but the landing site is within easy reach of the Japanese airfields at Kahili, Kara, and Ballale . . . here on the southeastern end of Bougainville. The enemy's main forces have been pushed northward in the past few weeks, but there are still sufficient contingents at these bases to threaten the Anzac brigade. We will fly a CAP today to ensure that no Japanese patrols pester the troops while they're occupied on the ground.

"We'll be taking two flights, with Blue Flight on station from 0730 to 0930 and Red Flight on from 0930 to 1130, when we'll be relieved by VF-17 out of Ondonga. Our run up will be at two hundred knots and we'll fly a ten-by-three-mile racetrack oval over the target at twenty thousand feet. If we make no contacts during the patrol, we have been authorized to make strafing runs on ground targets of opportunity."

Now a chorus of excited murmurs filled the ready room. Once the noise settled somewhat, I continued. "Take note of the reminder on the bottom of the board. In the event you encounter enemy fighters, do not press an attack if you don't have an altitude and speed advantage. Your F6F is maneuverable as hell, but a Zeke or Oscar will out-turn you in a low-speed dogfight. Do not try to turn with it, or you *will* die. Whenever possible, attempt a high side run with the sun behind you. If you don't make a kill on the first pass, don't get greedy and start playing around with him. Use your speed advantage to regain altitude.

"Wingmen, stay with your section leaders. I don't want anyone getting combat-happy and breaking off on his own. The Japs have traditionally flown three-plane divisions, but lately some of them have wised up and started using four-plane divisions, which will make it tougher to gain an advantage. What we know about the Japs is that they have some first-class pilots, but their team strategies are inferior. This is where we have the advantage."

All eyes and ears hung expectantly on my every word. My own pulse had begun to race as anticipation spread through the room like a contagion.

"This is what all our training has been about, so I don't expect any screw-ups. If you get hurt, you're nearly two hundred miles from home. You can head southeast to Munda or Ondonga if you're in bad trouble, but you may end up stuck there for a while if your plane's not flyable. Now, this is for both section leaders and wingmen: if one of you is hurt, the other stays with him, no matter what. I don't want anyone alone up there. Getting separated is the quickest way to get bounced."

Near the back of the room, a hand went up; it belonged to Ensign Armfield Hedgman, the number four man of Red Flight. With a name like that, it was no wonder he preferred to go by Hoagie. "Yeah, Hoag?"

"I've heard the Marines saying that the Japs are on the run from all the southern Bougainville bases. You really think there's a chance they'll send up any patrols?"

"Believe me, they've still got plenty of fight left. A lot of our best pilots have had the wind kicked out of them at Kahili."

The young blond shook his head. "It just sounds like a milk run to me."

I was glad to see these guys ready to fight, but the young

ones who had yet to face a Jap might find themselves rudely awakened. "You won't be bored out here, if that's what you're worried about. Now, I'm going to give the briefing over to Chuck, then we'll head to our planes. Good luck, everyone."

I stepped down from the lectern and Trimble took over to give the pilots the crucial weather information, radio frequencies, call signs, and navigational data. Each man had a small kneeboard on which he wrote down all the stats for easy reference while in the air. As Trimble began to address the pilots, I noticed a low, mechanical rumble outside the hut, soon growing louder and deeper. The Marine plane captains had begun starting up the Hellcats. Almost immediately, I felt that same cold fist of terror and ecstasy as when the engine of my old Wildcat had fired to life for my first combat mission aboard the *Lexington*. Even now, countless flights and several kills later, the thrill of anticipation had changed very little.

I found myself—almost unconsciously—offering a little prayer that on my first combat mission as squadron CO, I would fail neither my pilots nor the men who had entrusted me with this task. More than anything, I hoped that each of us would see the sunset over Conquest Island this evening.

As Trimble finished his presentation, I took my place again at the lectern and asked if there were any further questions. A tentative hand near the back of the room went up, and I saw the pale, pinched face of Ensign Kinney turned my way. "Yes, Mr. Kinney?"

His voice was barely audible. "Sir, just how many enemy planes are we likely to find at Kahili?"

All eyes had shifted to regard the young man, and all of them radiated disdain. I did not like this reaction.

"Our intelligence indicates something in the neighborhood of forty fighters," I replied. It was a legitimate question, for in the past few months, many a bold pilot had turned back to base before reaching the target with what had become known as "Kahili knock"—the sound of a rough-running engine, usually a product of shattered nerves rather than mechanical problems.

"If I may," Rook said, stepping forward into the midst of the men. "A week ago, Major Greg Boyington of VMF-214 led a group over Kahili and had to taunt the enemy on the radio to get them to launch any fighters. Then his flight swooped in and took out a mess of them, with practically no casualties. Like shooting ducks in a pond. Of course," he added with a little grin, "these were *Marines.*"

This had just the desired response. Faces lit up and a low chorus of chatter rose in protest. I saw Comeaux pound a fist into his palm.

"Marines. We'll show the Marines," he said, his pugnacious grin twice its normal span. "Marine pilots are a bunch of barnstormers that somebody with a lousy sense of humor handed fighter planes."

I had to chuckle. "Okay, Porthos, we're going to hold you to your word. But you don't fly till tomorrow." A smattering of laughter followed. "Now, are there any other questions?"

As the noise died down, one more hand went up. It belonged to Lieutenant Max Collins, a bright young fellow with longer-than-regulation brown hair and stark blue eyes who came from a small fishing village on the Maine coast; his distinctive accent had prompted our southern Colonel Rooker to good-naturedly call him a "fuckin' Yankee wharf rat"—not quite far enough behind Collins's back to go unnoticed. "Yeah, Max?"

"I hear the Marines owe a bottle to anyone who shoots down a Jap, and two bottles to whoever makes ace. Is that right?"

"So they tell me," I said noncommittally.

"Colonel Rooker," he said with a smirk, "you'd better pull out a case!"

There was no nervousness in the laughter now. But the moment I raised my voice and said, "All right. Let's mount up," the laughter trailed away.

I handed my reed baton to Trimble and clapped him on the shoulder. "Good work, Chuck. I reckon I'll see you for lunch. We'll have a beer."

"To be sure," he said with a smile. "Good hunting."

"Thanks."

As I started out after the men, Rook gave me a parting smile as well. "Show us Marines up, will you? Nobody here will much mind."

"Count on it."

Outside, a few brilliant stars still speckled the midnight blue sky, though a pale golden glow had begun to color the eastern horizon like a watercolor wash. A pleasant ocean breeze swept gently over the beach and through the camp, for one brief moment bringing to mind images of happy days from my youth in Hawaii. I made my way through the dark morning to the waiting jeeps and climbed into the back of the first one rather than taking my customary place next to the driver. I could vaguely make out the faces of Rufus Cox; Jimmy Penrow, the second division leader; and Eddie "Gummy" Gilliam—so named because of his missing front teeth—who slid behind the wheel. They said, "Morning, Skipper," in unison, and I replied with a terse, "Let's do it."

The overweight jeep bounced and sloshed mercilessly down the muddy track toward the revetments, and more than once, one or more of us felt the impact of a sharp elbow or shoulder. As we approached the line, I saw a pair of fuel trucks pulling away and several Marine crewmen scurrying back and forth among the planes. The smell of avgas had replaced the tang of salt in the air, and the roar of Pratt & Whitney engines thundered above the grinding of the jeep motor. The tableau was almost surreal, yet the scene was like so many I had experienced during my months with VF-3 aboard the *Lexington*. Here, only the surroundings were different.

In its revetment, my Hellcat rumbled with barely restrained power, as if bucking to take off on its own. As I hopped out of the jeep and strode toward my mount, the plane captain, a young fellow named Shaw, came out to meet me carrying my parachute pack. "Morning, sir," he shouted above the roaring engine, and I gave him a nod and a smile rather than attempt to be heard over the noise. He helped me sling the chute straps over my shoulders and around my waist, fastening them for me so that the pack hung rather awkwardly just below my backside. But once I climbed up onto the wing and into the cockpit, it served to cushion my seat; as long as the flight didn't last more than a couple of hours, the discomfort was tolerable.

Shaw helped me tighten the seat harnesses and made sure none of them were twisted behind me. I pulled on my snug, fireproof gloves, and looked over my instruments, or "clocks," which glowed warm red in the solid black panel in front of me. I firmly pressed each rudder pedal to make sure the tension was correct and then shifted the control yoke forward, backward, and side to side to check the action. Glancing to the east, I could see the hot rim of the morning fireball rising above the horizon and an array of sunbeams spreading like unfolding butterfly wings through the brightening sky. For a second, the view resembled all too closely the Rising Sun sigil of the Imperial Japanese Navy, and I debated whether to interpret this as a positive or negative omen. In the end, I chose neither and simply wished the Lord a good morning, asking that my men and I fulfill our duty to the best of our abilities and be delivered safely home afterward.

Finally, I pulled my goggles over my eyes and glanced at the other Cats to verify they were ready to roll. Satisfied, I gave my plane captain a thumbs-up; he, in turn, waved to the flight ops officer standing near my plane at the edge of the apron. He made a thorough scan of the planes, then lifted a hand, pointed at me, and swiveled quickly to point in the direction of the runway.

The signal to go.

I pushed the throttle forward, feeling the plane shiver and shake as power built up quickly, then my Hellcat went lumbering out of its revetment and taxied to the northwest end of the runway. I steered my Cat onto the metal matting and aligned the nose with the center of the runway, heading southeast, into the wind. Glancing back a final time to verify that the rest of the flight was falling in behind me, I gently pushed the throttle all the way up, and the Hellcat shuddered with power as it began to move. As the engine rpms increased, I applied pressure to the right rudder pedal to counteract the powerful torque. Old Grand-Dad gained speed quickly, and when the airspeed indicator read seventy-five knots, I nudged the stick forward slightly to raise the tailwheel; at ninety knots, I pulled the stick back, lifting the plane smoothly from the ground and into the air.

Pulling up my gear, I made a slow, climbing turn to the right, out over the ocean, watching my clocks and listening to the smooth roar of the engine. At 1,500 feet, I glanced over my right shoulder and saw the black silhouette of Cox's Hellcat lifting off the runway and turning to follow me. A tiny jet of blue flame spurted from the exhaust port just behind the engine cowling, and a dim red glow from his clocks illuminated his cockpit. I continued my southward heading, climbing steadily until I reached 5,000 feet, then I veered to the left to begin a slow orbit while the rest of the flight came up to form on my wing.

"Blue Leader to Blue Flight," I said, pressing my throat mike to activate it. "Radio check, please."

"Blue Two, copy five-by-five," came Cox's voice over my headset. One by one, the rest of the pilots confirmed they were reading me. At last, when all seven planes had formed on my tail, I cranked my canopy shut and began a full power climb to altitude on a northeasterly heading. From this vantage point, we were able to watch the sun rise above the ocean, its glare forcing me to don my well-used Ray-Ban sunglasses. At 20,000 feet, the cockpit was freezing and I had to wear my oxygen mask, for without it I would have blacked out in a matter of seconds.

Three-quarters of an hour away, at the southeastern end of Bougainville, Kahili awaited us. For many months it had been the most heavily defended enemy base south of Rabaul, and in conjunction with the neighboring airfields, Kara and Ballale, it presented a formidable bulwark against our air and sea forces. In the last few weeks, however, our concentrated assaults had come tantalizingly close to breaking the enemy's back in the region, and the name Kahili no longer inspired quite the degree of terror in our pilots it once had. Still, flying to Bougainville remained a risky endeavor. The antiaircraft guns at the Ballale airfield boasted legendary status, and enemy shipping in Tonolei Harbor, which supplied the Bougainville bases, continued virtually unchecked, despite our frequent—and deadly—anti-shipping raids.

We flew in silence the entire distance to the target, which I first glimpsed through a heavy cloud layer shortly after 0700. Our approach brought us into Bougainville at its southernmost end; the island extended some 150 miles to the northwest, and to my left, I could see a line of distant green mountains—the Crown Prince Range—jutting up through the clouds like the heads of sentient, watchful giants. I veered slightly to the right to begin our orbit above Kahili, keeping my eyes open for the first sign of enemy planes climbing to meet us. Rufus Cox clung tight to my wing, his head on a swivel; I knew that he—and everyone in the flight—must be feeling the adrenaline rush that comes when you realize you are deep in enemy territory, held aloft in a fragile machine that might at any moment be targeted for destruction, knowing that if you go down, it will be into shark-infested waters, or into territory governed by troops whose disposition is likely to be no less savage than the sharks'.

I liked to think that my nerves were steady and combat-hardened, but when I looked down and saw the tiny gray airstrip right at the ocean's edge and the myriad naval vessels choking the harbor, I remembered how many of our best young men had lost their lives in this precise spot, and I felt a quailing in my gut, almost severe enough to send me scurrying toward home base, caring little whether any of my flight followed or stayed behind. But it was for this reason we had been so thoroughly trained and conditioned before shipping out; up here, you did your job, shutting your fear into a tight little compartment where it couldn't do any harm. If you failed to do that, you were dead before you began to fight.

I flipped on my gun switches, charged the guns, and squeezed the trigger on the control yoke to fire a few test rounds. The gunfire crackled deafeningly, its recoil shaking the plane like a jackhammer. Six streams of tracers sliced through the air in front of me, three from each wing, indicating that all of my .50 calibers were working. Taking my cue, the rest of the flight followed suit and fired their test rounds, the very act of which bolstered everyone's confidence.

At 200 knots indicated airspeed, we made the first ten-mile leg of our orbit in about three minutes. We then turned slowly left to swing back in the direction we had come. For the next hour and a half, we flew this pattern high above Kahili, all of us constantly scanning the sky, the clouds, the sea, and the airfield below, our eyes never ceasing to roam, our necks growing sore from constantly turning our heads. During that whole time, none of us saw the first sign of enemy air activity, though a few flak bursts dotted the sky several miles to the northwest—probably in response to a raid on Kara by dive-bombers based at Munda.

By 0910, it seemed certain that no enemy fighters intended to challenge our flight; the chances of getting any kills today appeared bleaker by the minute. So, at 0920, ten minutes before Arsenault's flight was scheduled to relieve us, I led my group out over Tonolei Harbor and began a 1,500-foot-per-minute descent toward the airfield. As soon as we dropped below 10,000 feet, a few puffs of black smoke appeared ahead of us, gradually thickening as we descended. At 5,000 feet, we were screaming down at 300 miles per hour, and puffs of flak began exploding around us, shockingly close. But glancing back, I saw the flight spreading out beautifully to either side, to maximize the coverage of our guns. All the weeks and months of training and planning had served us well. Ahead, I could see the enemy base growing larger in my gunsights and even some tracers flashing toward us as the defenders began to fire in earnest.

I leveled out at 500 feet, my eyes frantically searching the field for any revetments or hangars, but as yet, I could see nary a plane on the ground. A few trucks zipped back and forth across the tarmac, and a number of tiny figures went scurrying for cover as our Hellcats screamed in. Unable to locate any enemy aircraft, I fixed my sights on a large wooden building in the center of the field and gave the trigger a squeeze. With a harsh clatter, my guns awoke, shaking the plane like a giant, pummeling fist, and streams of tracers poured straight and true into the windows and walls of the structure. I yanked the nose up as the building rushed toward me, and my vision went gray under the force of five G's, then I was climbing toward the clouds once again, leaving the enemy airbase and frustrated ack gunners behind. Cox, Vickers, and Rodriguez followed immediately and plastered the same building; a burst of black smoke erupted from its roof as something inside exploded. To my left, Jimmy Penrow, Gummy Gilliam, Ted "Tank" Wickliffe, and Rick Bellero cut loose on a couple of gun emplacements, sending up geysers of earth and flame as their bullets found their marks. I couldn't tell whether they had taken out the guns, but as we retired from the attack, no tracers or flak bursts pursued us as we climbed back to 5,000 feet.

We did not dare go back for a second strafing run, for then the gunners would certainly draw a bead on us. Turning southward, back toward Conquest, I loosened my collar and wiped the sweat that now dripped freely from my forehead; after flying in the cold, thin air for the last couple of hours, the heat in the cockpit felt stifling. I began to breathe easier as Kahili fell farther behind. But as the rest of the flight re-formed on my wing, I happened to glance up and received a nasty shock: eight fighters, high, rocketing in to attack. I started to roll out desperately, but then the newcomers broke off and swung southward to grab altitude.

Arsenault's flight, checking us out to make sure we were friendly.

Fortunately, Jasper had sharp eyes and quick reflexes. As his group climbed past us, he waggled his wings in greeting, then his Hellcats disappeared to the south to take over the orbit we had vacated.

As I looked back toward Kahili, though, I felt a real pang of disappointment. The airfield that had once been the bane of our pilots was now all but deserted. The forty-some fighters reportedly stationed there had apparently gone elsewhere—possibly to Kieta, to the north.

The Blue Devils' long-awaited premiere mission was coming

to its end. And it was a bust.

Saturday, October 30, 1943
1230 hours
The mess hall, known to the locals as the Conquest Island Supper Club, was a bamboo-frame structure covered only by a long tarpaulin and mosquito netting: the rightful domain of VMF-264's certified cook, Sergeant Clarence Podell. In all fairness, the old boy did the best he could with what he had, but after a couple of his best meals, I was almost ready to brave the dangers of the jungle to hunt some game of my own. Today's lunch specials were ham sandwiches on toasted (stale) bread, leftover Brunswick stew (a concoction of the previous three nights' dinners), or powdered eggs and (rubber) bacon strips left over from breakfast. Clarence looked like an old salt from the storybooks, with weathered brown skin, sunken, squinting eyes, a protruding lower jaw with a perpetual stubble, and a few missing teeth. He must have been somewhere between twenty-five and forty.

"You want a thamwish, Mr. McLachlan?" he asked as I stepped up to the less-than-elegant spread. He lifted a toasted ham sandwich on a spatula as if it were a rare delicacy.

"Sure, Clarence," I said with a forced smile. In spite of his rough appearance, the cook struck me as an oddly sensitive, almost meek individual. One hated to make a derogatory remark about the rations for fear of devastating him.

With a flourish, he dropped the sandwich onto my plate and then pointed to the trays of canned green beans and corn that seemed to be permanent fixtures at his table. "Vegables?"

"No thanks, just the sandwich."

Arsenault, Rook, Trimble, and I sat down at the end of a long table in one corner of the sparsely populated tent. I noted that Arsenault had taken a full portion of Brunswick stew, a sandwich, and a huge pile of corn and green beans. He noticed my look of distaste and said, "Never take for granted the Lord's bounty. May He bless this shit for the nourishment of our bodies."

Rook exploded briefly, then his usual deadpan expression slid back onto his face.

"Not one damn thing at that field," I said, after chewing on my leathery sandwich for a while. "Not so much as a broken-down Zero."

Chuck had brought our orders for the next seventy-two hours, hot off the radioteletype from ComAirSols at Munda. Tomorrow was to be another combat air patrol in the same area, a prospect I could only find depressing. The only thing more frustrating or fatiguing than an eventless CAP was a series of them. "Take heart," he said, scanning the pages he had brought with him. "Look at what we have for Monday. 'Operation Cherryblossom.' If all goes as planned, the Marines will be landing at Cape Torokina. We'll be covering."

Comeaux gave a little whistle. "Well, that ought to make for an entertaining morning. The Japs are not going to hand over that bit of real estate gladly."

"Definitely not," I said. "If anything, they'll be looking to work over the invasion fleet. That should put them down low for us to pounce on."

"Nothing like a bunch of Marines for bait," Comeaux said with a laugh, shoveling a heap of Brunswick stew into his mouth. "When we get into it, you guys are just going to have to hang back. I'd hate to frag somebody for getting in my way."

"Don't talk with your mouth full. But tomorrow, I'm going to put you in front of my second division. It'll be Penrow's turn as alternate." I glanced up to Arsenault. "So, Aramis, how did our boy Kinney do?"

Arsenault's face looked as if he had bitten into a lemon.

"He's the only one who scored anything. He took out an ack-ack in the strafing run."

"Well, good for him."

"He flew fine, Skipper, but I really wonder about him getting along with the guys. They say he's queer and such."

I shook my head. "I'm not going to have that going on around here. If he's a competent pilot, then we need him. Simple as that."

"I'd say he's competent. Of course, that was just a lucky shot he got in today."

"Well, the rumor mill isn't going to operate here. Especially with you senior guys."

"Roger that, Athos," Arsenault said with a sigh. "You know I don't condone badmouthing. But I can understand it. He's a strange little fellow. Keeps to himself all the time. He's got that weird way of looking at you . . . the way you or I would look at a woman. It's quite ungodly."

"Well, he may get his ass kicked. But I will not have a situation where somebody doesn't cover him in a fight, or he doesn't cover somebody else. That will not wash in this squadron."

"Understood."

"Likewise," Comeaux said. "But I sure hope he doesn't rile me. You know, I really despised Lefty Hazelhurst. But I miss him."

I nodded. "Yeah, me too. But we make the best of this. Some new guys take longer to adjust. He gets the benefit of the doubt until proven otherwise."

"I hope it doesn't come to that," Arsenault said.

"I think I'm going to take him with me tomorrow," I said, barely realizing what I was saying until it was too late. But I trusted my instincts. This was as good a time as any for me to watch him at work in the Cat.

"You're wearing your serious face," Comeaux said.

"Yeah, I reckon I am."

"I'm sure the CO knows best," Arsenault said.

I gathered the remains of my lunch and stood up. "Well, if you gentlemen will pardon me, I have administrative details to look after."

Comeaux and Trimble rose and deposited their lunch trays at the end of Podell's table; before getting up, Arsenault scooped up a few more mouthfuls from his tray, leaving it nauseatingly clean.

"No need to wash that one," Comeaux said, his face a little green.

"See you later," Trimble said. "Poker this afternoon?"

"Number one Tobacco Road," Arsenault said. "Be there."

Bidding my companions a good afternoon, I left the supper club, walked the short distance to my near-stifling little office building, and closed myself inside, where I sat down and loaded a dauntingly blank mission report form into the typewriter. This was one administrative duty that I looked forward to with as much enthusiasm as getting shot down in enemy territory. With an impatient sigh, I began to slowly type a description of the morning's mission, including the participants, relevant observations during the flight, and the results at the target. Despite my hatred of the task, I felt a sharp pang of disappointment that my first after-action report was going to be miserably brief.

As I typed, I thought for a moment that I heard a deep thumping sound somewhere in the distance, barely discernible over the clacking of keys, the chugging of the generator, and the whirring of fans. At first, I thought it must simply be some noise from the maintenance area, far beyond the intervening trees to the west. But then I thought, no, this was a rhythmic, deep percussion, like the beating of many drums—and it seemed to be coming from the deep jungle, well north of the operations area. I stopped typing, rose, and stood next to the window to listen, but the sound ceased before I could come close to identifying it.

I sat back down and resumed my typing, but recalling my initial apprehension about our quarters being so close to the wilds of the rain forest, I unholstered my .45 Colt and placed it on the desk next to the typewriter. I didn't honestly expect to need it for anything; after all, the Marines had been here for a month without experiencing anything particularly hostile.

But just in case . . .

Saturday, October 30, 1943
1930 hours

I had spent the rest the of the afternoon analyzing our upcoming mission with Trimble and then getting to personally meet most of Colonel Rooker's ground crew. Major Pearce also introduced me to the cavern that served as our fuel cache. The underground depot was easily accessible and provided the best cover for our stores in the event of a bombing attack. The main entrance was a semicircular mouth, large enough to drive a truck through, in the side of the nearly vertical rock wall. The surrounding teak and coconut palm trees obscured any view of the opening from above, so an airborne enemy would not be able to see it even if they knew where to look. I did not venture inside, for although I am not claustrophobic, as Rook professed to be, the dark interior looked like the perfect haven for bats or—worse—bugs.

Rook's men proved to be a spirited group, rowdy in much the same way as the Blue Devils and just as dedicated to their tasks. The crew chief was a sergeant named "Railroad" Bill Varn, a mountainous, craggy-featured behemoth from Missouri who took no guff from anyone, officers in particular. I wasn't sure I liked him, but he took the job of maintaining our fighters very personally, and I could not question his talent or loyalty.

When Rook boasted of having the best maintenance crew in the Pacific, he wasn't blowing smoke. These were tough men, who had overseen the care of dozens of aircraft under the most miserable conditions imaginable, oftentimes performing their jobs under withering enemy fire. It was not a rare event for them to devote all their efforts and resources to restoring a badly damaged plane, only to have it destroyed on the ground before their eyes by enemy bombardment. All of them had lost friends during their tour at Cactus.

We had finished our evening meal of almost-beef stew and stale bread an hour earlier, and the sun was starting its final descent toward the horizon. Rook and I were sitting together in the shade of the trees next to the Quonset hut, drinking the evening's final beer and reflecting on the exotic beauty of the tropical sunset, when I heard an odd, distant sound that I could not identify. It had the deep, vibrating rumble of multiple airplane engines, yet it rose and fell with an odd, warbling cadence, echoing strangely through the dark rain forest like the roar of some unimaginable, predatory beast. For a moment, I recalled the drumming sounds I had heard earlier, but this was different. I noticed that Rook's yellow-tinted face seemed to go pale, and he cocked one ear to listen intently. The sound did not repeat, but I realized that the calls of birds and insects in the jungle had fallen eerily silent. A strange, expectant atmosphere had gathered like a storm cloud over our shadowed encampment.

"What was that?" I asked, watching Rook take a nervous swallow of his beer.

He shook his head. "Don't know. I've heard it once or twice before in the evening."

"Something alive?"

"If it's something alive, it's as big as that mountain."

He had a point. Though distant and faint, the sound had had

a deep, thunderous timbre. Before long, though, the normal sounds of the forest picked up where they had left off, and the odd tension that had seized Rook dissipated like the remnants of a half-remembered dream. As if in defiance, he drained his beer and tossed the can into the darkness beyond the hut.

"That was weird," I said.

He nodded. "I'll tell you something. The first time I heard it, I was near the entrance to the caves. It almost sounded like it came from inside—from deep in the mountain."

"That mountain's volcanic, isn't it?"

"Yeah."

I "hmm'd" thoughtfully. "Maybe it's not extinct."

"Well, if it goes off while we're here, we can kiss this war goodbye. Now, I'm no expert, but I'm pretty sure that sound wasn't any kind of volcanic activity."

"You know, I thought I heard drumming earlier this afternoon. Ever hear anything like that?"

He raised an eyebrow. "Drumming? No."

"You don't suppose there could be other people on this island, do you?"

He shook his head. "I doubt it. The Marine landing force was here first, then the Seabees, then us, now you. All this time, there's been no sign of any other human life. Besides, even if there were other people here, what could they be doing to make a noise like what we just heard? No, I think it's something else entirely."

Now I shrugged. "Well. I guess it's our little mystery."

Cryptically, Rook said, "And I rather hope it stays that way."

Darkness fell quickly, with virtually no twilight. A few campfires sprang up among the trees, and Rook's men lit a row of tiki torches along the jeep track. The setting seemed so serene that, for the first time since my arrival, I felt fairly at ease, certain that—at least for now—we did not have to worry that our lights would be seen by the wrong eyes, or that the sounds of attacking enemy planes would shatter the evening's tranquility. The mellow strumming of a guitar soon drifted out of the darkness from the direction of the Marine City, indicating that one of Rook's mechanics aspired to become a musician. He still had a ways to go. Regardless, it was a warm and uplifting sound, and I was tempted to open another beer so that I might enjoy the relaxed mood and drift away. But while I have often overextended myself where alcohol is concerned, on this night my better judgment prevailed, mainly because I had no desire to be up and flying at the crack of dawn with a headache and dry mouth.

And while the setting overtly typified the tranquility of a storybook tropical paradise, I knew that, back in the communications center, the radar console was being carefully monitored and the radio operator kept his headset on, listening intently for any transmission, friendly or otherwise. Foxholes were kept clear, and antiaircraft gunners strayed no farther than a thirty-second sprint from their fortified emplacements. Rook had indicated that, just at the eastern perimeter of the camp, two powerful searchlights had been set up to illuminate the sky for our gunners in the event that Japs attempted to bomb us by night.

No, the balmy ocean breeze could not mask the air of preparedness and lingering anxiety that was a constant, twenty-four-hour companion to every man on Conquest, myself included.

But nothing more upsetting than a vocal difference of opinion between a few card players intruded on the evening, and at lights-out, I retired to my tent to find Arsenault and Comeaux already in the sack and snoring, the former lightly, the latter like a wounded grizzly bear. I considered an emergency tracheotomy using the bowie knife that I carried on my flight belt, but I wasn't sure even that could silence him.

I lit a single candle, stripped down to my shorts, and then rummaged through my belongings for my toothbrush. I found it only after making enough noise to wake the dead—not that this disturbed either of my tentmates. The evening's stew still filmed the inside of my mouth like old chalk, so I slipped back outside and took the kind of pleasure in brushing my teeth that can only be enjoyed by a man who has not been home for a very long time. I had just finished and was about to re-enter the tent when a low sound in the darkness from the direction of the mountain caught my attention. It sounded like a softer—but somewhat nearer—repetition of the grating, warbling rumble Rook and I had earlier heard.

I studied the dark trees thoroughly, listening intently for any further sound, but only the slight whisper of the distant breakers and susurrus of the wind overcame the silence of the night. Again I realized that no night creatures could be heard anywhere in the jungle, which seemed distinctly *wrong*. When I returned inside, blew out the candle, and slipped beneath the mosquito net tent over my cot, I found myself dwelling not on the mission coming up at dawn, or any other such notable cause of anxiety, but on the subtle, somewhat disturbing signs that these unfamiliar environs might prove to be more mysterious—even inhospitable—than we could have previously guessed.

Rooker hadn't said so, but the look in his eyes had been unmistakable: he believed that we were not alone out here. But even more disturbing—perhaps because I did not quite understand my own paradoxical thinking—my usually trustworthy intuition told me that learning the answer might be worse than not knowing.

CHAPTER 3

Sunday, October 31, 1943
0705 hours

"Bogey at nine o'clock low."

It was Comeaux's voice, slow and calm, scratchy-sounding over my headset. I looked to my left and down, carefully scanning the hazy horizon and whitecapped ocean. I had almost begun to believe he had merely seen a mirage when a tiny, rippling shadow moving over the waves finally caught my attention. Yes, there it was—a single, low-flying aircraft on a northward heading, moving rapidly away from us.

Damn his eyes! Comeaux could see a fly zipping around a room in pitch darkness.

"No way that's one of ours out here," he called.

"You and Dusty check it out. Everyone else stay high and watch for fighters."

Comeaux and his wingman, Ensign Donald "Dusty" Woodruff, peeled out of the formation and dove hard toward the retreating target. Now, all eyes were roving frantically around the sky for Zeros, in case the lone, low plane was a decoy to pull us down.

We were two-thirds of the way to our target, flying the same course as the previous day. We had received no notification of enemy air activity from Fighter Command. The bogey might be a Jap reconnaissance plane, hoping to escape our notice by dropping to wavetop level. I watched the two Hellcats steadily closing on the still indistinct shape. A second later, Comeaux's voice crackled over the headset: "Betty."

The twin-engine, Mitsubishi G4M bomber was a fast, elegant plane, with plenty of defensive firepower but no armor or self-sealing fuel tanks. Decoy or not, this one was doomed, unless its gunners had better eyes than Comeaux. I barely considered that a possibility.

Like bloodthirsty hawks, the two Hellcats screamed down on their target, commencing a high side run from the left, with Comeaux well out in front. Three seconds later, I saw a brilliant orange flash at the Betty's left wingroot, and three seconds after that, a huge, white splash as the bomber plowed straight into the waves and broke up, leaving only a spiraling plume of black smoke to mark its passing. Comeaux's first volley must have hit its fuel tanks. I would make book that poor Woodruff never even got to fire a shot.

I throttled back and made a slow, sweeping turn to the right, while Comeaux and Woodruff began climbing back toward the formation. True to his boast, Porthos had scored the squadron's first kill. I felt pleased for him, but at the same time certain that, for at least the next twenty-four hours, we would never hear the end of it. And on the off chance he had to share the kill with Woodruff, I would have little choice but to quarantine him until the verbal dysentery ran its course.

By the time the two fighters rejoined the formation, I could see the haze-streaked coastline of Bougainville in the distance, and the pale blue-green caps of the Crown Prince Range beyond. We had strayed slightly north of our anticipated course, so I veered southeast, toward Tonolei Harbor. After a few minutes, I could see the tiny pair of Treasury Islands below and to my right, but no air activity or plumes of smoke to indicate conflict. The Anzac brigade had apparently established itself there without appreciable resistance.

I led us into the same racetrack-oval orbit we had flown the previous day but, after a short time, swung south to eyeball the airfield at Ballale Island, about fifteen miles southeast of Kahili. As expected, I saw no sign of aircraft in the air or on the ground. However, under no circumstances could we relax our guard or take for granted that the skies were free of enemy. That Betty back there proved that we needed to keep our eyes open; if not for Comeaux's keen vision, it might have passed unnoticed.

The runway on Ballale spanned the length of the island, making it the equivalent of an anchored carrier. Craters from our many recent bomber strikes pockmarked the apron and beach. The ever-resourceful Japanese, however, never let anything so paltry as air raids dissuade them from using an airfield if their hearts were set on it. Frequently, our bombers would pound them mercilessly, leaving nothing but smoking ruins in their wake, only to come back the next day and find the damage repaired and the runway functional again.

For our side's sake, I couldn't help but hope that the days of such herculean persistence had come to an end. On the other hand, I did not relish the idea of flying over this ghost of a stronghold day after day if the enemy were not going to mount a counteroffensive.

The sight of something moving far to my right, at a slightly lower altitude, derailed that depressing train of thought. Focusing on that part of the sky, I finally detected six tiny, dark silhouettes flying on a northeast heading, seemingly unaware of us. I rocked my wings, then banked to the left to establish an intercept course, maintaining altitude and approaching cautiously, for I could not yet identify the plane type; I knew only that they were not Navy blue fighters.

Unfortunately, to get the sun behind us, we would have to veer far to the north and east, and by then, the bogeys would certainly have seen us. So I nosed down and nudged the throttle, increasing my speed to 250 knots, setting up an approach from their seven o'clock high position. They still showed no sign of having noticed us.

As we closed the distance, I finally ascertained—very nearly to my chagrin—that these were sleek, sharp-nosed Curtiss P-40s, painted olive drab and bearing the blue, white, and red roundels of the Royal New Zealand Air Force. The white stripes on their wings and vertical stabilizers identified them as members of the RNZAF 15th Air Squadron, no doubt up from Munda on a CAP of their own. Having verified that the newcomers were friendlies, I banked away to the left, leading my flight back to our designated patrol zone.

It would have been a sad situation had we been a group of enemy fighters; by all indications, the RNZAF pilots never saw us.

And so, again, we spent the rest of our shift orbiting Kahili and Ballale, never spotting so much as a cloud shaped like an enemy plane. Fifteen minutes before we were due to be relieved, a flight of Marine F4U Corsairs passed overhead, but they were too fast and too far away for me to identify their markings. As on the previous day, just prior to finishing our patrol, I signaled my flight to follow me down, this time in the direction of Ballale. I figured the least we could do was go down and shoot up the place to relieve our frustration.

Today, I had put Ensign Kinney on my wing and paired Rufus Cox with Lieutenant Max Collins, the second division leader. I could see the young, pinch-faced Kinney peering anxiously toward the island below as we descended rapidly; so far he had hugged my wing as tightly I could have expected from anyone. His head moved constantly, and his eyes roved the sky to check for bandits as we went into our dives. I certainly could not criticize his observance of procedure.

As expected, thick puffs of black smoke began to erupt

around us the moment we dove through 10,000 feet. Today, however, the violent flak bursts erupted squarely amid our formation, battering our planes like sledgehammer blows. I found myself enveloped by a dense black cloud and heard the metallic clatter of shrapnel over my wings and fuselage. When the smoke cleared, I saw a nasty, jagged gash about ten inches long in the blue metal skin just in front of my windscreen. If the projectile had come through the glass, it would have taken off my head.

But dwelling on close calls only undermined one's resolve, and in my combat experience, I had had many; I drove the horror of what might have happened from my mind and focused only on the tiny island below, scanning every quadrant of the airfield for appropriate targets. As at Kahili, there appeared to be no aircraft anywhere on the ground, and tracers were streaming up hot and heavy from numerous gun emplacements. However, off to the left, out in the harbor, I saw a large number of black, boxy-looking vessels and finally recognized them as barges. They appeared to be moving in the direction of Kahili, probably filled with troops or supplies. Bingo! I dipped my left wing to indicate a change in target, and then banked hard to set up an approach. I estimated there were at least a dozen of them, slowly trawling through the choppy waves in a tight cluster. One would think that a combat-savvy enemy would have learned better by now, but the Japanese constantly surprised our side by one day exhibiting brilliant, masterful military tactics, and the next blundering with all the panache of intellectual pygmies.

I nosed down, hit 300 knots, and leveled out just above the waves; the flight spread out to either side in line abreast formation. A few meager tracers streaked from the barges' rifle-caliber machine guns, but none came close enough to be worrisome. As the lead barge grew in my gunsight, my finger closed on the trigger; at 500 yards I opened fire. The tracers splashed into the water a few yards short of the target and then simply walked over the hull and deck, throwing up flowers of sparks and smoke. Several tiny figures scampered over the sides and dropped into the sea, and a second later, the middle portion of the barge buckled like a tin can struck by a club. Within two seconds I had rocketed past the target and roared into a left-hand chandelle (a steep, climbing turn). Swiveling my head, I saw that the barge's hull had been smashed and was taking on water; slowly, it rolled onto its left side like a lethargic whale and then began to settle into the oil-filmed ocean. Nearby, I saw many white eruptions of foam and flashes of flame as the other fighters hammered their targets. Dozens of tiny heads now dotted the surface, and I guessed that these vessels must have been laden with troops.

The flight clung to my wing beautifully as we swung around to the east and prepared to make a second pass. Out here, we had not been subject to the shore-based antiaircraft fire, and the barges' guns were too small and inaccurate to pose much of a threat. But as I bore down on the remaining vessels, a nearby explosion rocked my plane, and something smashed through the Plexiglas behind my head, leaving a hole the size of a golf ball. I frantically looked right and left, and there it was. Destroyer! Less than a mile to my left and aft, cutting quickly across the waves, the warship came steaming toward us, its guns spitting flames. It was too late to break off the run, so I scrunched myself down in my seat to present the smallest pos-sible target. Another hot burst of flame and smoke shook my plane as the destroyer's gunners opened up on me, and I began to regret accusing the Japs of tactical ineptitude. Had I been wise, I would have settled for making one pass and retiring.

But then an amazing thing happened. Ensign Kinney's Hell-cat, tight on my right wing, abruptly nosed up, rolled inverted, and then somersaulted sideways over the top of my plane, taking up a position on my left. An incredibly dangerous but skill-ful move that I would have expected from no one other than perhaps Comeaux. Kinney did not even look my way, but dipped his wings from side to side, using his plane as a shield. Shrugging to myself, I turned my attention back to the target and opened fire the second I was in range. My shots smashed into the barge's hull and opened it, and again I saw a number of men leaping into the water as their transport came apart at the seams. Then I was zooming past the stricken vessels and out toward the open sea.

"Damn it, I'm hit," came a voice over the radio. It was Dusty Woodruff.

"How bad?"

"Controls sluggish. Looks like he hit an aileron."

I looked back to my right and saw the flight re-forming into finger-four formation, with one plane—number 14—straggling. Thankfully, he wasn't leaving a smoke trail.

"Can you keep up?"

"Roger that, as long as I don't have to maneuver."

I led us in a slow climb to a more comfortable 5,000 feet as the adrenaline rush from combat began to wear off. Well, it hadn't exactly been dogfighting, but it was action. Successful action. We had inflicted major damage to the enemy flotilla and almost certainly taken out a fair number of personnel intended for the defense of Bougainville. I did not dwell on the loss of human life, though I could not help but feel a temporary sense of dislocation, as if I were somewhere else, looking down at myself from a distance. I had no personal animosity toward the enemy. They were doing their jobs and I was doing mine. Our duty to our respective countries necessitated the taking of lives; we did what was expected of us, and that was that.

I reached into my pocket, took out a cigarette, and lit it, deeply inhaling the sweet, refreshing smoke. The cockpit felt like a furnace, so I cranked back the canopy and reveled in the cool windstream. Right now, it was the most pleasurable sensation I could imagine. We had done a good job, and I fully anticipated Dusty Woodruff landing safely at the end of it all.

Had I been able to see directly back and some 10,000 feet above, however, I would have been shaken to discover that we were no longer alone in the sky. From what I came to understand later, our flight had been spotted by a lone enemy scout plane, whose pilot was even now making notes of our heading. Even if I had seen it, I would most likely have mistaken it for one of our new P-51B fighters; until now, no Japanese plane that we knew of bore the sharp, streamlined silhouette of an inline, water-cooled engine. This was a Ki-61 Hien, or "Tony" as the type came to be known: a fast, capable fighter that would have surprised us nastily had we encountered a group of them in combat. But as it was, the single scout merely shadowed us until we reached Conquest Island's radar range.

Ironically, the skies were clear until just before we reached home base, making it easy for the Japanese pilot to keep track of us. Ten minutes before landing, heavy cumulus clouds began to roll in that would have earlier shielded us from the enemy's view. I ordered Woodruff to hang back and land last; if he did have problems, I didn't want a blocked runway stranding the rest of us in the air. Woodruff radioed that he still had control of the plane but was having to fight to bank without stalling.

"If you don't think you can make it in, bail out over the lagoon and we'll send a boat out to you."

"I'll be okay."

"Roger that. Okay, the rest of us are pancaking."

I led the flight into the landing pattern while Woodruff maintained a wide, sweeping orbit a couple of miles out. I notified Conquest tower that we had a potential problem and requested that they get the ambulance and flight surgeon down to the field—just in case. By the time I brought my plane down to the runway, I saw a pump truck and a jeep bearing a litter sitting on the apron, surrounded by base personnel holding fire extinguishers, shovels, ropes, and blankets. It was an obvious precaution, but I could imagine poor Woodruff being unnerved by the display as he brought in his stricken Cat.

Once I had landed and parked my plane, I hopped out without waiting for the plane captain and hurried toward the gathered crewmen, all of whom were anxiously watching each Hellcat land and quickly clear the runway. Finally, Woodruff began his approach, and even from a mile away, I could see his wings wobbling as he struggled to maintain stability at low speed.

Rook stepped up to me, his face shadowed with concern. "Get into a fight out there?"

"Ack-ack. No fighters."

"How bad's he hit?"

"He's not injured. Fouled-up aileron."

Rook watched the plane approach with a critical eye. "He's gonna make it."

Woodruff's Cat was now cleanly aligned with the runway but coming in a little hot. The aileron damage forced him to steer mostly with the rudder, but now that he was in the groove, I expected he would be able to land more or less normally. I noticed with slight alarm that some of the nearby palms had begun bending in a swift cross-breeze, which seemed to have only just picked up; Woodruff had to jink the rudder several times to keep his nose in line. His landing gear lowered normally, though, and he managed to cut his speed a little. Everything looked good.

But just as his Cat reached the runway, its tail swung to one side, and the left wing dipped slightly. As the wheels touched down, the tail slewed violently, and to my horror, the right gear snapped and collapsed, and then the Hellcat was sliding sideways down the runway, spraying sparks like an ax blade in a grinder.

The remaining gear crumpled, and the left wing slammed to the ground. The prop struck the metal matting with the sound of a cannon shot and abruptly jerked to a stop. The Cat spun 180 degrees on its belly, still spewing sparks, and finally skidded to a halt halfway down the runway, facing back the way it had come. The pump truck lurched forward and rattled toward the wrecked plane, as the ground crew broke into a frantic run to rescue the pilot.

A few streamers of smoke curled from beneath the engine cowling, and, immediately, several men uncoiled a pair of hoses from the truck and began dousing the plane with water. I saw the canopy fly open, and as if propelled by a rocket, Dusty Woodruff leaped onto the wing and went sprinting madly down the runway—in the opposite direction of his approaching comrades—never so much as glancing back to see if his plane had actually caught fire. The ambulance, which had started toward the wreckage, changed course and began chasing Dusty down the runway.

Finally, when Woodruff realized which way he was going, he turned back toward us, forcing the baffled ambulance driver to wheel around yet again. Rook and I hustled the hundred yards or so out to meet him, and I saw Doc Bob McCall, our flight surgeon, jump out of the jeep, figuring the most direct route to his potential patient was on foot. When Woodruff came huffing to a stop in front of us, he pulled off his flight helmet, nodded wearily to indicate he was all right, and finally turned to take a look at his ruined Hellcat. He appeared unhurt, but his face turned white when he saw the condition of his plane.

"Christ on a cracker," he groaned.

"Take some deep breaths," I said, giving him a sympathetic

pat on the shoulder. "That was good for one official scare."

"She was shuddering bad, all the way in," he said in a tremulous voice. "Just before I set down, it felt like all the air had just gone out from under me. One wing dipped, and that was all she wrote."

"Crosswind," Rook said. "And made to order just for you. It only picked up as you were coming in to land."

"Figures, don't it?"

The rather hefty Doc McCall finally jogged up to us, panting heavily. "I guess there's nothing wrong with you," he said to Woodruff. "Me, I'm gonna have a heart attack."

"Well," I said with a little sigh. "The Japs get in one last laugh after all."

Woodruff's eyes widened apprehensively. "You're not gonna ground me, are you, Skipper?"

I shook my head. "Not your fault. You did well to get her as far as you did in one piece."

He nodded grimly. "Yeah. Could've been worse."

"It is worse," Rooker said, giving Woodruff a stern glare.

"How's that?"

"You owe the United States Marine Corps a half a case of your finest brew."

Sunday, October 31, 1943
1245 hours
Arsenault's flight returned after an uneventful CAP. On their way back, they shot up Kahili again but couldn't claim to have knocked out so much as a flak gun. On the other hand, all of Red Flight's planes came back without so much as a nick from enemy guns, and all landed safely.

The wreckage of Woodruff's Hellcat had been towed off the runway, and the Marines hurriedly laid down a couple of new sections of metal matting to replace those ruined by the crash.

After Doc McCall had pronounced him healthy, Woodruff had retired to his tent and promptly passed out from exhaustion.

And now I found myself in an odd and distinctly awkward position. Following a lunch of canned ham and beans, I called Ensign Elmer Kinney to my office and sat him down in front of my desk. A more uncomfortable-looking young man I had never seen.

"Relax, Mr. Kinney," I said as he fidgeted in his chair, his eyes alternately squinting and widening, his fingers tapping nervously on his knees. "You feeling all right, son?"

"Yes, sir, I feel all right," he said, shrugging his shoulders uncertainly. "Did I do anything wrong?"

"No, you didn't do anything wrong."

"Oh."

"Quite the contrary. You did a hell of a job this morning. Your flying was exceptional."

Kinney's paper-white face changed to alizarin. "Oh. Thank you, sir."

" 'Skipper,' if you please."

He nodded abashedly.

I couldn't help but stare at him, which made him all the more uncomfortable. "Where do you come from, Mr. Kinney?"

"Oklahoma. Near Enid."

"Is that where you learned to fly?"

"Yes, sir."

"And you did this how?"

"I was a crop duster."

"I see. Did you enjoy crop-dusting?"

"No, sir."

"And why is that?"

Kinney gulped. "It bothered my sinuses."

"So you decided that flying fighters would be more down your line?"

He nodded hesitantly. "Yes, sir."

"Flying fighters plays hell on your sinuses—the rapid changes in altitude, and all. Your sinuses been bothering you here?"

"No, sir."

"Good." The fact that I could not make eye contact with him for more than two seconds at a time was beginning to frustrate me. "Tell you what, Mr. Kinney. I'm going to make you my wingman on a more permanent basis. What do you think of that?"

"I—I think it's an honor, sir."

"Skipper."

"Skipper."

"You showed a lot of initiative when you moved to cover me on our strafing run. But that was a very dangerous maneuver."

"Oh . . . I'm sorry about that."

"Don't be. We need that kind of confident, aggressive flying. Tell me something. When you rolled over the top of my Cat, did you even for a second doubt that you could pull it off successfully?"

"Well, no, sir, I just did what came naturally."

"You ever do that in a Hellcat before?"

"Um, no, sir."

"I guess you know that flying a Hellcat's nothing like flying a crop duster."

"Yes, sir. I just took into account my speed and the space I had to work in and compensated for it."

"I see."

"I'm sorry if it startled you."

"Forget it."

"Thank you, sir."

"Well, Mr. Kinney, you're my wingman now."

He nodded and actually met my gaze for perhaps three seconds. "That's very kind of you."

"I make decisions that I feel are in the squadron's best interests. I'm counting on you to prove that I've made the right one."

"Yes, sir, I will, sir."

"Thank you, Mr. Kinney. Dismissed."

He stood up, saluted stiffly, and then disappeared silently through the mosquito-netted door. I shook my head to myself, not entirely certain I had done the right thing. I could not deny that the young man was a hell of a flyer, but he appeared so high-strung it was a wonder he could walk across the camp without having a panic attack. I could only marvel that he had made it through the Navy's basic training, where his flying skills would have meant squat. Well, now that he was here, I could hardly put him on someone else's wing if I were not willing to have him on mine.

Once again, I had only a brief mission report to type, and my remarks regarding Woodruff's crack-up were intentionally terse. He was a fine pilot, and I figured he would come around all right. But if he didn't, I would not put him back in the air; I couldn't let anyone who was inordinately rattled by a crash landing go up against the Japanese.

Determining how a person would react in combat was a tricky job for a squadron commander. Even a man who had proven to be an aggressive, skillful pilot and marksman during training might quail once he actually flew into a fight. And sometimes a pilot who had shown marginal skills in training might go on to exhibit a cool head and the ability to reliably knock down targets in live combat. But it was distinctly rare for someone like Elmer Kinney, who showed all the signs of being a near, if not already full-fledged, neurotic, to even make it as far as the cockpit of a fighter plane.

Tomorrow, I knew, could bring a change in our fortune—for better or for worse. The Fighting 39 had been assigned to cover the Marine landings at Cape Torokina, and I would be more than surprised if we didn't finally see some aerial action. Torokina, midway up the western coast of Bougainville, was a Japanese bastion that our forces intended not only to neutralize but to capture. If the attempt succeeded, we would be in position to deliver a lightning thrust at Rabaul, the largest and strongest enemy fortress in the south Pacific. Conversely, it would put our forces within easy range of Japanese attack planes both from Rabaul and from carriers assigned to bolster its defenses.

I covered my typewriter, stepped outside, and lit a cigarette. The chugging of the generator behind the hut barely drowned the buzzing and chirping of the jungle's inhabitants, whose vigor seemed to mock my pensive mood. Out of the blue, the brutal, crushing fear that I might not survive this tour fell upon me, and my hands began to tremble as if with palsy. Although every pilot wrestles with the concept of his own mortality, this onslaught of doubt hit me more savagely than any I could remember. Ironically, I knew—at least consciously—that I had a better chance of surviving now than I had during my previous tour aboard the *Lexington*. But like a wild colt released from long confinement, this unbridled sentiment simply beat down my fiercest resistance, leaving my nerves jangling and raw.

I sucked down my cigarette, unable to uproot myself from the spot where I was standing. When it was spent, I lit another. And another one after that.

Sunday, October 31, 1943
2350 hours
I rarely have vivid nightmares, although a certain few have etched themselves into my memory with disturbing clarity. So it was with the one that dragged me back to wakefulness just before midnight—appropriately, on Halloween night, although

71

that fact eluded me at the time. I had been asleep for perhaps two hours when steel claws clutched my chest and ripped me like a piece of carrion from the comfortable darkness of slumber, shocking me so that for several confused moments I had no clue where I actually was. Eventually, the irregular, buzzsaw-like grating of air through Comeaux's pipes reminded me that I was in my tent, laid out on my cot beneath a protective web of mosquito netting. The jungle was alive with insect and animal noise, now more than ever creating the impression that the night creatures were actually laughing.

In the dream, I had been walking at night on a torchlit path through the tropical flora, apparently searching for someone or something; in one of those nonsensical transpositions of time and place that happen in dreams, I believe it was supposed to be my younger brother, Robert. As I wandered, I eventually came to a clearing, and at its far end I saw a cave mouth in the side of a huge granite wall that extended into impenetrable darkness high above my head—much like the actual location on the island, only far larger. From the cave, a shadowy figure slowly emerged, seeming to glide on legs that did not move. The figure was draped in a robe of blood-red material that looked like satin and that rippled and rustled strangely, as if beneath the fabric, several arms or other appendages were engaged in a struggle with each other. I could not see his face, even though the torchlight otherwise fully illuminated his body. His arms lifted, and when the sleeves of the robe fell back, I could see that his skin was onyx black and glistened as if coated with oil.

Although he presented no overt threat, I felt terrified of him; he was inhumanly tall—at least eight feet—and seemed to be studying me, even though I could not see his eyes. I crept closer, strangely compelled to view his peculiarly hidden face, but as I approached, he lowered his hands and motioned for someone—or something—behind him to come forward. Now, two squat figures that looked like huge toads appeared at the cave mouth, loping oddly on stiff, bipedal legs, and settled themselves at the figure's sides. He held his black hands to their mouths, and each of them spread its wide jaws to reveal a gray, wormlike tongue that flicked forth and began to lap at his fingers. A deep, cavernous voice said, "I look forward to getting to know you."

The toad-like creatures leered at me with their bulging eyes, as if ecstatic to simply be in the presence of their tall, faceless master. From the dark depths beyond the figures, a low, flute-like piping began: a discordant melody that was at the same time eerie and profoundly melancholy. Though I perceived the sounds to be a product of musical instruments, after a time, the tones took on the timbre and cadence of a voice speaking in some grotesque, chirping, alien tongue. And, somehow, of all these sounds and images, it was this piping that shattered my nerve and sent me retreating into blindingly dark wakefulness.

The night air felt comfortable, for a low breeze whispered through the camp, dispelling the humidity. But my nerves could not have been more unsettled if I were in the cockpit and under fire; thus sensitized, I actually jerked upright when I heard a soft rustle just outside the entrance to the tent. It sounded like a furtive footfall. I couldn't see what time it was, but I doubted anyone from the camp would be up and about at this hour unless they were on their way to the head.

I have never been prone to overreacting. Nevertheless, I slipped my hand beneath the mosquito netting, reached for my .45, which lay on an upended wooden crate at the head of my cot, and crept from my bed to the closed tent flap. I stood still and listened for a full two minutes, half-convinced that I could hear the faint sound of measured breathing just beyond the layer of canvas. Then, with an unsteady hand, I unfastened the flap and mosquito netting and thrust my gun hand through the opening. When I poked my head out, I saw no one loitering around the tent or amid the faint, moonlit trees. But as my eyes adjusted to the darkness, I thought I saw a silhouette, black against black, a few yards to my right. It was obviously not a tree, for it was shaped like a man—a very tall man—and as I watched, it seemed to glide into the black forest on legs that never moved.

Only my well-honed, ingrained self-discipline and the halfhearted conviction that I had merely experienced the last vestiges of some weird, waking dream kept me from raising my gun and emptying the clip into the mocking, leering night.

CHAPTER 4

Monday, November 1, 1943
0645 hours

As the sun's face peeked over the horizon, the blinding glare hit us squarely in the eyes, and I had to frequently block it with an extended thumb so I could scan the sky for bogeys. Elmer Kinney clung tightly to my left wing, while Willy Vickers and José Rodriguez flew slightly above and behind to the right, completing my division. Jasper Arsenault led Danny-Boy Grogan, Dusty Woodruff, and Hoagie Hedgman in the second. Comeaux's flight consisted of himself, Jack Bartholomay, Tank Wickliffe, and Timmy Asberry in the first division; and Max Collins, Mike Dillon, Jimmy Penrow, and Gummy Gilliam in the second. For today, I had put Rufus Cox on the list as first alternate, but I think he was a little miffed that Kinney had usurped his place on my wing. As something of a balm, I planned to make Rufus a division leader, replacing Lieutenant Hank Hubbard, who had at first made a fine impression with his aggressive flying style but was well on his way to becoming a rogue, according to Arsenault.

Just now, however, my main concern was navigating, managing my fuel, and making sure that everyone else was following my lead. My concentration wanted to waver, for I had dragged myself out of bed that morning feeling as if I had been in a fight that lasted all night. More than once, I had to forcibly sweep the strange dread, if not the details, from my nightmare into a dark, distant place in order to focus on the matters at hand. And focus I must, I knew, because the day promised to be a momentous one for the Blue Devils. This morning, over 14,000 men from the Marine Amphibious Corps would begin their landings at Cape Torokina—code-named "Cherryblossom"— and we were assigned to fly a CAP over them from 0715 until 0915, and then again from 1200 to 1400. Several air groups— including Army, Navy, Marine, and New Zealand Air Force squadrons—would cover the landings over the course of the day.

The previous day, Task Force 39, which included four heavy cruisers and eight destroyers, commanded by Rear Admiral A. S. "Tip" Merrill, had steamed into position to bombard the Bonis and Buka airfields at the northwest end of Bougainville, thus preventing the enemy from launching counterattacks. Now, Merrill's force was on a fast haul toward Torokina, while Task Force 38, under Rear Admiral F. C. Sherman, took over the assault on Bonis and Buka. Our intelligence indicated that virtually all of the enemy's 40,000 troops on Bougainville had been dispersed to the northern and southern ends of the long island, so the Marines expected to encounter only a small number of defenders at Torokina; however, they would be fierce and extremely well dug in. Furthermore, we could make book that the Japs would counterattack with large numbers of aircraft from Rabaul.

Here we were, I thought, a tiny cog in a giant operation in what most people would consider an unimaginably remote corner of the globe. Yet the outcome of this operation had far-reaching implications for the war effort, and thus our entire nation. I had not felt such a mélange of excitement and anxiety since the day of my final flight with VF-3. That day, at the end of the combat mission, I had been forced to land aboard the U.S.S. *Yorktown*, for during the battle, the *Lexington* had been critically damaged by enemy bombs. And now, the *Lexington*—and many of the people I had known and called friends—lay at the bottom of the ocean.

Just after 0700, I could see the distant peaks of the Crown Prince Range rising from a milky haze. And now, I began to hear chatter from other patrols and "Cocker Base"—the Fighter Direction Officer aboard the destroyer U.S.S. *George Clymer*, the flagship of Rear Admiral T. S. Wilkinson's 3rd Amphibious Force at Empress Augusta Bay. From what I could gather, the Marine landing craft were at this moment slogging their way through the choppy ocean toward the Cape Torokina coast. My pulse had begun to race, and I was breathing heavily in my oxygen mask. But with steady fingers, I charged my guns, switched on my gunsight, and fired a few test rounds, prompting the rest of my pilots to do the same. We were less than ten minutes from our patrol zone.

"Conquest squadron, I have your contact," came the FDO's voice. "What's your call sign, over?"

I pressed my throat mike. "Cocker Base, this is Blue Devil One, reading you five-by-five."

"Roger, Blue Devil One. Proceed on your current vector."

Ahead, the crescent-shaped coastline of Empress Augusta Bay materialized out of the haze, and soon I could make out the white foam wakes of what looked like a hundred ships aimed at the southern arm of the bay. I turned my group northeast to begin the first leg of our orbit, keeping the vessels below in sight to my left. Far to the right, I saw another flight of eight aircraft approaching from the south, a thousand feet or so above us; as they drew nearer, I recognized them as Corsairs, their engine cowlings emblazoned with the grinning skull and crossbones insignia of VF-17—the Jolly Rogers—stationed at Ondonga, New Georgia. They crossed our path close enough for me to see that the lead plane bore the name "Big Hog" stenciled in white on the sea-blue tailfin; it belonged to Lieutenant Commander Tom Blackburn, whose squadron had shipped over from the States about the same time as us. He waggled his wings as his flight passed us and zoomed east to take up their station high above the landing sites.

More excited chatter over the radio described the withering fire that was even now falling on Bonis and Buka; I later learned that the narrator was Lieutenant Commander "Jumpin' " Joe Clifton of VF-12 from the U.S.S. *Saratoga*. Clifton was a fine and respected pilot, but according to some, his chronic nonobservance of radio silence bordered on the treasonable.

Then the voice of the FDO called: "Blue Devil One, this is Cocker Base. Many bogeys at angels one-five, heading one-four-zero. Vector three-one-zero, two-five miles. Proceed to intercept, buster."

Bogeys! The message meant that radar indicated a large number of unidentified aircraft, heading southeast at 15,000 feet, twenty-five miles to the northwest; we were to set a course to intercept at top speed. Apparently, the Japanese had wasted no time in launching a counterattack, probably from Rabaul. I pushed the throttle up to full combat power, banked left, and rocked my wings to signal that we were changing course. My two divisions closed in tight, while Comeaux's planes dropped back and climbed a thousand feet, spreading out to provide high cover. At most, we had five minutes before making contact.

I scanned the sky by drawing an imaginary sector, studying it quickly but thoroughly, then moving to an adjacent sector; without a methodical system for maintaining situational awareness, you were likely to miss spying a distant target. Comeaux was the undisputed master of this procedure, and once again, even though he was behind me, he was the one to call out, "Athos, bogeys at ten o'clock low."

I saw them a split second after his announcement: an

ominous mass of dark shapes in the distance like a flock of huge crows, winging toward us some 8,000 or 9,000 feet below. The sun had crawled far enough above the horizon to be behind us; there was a good chance the enemy pilots had not seen us yet. My heart slammed into overdrive and my fingers clutched the yoke in an iron grip. There were so many of them! I counted at least twenty dive-bombers—fixed-gear Aichi D3A "Vals"—escorted by as many Zeros flying above but slightly behind the formation. As we sped toward them, the lead Zero, still over a mile away, began to climb toward us with his wingmen glued to his tail. We had been spotted.

I pressed my throat mike and said, "Okay, they've seen us. Porthos, stay high and handle the fighters. Blue Flight, we'll take the dive-bombers. High side runs to the left. Mr. Kinney, stay tight with me."

"Roger that, Skipper," came his voice.

Holy shit, the boy had called me "Skipper." I glanced up to make sure the sky wasn't about to fall.

I banked left and swung around the bomber formation, paralleling them above and to their right. This put us dangerously close to the Zeros, but we still had a fair altitude and speed advantage. I could see the Vals clearly now: dark green, broad-winged wasps with blood-red suns blazing on their wings and fuselages. Each dive-bomber carried two men—pilot and rear gunner—and I saw the lead plane's gunner swivel his 7.7mm machine gun to draw a bead on me. I rolled inverted, then pulled back on the stick to complete a split-S maneuver, which sent me hurtling down at a sixty-degree angle. Like the hand of a brutal giant, the force of six G's crushed me into my seat, so I clenched my stomach and neck muscles to keep the blood from rushing out of my head and causing my vision to go black.

I was barreling in now at 350 knots, so I chopped the throttle to keep from overshooting my mark. At 300 yards, I squeezed the trigger and watched my tracers arc toward the hazy blue ocean below, my Hellcat rattling and shaking with the recoil. Then, there was the Val, flying right into the tracer stream, its right wing and fuselage sparking and smoking as my .50-caliber bullets slammed home. I saw a piece of green metal go whirling into space—one of his ailerons, I thought—then I firewalled the throttle and pulled hard on the stick to zoom above him. Six G's again pressed me into my seat and dimmed my vision; when my eyesight returned a few seconds later, I saw only empty blue sky as I climbed away fast and free. Looking back, I glimpsed twin trails of white and black smoke, which meant my target was leaking coolant and probably burning oil.

I banked left and saw Kinney coming around just behind me, still holding tight even after my fast run on the Val. Vickers and Rodriguez now dove into the formation, each of them picking out targets just behind the leader. A huge ball of flame erupted from one of the dive-bombers, and a second later, José called in his calm, Spanish-tinged voice, "Splash one meatball."

With Kinney trailing like a faithful hound, I sped back toward the formation to set up another run from the opposite side. The Val I had shot up still held its place, but it was smoking badly and its wings were wobbling erratically. This time, I didn't split-S but nosed down to make a fast and hard final pass on him. Again, I saw the rear gunner taking aim at me, and a line of tracers flashed dangerously close to my cockpit. I held my fire to 300 yards, then, when the Val's wings completely filled my gunsight, I squeezed the trigger. As the tracers struck home, one wing blew into the air and fluttered away like a lost feather, and the now-unrecognizable, blazing husk of the fuselage began spinning wildly toward the earth, trailing thick, black smoke.

I had just earned two bottles of scotch.

"Athos, two Zekes closing on your six," came Comeaux's voice.

I swiveled my head and saw a pair of mottled green and gray fighters diving rapidly toward me, perhaps a half mile back. If necessary, I could roll out and lose them, but I didn't want to let the dive-bombers get away while I was trying to avoid their little friends. I pushed up to war emergency power, which gave my engine an extra ten percent boost, though it couldn't handle the extra strain for long.

Kinney's Hellcat sailed into view on my right, banked to the left, extended a few hundred yards, and then veered back to the right. I understood his purpose immediately and turned toward him at high speed, crossing his path just behind him; I extended a quarter mile or so and then banked back in the opposite direction. This time he swerved and crossed my path just behind me. This was a defensive play called the beam defense maneuver, or "Thach Weave," named after my former CO, Lieutenant Commander Jimmy Thach, who had perfected its execution. Maneuvering back and forth this way, a pilot could set his sights on any enemy that attempted to lock onto his partner's tail, and vice versa. Pulling into the weave cost us some speed, however, and the pursuing Zekes were almost in firing range. But in another inexplicable, uniquely Japanese maneuver, both of them selected me as their target, apparently ignoring my wingman. Before I could even register what he was doing, Kinney had pulled in tight behind the trailing Zeke and fired a burst of his Brownings, which sheared off both of the Zeke's wings like the hand of a mischievous god. The wingless fuselage spiraled away, and I caught a glimpse of the pilot struggling to escape the cockpit. However, his partner didn't even pause to take notice and instead opened fire on me.

A foolish move; he was still too far back for his shots to come close. I nosed down a few degrees to gain more speed, and again Kinney's Hellcat swerved, ending up on the Zeke's tail so fast I thought he was going to collide with it. His gun muzzles flashed, and, with no armor to speak of, the Zeke's fuel tanks torched off, and the plane exploded in a huge, brilliant fireball. When I glanced back, I saw the nose of Kinney's Hellcat magically appear amid a roiling cloud of black smoke, his windscreen coated with oil from his kill.

"Mr. Kinney, you all right?" I called.

"Okay," came his shaky voice. "Can't see too well at the moment."

"That was close."

"Yes, sir." A long silence followed. Then: "Um, Mr. McLachlan, could you cover my wing for about one minute?"

I hauled back a little, pulling up beside Kinney's Cat, glancing around at the enemy formation. I could see several smoke trails and a few fighters swirling above the bombers; we were heading away from them, though, and needed to turn around quickly.

"Got it, Kinney. Make it fast."

Then I saw the damnedest thing I had ever encountered in combat. For a few seconds, Kinney's head disappeared in the cockpit; when he reappeared, he cranked open his canopy, unfastened his harnesses, and then stood up on his seat. Leaning blithely out into the windstream, he reached over the front of his canopy and began to wipe away the oil with a white rag. Then I realized the little bastard had taken off a boot and was cleaning his windscreen with his sock. The backwash from the prop pummeled his face like a fist, but he simply ignored it and, with effeminate fastidiousness, wiped down the glass until it was clear. Then, just as he started to carefully lower himself back into his seat, his sock went flying into space, and for a second it looked as if he were going to leap out after it. I saw him quickly glance my way, his face dark with that damnable, perpetually worried expression of his.

Once he was safely back inside and had closed the canopy, he called in a meek voice, "I lost my sock."

"I saw that."

"Sorry, sir."

"Can you see now?"

"Yes, sir."

"Okay, then." I swung the plane back in the direction we had come, mentally plotting a course to intercept the bombers again. I wanted to avoid the Zekes if at all possible, but it was going to be tougher now, for they had been stirred up like a swarm of angry hornets. But glancing over at my wingman, I could barely suppress a bark of laughter. Little Elmer Kinney had just saved my life by flaming two enemy fighters, risked death by hanging halfway out of his cockpit 15,000 feet above the Pacific Ocean, and now appeared to have sunk to the depths of depression because he had lost a sock.

As we rocketed back toward the formation, I heard Comeaux's exultant voice calling, "Got one! The sumbitch is spinning in."

I could now make out two Hellcats diving into the rear of the bomber formation, their tracers streaming unerringly toward their targets. A Val exploded, and I heard Max Collins mutter, "Killed by a fuckin' Yankee wharf rat."

In the distance beyond the bombers, several black dots were zooming southward with another set of dots in pursuit. I could not tell who was chasing whom, but the Hellcats and Zekes were now obviously mixing it up. I could spare them no attention, however, because Kinney and I were fast gaining on the slower Vals and my eyes had begun to seek an appropriate target. The formation was gradually breaking up, but the Japs were at least marginally maintaining their *vics,* or wedges of three planes each. I selected the nearest, outermost vic to attack and began a shallow climb to get above them.

Just then, I heard Comeaux exclaim again, "Flame another

Zeke. I'm a goddamn ace!"

Arsenault's voice replied, "The sin of pride weighs heavy upon you, Porthos."

"Screw you, Aramis."

"Cut the chatter, gentlemen," I said, taking my eyes off the target long enough to look around to make sure no Zeros were coming in to bounce me. I trusted that Kinney, who surely now had a crystal-clear field of vision, could cover my backside.

I was not high enough above the Vals to split-S into them, so I nosed down a few degrees until I hit 335 knots. I set up my intercept point and prepared to open fire, but then the three Vals began to veer to the right, turning into my attack. I honked my Cat's nose around as hard as I could, rolled onto one wing, and let loose a wild deflection shot, hoping my fire was somewhere near accurate. It was—beyond all expectation. The nearest Val angled straight into my tracers and shuddered under their impact. The rear gunner danced in his seat like a marionette in the hands of an insane puppeteer and then slumped over.

Now, to keep from colliding with the banking dive-bombers, I quickly rolled left and hauled back on the stick, straining so hard that my vision shrank to a tiny tunnel in a field of gray and black. Metal and muscle groaned in the grip of six G's; I could not move my head or arms until the plane began to level out and the force of acceleration diminished.

Looking back, I saw the Val I had hit trembling like a wounded bird, smoke pouring from its engine cowling. I saw no sign of his wingmen; they must have broken away and dove once I commenced my attack. Even up here in the cold, I was sweating bullets now, and I had to lift my goggles to wipe my stinging eyes. When I looked out again, I no longer saw the Val. Rolling, I scanned the choppy sea below but there was no sign of it. A quarter mile to the left, a thick cloud was drifting lazily toward the coast; perhaps the Val had flown into it.

"You see him, Kinney?" I called.

"Negative. Lost him in the turn."

I sighed. I was certain my attack had fatally damaged the dive-bomber, but if neither of us saw him go down, I would only be able to claim a probable kill.

Now, near the horizon, I could see only a scant few dots moving away to the south. I was heading west, still tooling along at nearly 300 knots, struggling to get enough oxygen until the hot flow of adrenaline abated. Disjointed chatter crackled occasionally on the radio, and finally, Arsenault's voice said, "The Zekes are running. Vals have split and are moving south."

Then I heard a new group of voices calling out their targets. The Corsairs of VF-17 were now in on the formation, taking up where we had left off. Soon, a pair of Hellcats appeared in the distance, flying toward me: Vickers and Rodriguez, I soon saw. As they fell in on my wing, I ordered the rest of the squadron to orbit over the landing area so we could regroup. As often happens in combat, one minute the air had been swirling with airplanes, and the next, it was empty. I still wondered what had become of the Val I had hammered only a few moments before.

"Everyone all right?" I asked.

"Mine are all here," Comeaux said, still breathless from excitement.

"I still see a few Vals," Arsenault called. "They're heading right into the Jolly Rogers."

"Roger that," I said. "Hold over waypoint Baker."

I raised my goggles again and wiped my eyes, sucking in a few deep breaths from my oxygen mask. My heart was still pounding and my hands were shaking. By God, we'd been in a fight, and a good one, too. We had broken up the bombers and knocked out at least a few Zekes. And the Jolly Rogers were already picking the remaining formation to pieces, which meant that few, if any, of the dive-bombers would get through to their targets. But the mission wasn't over yet, and once my two flights had regrouped over Torokina, I led us back into our orbit, still vigilant for any sign of surviving enemy planes or fresh attackers from the north.

Above the ships in the bay, clusters of black flak began to dot the sky, indicating that some of the Vals had begun to dive. A few miles to the south, I saw a magnificent explosion high in the air; something had certainly gone up with a bang. One of the Jolly Rogers called a kill, but I didn't know if it was in response to the blast I had seen.

That was it for our contacts. The next hour passed uneventfully, at least for my group. However, we could see considerable activity far below in the landing zones—lots of smoke and occasional explosions. And on our radios, we heard Jumpin' Joe Clifton reporting a new wave of enemy attackers, but they were far north of our patrol zone. At one point, I spied a Zero some 2,000 feet below, fleeing northwest with a pair of Corsairs on its tail; I never saw the outcome, but a few minutes later, an anonymous voice called "Kill," and I'm reasonably certain the Zero had come to a bad end.

Right on schedule, at 0915, I turned the flight back to Conquest. It was an easy cruise westward, on a tailwind that sped us along in an exuberant mood. We landed ten minutes early, to jubilant greetings by our ground crew and other pilots—with the exception of Rufus Cox, whose face had grown about five miles long. I knew he was feeling put out at being denied the chance to fight, so I decided that, right after some chow, I would break the news to him that I was promoting him to division leader.

That little meeting did the trick. Once I informed him of his new responsibility, his face shrank to its normal size. He didn't even look perturbed when I charged him with the task of breaking the news to Hank Hubbard; in fact, I think he rather looked forward to it. As for me, it was one less headache to deal with.

When I sat down to write up a hasty after-action report, I tallied the claims that had been submitted to me. The numbers were impressive, too impressive, in fact, to accept at face value. I knew that two each could be confirmed for Comeaux and Kinney, one each for Rodriguez, Collins, Arsenault, and me—plus my probable—but all totaled, the squadron was claiming sixteen kills. By taking into account typical pilot exaggeration, several pilots claiming credit for destroying the same plane, and outright error, nine or ten was a more realistic figure. Looking over the claims, I settled on a preliminary figure of twelve, listing the other four—submitted by Asberry, Grogan, Bartholomay, and Dillon—as probables, since they could not be verified by other squadron members. Chuck Trimble, as intelligence officer, would evaluate and then sign off on the valid claims, making them official.

Still, regardless of any errors or exaggeration, we had made an impressive debut in aerial combat. The Fighting 39 had struck a fair blow to a superior enemy force and come away without a single casualty.

I could only hope our good fortune would hold out. I also knew that this was, of course, quite impossible.

Monday, November 1, 1943
1435 hours
Our second patrol over the landing zone was far less eventful than our first, for it looked like we had knocked the fight out of the Jap air raiders during the morning. The opposite, however, was the case with the naval vessels some 20,000 feet below. Task Force 39 had steamed south from the Bonis-Buka area and now, along with two destroyer divisions, blocked the entrance to Empress Augusta Bay. The Japanese had attacked with two

destroyer divisions, two light cruisers, and several scattered destroyers, fighting ferociously but with little success. From our vantage point, we could see the spectacular fireworks display going on below, but toward the end of our CAP, heavy clouds began to move in from the east, spoiling not only our view but the chances of the enemy attempting any further air attacks. As we turned west toward home, the clouds thinned, but we knew they would be following us all the way back. We could be in for a storm just about chow time.

We were nearly halfway to Conquest, cruising at 9,000 feet, when I heard Arsenault call on the radio, "Athos, bogeys at four o'clock high."

I cranked my head around to the right. Sure enough, about two miles back and 2,000 feet above, I espied a large wedge of black dots, heading directly toward us at high speed. *Christ!* Out here was the last place I would have expected to encounter an enemy patrol. However, I could tell by the three-plane vics that these were not friendlies—and they had a substantial altitude advantage. "Blue Flight, tighten up," I called. "Red Flight, spread out. Full combat power."

Our guns were charged and we had enough altitude to gain plenty of speed; still, the prospect of fighting high Zeros sent a cold worm of dread wriggling down my throat. I banked into a gradual, full power climb, hoping to get my nose to the enemy while maintaining sufficient speed to zoom past them after the merge; if we didn't blow through at high speed, the maneuverable Zeros could simply reverse and drop in on our tails. But if we went in head to head, our superior firepower could shatter their attack just as it began. The danger in a head-on confrontation was that the Japanese would not break off under any circumstances. They would collide with us and destroy themselves in the process before losing face by veering away. Our best hope against them was the sheer firepower of our massed .50 calibers.

Our ammo belts were loaded so that every third round was a tracer; between them were an armor-piercing shell and an incendiary round. It was the invisible rounds between the tracers that actually did the dirty work; the tracers simply lit the way. The Zeros, however, in addition to two 7.7mm peashooters, carried a pair of 20mm cannons that could shred even our Hellcats' armor if they found their marks. But they had a slower rate of fire and less range than our .50s. To survive, we had to get the first shots in.

I counted twelve planes in the enemy formation. If they didn't have cohorts hiding in the sun, then we owned the numerical advantage. I glanced high and west and held up a thumb to block the sun; I could see no sign of any other attackers. So, casting aside all fear and doubt in my accustomed manner, I hunkered down over my clocks and peered through the illuminated gunsight on the glass panel in front of me. The bandits were closing the distance at horrifying speed; they must have seen us long before we became aware of them. As the Zeros zoomed in, I jinked my rudder to the left, lined up my sights on the first one, and opened fire, only to see my tracers streaming far beneath it. There was no time to adjust my aim, either, for within a second, the fighter filled my entire windscreen. With an involuntary cry of surprise, I pushed my nose over and heard a deep *vroom* as the Zero rocketed past, only inches overhead. His propwash shook Old Grand-Dad so violently I barely kept it from snap-rolling out of control.

"Jesus!" I shouted, unabashedly rattled by the close call. But three more planes were bearing down on me, and I honked my nose up to fire off a shot, hoping to hit at least one of them. No joy. The Zeros roared over me, almost as close as the first. Then, glancing back, I saw them stand on their tails and go into a high-G climb that by all rights should have ripped their wings off. There was no way our Cats could match such a move, so I kept my nose down and pushed up to war emergency power. The acceleration smashed me into my seat and within three seconds, my airspeed indicator read 400 knots. No way the Zeros could reverse and catch us at this speed.

Kinney clung to my right wing, but I could not see Vickers or Rodriguez. Far to the left, Collins's division was hauling away at high speed, but three Zeros were closing in from above. I called out, "Max, check six." Immediately, his division split, the two sections banking away obliquely and swerving into a Thach weave. I could no longer see the bandits that had zoomed up and over me, but I felt certain I had enough speed to escape them even if they remained in pursuit.

Clang-thunk!

I looked at my right wing and saw a long, silver furrow in the dark blue skin. A few tracers zipped past, inches from my Plexiglas canopy. Jesus, but these bastards were determined! Rolling to the left, I stomped right rudder, throwing the plane into a skid that I hoped would throw off the enemy's aim. I looked back, and there he was—a single Zero some 500 yards behind, still spitting ammo at me; his wingmen were at least 200 yards behind him. But I was losing them now, for even with their initial altitude advantage, the Mitsubishis couldn't match the Grumman's speed. I called, "Mr. Kinney, straighten out and extend, please. We'll outrun them and then start climbing."

"Roger that, sir."

Kinney and I were now beyond the range of the Zeros' guns, so I began looking around for the remnants of my scattered flight. To the right, I saw two more Cats, several thousand feet below: Vickers and Rodriguez, who had gone into steep dives to lose their pursuers. I didn't see anyone chasing them, but they were too far away to be of any assistance. Surprisingly, I hadn't heard anything out of Comeaux; I hoped he had been able to get his flight out of harm's way and set up a counterattack.

Once I had gained a good half mile on the pursuing Zekes, I pulled up into a 2,500-foot-per-minute climb, which would bleed my energy quickly; however, if the slower Japs attempted to follow, they would stall before me and I could drop right down on their heads. But when I looked back again, they were breaking off, obviously wary of my ploy. They lowered their noses and zoomed off in search of less formidable quarry, leaving Kinney and me to bank right and climb away, no longer the hunted. I saw a swirl of dots against the horizon several miles away, so I set my sights on what I took to be the nearest group of Zeros, still keeping an eye on the blue ceiling above. I didn't want to get bounced again.

"Got trouble here," came Comeaux's voice at last. "Three high ones on my six. They came in after the others."

"Where's your wingman?"

"Don't know, I've lost him."

"On the way."

Within a minute, I picked out three green planes circling and diving on a lone Hellcat, some two miles to my left. Fortunately, Kinney and I had gained enough altitude to come in on top of them, and it didn't look like they had seen us yet. The arrogant bastards probably figured their partners had hit my flight and either finished us or sent us running. So when Kinney and I dove in at 300 knots, two of the Zekes were doing slow rolls at the top of a half-loop, more intent on showing off for the doomed Hellcat driver than watching out for their own asses. I closed to within 200 yards of the nearest plane, took careful aim at its wingroot—and its vulnerable fuel tanks—and squeezed the trigger. My armor-piercing .50s chewed up the aluminum skin, and the incendiaries torched the avgas. He went up so fast that I found myself flying right through an expanding ball of flame. Pieces of the Zeke clattered over my wings and fuselage but, to my relief, did no more damage than scratch the paint, though the fireball scorched Old Grand-Dad's blue engine cowling charcoal black.

Kinney's aim on the second Zeke was almost as perfect. Out of the corner of my eye, I saw the enemy plane falter like a pheasant shot through the heart. Black smoke erupted from its engine cowling, and the fighter began to spiral earthward. Its canopy slid open, and the pilot's head popped out, but he never emerged from the cockpit and ended up riding the blazing wreck all the way down to the ocean, where it shattered the blue surface with a splash of white and gold.

Now, the remaining Zeke driver realized his predicament and, in an elegant move, rolled his fighter inverted, dove, and began barrel rolling. His dive, however, brought him too close to Comeaux, who had recovered speed while we engaged his attackers. He lifted his nose, honked it around toward the retreating Zeke, and snapped off a quick burst that any observer would have thought to be a wild, random shot. Not our Porthos, however. His tracers arced as if in slow motion right into the Jap's flight path and intercepted it with uncanny precision. The Zeke's vertical stabilizer shredded like tinfoil hit with buckshot. The plane shook violently and started to roll over, but somehow the pilot managed to maintain control. He nosed down and beat a hasty retreat. For a second, it looked like Comeaux was going to take up the chase, but he wisely thought better of it. For all we knew, the fleeing Jap could lead us right into another ambush. With his plane in such condition, I doubted the little yellow bastard was going to make it home in one piece anyway.

"Let's get the hell out of here," I breathed as I once again saw clear skies around us. I knew that other members of the flight were probably still engaged with the enemy but I had no idea where they were.

Then my headset crackled and I heard the dreaded call,

"Dammit, I'm hit."

It was Dusty Woodruff.

"Where are you?"

"About five miles southwest of intercept point. I got two on me. Christ, here they come again."

I quickly banked to the left, heading south, hoping but doubting I would be able to find him in time to save him. Vickers and Rodriguez soon formed on my left wing. I didn't even have to look to know that Kinney still clung to me like beggar lice. I called to Woodruff, "Where's Hoagie?"

"Don't know, he dove and I lost him."

Dammit. The price of getting separated from one's wingman was becoming painfully obvious. "On the way," I said. "How bad are you hit?"

"Elevator's tore up, rudder not responding. Jesus, she's shaking like a motherfucker."

"I see him, Skipper," came Arsenault's voice. "Going in."

I still couldn't see any sign of the fight. Three more Hellcats joined on my right wing—Max Collins's division, sans Gummy Gilliam—and I saw a couple of others far to my left. The enemy attack had ripped us apart, that much was certain. At the moment, I could not be sure whether any of us had actually been shot down.

"Got one," came Arsenault's cool voice. "Dusty, roll out left. Roll out!"

"Can't do it," Dusty replied, his voice quavering. "Jesus, help me out."

"Hold on a few seconds more."

Now I saw a trail of black smoke far in the distance and aimed my plane toward it. I hoped the smoke was from the Zero that Arsenault had flamed. Finally, I could see several dots in the blue haze ahead, a couple of thousand feet below. I bent the throttle forward, and as I began to close the distance, I saw

Dusty's damaged plane hobbling along with a Zero in hot pursuit—and Arsenault's Cat bearing down on it from above and behind. But from the north, another wedge of three green planes was closing in at high speed.

It was going to be close.

Arsenault popped off a shot, but he was too far away to hit the Zero. The Jap, however, must have seen the tracers and realized he was in a bad situation. With astonishing agility, the Zero simply raised its nose, flopped over on its back, and went into a barrel roll that carried it under and away from Arsenault. He wisely chose not to pursue and instead sidled up to Dusty Woodruff's stricken Hellcat.

"You got some real damage there," Arsenault said. "You're going to have to nurse that thing home."

"Aramis," I called, "there's three more incoming. I'll try to keep 'em off your backs."

"Roger that."

I now had six Hellcats attached to my wing. The three Zeros roared in, gun muzzles flashing, and I saw tracers streaking past the nose of my plane. But these Japs were less audacious than their predecessors, and once they made their pass, they zoomed away to the east, their resolve apparently broken when they realized they were significantly outnumbered.

"All right," I said, "let's see if we can get this parade home in one piece."

"Thanks, Skipper, Jasper," Woodruff said somewhat abashedly. "I'll try to keep up."

The fight had dragged us far off course, so I led us on a west-southwest heading, hoping my calculations were somewhere close to accurate. Out here, over empty ocean, with no landmarks to steer by, navigation was by dead reckoning. Fortunately, visibility was still good to the west, though the clouds were rapidly stacking up behind us. I figured that, if my plotting was halfway reliable, we should see Conquest in about twenty minutes.

I wasn't far off. Twenty-five minutes later, I saw a hazy green hump protruding from the ocean far to the right. We were somewhat south of our destination, but after all we had been through, the distant island was the most welcome sight in the world. A few planes were still missing from the formation and I had been unable to contact them by radio. I just hoped they were safe and could make their own ways home.

Today, Dusty Woodruff's plane was too shot up to orbit while the rest of us landed, so I directed him to go down first. But when he attempted to lower his nose, the Cat immediately dropped one wing and almost fell into an uncontrolled spin; by some miracle of luck or skill, he was able to recover.

"That's it, Dusty. Just get over the lagoon and bail."

"I think I can make it, Skipper."

"No, you can't. Get out of the pattern and hit the silk. That's an order."

"Skipper, I don't want to lose another plane . . ."

"And I don't want to lose a pilot. Out you go."

"Roger that . . . sir."

Woodruff gingerly steered his plane to the right, and again his wing dipped. This time, the wing continued to roll over as if the cushion of air that held his plane aloft had been ripped from beneath it, then the Cat began to tumble lazily earthward, completely out of control. My heart froze for a moment as the tumble became a mad, dervish-like spin, but then the canopy flew open and Woodruff's head emerged. He somehow kicked himself free of the whirling deathtrap and pitched into space; a few seconds later his chute blossomed like a snow-white lily, and I saw him wave to indicate he was all right. I whistled a sigh of relief that probably pierced a few eardrums, but my jaw involuntarily clenched like a vise when I saw the ruined Hellcat shatter the azure surface below with a splash of white foam and then instantly disappear.

Dusty Woodruff was three planes shy of becoming a Japanese ace.

Despite the fact we had destroyed many of the enemy attackers, I brought my plane in to land with a heavy heart. We had lost another fighter, and I would almost certainly have to ground Woodruff for a few days. Maybe his flying skills weren't as well-honed as I had thought, or maybe he was just unlucky; regardless, the loss of two planes in as many days was a heavy burden to bear, and I didn't intend to send him up in another one until I was satisfied he was fully fit to fly and fight.

The pilots that rode in with me put their planes down without incident, and within ten minutes, a few more stragglers—including Comeaux—appeared off the end of the runway on approach. But it wasn't until they were all down that I realized we were still shy one: Eddie "Gummy" Gilliam, Max Collins's tail-end charlie. He had gotten separated in the mêlée and could not be contacted by radio. No one had seen him go down, but it was possible he had been hit by a bullet and killed in the cockpit. As near as anyone could tell, Gilliam had gone into the fight with everyone else, then flown into oblivion without even a final farewell.

Sometimes in combat, a lucky pilot might make his way into friendly territory and show up again, unscathed, hours or days later. We held out hope for Gummy Gilliam for as long as we could, but in the end, it was for naught. No one ever saw the hapless young man again.

Monday, November 1, 1943
1945 hours
"There's only one answer," Comeaux said, jabbing his thumb dramatically over his shoulder and very nearly poking Colonel

Rooker squarely in the eye. "They know we're here. That patrol was too far west to have just happened upon us. They were looking."

"I expect you're right," I said with a grim sigh. Comeaux, Arsenault, Trimble, Rooker, and I were sipping beers as we sat around a folding table the Colonel had placed outside the Quonset hut and surrounded with blazing tiki torches. The sun had dropped behind the mountain to the west, and the eastern sky hung like a purple cerement over the gunmetal ocean. A fierce but short-lived squall had hit us just before chow and left a coating of sparkling water droplets on the surrounding foliage. Low cumulus clouds lingered, though, and every now and then an impish gust of wind swept over the base, whipping the torch flames and sometimes extinguishing them; each time, Arsenault dutifully relit them. The temperature had turned downright pleasant, though, and the intermittent breeze kept the mosquitoes away. I had smoked three cigarettes in rapid succession, and I lit a fourth even as I tossed away the butt of the third. "They had to find us sometime," I said. "But I was hoping to keep our presence here a secret long enough to do some good."

I noticed that every time Rooker took a swallow of beer, he peered with narrowed eyes into the darkness beyond the Quonset hut. "It would be wise to keep the lights to a minimum at night," he said in a low, almost conspiratorial voice. "Can't say as I much like the idea. But we don't want to provide the Japs with an easy homing beacon."

"Agreed," I said. "I still don't think they're going to waste any resources attacking us directly. But their patrols could make our trips coming and going pretty hairy."

"I have an idea," Arsenault said. "Send up an extra division on each patrol. Launch them ten minutes after everyone else and have them grab an extra three to five thousand feet. That

97

way if we get hit on the way to the target, we'll have backup in no time."

"That's not bad," Trimble said, "as long as we have the planes to do it."

I nodded, thinking of Dusty Woodruff. The Marines had picked him up just off the lagoon after he had bailed. He had come out waterlogged and depressed, but otherwise unharmed. And poor Gummy Gilliam was probably sleeping peacefully fathoms deep on the ocean floor. In two days' time, we had lost three planes and one pilot. "The Japs never launch before dawn," I said. "That's pretty much engraved in stone. Early patrols will go status quo. On later patrols we can put up the extra planes."

"What if the Nips hit our backup first?" Comeaux asked. "That's only four planes."

"They just haul ass and draw them off," Arsenault said. "Zekes are no good at high altitude."

"They coming from Rabaul, do you think? That's one hell of a long haul just to intercept a single squadron," Comeaux said.

"More likely Bonis and Buka," Trimble said.

"If they came from Bonis and Buka, they took off under bombardment."

"No," Rooker said. "I'm betting Rabaul. Zeros can fly forever on a tank of gas and Japs don't seem to mind going the distance."

"Well, wherever they're from, I don't intend to see us get bounced. Even on the early flights, we're going to start pulling some extra altitude. And on days we don't have an assigned afternoon mission, I may put up a patrol or two just beyond our radar range. Maybe beat them at their own game."

Arsenault nodded approvingly. "Little is more fitting than beating the Japs at their own game."

As we drank our remaining beers, I saw a heavy figure

shambling toward the nearby tents. Before he disappeared into the shadows, I recognized him as our crew chief, Sergeant "Railroad" Bill Varn. I called, "Hey, Bill," and he detoured to our table.

"What's up, Mr. MacLachlan?"

"How's Old Grand-Dad looking?"

Varn shrugged his broad shoulders and squinted disapprovingly at me. "Your wing took a few good hits, Mr. Mac. Lucky for you they were from 7.7 millimeters. If they was from the cannons, you'd be out there right now." He pointed toward the ocean.

"You patch them?"

"Yes, sir. But you'd best watch yourself out there."

"I'll do my best."

"I got enough to do already. I hate having to patch up a plane because some reckless Navy daredevil decided to test the Nips' marksmanship."

"I'll keep that in mind, Bill. Thank you."

"Don't mention it."

He ambled away into the darkness and the rest of us stood up at once, signaling the end of our little skull session. I had yet to write the report of the day's second mission, and I dreaded the ordeal of composing a letter to Gilliam's next of kin. I decided I would hold out hope a little longer, but my gut told me it was pointless.

I went to my little shack behind the Quonset hut and flicked on the overhead electric light. Sitting at my rickety desk, I typed out a brief account of the afternoon's events, signed it, and dropped it in the "out" tray. The mission reports would be delivered to my immediate superior, Marine Colonel Oscar Brice, at Fighter Command at Munda, New Georgia, when the next scheduled supply gooney came and went, three days hence.

I was just about to close up shop when a sharp rap sounded

at the door; a second later, Colonel Rooker stepped inside, his face as clouded as a rainy evening sky. He barely glanced at me before going to stand at the window and peer into the dark night.

"I don't think we're alone on this island," he said in a low, grave tone. "In fact, I'd wager that we're being watched even as we speak."

I found myself strangely unnerved, perhaps more by his manner than by the statement itself. "I've almost thought the same thing," I admitted, going to stand by his side. "Nothing I can put my finger on. Just a feeling."

He nodded. "I'm sure I saw a figure in the trees this afternoon. Just beyond the perimeter."

"A tall black man?"

Rook turned to me in surprise. "No. A very short man, actually. Nothing more than a shadow, really. But it wasn't any illusion. So have you seen someone too?"

I shook my head. "Not for certain. I thought I had. But then I figured it was just a dream."

"Perhaps it wasn't."

"What do you suggest?"

"Well, I don't have the manpower to do extensive recon," he said, rubbing his chin thoughtfully. "I think it's safe to say there are no Japs on this island. But if there are natives, they could be hostile. If they were friendly, it seems we would have made contact by now."

"I don't know about that. If I were a native and my island was suddenly turned into a military outpost, I might not want to go marching up to the people working it."

"Maybe. But our original recon reported that this island was uninhabited. They don't usually make mistakes like that."

"But they do happen."

Rook nodded. "Yes, they do."

"Tell you what. Tomorrow, I can do a few passes over the island to see what I can see. If there's any kind of settlement here, I should be able to spot it."

He shrugged. "Good idea. I don't know what you might find that our original scouts missed, but it couldn't hurt. What's your schedule tomorrow?"

"CAPs over Cherryblossom, morning and afternoon. I'll put Comeaux in front of the afternoon run and do some local sweeps myself."

"Sounds like a plan."

Just then, I heard a distant burping sound, and the hand-cranked air-raid siren sighed to life, its voice climbing to a mournful, high-pitched wail. Rook and I glanced at each other in surprise, then rushed out the door of my shack and over to the operations hut, where we found an anxious-looking Marine private hunched over the radar monitor, his fingers nervously tapping Morse code on the tabletop. When he saw Rook and me, he spun around and said, "Sir, bogey approaching from the northeast. Fifteen miles out, about one thousand feet."

"Just one?"

"Yes, sir. So far. He came in low, under radar."

Rook nodded. "Washing Machine Charlie, we call him. Back at Cactus, the fucking Japs sent over a lone bomber just about every night. Sometimes well after midnight. Didn't hit much, but he sure kept us awake."

"Well, they know we're here now, that's for sure."

"No question about it."

"A scout must have spotted us the other day and followed us. But damned if we ever saw anything."

I could now hear excited shouting above the siren. When Rook and I emerged from the door of the shack, I saw the beams of flashlights strobing crazily through the darkness. Nearby, at the edge of the trees, a pair of shadowy figures was pulling the camouflaged tarpaulin off of a 20mm gun.

"Just get your guys under cover," Rook said. "And turn out all the lights."

"Roger that," I said, and rushed off along the dark path toward Tobacco Road. The tiki torches had already been extinguished, and I stumbled two or three times in the short distance I had to run. Then a solid figure abruptly materialized from the shadows in front of me, halting my forward momentum.

"Careful, Athos," came Comeaux's voice. "I'd hate to break any of those brittle bones of yours, however inadvertently."

"Porthos," I said by way of greeting. "I suggest taking cover. Inbound bogey, three minutes out."

"They've found us out. So soon!"

"Bitch of a life, isn't it?"

A disheveled Rufus Cox appeared a second later, wearing only his khaki shorts, apparently having been rudely dragged from a sound sleep.

"Air raid, Skipper? What gives?"

"You guys dig your foxholes?"

"We did."

"Good. Make use of them."

"Then it's for real!"

"It's for real."

"For crying out loud. I was just on my way to dinner with Joan Fontaine."

"She'll wait for you," Comeaux said, clapping Cox on the shoulder. He then gave the smaller man a sour look. "Well, she's always waited for *me*."

"What a pal."

"Let's go!"

I made my way toward the tents with Comeaux in tow. He and Arsenault had dug a narrow trench alongside it and woven together a few palm fronds like a parasol to cover our heads. Arsenault had already dropped into the trench and was motioning for us to join him.

"That little roof isn't going to keep out shrapnel," I told him.

"Ah, but Athos, it will keep the dirt out of our hair. I would hate to be laid in hallowed ground with Conquest Island earth prickling my scalp."

I chuckled and then made a quick inspection of the nearby tents. The men were frantically extinguishing their lanterns and torches, so after a minute, I couldn't see anything farther than ten yards away. But many confused and irate voices continued to emanate from the darkness as the Blue Devils made their way out of their tents and into their foxholes. I had Comeaux to thank for seeing that everyone had followed Colonel Rooker's advice to dig their holes right outside their tents; the precaution was apparently timelier than any of us had anticipated.

I had just dropped into the four-foot-deep foxhole next to Arsenault when the air-raid siren stuttered and died. Once its lingering echoes had whirled away into the darkness, I could hear only a faint whisper of breakers from the ocean and the low breath of the intermittent breeze through the dense trees behind me. The whole camp had fallen deathly silent in anticipation of the coming raid. Finally, from far in the distance, I made out the distinctive *rattle-rumble-thud* of approaching unsynchronized radial engines.

"Betty," Arsenault whispered. He pulled the umbrella of palm fronds close over our heads as if it could shield us from the bomber's payload.

The engine sound seemed to be heading unerringly toward us. The gibbous moon hid behind a layer of stratus clouds in an otherwise hazy sky, so to airborne eyes, Conquest Island would be all but invisible in the black sea below. But a single light—even a reflection on the canopy of a parked fighter—could give us away to scrutinizing eyes if they were sharp enough. I judged from the sound that the bomber was cruising at slow speed, at about 2,000 feet. Evidently the pilot was either oblivious or apathetic to the possibility of antiaircraft fire coming up to meet him.

The engine sound seemed to be right above us when I heard the shrill scream of falling bombs. I automatically covered my head with my arms and made like a mole, pushing my body as deep into the damp, sandy earth as humanly possible. Then the ground shook as if a portion of it had opened to swallow the whole base, and an avalanche of sand poured over my head and into my ears; the deafening boom of the blast didn't come until almost two seconds later. The inside of my eyelids turned orange as a wave of light and heat swept over us like a new, small sun bursting to life in the night.

My ears were ringing like a church bell at noon on Sunday. But above the sound, I heard Arsenault quip, "Gracious. There goes the neighborhood."

Suddenly, a stark beam of white light pierced the darkness to my left, and lifting my head from the foxhole, I saw a powerful searchlight sweep quickly across the northern sky. The Marines had sensibly positioned the light off the northeast end of the field so that a bomber targeting it would miss the base itself. A second searchlight flared to life down by the lagoon, south of the runway, and began to rove toward the source of the engine sound. And then the beams converged upon it—a single, gray-green, twin-engine Mitsubishi G4M moving slowly to the southwest, no more than a thousand feet overhead. The engine sound rose in pitch as the pilot throttled up now that he had delivered his package. But then I heard a new, deafening sound—a heavy, bass pounding—and from my left, a stream of orange tracers rocketed skyward, latching onto the tail of the bomber. Another stream began firing from a point on the beach to my right, but neither gun appeared to register any hits. A few seconds later, the Betty sailed beyond the range of the searchlights, leaving the 20mm to fire uselessly after it for a few more seconds before falling silent.

Washing Machine Charlie had come and gone unscathed, hardly an encouraging portent of things to come.

I could see flames to my left and behind me, which meant the bombs had hit in the jungle, well away from our facilities. At least we were lucky on that count. The foliage was still wet from the afternoon rains, so the fire wasn't likely to spread.

"Those were thousand-pounders," Comeaux said, pushing the little canopy of vines and leaves off to the side of the hole. "Heavy stuff."

"Think again, Porthos," Arsenault said. "Those would be five-hundred-kilogrammers. They're Japanese."

I crawled out of the hole and rose to my knees, brushing the sand from my khaki shorts and shirt. I heard a few panicked birdcalls in the jungle and excited voices nearby as the men emerged from the earth. The flames in the forest crackled and sputtered noisily amid the wet flora.

Then, with the insidiousness of a serpent questing for prey, something in the air seemed to change. It was not so much a sound—not yet, anyway—as a vibration, or alteration of atmospheric pressure. For several seconds I felt as if ants were crawling over my body and creeping into my ears. And then, finally, a low, grating rumble began somewhere deep in the jungle, slowly rising in pitch and timbre, eventually becoming a harsh, warbling wail, not unlike the air-raid siren. The sound continued to rise, becoming a shrill, eerie scream, like the voice of some gigantic, furious bird.

To my mind, there was no question that the source of the sound was something alive. Yet nothing that I knew to exist could utter a noise so monstrous—so big—that its intrusion upon the night made the bomb blasts puny in comparison. As if it would never end, it pealed to the sky, on and on, in a current of unmitigated anger, torturing my eardrums until I thought they would rupture. When I glanced at Comeaux and Arsenault, I saw them peering toward the jungle in confusion and disbelief, their faces contorted in pain.

I can't imagine how many seconds or minutes passed before the bizarre cry fell silent. In fact, I never seemed to actually hear the sound cease, or even soften. One moment it was there; the next, the air was simply quiet again. Even the crackling flames now seemed tenuous and muted, as if humbled by the sound's sheer power. Less than a minute later, the fire in the jungle began to dwindle to a smoldering glow, and a thick cloud of smoke came wafting through the camp like a filthy fog. Torches, lanterns, and flashlights soon dotted the darkness again, and the sounds of life returning to the camp finally replaced the eerie silence left in the wake of the terrible cry.

A few seconds later, I found myself surrounded by startled, curious pilots, with more appearing from the darkness every moment.

"Say, Skipper, what the hell was that?"

"The Japs dropping noisemakers on us now?"

I shook my head, still peering into the jungle. "I wish I knew."

"That sounded like it came from the caves," Max Collins said. "There must be something inside the caves."

I realized Max was correct. If the noise hadn't actually come from within the caves themselves, it was damned near. But that revelation set my mind grasping for some logical conclusion—something to reassure us that nature had not gone awry, even if it were improbable or downright far-fetched.

"What do you think, Skipper?" Hank Hubbard asked, giving me a critical stare.

"Sound can travel strangely in caves," I said with a shrug.

"Colonel Rooker has indicated there might be volcanic activity on this island."

It sounded okay, but I didn't think I believed it. And no one else did, either. I recalled the eerie, distant rumbling I had heard the night before, and Rooker's cryptic statement, *"If it's something alive, it's as big as that mountain."* This time, the noise had been infinitely louder and seemingly imbued with what I could only describe as *emotion.* But I could not doubt that the source of this sound was the same as the first.

"The Japs must have dropped something," José Rodriguez offered. "Something that came down with the bombs."

"It sounded like an animal," Hubbard said, but several other voices shouted him down.

"That was no animal," Jack Bartholomay said, giving Hubbard an exasperated glare. "No animal could make a sound like that."

"It sounded like a giant bird."

"More like a big cat screaming."

"A dinosaur!"

Everyone fell silent, and all eyes locked on the speaker. It was Ensign Elmer Kinney, his eyes big, his arms folded nervously in front of his chest. And, as I feared, an eruption of laughter drowned anything else the young man might have had to say. He hung his head and dug one heel into the ground.

"Quiet down," I said, unable to help feeling sorry for the lad. "Well, Mr. Kinney, I don't know if I'd go so far as to say there are dinosaurs on the island. But it was obviously no bird. And I doubt we have giant cats here."

"Whatever it was, it didn't sound at all happy." Arsenault stepped up beside me, following my gaze into the darkness. "I just hope it doesn't decide to take its frustrations out on us."

Another figure appeared at my side, and the red glow in the jungle faintly limned the angular features of Lieutenant Colonel

Rooker. He said, "So, you subscribe to the idea that something out there is alive, Mr. Arsenault?"

Arsenault shrugged. "Do you have an alternative theory, Colonel?"

Rook just shook his head and said, "No. No, I do not." But for the first time, I got the strong impression that the Colonel might actually have suspicions he had yet to share with me.

From that point on, the night remained quiet, and the fire in the jungle died without further incident. We finally dispersed and returned to our tents, everyone now uncharacteristically subdued and thoughtful. But no one mentioned the sound again, not even Comeaux or Arsenault in the privacy of our tent—a sure sign that the island's voice, as I had come to think of it, had profoundly rattled our nerves. When we extinguished all the lights and I lay back on my cot to go to sleep, I again had the distinct, uncomfortable impression that unseen eyes were watching us from a distance, eyes that were cold, calculating, appraising, and assuredly hostile. Now more than ever I felt that, whatever we shared the island with, it was alive and sentient, but certainly not human. In the all-but-silent darkness, even Kinney's suggestion of a dinosaur in the jungle hardly seemed ludicrous.

As I finally began to drift off to sleep, I became aware of a slight scratching against the fabric of the tent, somewhere behind my head. I turned and peered into the nearby abyss several times to see if I could discern any movement, but there was nothing. The noise was soft, subtle, and intermittent, and since I had finally made myself reasonably comfortable beneath my covers, I decided to ignore the disturbance and go to sleep. Most likely it was a stray palm frond swaying in a light breeze, occasionally brushing against the canvas. Or perhaps it was a large insect of some sort, searching for any delectable item we humans had unwittingly left out for it to find.

The latter possibility was only slightly less horrid than some unknown monstrosity lurking in the darkness, so I opted to believe in errant palm fronds. Having made that comforting decision, I eventually managed to drift into a sound, dreamless sleep.

CHAPTER 5

Tuesday, November 2, 1943
0730 hours

The morning sun had climbed into a cerulean blue sky, clear but for a single, extensive cloudbank that cloaked the southwestern coastline of Bougainville. Because of it, I missed seeing the formation of ships 20,000 feet below until we had flown past Empress Augusta Bay and were circling back to the west to begin our patrol. Then I noticed a string of dots off to the south and steered toward them, only to find that we were latching onto the tail of a flight of twin-engined, olive-green P-38 Lightnings, hanging in two tight echelons. I veered around them and took up a position at their two o'clock position, buzzing in so close that their leader doubtlessly devised a few creative epithets for me, "Brittle Bones" not among them.

"Hellcat leader, you want to spread out, please?" came an obviously piqued voice over my headset. The Army apparently had our frequency.

"You want to mind the radio chatter?" I called back.

"What's your call sign, Hellcat?"

"Blue Devil One, at your service."

"This is Pitchfork One. Your services would be more appreciated elsewhere."

"Suggestion noted," I said tersely. "Holler when you get in too deep. We'll be around. Blue Devil One, out."

So went the rivalry between branches of the armed services.

The P-38 leader wisely kept his mouth shut from that point on, though maintaining radio silence was largely superfluous with so many patrols flying directly over the beachhead. Soon, Task Force 39's FDO reported that his radar was tracking high-alt bogeys heading our way from the vicinity of Kieta, on the eastern coast of Bougainville. I pushed up to combat power and began the climb to 25,000 feet.

The radio crackled a few times, and Rufus Cox's voice called, "Bogeys at two o'clock low." A few seconds later, I saw the tiny dragonfly silhouettes a few thousand feet below, standing out in stark relief against the pure white clouds: a group of Vals, on their way to hit the task force again. I was just about to nose over to attack when I noticed another group of dots far ahead, at least 2,000 feet above us, struggling to get the sun behind them. They were not far from succeeding.

Pressing my throat mike, I called, "Bogeys, one o'clock high. Blue Flight, follow me. Red Flight, stay upstairs and stand by to assist."

"Roger that, Athos," came Arsenault's reply.

I banked to the right and dropped my nose to gather speed. Now I could see that the approaching fighters were Zeros, still slow and climbing. The Mitsubishis performed poorly at high altitude, and we had the speed advantage at any alt. I figured we could hit them quickly and get away effortlessly, as long as they didn't attack while we were still climbing.

Within seconds, however, it became obvious that the Zekes were already targeting us.

"Blue Flight, split," I said, watching the enemy fighters turn directly toward us. I counted eight of them. As they approached, I realized that these were A6M3 "Hamps"—a version of the Zero with squared rather than rounded wingtips. "Red Flight, come on in."

"On the way."

111

The Japs were closing fast, and they still had a slight altitude advantage. All we could do now was attempt to get the first shots in and cripple their offensive. Cox and his division—Jack Bartholomay, Todd "Tubby" Willis, and Timmy Asberry—veered wide to the left, hoping to hit the attackers' flanks. But the Hamps were closing too fast; we could not risk turning to engage them until Arsenault's flight joined us. I saw that, rather than vics of three, these Japs were grouped in four-plane divisions, like ours.

Smart. Smart sons of bitches.

The leading pair appeared to be targeting me, so I pushed my nose down even harder and shoved my weight onto the left rudder, throwing my Cat into a skid. The two Hamps attempted to realign their sights, but to no avail; they zoomed over my head fast and close, unable to draw a bead. As the following pair rushed in, I honked my nose up and snapped off a quick burst, but they were too fast to hit.

When I looked back, I saw Arsenault and his flight above and to my right, still most of a mile behind me. But like hawks on sparrows, they dropped down on the first group of Hamps, their guns spitting tracers. One Hamp exploded in a ball of orange flame, and another shed a wing and began spiraling toward the ocean below. I had lost sight of the second Jap division, which probably meant they had climbed and reversed to get on our tails. We didn't dare turn around; maneuvering would cost us speed, and we couldn't afford to give up any to the Hamps.

"Aramis, where's that second group? I can't see them."

A second later, he replied, "Don't slow down."

Frigid fingers clawed my back, for the Jap fighters were apparently on my six, just out of sight.

"Jesus Christ, I'm getting peppered here!" Willie Vickers, just behind me, called in a shaky voice. "I need a hand!"

Max Collins replied calmly, "I'll have 'em off you in a second."

"Hurry, please."

A flash of sunlight on metal caught my eye off to the right. Another group of fighters was closing in from above.

"Bandits, two o'clock high!" I cried, but we were now hemmed in. If we turned to engage the new enemy, the pursuing fighters would have us like sitting ducks. If we kept running, the high ones had enough energy to catch us.

"Blue Devil One," came a familiar voice. "Duck, you swabbie!"

I heard a rumble and looked up just in time to see eight fork-tailed, olive-green P-38s roar past on course for the new bogeys. Saved by the Army. What a disgrace!

"Go get 'em, Pitchfork," I said with a little sigh of relief.

"Tally-ho, eight Zekes!" he called. "I'm in."

Now, our pursuers broke off to assist their comrades, who were about to become prey to the Lightnings. Then, off to my left, I saw a pair of Val dive-bombers, just above the water, apparently trying to make a surreptitious exit from the scene of battle. I turned toward them, grinning hard behind my mask. When fortune smiled, she smiled with a vengeance.

The Vals were no more than twenty feet above the waves when Kinney and I caught them. We opened fire simultaneously, and I felt a triumphant surge of adrenaline as I saw my target shiver under the onslaught of bullets. Several pieces of gray-green metal spun away from the fuselage, and the rear gunner thrashed in his seat for a moment before dying. Then the strangest thing happened: just as I thundered past the disintegrating plane, the pilot looked up at me, his almond-shaped eyes plainly visible behind his goggles, then he waved wistfully, like an old friend at a bittersweet parting of the ways. Then the broken Val flopped clumsily into the water, split into pieces, and began to sink.

What peculiar, inscrutable bastards, these people.

A minute later, I saw Cox's division winging in from the right to rejoin our little band. I had to admire the discipline with which my group had stayed together; so often in the chaos of combat, even the most durable formations came apart at the seams. However, when I got a close look at Vickers's Hellcat, my stomach went queasy; his right wing and horizontal stabilizer were so chewed up from the Hamp's bullets I couldn't believe he was still flying. I doubted that even Railroad Bill's best efforts could hold that plane together for another flight.

"Mr. Vickers, head on back to the barn, please. You're looking a little threadbare."

"I'll be okay," he said confidently.

"José, see him home. I'd really hate to lose that Cat out here."

"Si, señor Skipper."

Vickers waved, scowling behind his mask, and broke away to the left, the flap dangling precariously from the trailing edge of his right wing. Jesus! Willy had to be fighting with the controls but didn't want to let on. Dutifully, Rodriguez tucked in tight with him and the two F6Fs zoomed away to the southwest, toward home. I could only hope that Vickers wouldn't end up pulling a Dusty Woodruff when he attempted to land.

The rest of us climbed back out over the fleet, which was mercilessly pounding the enemy gun emplacements on the Torokina coast. As the heavy cruisers and destroyers strung out across the crescent-shaped Empress Augusta Bay fired their guns, orange, gold, and red flowers began to bloom along the ridge above the beach, followed by thick knots of black smoke that grew into tall, ascending columns. The enemy had dug in and built tunnels several hundred yards in from the battered coastline, keeping the amphibious raiders from pushing their way beyond the beachhead. As I watched, a particularly grand mushroom of brilliant yellow hue, followed by an eruption of dancing, spiraling white sparks, suggested that the ships' guns had torched an ammo dump; within a minute, an opaque cloud of black smoke smothered the entire length of the bay.

For the rest of our CAP, we were merely spectators to the awesome display of firepower below. By the time we swung around to the southwest, my backside had begun to ache, and my neck felt as if it had been wrung from swiveling. While I wouldn't have minded knocking down another Jap or two, I now hoped we could just get back to base without further incident for a well-deserved break. Some of the guys would be returning later this afternoon to continue the CAP. I would be flying again too, but for a very different reason.

Fortunately, we encountered no more fighters, and though our fuel was running dangerously low, all of us made it home safely, even Willy Vickers. After I had parked my Cat and climbed out of the cockpit, he was the first person I saw, for he came down to the line to fuss at me for having made him come home early. And when Willy was finished, Railroad Bill came over to fuss at me for having allowed another Hellcat to be shot up. He figured he could make it fly again, but that much energy could be better spent fine-tuning the planes that were still combat-worthy.

"You know how long it's going to take me to patch this kitty up, Mr. Mac?"

"How long, Bill?"

"Too long. So don't you bring me another one unless you want me to put this one in front of the bulldozer. That acceptable to you, Mr. Mac?"

"If you say so, Bill. I dislike the bulldozing part."

"I'll be much obliged."

"Don't mention it."

I clambered into the nearest jeep chuckling, but Bill's point was not lost on me. Despite the fact we had downed an exceptional number of enemy planes over the course of a scant few missions, at this rate of attrition, in no time at all, we would find flyable planes in short supply. And we had already lost a valuable pilot. I couldn't help but picture Gummy Gilliam's youthful, homely face and awry, toothless grin in my mind's eye. I still hadn't written a letter to his parents, but I could not put it off much longer. The supply gooney that would bring our mail and other goods—and take any outgoing parcels when it left—was scheduled to arrive the day after tomorrow.

At the moment, though, the very thought of putting pen to paper seemed as daunting as flying alone into a swarm of murderous enemy aces.

Tuesday, November 2, 1943
1435 hours

Conquest Island was not particularly large, but our airfield occupied only a small portion of its southeastern quadrant. Should one attempt to explore the entire island on foot, it would require several days to get a halfway accurate picture, never mind the fact that much of the terrain appeared quite impassable. On the northern and western coasts, huge, craggy outcroppings of rock grew right out of the jungle and tumbled into the ocean, forming a natural barrier against any sort of landing there. The sides of the mountain that rose from the center of the roughly oblong island were steep and pitted in places as if gouged by a huge pickax. Coconut palms grew thick around the island's perimeter, but farther in, the dense mangrove, teak, and mahogany growth was more characteristic of the jungles of Burma or Thailand than an isolated spot of land in the Solomons.

Flying slowly over the island at 2,000 feet, I could not see a single open area large enough to accommodate a settlement of any kind, much less a native village. Yet both Rook and I had experienced moments when we were convinced that someone besides us must reside here, and where else could they be but somewhere down in that thick chiaroscuro of green, brown, and black? I could not deny a lingering uneasiness after hearing those strange sounds in the jungle. Yet, as had been so aptly pointed out, even if there were other humans on Conquest, how could they be responsible for so shocking a noise, one so alien to civilized ears? Somehow, even Mr. Kinney's dinosaur theory seemed too prosaic to explain the suggestion of awesome, raw power in that vast, voluminous tone.

And then there was the cavern—or more precisely, the tunnel—in the mountain. To my mind, no volcanic activity could have produced the noises we had heard. For safety reasons, the cavern had been thoroughly explored prior to our fuel being moved into it. But both Colonel Rooker and I suffered a strong aversion to its dark depths that seemed to go beyond mere phobia. A small, increasingly insistent voice in my mind suggested we might be terrified on an instinctive level because we *needed* to be.

I dropped my nose and descended to a thousand feet as I flew along the island's northeastern edge. Here, the ocean was aqua and clear, and I could see the sandy bottom for several hundred yards beyond the shore until it dropped off to impenetrable blue depths. In the shallows, a half dozen sharks— big ones—were gliding along just beneath the surface, questing for prey. (So much for any desire to go swimming!) Sunlight reflected brilliantly on the pure white sand that led to the jungle's edge, but there the dark, verdant canopy swallowed it greedily. If human beings could actually survive in that dense, hostile growth, they would be virtually impossible to detect from above. But I saw no smoke, no trace of any dwelling, no concentration of refuse that would inevitably accompany even the most primitive settlement.

By all appearances, Conquest Island was just as desolate as the original reports indicated.

For good measure, I flew around the island's perimeter a second time, and then over the center, climbing to 5,000 feet to clear the mountain's rocky summit. And as I passed over the knobby crest, something at the corner of my eye caught my attention. A movement, perhaps, or something out of place; I couldn't immediately identify it. I carefully studied the terrain, but the effort was for naught. Nothing unusual lurked down there.

Or did it? Again, when I turned away, something struck a nerve, and this time when I looked down, I thought—just for a second—that I saw a large, dark object on the mountainside that might have been a structure of some sort. Figuring a cloud might have cast a shadow on the mountainside, I glanced up but found the sky quite empty, apart from a large bank of cumulus clouds far to the east. Now I was beginning to seriously question the veracity of my senses—an unacceptable situation for a fighter pilot. Frustration was giving way to outright anger.

"Conquest Base to Blue Devil One, copy?"

"Roger, Rook, go ahead."

"See anything, Drew?"

"Negative. Wait a second." I banked to the left, looking down at the mountainside. Again, so quickly that my eyes could not apprehend it, *something* blinked in and out of existence, like a person's face, briefly illuminated by lightning. I cranked open the canopy, leaned out into the windstream, and thoroughly examined every crag, every boulder, every crease in the steep, rocky face of the mountain. There was nothing. Absolutely nothing.

"Nope," I said with a disgusted sigh. "I suppose I'll come on in."

"Drew, fly over the northern perimeter of the base. Just beyond the caves."

"Why, what's up?"

"Tell me what you see."

Once I cleared the southern slope of the mountain, I descended to just above treetop level and peered hard into the leafy canopy. It might help, I thought, if Rook were to tell me what I was looking for.

"Don't see anything."

"Okay, I'm eyeballing you. Veer northwest just a little and look down to your left. See if there's not something there."

I searched in vain. "Nada."

"Damn."

"What is it? What's up?"

"We hear drums."

"Drums!"

So, I *had* heard drums the other day.

"At first we thought it was just some weird echo of your plane engine. But it's not. Definitely the sound of drums. Pretty far off, but distinct."

I briefly entertained the idea of firing a few volleys into the jungle just to shake the place up, but if there really were people down there, it wouldn't do to cut loose on them without justification. So, disappointed with my lack of results, I turned back toward the field and put my plane down, noting by my watch that the afternoon flight would be returning within a half hour or so.

"Interesting timing," Rook said, when I met him outside the Quonset hut. "The drums started just after you took off and ended just as you were lining up to land."

"Like they're signaling someone, maybe?"

"Quite a question."

"You going to send a team to check it out?"

Rook thought for a moment. "No. Going deep into the jungle could be risky, and I can't afford to lose anybody. But I'll post some of the crew as guards each night. We don't want any nasty surprises after lights-out."

"I'll assign some of the pilots who aren't flying morning missions to night duty as well."

He nodded. "I think I'm going to run barbed wire along the perimeter beyond the tents. Hell, I wish we had some land-mines."

Through the dense palm fronds that overhung the Quonset hut, the knobby mountaintop gazed down at us like a leering giant. "We'd better report this to ComAirSols," I said with a sigh.

"Agreed."

Just then, I heard the distinctive growl of a Hellcat engine in the distance, and stepping from beneath the trees, I looked east to see a lone F6F drifting toward the runway. Disturbingly, its engine was blowing smoke. Red Flight must have run into trouble over their target.

Leaving Rook without a word, I hauled down the trail to the mechanics' shed, flung myself into a jeep, and bumped my way down the track to the runway apron. Railroad Bill was already standing by with a fire extinguisher in hand, and a couple of plane captains were hustling down to the line.

"Know who that is?" I asked.

Bill shook his head. "Nope. You people got no respect for my job, Mr. Mac."

"*C'est la guerre*, Bill."

"*Gesundheit.*"

Once the Cat got close enough to see clearly, I made out the number 17 on its tailfin. Ensign Timmy Asberry. He was a quiet young Virginia boy, an aggressive but level-headed pilot, possibly division leader material. To my relief, he managed to nurse his plane safely down to the runway, but as the Cat rolled toward the apron, I could see the glow of flames in the engine cowling behind the cylinder heads. Bill ran with surprising speed for so bulky a man, hefted the fire extinguisher, and cut loose with the foam spray. With a sizzling hiss, the flames quickly died and the engine spat a thick wad of smoke right into Bill's face. Unperturbed, he continued to spray.

The canopy flew open and Asberry leaped onto the wing, tugging off his goggles and flight helmet to reveal a smudged, blackened face. The fringes of his blond hair had turned sooty gray.

"You okay, Mr. Asberry?"

He nodded, coughing up a black ball of phlegm. "Christ," he groaned, clearing his throat with a harsh rattle. "No more smoking for me."

"What happened?"

"Ack-ack. So thick you could walk on it. The fleet hasn't put down those guns yet."

"Any fighter action?"

He shook his head. "Just the triple-A."

"Anybody else hit?"

"I don't think so. Mr. Comeaux told Hoagie to head back with me, but I told him to stay put. I figured if I got jumped on the way back, better to lose just me, not two of us."

My ire started to rise at Asberry flying off alone, but his reasoning was sound. I settled for telling him, "That was a big risk, since the Japs have proven they may be out here waiting for us. I wouldn't advise doing that again."

"I think your high cover did the trick. Nothing out there today."

"You were lucky."

"Yes, sir, I'll grant you that."

"Go get cleaned up. Take the jeep. And we'll see what Railroad Bill has to say about your plane."

Asberry's eyes got big and he glanced warily at the crew chief, who gave the young man an icy stare. "I think I'll go clean up now."

"Good idea."

I stepped up to the exasperated-looking sergeant and peered into the smoking, foam-coated cowling. "Well, Bill, what do you think?"

"I'm gonna have to tear it apart to see how much damage we got in there. But you got another plane out of action. We're gonna exhaust our supply of spare parts at this rate. Does that make you happy, Mr. Mac?"

"Not particularly, Bill."

"So. How 'bout you sit your boys down and explain to them who's s'posed to be doing the shooting and who's s'posed to be doing the dying. I'm gonna start stenciling American flags under your cockpits."

"Tell you what. I'll have Mr. Asberry send the half case of beer he owes directly to you. How's that?"

"Much obliged, Mr. Mac."

"Don't mention it." I started to turn away and then paused. "Say, Bill. Did you hear the drums a while ago?"

"Well, I was working in the shed. But yeah, I could hear 'em."

"What did they sound like?"

Railroad Bill scratched his bony, flat-topped crown and squinted at me. "Well, sir, they was a long ways off, but plenty loud. Playing fast and hard, too, like a goodly number of people banging all at once. Big ones, little ones, you name it. Quite a racket, what I heard of it."

"I see." I gazed up toward the mountain. "Well, thank you, Bill."

"Mr. McLachlan?"

"Yes?"

"I don't get the feeling they was beating them drums to say hello."

"No?"

His face darkened. "No. I took them about the way I'd take a rattlesnake shaking his tail before he bites you."

"A warning?"

Bill just shrugged.

Without a word, I began walking back up the track toward the camp, leaving the crew chief to tend to Asberry's damaged Hellcat. Although Rooker hadn't expressed the crew chief's sentiments about the drums in so many words, I had seen it in his eyes. And there was every reason to be wary. We were not prepared to organize a dedicated ground defense. Although every pilot and crewman on the island was fully combat trained, we had neither the personnel nor the equipment to contend with an enemy on the ground, however primitive. We had no proof that our unidentified neighbors posed an actual threat, but we could hardly just ignore them and hope for the best.

As I plodded along the rutted track toward the camp, I thought I heard something rustling in the underbrush off to my left. I kept walking but softened my steps, keening my ears for any further sound. Just to my left, several huge clusters of brilliant, wild orchids grew like a long, thick hedgerow, obscuring anything that might be moving on the other side. I paused and gave the orchids a quick glance—and then nearly leaped out of my skin, for standing next to a nearby palm tree was a distinctly recognizable, ebony black, stick-like figure wearing a brilliant crimson robe, its face obscured by the shadows of the overhanging fronds. I drew my .45 and took a few decisive steps forward, but the words "You there, step out of the trees!" froze on my lips, for as I approached, the figure simply vanished. With an explosion of crimson, a thousand or more huge, red-winged butterflies took flight, all swirling, diving, and dancing around me before scattering into the shadows of the jungle. They left behind only an ordinary, spindly palm tree.

I stood there, dumbfounded, for a long time, unable to accept that my imagination could have so drastically misinterpreted my eyes' input. When I slowly started toward the camp again, I resisted the compulsion to turn around and peer into the trees, angry and frustrated by my apparently warped perceptions. As the rows of tents came into view just ahead, I noticed that goose bumps had broken out all over my arms. It was damn near ninety degrees, yet I felt as if I had emerged from a refrigerator.

Something was tickling my eardrums. It took too many seconds for me to understand that it was a barely perceptible thudding sound, reverberating subtly through the earth itself.

Drumming.

Yes! Somewhere far away, the drums were still beating. Distant, barely heavy enough to detect. But this was no flight of fancy, no misperception of combat-fatigued senses. The sound was truly, unmistakably, 100 percent certifiably real.

And I knew now that, without question, it was coming from the direction of the cave that housed our supply of aviation fuel.

Tuesday, November 2, 1943
2030 hours

Until now, I had never actually set foot inside the underground fuel depot, and even with an array of light bulbs burning inside and two well-armed Marines guarding the entrance, the prospect caused my stomach to flutter. As I stepped through the gaping maw in the living rock, the temperature plummeted a good ten degrees, and even the sharp smell of avgas could not disguise a dank, musty undercurrent, a sour, organic odor that seemed to seep from the very stone itself. Just inside the entrance, I looked up, half-expecting to see countless bats clinging to the ceiling, leathery wings folded around their hairy bodies, tiny red eyes focused directly on me, but I saw only a knobby, charcoal-hued surface fifteen feet above that glittered as if encrusted with fragments of mica or even diamonds. Twenty feet ahead of me, through an almost perfectly symmetrical stone archway, a sphere of golden light dispelled the thick darkness with a friendly, welcoming warmth, and I could hear the distinctive drone of men conversing softly.

The tunnel widened into a semi-spherical chamber a good hundred feet in diameter, the ceiling rising some twenty feet in the center. Several strings of 100-watt bulbs had been rigged overhead to provide illumination, and all around me, scores of dark green, fifty-gallon drums of aviation fuel stood in dozens of immaculate columns and rows. I felt a slight draft across my cheek, which suggested to me that this chamber might be a mere portion of a much greater subterranean network. However, at first glance, I saw no opening in the walls to indicate that this was anything other than a single, self-contained pocket in the mountainside.

A pair of slouching Marine PFCs at the far end of the chamber snapped to attention when they saw me enter. "As you were," I said with a dismissive wave, and they returned to their relaxed positions. As I approached, I motioned to the nearest row of fuel drums. "I don't guess any of these have tried to escape, have they?"

One of them chuckled. "No, sir. They're behaving."

I glanced at their nametags. Hauschildt and Dietz. Both of German descent, I thought. Axis beware. "Boring job, I guess."

"Yes, sir."

"Tell me," I said, looking around at the arched walls. "Besides the main entrance, are there any other openings in here?"

Hauschildt pointed to the shadows behind him. "Well, there's a couple of passages back over there, and one there, to the right. But they're just dead ends, as far as I know."

"Got a flashlight?"

"Yes, sir." The young man handed me a heavy-duty, high-powered flashlight, and I stepped around the barricade of drums into a narrow, shadowed aperture. Here, the ceiling fell so low that I had to crouch as I moved toward its farthest end, playing the ghostly beam over the rough, basaltic walls. If this were part of a volcanic passage, its roof must have collapsed a long time ago. It was a dead end, all right. I backed out and walked around to the other extensions Hauschildt had pointed out, and fifteen feet into the last one, the walls and ceiling converged into a small cubby no more than eighteen inches in diameter. But through that opening, my flashlight beam revealed only pitch darkness.

"I'll be damned," I whispered to myself, dropping to my hands and knees to peer into the tiny opening. Plainly, it was too small for a full-grown man to squeeze all the way into it. I lowered myself onto my belly, my skin shuddering at the touch of cold stone, and aimed the flashlight beam into the inky depths. It revealed a long, tubular passage, like a gullet leading into the bowels of the mountain. The sides of the narrow tunnel were smooth and worn, resembling an oversized wormhole, no doubt the results of lava flow, countless years in the past.

Well, this proved there was another opening—but too small for any human to make use of it. Still, the fact that it existed gave me a strange, uneasy feeling. As I crawled out of the cubbyhole and rose to my feet, my knees cracking sharply, I called to Private Hauschildt, "Have you been back in here?"

"No, sir."

"Well, there is a passage beyond this wall. It's very small."

Hauschildt looked perplexed. "Well, I'm sure it was noted

during the initial inspection. It must not have been considered a safety hazard."

"I think it ought to be sealed up."

The young man shrugged. "I guess we can arrange that."

"Right away," I said. "We have everything we need to make concrete here, right?"

"Yes, sir."

"Good."

I waved them a little salute and turned to leave the chilly cavern. I wanted to get that opening sealed before sunrise.

The humid warmth of the tropical night was a welcome relief after even so brief a period in the dank depths of the cave. The two Marine guards still stood their vigil just outside the entrance, and they saluted as I went past. Darkness swallowed them before I had gone ten paces.

I had retreated from that place so quickly because, as I had thrust my light into that organic-looking passage in the rock, I was certain I had heard, at the very edge of detection, a deep, rhythmic hiss of air, rising and falling slowly.

The unambiguous sound of breath passing in and out of inconceivably huge lungs.

CHAPTER 6

Wednesday, November 3, 1943
0115 hours

I had been asleep maybe a couple of hours when I woke to the shrill, bitter sound of the air-raid siren rising in the night.

The chances of Washing Machine Charlie hitting anything were remote, and I doubted it was worth my bother to evacuate my bunk. Perhaps we would win the greater victory by not allowing him to disrupt our sleep for any longer than it took him to drop his eggs and beat his retreat, I thought. But my tentmates were stirring sluggishly in the darkness.

"I look forward to the day when I can repay Tojo for these breaches of etiquette," came Arsenault's sleepy, grumbling voice. "Positively Philistine behavior."

"And I should very much like to plague him with your existence," Comeaux groaned. "No one else could be more deserving."

"I'm thinking of boxing you both up and sending you to Tojo air freight," I said, forcing myself out of my little tent of mosquito netting. "He would surrender out of sheer exasperation."

"Would you at least spring for return postage?"

"Not for all the alcohol in the world." I tugged on my trousers and Brogan boots, and poked my head out of the tent flap. The sound of men moving nearby crept out of the darkness, but I literally could not see a damned thing. Fortunately, the chap

128

cranking the siren had given it a rest after only a few turns. Its noise was as bad as anything Charlie could drop on us.

"You know," Comeaux said, "when you're a kid, they tell you about the sandman who sprinkles sand in your eyes to make you go to sleep."

"Yeah?"

"That's horseshit. It's a squad of men in trucks who pour cement over you, so you have to chisel your way out."

"Ten bucks on the cement men," Arsenault said.

"You're out that bet," Comeaux said, dragging himself off his cot. "Well, shall we make ourselves comfortable in our outdoor digs?"

Pushing my way into the humid breeze, I saw a few lanterns and flashlights moving through the nearby trees, but within seconds, the lights vanished. A minute or so later, I heard the distant *thrum-rattle-thud* of the Betty's unsynchronized engines approaching. By then, the three of us had settled snugly into the foxhole and covered our heads with Arsenault's leafy parasol.

"Jesus, he's low," Comeaux said.

"Maybe he'll run into the mountain."

I keened my ears, realizing I was listening for something other than the bomber's engines. Something in the jungle . . .

Above, a black silhouette briefly blotted out the stars, and a few seconds later, a shrill, warbling whistle split the night air—but it was not the scream of bombs falling. This was something different.

The whistle became a chorus of thin, ear-piercing shrieks, like a hundred children screaming at once. Then, from somewhere near the beach, I heard a series of tinkling, shattering, splashing sounds, like innumerable panes of glass being smashed with hammers.

"Sake bottles," Arsenault said. "The scurvy knave is dropping sake bottles on us."

I nodded, realizing he was correct. "Yep. It's cheaper than bombs and does about the same thing—keeps us awake at night so we'll be exhausted during the day."

"It's working," Comeaux said with a yawn.

Just then, the searchlights blazed to life and a couple of the .50-caliber guns cut loose, sending gold tracers streaming toward the cigar-shaped, broad-winged bomber caught in the silver disks of light. But, again, none of the shots found their mark—and the 20mm wasn't even firing. Half a minute later, Washing Machine Charlie passed out of range, and the thrum of his engines gradually faded in the distance.

I half expected to hear a repeat of the previous night's terrible scream from the jungle, but it never came—only agitated, cursing voices and the rustling of bodies in the distance. As I crawled out of the foxhole, I decided that, from here on out, the hell with Washing Machine Charlie. If bombs actually fell on us, we were as likely to die in the hole as in the tent. As far as I was concerned, the precious few minutes it took to get out of the sack, into the hole, then out of the hole, and back into the sack could be better spent just plain in the sack. At worst, Arsenault would be insulted that we should spurn his painstakingly engineered foxhole.

Above all, that damned air-raid siren simply had to go.

I was just about to crawl back into the tent when I heard a commotion far off in the darkness, somewhere near the operations hut. I contemplated ignoring it, but better judgment overcame my urge to slip back into the sack and shut out the world. I plodded down the dark path toward the Quonset hut, once slamming painfully into a palm tree that had somehow planted itself in my way. Grumbling loud enough to make sure God heard it, I maneuvered through the trees until I found myself facing a trio of gesticulating silhouettes, now speaking in hushed tones. When they noticed my approach, I heard Colonel

Rooker say, "Commander McLachlan. I was just about to send for you."

Once I was close enough to make out a few features in the dark, I identified Rooker's companions as Major Pearce and Railroad Bill. Then Pearce flicked on a flashlight, and I saw that they were wearing their gravest expressions.

"What's up?"

"I wish I knew," Rook said. "Come with me." He took the flashlight from Pearce, then turned and led me around the Quonset hut to the outcropping where the 20mm gun was mounted; the other two men followed silently. When we came upon the sandbag-encircled emplacement, the only thing I noticed was that the gun wasn't crewed. My first thought was that the men simply had not gotten to it in time to open fire on the Betty. However, I realized that the camouflaged tarpaulin that usually covered it lay on the ground next to the sandbags. Then I saw, in the beam of the high-powered flashlight, that a glistening, dark liquid had splattered the gun's breech and muzzle.

Blood.

"What the hell?" I exclaimed, seeing a thin streamer drip from the gunsight onto the muddy ground.

"As near as I can tell," Rook said, "this is all that remains of the gun crew. That would be Privates Lester and Malloy." He pointed the light at the ground, and I saw a disturbingly long trail of blood that disappeared into the thick undergrowth just behind the emplacement.

Railroad Bill, expressionless, knelt to examine the trail, then peered into the dark jungle. He glanced up at Rooker. "Look here. Here's the footprints of the men as they got here and pulled off the tarp. But there's none leading away. Just that blood trail."

"That can't be," Pearce muttered. "They're just obscured by the blood."

Rook knelt next to Bill, dipped a finger into the still-warm liquid, and then wiped it away on the broad leaf of an overhanging creeper. He shook his head. "No. No prints."

"I don't buy it."

"Well, it's right here in front of our eyes."

"The bodies must have been dragged. Wiped out the prints of whoever took them away."

"Doesn't look like any drag marks to me," Railroad Bill said. "What do you think, Mr. Mac?"

"The blood is splattered, not smeared, which would be the case if they had been dragged. But you're right. I don't see any footprints other than theirs."

"Doesn't make a whole lot of sense, does it, gentlemen?" Rooker said.

"Not a lick," Pearce said, his scowl brilliant in the darkness.

"Who found this?" I asked.

"I did," Railroad Bill said. "I came over to see why the gun wasn't firing."

"So this happened while the Betty was still overhead."

"Near as I can tell, yes, sir."

"And no one saw or heard anything."

"Nothing."

The atmosphere of alarm and foreboding seemed almost corporeal as we peered into the inscrutable jungle. Finally, Pearce said, "Judging by the amount of blood, I'd say the chances of finding those men alive are zero."

I heard a crunching in the underbrush behind us and turned to see Comeaux and Trimble appearing out of the trees. "What the hell gives over here?" Comeaux asked, his eyes widening at the sight of the gore-coated cannon. "Holy fuckin' sheep shit."

"Get Doc McCall over here," Rooker said. "And Bernie,

keep the rest of the men away for now. I don't want a three-ring circus."

"Agreed," Pearce said. "Mr. McLachlan, why don't you make sure all your men are accounted for. God help us if anyone else is gone."

"Yeah. I think I had better," I said, shuddering at the possibility. "Chuck, go see if any of our guys are in the head, will you? We don't know who or what might be roaming around camp."

"Aye, sir, thank you, sir," Trimble said.

"Just watch yourself."

Trimble grumbled something and scurried off into the darkness. Comeaux and I hurried back to Tobacco Road, where I motioned to the nearest tents. "Porthos, I want you to do a tent-by-tent check. Make sure everyone is all right and has weapons. One man per tent is to be awake at all times for the rest of the night. Got that?"

"Got it. And you're going . . . ?"

"To the cave. Two of our guys are on shift."

"I oughta go with you, then."

"I'll be all right."

"You'd better be." He hurried off on his task, while I slipped into my tent to grab my flashlight and .45. Ensigns Hart and Dillon would be pulling guard duty at the fuel dump, and I worried that they, more than anyone else, faced the gravest risk if an unknown predator were about. As I set off toward the cave, I rather regretted refusing the offer of company, but I could not deny a strange thrill of anticipation and exhilaration, as if by confronting the darkness I might somehow render it impotent. Maybe not the world's best idea ever, but I told myself that whatever had killed those men was long gone, and if it were not, I would not face it empty-handed. My fingers tensed expectantly on the grip of my gun. As I approached the cave entrance, the sight of the faint, warm glow from inside offered me some small relief.

But the moment I entered the antechamber, the temperature plummeted, and every step seemed to be taking me deeper into a forbidding, menacing crypt. However, being bushwhacked by overzealous friendlies posed the most immediate danger, so I called out, "Skipper in the cave."

When Lew Hart called back, "Roger, Skipper," my relief was profound.

In the glow of the overhead lights, the cavern looked the same by night as it did by day. Hart stepped out of the shadows, his Marine-issued M-1 carbine at the ready. He was tall, slim, and muscular, with scraggly sienna hair and the beginnings of a bristly beard. He cut a thin grin as I walked in. "Washing Machine Charlie disturb your sleep, Skip?"

Before I could answer, a second figure, also brandishing a rifle, appeared from behind a column of fuel drums. Ensign Dillon was stocky, wide-eyed, and heavy-jowled; his chin sported a tangle of dark fuzz that could not decide which direction to grow. "Hey, Skipper. All secure here."

"Good," I said, but both of them realized something was wrong by my taut features.

"Jesus, what's up, Skipper?"

"Bad situation," I said. "Two dead Marines."

"God almighty. Who?"

"Privates Lester and Malloy. Mechanics. Rooker's 20-millimeter crew."

"What happened?"

I shook my head. "I wish I knew. There was so much blood . . ." I choked. "Christ, there's nothing left of them. Something out of the jungle . . ."

Both faces went pale. "What do we do?" Hart asked.

"I'm going to get some more men up to stand watch. I'm

sure Rooker will too. Can't afford to have the early crew losing all their sleep, so we'll keep it as quiet as possible. But come sunup, all hell's going to bust loose."

"Yeah. I'd say so."

"You haven't seen or heard anything . . . unusual, I take it?"

"No, nothing. Just that damned noisemaking bomber."

"Okay. Be extra alert. Anything happens . . . anything . . . you fire a couple of rounds—preferably outside, where you won't blow everything up."

"Okay, Skipper."

"Don't you dare get caught with your pants down."

"Not likely, Skipper."

"Hey. Did that opening get sealed up over there?" I pointed to the shadowed recess that hid the tiny passage.

"Yes, sir. They were closing it up just as we came on duty."

"Good. Stay alert, gentlemen."

"You got it, Skipper."

I turned and started toward the exit. But then I detoured, stepped around the nearest fuel drums, and aimed my light into the aperture toward the tiny opening in the wall. I was relieved to see that a thick, organic-looking mound of concrete glistened wetly in the beam of my flashlight. On the surface, it seemed an excessive precaution. But knowing the job was done set my mind at least marginally at ease.

As I hurried back toward Tobacco Road, the darkness seemed to smother my flashlight beam, and once I heard a shuffling sound somewhere beyond its range. Unable to do otherwise, I paused a few moments to listen, straining to hear over the pounding of my heart. For several seconds, there was nothing, but when I heard the distinctive *snap* of a twig only a few feet away, I broke into a run, my bravado finally buckling. Only when I nearly barreled into the side of a tent did I realize I had reached our quarters. A moment later, a dark figure came shuffling toward me from the direction of operations. My flashlight beam swung upward and hit Comeaux squarely in the face. He squinted in annoyance and shielded his eyes.

"Yeah, okay," he said. "That's a mean thing to do."

"Sorry."

"Cave secure?" he asked.

"Yeah," I said. "Everyone here all right?"

He nodded. "All accounted for. Albanese, Grogan, and Staunton are stationed on the western perimeter—down yonder." He pointed to the far end of Tobacco Road. "And we're putting up lanterns and tiki torches. If anything gets into camp, we'll see it."

"Good work. Now, one more thing. Tell Albanese to get you and Aramis and me up two hours before dawn. We'll take a watch ourselves."

"Christ. No rest for the wicked."

"We're in deep shit, Porthos. Nobody expected anything like this."

"We're not going to get any shut-eye tonight."

"Probably not."

"You've got escort duty in the morning. You need to sleep."

"I'll sleep en route."

"What else would be new?"

"Go do your job."

"Aye, aye, sir."

Comeaux turned and vanished in the darkness, and I headed back toward the operations hut. A few lights had come on here and there, but the camp remained reasonably quiet. Our night had already been shot to hell, but for at least a few of the men, some of it might yet be salvaged. I had no desire to lead into combat a group of pilots as exhausted as I.

"Hey, Drew," came Rook's voice from nearby. I saw him approaching from the direction of the ack emplacement. "All your men secure?"

"Yeah," I said. "I've got a few extra men up to stand watch."

"So have I. Bernie's taking care of it."

"Good."

Rook peered toward the distant beach, invisible in the darkness. "This may not leave me any choice, Drew. We may have to make some kind of offensive move. I'm not going to sit back and let my men get chewed up in the dark."

"We don't even know who or what we're looking for, Rook."

He gave me a knowing glance. "That's true. But I'm willing to bet that we've heard what did it."

I nodded. "My thoughts exactly."

"You know, your Mr. Kinney's rather peculiar suggestion might not be as outlandish as it seemed."

"Who can tell?"

"Well. You've still got to lead a flight in the morning. No matter what happens here, that's your job. You need to get some sleep."

"Doubt it."

"Try."

Pressure to get some sack time was mounting from all quarters. I decided to give it a go, even though I knew the chances of success were slim.

Somehow, I was asleep practically before my head hit the pillow.

Wednesday, November 3, 1943
0443 hours

It wasn't the raucous blare of reveille that woke me. It was the sound of a man screaming, his voice shrill with horror.

I shot up from my cot and, without pausing to put on my trousers or boots, grabbed my gun and stumbled out of the tent. It was dark, still well before dawn. Comeaux and Arsenault followed a half second behind.

"What the hell?" Comeaux muttered. "Where's that coming from?"

"Beach," Arsenault said groggily.

The three of us hustled through the trees in the direction of the scream, which finally trailed away. From the nearby tents, several other pilots were poking their heads out to see what was the matter, and farther down, in Marine City, I could hear men calling curiously to each other. To my right, in the light of several tiki torches, I saw Major Pearce—like me, still in his skivvies—rushing toward us, his .45 in one hand.

As we emerged from the trees and hustled toward the lagoon, I saw a dark silhouette kneeling in the sand in front of two odd-looking objects that I could not immediately identify. After a moment, I recognized the figure as Danny-Boy Grogan. When he saw us approaching, he stood up and with exaggerated deliberation brushed the sand from his trousers. Very calmly, he said, "Hey, Skipper."

"What the hell's going on?"

Grogan, a chunky, ruddy-faced lad of twenty-two, gazed at me with deep brown eyes that looked like wells of black ink in the darkness. "I found these." He flipped on his flashlight and turned the beam onto the objects I had seen:

Two heads mounted on six-foot bamboo staves. The heads of Privates Lester and Malloy. Drying blood ran down the shafts to form black pools at their bases.

My breath caught in my throat. We stood transfixed, and only Comeaux managed to breathe, "Jesus Christ almighty."

I heard heavy footsteps behind me and turned to see Rooker, Trimble, and Railroad Bill jogging toward us. When their eyes fell upon the horror that had sent Grogan into a screaming frenzy, they issued a collective groan of shock and disgust.

When Rooker recovered his wits, he said, "Did anybody see anything? Anyone?"

Grogan answered, "I just walked down here, you know, to make sure everything was okay. And I found . . . these."

Rooker aimed his flashlight at the base of the staves, toward the ocean, and back toward the jungle. He sighed. "Well, unless whoever did this followed our exact paths here, they left no prints." He pointed to our tracks in the sand. "There's Grogan's, and there's ours, right there. No others."

Pearce shook his head, incredulous. "Human beings did this. They had to have left some sign."

I couldn't repress a shiver. "Whether the actual killer was human remains to be seen. But Pearce is right. This could only have been done by men."

"This was a ritualistic murder," Arsenault said grimly. "And these are meant as a warning."

Rooker nodded. "Like the drums."

Railroad Bill growled, "Well, I got news for these bastards. There's a war going on, and they just joined it. On the wrong side."

"From this point on," Rooker said, "we can no longer be reactive. We have to act."

"What can we do?" Grogan asked.

"What we need is a platoon to scour the jungle," Pearce said. "Maybe a whole damned company."

Rooker shook his head. "We won't be getting any additional forces. Everything and everyone is tied up in theater operations. I'm afraid we're going to be on our own, gentlemen."

"Well, I suggest we get these . . . things . . . taken down," Pearce said, his voice heavy with dismay. "The least we can do is give them—what's left of them—a decent burial."

"Let us take care of it," Arsenault said, motioning to Comeaux. "We can spare you that small detail, at least."

Rooker nodded and took several steps into the darkness, toward the rushing breakers fifty yards away, bowing his head as if in prayer. Dawn was still a couple of hours away. But none of us would be able to sleep again, not for quite some time. And we could not scrub the day's mission. Like it or not, no matter what happened on Conquest or how devastated we felt, come daybreak, the Blue Devils still had to fly.

Wednesday, November 3, 1943
0715 hours
So blurry-eyed from lack of sleep that I could barely see straight, I managed to lead eight fighters through dawn's early light to a point northwest of Vella Lavella, where we rendezvoused at 18,000 feet with eighteen TBF Avengers and twenty-one SBD Dauntless dive-bombers out of Munda. Twenty other fighters, including Corsairs from VF-17 and Hellcats from VF-38 comprised the escort, and by the time we hit Kahili, my blood had finally begun to stir again. As anticipated, the ack came up hot and heavy on our approach, but also as anticipated, not a single fighter rose to challenge us. Prior to attacking, the bombers dropped to 12,000 feet, and we dove to treetop level ahead of them to shoot up any gun emplacements we could locate. There was no shortage of targets.

Countless streams of tracers cut loose to welcome us as we zoomed in with guns blazing, and I heard José Rodriguez spout an angry string of Spanish that I interpreted to mean he had taken hits. But he pressed his attack without wavering and let out an enthusiastic whoop when his .50 calibers obliterated a gun emplacement like a broom sweeping away an anthill. As I homed in on a sandbag-covered mound from which a .20 cannon was pumping shells skyward, I discovered how critically Old Grand-Dad needed an appointment with Railroad Bill, for my shots surrounded the target but never hit it, indicating my

Brownings were severely out of alignment. I soared away with irate Japanese tracers streaking after me; with a few evasive jinks and rolls, I managed to escape unscathed.

The same could not be said for Jimmy Penrow, leading my second division. As he zoomed down on his target and then past it, he shouted "Shit!" over the radio and then, in a calmer voice, said, "I'm hit. Throwing oil."

"Grab some alt and head for the barn," I said. "Blue Six, go with him."

"Roger, Skipper," called Emmett "Smitty" Hensley, his wingman. "Got you covered, chief."

"Roger," came Penrow's dismayed voice. "Heading out."

I led my remaining flight to the southwest to regain some altitude. Glancing back, I saw Tommy Blackburn's Corsairs roaring in just behind us, blasting away exuberantly. Big Hog made a run on the cannon I had missed, destroyed it, and went into a barrel roll to avoid the retaliatory machine gun fire. Blackburn and his flight now retired to the northwest, leaving the field open for the bombers to deliver their packages. As I began a gentle climbing turn to the left, I looked up and saw the Dauntlesses hurtling downward with their divebrakes spread wide, their noses almost vertical. They released their 500 pounders so low I didn't think they could possibly pull out of their dives, but with the aplomb of seasoned professionals, the pilots smoothly brought their noses up and firewalled their throttles, carrying the planes back up and out of harm's way. Seconds later, their bombs began to plaster the field, taking down hangars, barracks, towers, and fuel tanks with almost surgical precision.

Then, as the Dauntlesses roared away to the west, I saw the Avengers, still accompanied by VF-38's Hellcats, thunder in at 2,000 feet and release their thousand pounders, many of which fell directly onto the airstrip, sending up huge gouts of earth and coral, leaving rows of smoking craters that would render the strip completely unusable—at least until the Japanese took it to heart to begin renovations.

This type of raid had by now become routine for our bombers, and all too often, the enemy's fast and skillful repair work turned a pitted wreck back into a viable airfield within a few hours or days. But after this raid, I didn't think that was going to be the case. More and more, the evidence pointed to the enemy soon writing off Kahili as a total loss. In the face of our increasing air superiority, the Japanese could no longer mount an effective aerial offensive from southern Bougainville. The only remaining function for the Kahili forces would be to support their crumbling defenses at Torokina, and I suspected that within the next few days, even that task would be impossible.

We flew to the rallying point southwest of Kahili, where we re-formed with the bombers and stuck with them for half an hour, to ensure that no long-range enemy patrol could jump them. Then, with our fuel approaching the critical point, I turned my six Cats back toward Conquest, my body aching and desperate for uninterrupted sleep. However, I dreaded to think what might be waiting for us there; insidiously, an unknown enemy had turned our supposedly safe haven into a place of unknown pitfalls and deadly terror. I could only hope no new complications had arisen while my flight was away.

We landed without incident, and I was relieved to learn that Jimmy Penrow and Smitty Hensley had arrived safely—although Penrow had disappeared immediately afterward to avoid facing Railroad Bill's wrath.

As soon as I climbed out of my cockpit, I saw the husky crew chief striding toward me, sporting only a minor scowl. After all we had been through the night before, I figured he was too tired and shaken to be at his querulous best.

"Mr. Mac," he said, giving me a little nod. "I'm happy to say

I got two of your birds back in service. Of course, now you've up and sent me another one."

"How bad is it?"

"Well, if you don't bring me no more business this afternoon, I might have her ready to fly again tomorrow."

"That's not so bad."

"She took a few good pings. And I'm gonna ping Mr. Penrow when I find him."

"You might want to wait till he pays up the beer he owes."

"Some deal."

"Everything else all right?"

"Far as can be. Mr. Rooker's stringing up barbed wire from one end of the base to the other, at least till he runs out."

"By the way, I need to have my guns realigned. They're way off."

"They wouldn't be, if you weren't sending me so much other business."

"Sorry about that."

"I reckon I can pencil you in."

"Thank you, Bill."

"Don't mention it."

By now, the rest of the flight had landed, and the pilots were converging on the waiting jeeps. I wearily made my way toward them and flopped into the back of one with Vickers, Rodriguez, and Kinney. At the moment, all I wanted was to disappear into my tent and shut out the world for a few hours. I wasn't sure I could hold my eyes open even as long as it took to get there.

Somehow I did, and I met Comeaux and Arsenault on their way to the afternoon mission briefing at the operations hut. They would be taking twelve planes up to Matchin Bay, on the northeastern coast of Bougainville, to knock out supply and troop barges reportedly gathering to contribute to the defense of Torokina.

"Athos, you look ugly," Comeaux said. "Take a nap, for crying out loud."

"That's the plan."

"They're calling for bad weather this afternoon," Arsenault said. "I suspect we'll run into it."

"Be careful out there," I said, slipping into the tent. "We can't afford to lose anybody to an act of God."

"I'll put in a good word," Arsenault called, the sincerity of his tone giving me the first reason I'd had all day to chuckle. Sometimes I had to wonder if he didn't honestly consider himself the divinely appointed liaison between the Almighty and the rest of us. I sat down on the edge of my cot, pulled off my boots and shirt, and lay back on the scratchy pillow, trying to forget that I still had to file an after-action report. I would also need to get with Chuck Trimble later in the day to outline tomorrow's missions. Plus, with the assistance of the appropriate officers and Marine personnel, I'd have to compose comprehensive reports for Fighter Command about the condition of our aircraft, the efficacy of our missions to date, and the adequacy of our stores, ammunition, and fuel—all the little bureaucratic details I detested—to go out with the supply gooney the following day.

Somehow, even after the previous night's horror, it was these niggling tasks that weighed most heavily on my mind as I closed my eyes and tried to relax. Though thoroughly exhausted, I could not immediately drop off to sleep. My ears seemed acutely sensitive to noises from around the camp: the voices of men at work, the distant hammering and banging from the maintenance shed, the occasional roar of engines as they were tested and tweaked. I believe I half-expected to hear *something* in the jungle that would remind me that we were most assuredly neither alone nor secure in our fortified encampment.

Eventually, though, the late morning noises softened, and my mind began to drift away. The last thing I remembered hearing was the soft rush of a breeze as it swept through the trees and over the tent, subtly hinting that, before the day was out, nature might yet reveal herself as a force to be reckoned with.

Wednesday, November 3, 1943
1420 hours
The sharp, repetitive crack of machine gun fire tore me abruptly out of dreamland, and I nearly tipped over my cot as I bolted upright in surprise. After a few seconds, I realized that the sound came from a Hellcat's guns. Down by the runway, the gunnery crew had set up a target range for adjusting the convergence of our planes' .50 calibers. Once my dream-muddled brain began to form cohesive thoughts, I recalled that Old Grand-Dad was among several F6Fs that the crew would be attending to this afternoon. I could be hearing gunfire for quite some time to come.

But my thoughts soon returned to the dreams the shooting had interrupted. Though cloudy, certain images, sounds, and sensations lingered in my consciousness like the aftermath of a storm. Prominent among them was the sight of the now-familiar tall, crimson-robed black man. I now recalled that he had been speaking to me in a deep, sonorous voice that was both hypnotic and unsettling, and though I couldn't remember his exact words, I understood that he wanted me to accompany him somewhere. I had half-willingly walked with him for a long distance in complete darkness and, after a time, realized I was no longer walking but floating. Though I could not see where I was going, I had the distinct impression that I was moving faster and faster, and that I had no control over my speed or direction. I began to experience vertigo, and at the farthest range of my vision, a dot of pale blue-green light sprang out of the darkness. It slowly expanded, and as I drew nearer, I heard a shrill, discordant piping, as if a large number of inexperienced lips were blowing raucous notes from flutes.

No, not inexperienced. The sounds were too deliberately inharmonious. *Insane.*

I lay on my back for several minutes, listening to the normal sounds from outside: assorted birdcalls, a few haranguing voices, some arrhythmic hammering from maintenance. I heard no more gunfire. Then a sharp clattering sound rose in the distance, and I realized it was rain coming down fast and hard in the jungle. Gradually, it grew louder as it drummed its way through the trees, and then, as if the clouds had exploded, water began to batter my tent with a ferocity exceeding anything I had experienced so far. I heard some shouts as the Marine crews began to seek shelter, and I examined the seams of my tent, hoping against hope to see no water oozing through them. So far, so good.

The wind rose with a whine, huffing against the sides of my tent like the breath of some giant animal. Thunder began to rumble: a continuous rolling *boom* that approached steadily from the northeast. I dragged myself up and gazed out the mosquito-netted windows, struck by the sheer power of the water as it drove through the leafy canopy, batting fronds and limbs about like invisible clubs. Lightning crackled above the trees, briefly illuminating the dark day like a magnesium flare. Then I felt a wet spray in my face, so I laced the canvas flaps over the windows, which left me in a thick, humid darkness, feeling strangely alone and vulnerable. For a few seconds, my lungs felt heavy and bereft of air, almost as if I were drowning. Perhaps strangely, the sensation brought to mind an image of Gummy Gilliam's homely face, and I wondered if he had met his end being dragged helplessly with his plane into the dark depths of the ocean. Or had a bullet mercifully ended his life before he went down?

A sense of the sheer fragility of life overwhelmed me, a rush of paranoia that turned my knees to mush. Backing up awkwardly, I dropped onto my cot, near to hyperventilating. I could not allow myself to succumb to such weakness, I thought angrily, not even for a moment, or my days as a squadron commander were finished. I had learned how to deal with fear a long time ago, but now I felt like a child, quivering helplessly on my bed. This would never do.

Outside, the gale had begun to increase, and now the canvas siding was shuddering so violently I began to worry my whole tent would collapse. Water splashed in even through the closed window flaps, and thunder rumbled continuously like a barrage from a battleship's sixteen-inch guns. I recalled Rooker telling me how violent some of these storms could be, and the memory of him saying "You don't want to be flying when they hit" reminded me that it was nearly time for Comeaux's group to return from its barge-busting mission.

Anxiety for my men's safety quickly replaced my personal fears—at least until I heard a slow, heavy clumping sound in the foliage somewhere outside the tent. At first I thought one of the Marines or pilots must be making his way to shelter from the rain, but this was a measured, deliberate, *unhurried* tread, so heavy that only a huge man could be making such a noise over the sounds of the storm. And it was coming from the direction of the jungle, now separated from the tents by a tangled barricade of barbed wire.

Automatically, I reached for my .45 and crouched at the foot of Arsenault's cot, next to the side of the tent that faced the rain forest. I estimated that whoever or whatever was out there couldn't be more than a dozen feet away. To my disbelief, the footsteps approached without breaking their rhythm—as if the walker had passed through the barbed wire without missing a step. Most disturbing of all, the footsteps were heading directly for my tent.

Had Privates Lester and Malloy heard the same thing just before meeting their fates?

Well, there was nothing to do now but attempt to escape or hold my ground. No matter how badly my nerves had been shaken, I could not bring myself to turn and run. So, drawing on all my training and experience, I swallowed my fear, stood up, calmly unfastened the flap over the window, and raised it with one hand while thrusting my gun against the mosquito netting with the other. Somehow, I almost knew what I was going to see.

But steeling my will did not prepare me for the sight of the crimson-robed figure standing just on the other side of the window, his arms spread at his sides in a beckoning gesture. He was so tall I had to crane my neck to see his head, and when I did, I saw only a pitch-black, featureless void where the face should be, like a hole punched in space itself, radiating cognizance more intensely than if a pair of blazing eyes were staring directly into mine. I took an involuntary step backward, releasing the window flap so that it dropped and thankfully hid the figure on the other side.

Then that deep, familiar, sonorous voice spoke—but only in my head, for the words did not rise above the sounds from outside; they somehow took shape in my brain as if they'd been whispered in my ear.

"We are not finished."

My finger automatically closed on the trigger of my .45, which discharged with a deafening blast. In the ringing echo that followed, I kept hoping to hear the sound of a heavy body dropping to the ground. But it never came.

Gripping my Colt in bone-white fingers, I unfastened the canvas door flap, pushed my way out into the battering rain, and sloshed in my bare feet through three-inch-deep mud to the back of the tent. I prayed to see a body splayed on the rain-soaked earth, but—hardly to my surprise—there was nothing. No sign of a crimson-robed figure anywhere within view.

And not a single footprint in the muck where the faceless figure had been standing.

I heard voices now, some yelling my name. I ignored them and peered into the rain-shrouded depths of the trees, searching for any sign of movement, some indication that my visitor had been anything other than a vivid figment of my overwrought imagination.

Nothing.

The sharp smell of cordite assured me that I was awake and no longer dreaming. Cold rain slapped my face angrily, as if to rebuke me for trespassing where I had no business. The stinging raindrops soaked me through to my bones, but I barely felt them now. I could no longer be sure of the validity of my senses.

"Skipper, what the hell?" came Rufus Cox's voice. He hustled up next to me, wiping water out of his curious eyes. "You see something?"

Major Pearce appeared a second later, wearing a poncho, his dripping, bushy brows clenched over concerned, if suspicious-looking, eyes. "Commander McLachlan?" he asked, his gaze roving among the trees in the direction I had fired. "What did you see?"

"A man. I think it was a man."

"You think?"

I turned to Pearce and shook my head. "I've seen him before. But I'm not certain that he's real."

"You're not making sense, Commander."

"Yeah, I know," I muttered. "But I think he—or it—is what killed your men."

A few seconds later, Colonel Rooker came sprinting up the

path from the operations hut. He looked thoughtfully at Pearce and then at me. "I don't suppose you got him?"

"Doesn't look like it."

A few other pilots and Marines came rushing up to see what was going on. Naturally enough, after having lost two men so brutally to an unknown predator, everyone was on edge and curious. And while my vague explanation could satisfy no one any less than it did me, there seemed to be an unspoken sentiment among these men that we were, in fact, dealing with something that defied conventional explanation. Anywhere else, I might have been regarded as unbalanced, but not here. Not now.

Rooker gave me a quick tap on the shoulder. "Your flight's on its way in. The worst of the storm has passed, but it's not over yet."

"Okay," I said. "Hey, do something for me. Have somebody go check in at the caves and see if everything's all right."

Rook's face clouded. "You think something's wrong?"

"Just a hunch."

"Yeah, okay," he said, giving me a parting nod.

I was already waterlogged, so I saw little point in attempting to stay dry now. I went back into my tent just long enough to pull on some socks and my boots, then I closed it up and began hiking down the jeep track toward the flight line. As I passed the patch of orchids where I thought I had seen the black man yesterday, I paused to study the tangle of growth, briefly wondering if there might be some chemical or organic substance on this island that could produce hallucinations—thus leaving us vulnerable to whatever deadly entity lurked in the jungle.

Something devised by the Japanese themselves?

No. It was too pat an explanation. My gut told me that we were dealing with a thing—regardless of its veneer—that was decidedly inhuman.

Something evil?

But only humans could be truly evil, I thought. Anything else was just the way of nature. Arbitrary in its destructive capacity, perhaps, but not evil.

So I had always believed. Now I was not so sure.

I continued on my way, my feet sinking into earth that only a short time ago had been as hard as concrete. The gray, ink-washed sky appeared to be brightening slightly in the east, but the rain was still falling in sheets, and my scalp tingled from the continuous impact of cold droplets. Off to the right, I could see the maintenance shed and the pair of frame buildings that served as hangars; a few figures moved about beneath the roofs, still engaged in their jobs, seemingly indefatigable and un-daunted by either weather or unknown enemies. It was a heartening sight.

The plane captains had already driven the jeeps down to the flight line and were gathering next to the aircraft revetments to meet the incoming planes. My heart had begun to race at the thought of a dozen planes having to put down into the morass the runway had become, even with the steel matting. Above all, I hoped that Comeaux was coming home with his entire group. They could have conceivably encountered fighter resistance at the northern end of Bougainville. And furious enemy ack-ack on these missions was a given.

Only a few minutes later, I heard the faint roar of engines in the distance, and I searched the low, thick clouds in the southeastern sky for the first sign of the inbound fighters. Finally, I saw it: a hazy shadow forming inside a roiling mass of gray and white just off the end of the runway. Comeaux's gear was already down; how he had managed to home in on the runway so precisely was a marvel to me. God, to have eyes like his!

The Hellcat materialized fully just before it set down in a

perfect three-point landing, its tires throwing up a plume of water that looked like the explosion of a 500-pound bomb. My stomach lurched for a second as I saw the F6F swerve drunkenly to one side before straightening out, its whirling prop sending a spiral tube of vapor back over the canopy and fuselage. Comeaux's engine deepened to a slow thrum and he steered his plane toward the apron, throwing his canopy back before the plane even stopped rolling. One of the plane captains hurried out to meet him, but he had hauled himself out of the cockpit and jumped onto the wing before the man got halfway.

When he saw me, he gave me one of those broad grins that assured me all had gone well.

A second Hellcat—Timmy Asberry's—appeared at the end of the runway and settled into the slop, also slewing to one side before straightening out and slowing. It began rolling toward us as Comeaux stepped up to me and pulled off his flight helmet, letting his hair and face get soaked by the rain.

"We blew the hell out of 'em, Athos. Troops, ammo, fuel, you name it. All at the bottom of the bay."

"Everybody come out all right?"

"Not a scratch."

I looked over his shoulder at the next approaching fighter. "So far," I said.

He glanced back with a thoughtful grunt. "It is a mess out there."

We stood together and for the next ten minutes watched each Hellcat appear out of the mist like a ghostly bird of prey and splash onto the matting. By the time the last one was down, the rain had thinned to a gentle shower, and when Jack Bartholomay, riding tail-end Charlie, pulled up at the flight line, a brightening patch of blue had appeared in the east. Ten minutes later, the rain stopped altogether.

Arsenault and his section leader, Lew Hart, came walking

toward us, both gesticulating spiritedly as they described their diving attacks on their targets to each other. Arsenault was beaming almost as shamelessly as Comeaux. "I dispatched three of the heathens," he said, holding up three fingers. Then he pointed to Hart. "I would have sank a fourth if this heretic were to heed the commandment, 'Thou shalt not steal.' "

"You missed on your first pass," Hart said with a smirk. "I was merely obliged to finish the job."

I felt Comeaux's eyes on me as we began walking toward the parked jeeps. No doubt he had noticed my wan complexion and drawn features, but I didn't want to mention the incident with the strange figure at the tent quite yet. He flicked a Camel from his pack, stuck it between his lips, and lit it. Then he handed the pack to me. "Athos, you need a smoke," he said.

"Thanks." I took one and accepted a light. The first deep breath of smoke worked like a tonic.

"Didn't you get any sleep?" he asked.

"A little."

"You look worse than when we left."

"I was worried about you."

"He isn't worth it," Arsenault said. "The energy spent worrying over his unworthy skin could be put to better use. Such as in devising a plan for a few days' leave on Espiritu. Give me a pass, Athos."

"I will not."

"You didn't meet the nurse I met when we were laid over. If you had met her, you would surely give me a pass."

"We don't have any leave time yet."

"If I were CO, I would give you a pass."

"If you were CO, this base would by now be the property of the Japanese."

"You are a cold and heartless CO."

"You can't have a pass."

Comeaux nodded his approval. "You are a wise and noble CO, Athos. Don't let anyone except me tell you otherwise."

I got behind the wheel of the jeep and Arsenault took the passenger seat. Comeaux hopped into the back.

"I'll have you a mission report by sundown," he said. "And unlike his, mine will be accurate."

"Thank you."

Arsenault frowned. "Athos, do not give *him* a pass."

"I won't."

He cut a little smile. "Perhaps not wise and noble. But fair."

I drove us up the muddy track to Tobacco Road, parked the jeep, and led the way to number one. As we stepped inside, Comeaux immediately noticed the shredded flap and mosquito netting over the rear window.

"God almighty, what happened here?"

"Sit down. And I'll tell you all about it."

As we sat down on our bunks, I proceeded to describe everything that had happened while the flight was gone, including as much of my dream as I remembered. If there was anyone who would believe the whole account, these two would. When I finished, Comeaux gave a low whistle.

"No wonder you're so goddamn rattled. Anybody else, I'd say they were crazy. But I know better."

Arsenault nodded. "Does Rooker know?"

"Yes."

Just then, I heard Rook's voice. "Drew, you home?"

"Yeah, come on in."

The flap opened and Rook, crouching, slipped inside. His face looked ivory in the dim afternoon light. "Drew, how did you know something was up at the caves?"

I shook my head. "I didn't. Not really."

"What is it?" Comeaux asked. "What's wrong?"

"The concrete seal we put in last night."

"What about it?"

"It's busted up," Rook said, giving us all a look that shadowed despair. "From the other side."

Wednesday, November 3, 1943
1530 hours

"Sure looks like something must have come out through here," Comeaux said, shining his light at the shattered fragments of concrete that littered the floor of the small recess. The air was still thick with chalky dust. When I knelt low and peered into the little alcove, I could see the gaping mouth that led into the unknown depths of the earth itself. Not a piece of the concrete seal larger than a golf ball remained. Two Marine guards hovered nervously while Rooker, Pearce, and I examined the scene.

"All your men all right?" I asked.

"Yes," Rooker said. "Everyone's all right."

"What happened?"

"It was just a few minutes ago, sir," one of the Marines said, and I realized his voice was familiar. I recognized him as Sergeant Shaw, one of the plane captains. "When we came on duty, that opening was sealed up tight. Then, after the storm had ended, we heard two loud booms. When I came to check out the noise, I found the slab all smashed up."

"You didn't see anyone? Nobody in the cave, or outside?"

"No, sir. I checked thoroughly."

I clicked my tongue. "It would have taken tremendous energy to pulverize concrete this way."

"All we heard were those two booms. At first we thought another thunderstorm was coming, but it was too close." He pointed at the rubble.

"Volcanic pressure? Gas, maybe," Pearce said.

"If that were the case, it would have blown concrete pieces all the way into the cavern," I said.

Rooker's face looked as if he had swallowed poison. "Gentlemen, let's move outside. This place is not sitting well with me."

I nodded, recalling Rook's claustrophobia. Was that really what was causing him so much discomfort?

Once we had made our way into the late afternoon sun, we all seemed to breathe easier. Pearce produced a small hip flask and handed it to the Colonel, who took a grateful swallow.

"Drew, you suggested that I check out the cave," Rooker said, handing the flask back to Pearce. "So. What *do* you know?"

"Only that whatever's happening here is linked to this place. And that little opening is the only way I can see for something to come through from anywhere else on the island."

"We'd better start thinking about moving the fuel."

I shrugged. "Maybe. Though I honestly don't believe it'll be safer anywhere else on this island. The main thing is the men."

"Will they be safer anywhere else on the island?"

After a few moments, I shook my head. "I would have to say no."

Pearce sighed. "Well, this is enough to make the Pope cuss."

"Well, for whatever good it does, let's seal it back up," Rooker said. "Maybe we can rig a booby trap that won't blow up the whole place. So—if something does bust its way out of there—it'll either go up in smoke or alert us that something's on the move."

"But if something did come out through there," Pearce reminded him, "it must still be outside."

"Then we'll try to catch it going either way."

"Whatever."

Rooker's eyes went back and forth between Pearce and me. "So, Drew, just what is in there, do you think?"

"Something very old," I said softly. "I believe we've woken something up. And it is not happy. No, it is not happy at all."

CHAPTER 7

Thursday, November 4, 1943
0725 hours

The frenetic blare of reveille had drawn me out of a sound sleep that, for what seemed like the first time in ages, had been free of either disturbing dreams or rude intrusions by Washing Machine Charlie. Yesterday's storm had apparently been severe enough to keep our more familiar enemy grounded. I could only bless our good fortune, for I doubted that the extended forecast called for many such nights.

This morning, I was leading eight planes on a high-altitude CAP over Task Force 38 as it continued its campaign of bombardment at Bonis and Buka. My flight, consisting of Kinney, Vickers, Rodriguez, Collins, Hensley, Staunton, and Bartholomay, took off at 0630 in a light drizzle that, before we climbed above the clouds, turned to a torrential downpour. The cloud cover was low and solid all the way to our destination, so I doubted the enemy would be launching any bombing attacks against our surface vessels. However, clearer skies were reported over Rabaul, so we could not discount the possibility of Japanese fighter sorties.

And so it was that we had just taken up station over the task force, which was visible only through sporadic breaks in the clouds, when Ensign Kinney called out bogeys at ten o'clock high. I searched the sky frantically and, after a few seconds, saw a cluster of dots some three miles out and 2,000 feet above us. I

157

counted ten of them, and as they approached, I saw that these planes had long, tapered fuselages and small, bulbous canopies; they were not Zeros, but Ki-43 Hayabusas—"Oscars," by our lingo—painted solid green except for yellow panels on the leading edges of their wings and orange diagonal stripes on their tail fins. Like Zeros, Ki-43s were highly maneuverable, but with only two cowl-mounted 12.7mm machine guns, they had barely a third of the firepower of our Hellcats' six .50 calibers. Also like Zeros, they provided no protective armor for their pilots. We could make short work of them if we gained the tactical advantage—but that was no small feat against such nimble adversaries.

I throttled up to full combat power and shoved the nose down to build airspeed. "Blue Five, split low," I said, directing Max Collins to move his division away from mine and descend a thousand feet, figuring that if he could drag the attackers down and keep them engaged, my division could then reverse and blast them out of the sky. That meant using his division as bait. His planes banked to the right and began to dive; several enemy planes swung away from the main body to counter the move. We were closing with the Oscars at a combined speed of over 500 miles per hour and ate up the distance in a matter of seconds. They zoomed in with guns spitting tracers, and I involuntarily ducked as they screamed over us, the sounds of their engines briefly drowning my own.

Six Oscars were now bearing down on Collins's group. "Blue Five, break right," I called, leading my planes into a wide, climbing turn to the right, all the while searching the sky to make sure none of the remaining Oscars had slipped onto our tails. As the enemy closed in, Collins led his four planes into a tight Lufbery circle: a kind of defensive ring-around-the-rosy, where any enemy that attempted to get in a shot exposed itself to another Hellcat's guns. It was a risky move on Collins's part, but his only alternative was to simply dive away and escape.

The Oscars went for the challenge. Three of them banked hard, rolled out over the Lufbery, and dove in firing, targeting Archie Staunton. I saw his Cat take hits, and he cried, "Jesus, somebody get them off me!" Jack Bartholomay nosed up to try to clear Staunton's tail, but this merely put him squarely in the sights of the three Oscars that had remained high; one of them dropped directly onto him, its twin 12.7mms blasting away. Bartholomay's cockpit exploded under the barrage of arrows, and his Hellcat rolled over like a dead fish in the water. The next two Oscars fired simultaneously at his exposed belly, and the F6F came apart, one wing hurtling into space, the tail assembly splitting off and spinning down like an ungainly top. The rest of the wreckage plummeted toward the ocean, trailing black smoke.

"Oh, God, no," I groaned, pushing up to war emergency power. I was only a few seconds shy of firing distance when Archie Staunton's Cat took another round of hits and broke up, shedding panels from both wings and stabilizers. I saw the canopy fly open, and Staunton scrambled out, fingers of flame groping lustfully after him. He hit the silk immediately, and I saw the white chute bloom below me while his Hellcat fell away, twisting and burning. I had no time to watch him drop or to lament our grievous loss; the first three Oscars were banking hard to the left, while the second three stood on their tails and grabbed altitude as if they were rocket-propelled.

"Stay with me, Mr. Kinney," I called. "In on Oscars at ten o'clock."

"Roger, Mr. McLachlan."

"Got your six, Skipper," Vickers called.

Their attack on the Lufbery had pulled the Oscars low, and I roared in behind the trailing Ki-43, fiercely squeezing the trigger on my control yoke. My plane shook and shuddered as the guns rattled to life, but my aim was true; with only a few hits to his wingroot, the Oscar exploded in a massive fireball, hurling wreckage back toward my cockpit. Something bounced over my right wing and clattered away, but I didn't even look to see if I had taken any damage. The next Oscar in line started to roll into a split-S to escape, but I was still gaining at breakneck speed. Another trigger pull sent him flaming toward the clouds below, and I felt a moment of grim satisfaction when I saw that the cockpit was nothing but a mass of writhing flames.

Another target loomed in my sights, but now the first group of Ki-43s was closing quickly from both right and left. Collins and Hensley took the opportunity to break free from the Lufbery and haul away to the north to gain speed and altitude before circling back to re-engage the enemy. I needed their firepower, though I knew that if they came up to clear my six, they would be sitting targets. I lowered my nose a bit more, hoping to outrun my nearest pursuer, but then I saw tracers zipping past my canopy, and something dinged sharply behind my head. Glass fragments hit me in the face, and looking down, I saw that a jagged hole in the instrument panel had replaced my altimeter.

Kinney rocked his wings once and then swerved to the left. A split second later, I broke right, hoping to commence a Thach weave; if Vickers and Rodriguez began a simultaneous weave of their own, we stood a good chance of throwing the Oscars off-kilter and evening the odds.

But then Rodriguez's voice blared, "God almighty, Skipper, dive! Dive!" Another stream of tracers lit up my peripheral vision, and a section of my Plexiglas canopy, just to the right of my head, imploded with a loud bang. Then I heard a sharp *blam* and saw a large, shapeless chunk of something black bounce off my clocks. I didn't even realize what it was until I felt air whistling past my right ear and saw that my goggles had fallen into my lap.

A bullet had zinged through my flight helmet and smashed my headset. It was only then that I realized my ears were shrieking. I tentatively touched my right temple.

No blood. My heart nearly exploded with relief. But still three-quarters convinced that my number was up, I stomped left rudder, then right, hoping that some wild jinks would at least throw off the enemy's aim. A sharp clang in the armor plate just behind my head told me the plan wasn't working. So, fully aware the maneuver itself might kill me, I tugged my control yoke to the right, smashed right rudder, and rolled inverted, then I pulled the yoke into my stomach, going into the split-S so fast that the metal airframe groaned and screeched under the force of acceleration. My vision became a tiny pinpoint of light in a tunnel of gray, then all went dark, and for a few seconds, I was completely blacked out. When I came to, an invisible weight was crushing me into my seat, preventing me from even moving my arms.

Through the windscreen, I could see only white cloud below. "Oh, shit, oh, shit," I muttered, trying to pull the stick back, with little success. The pressure on the external control surfaces had almost totally locked up my yoke and pedals. With a supreme effort, my left hand somehow found its way to the throttle lever, and I dragged it back to idle, which decreased my speed only slightly. But I now managed to slowly pull my bucking Hellcat's nose up, and I leveled out just as Old Grand-Dad broke through the bottom of the clouds—which I knew to be at 6,000 feet. I had no idea where the enemy had gone, but I knew where they were not. There was no way a Ki-43 could match the maneuver I had just made.

A second later, I saw a fluttering movement to my right, and when I realized what it was, my heart swelled with jubilation. The Oscar that had come so close to shooting my tail off had attempted to follow me, and the G-force had plucked his fragile wings right from their roots. The dark green fuselage was spiraling downward like a dart, and for a second I saw the pilot pinned awkwardly in his seat; he had also blacked out from the acceleration, and at the rate his plane was falling, I doubted he would wake up until seconds before he hit the water—if then.

I'll take that as a kill.

I pulled off my oxygen mask and sucked in several deep breaths to slow my clamoring heart. Then I cast my eyes upward, hoping to get some idea where the rest of my flight had gone; my wild dive had carried me so far that my chances of rejoining the fight were exceedingly slim.

Then, to the north, I saw a white flash at about my altitude and began banking toward it, thinking it might have been sunlight reflecting off a wing or canopy. As I approached, however, I saw that it was a parachute—probably Archie Staunton. Sure enough, I could soon make out his tiny figure dangling beneath the billowing silk. He was alive and appeared to be unharmed.

I slowed a bit and waved as I passed him; out of the corner of my eye, I saw him return the greeting. But then I looked up, and my heart stuttered when I saw two green hornets coming down in a slow, relaxed spiral, probably looking for me. As yet, they had not seen me, so I leveled out and increased my speed again, figuring that if they came to engage me, I would happily oblige.

What I didn't count on was their noticing Staunton as he drifted leisurely toward the clouds. Like greedy vultures, the two Hayabusas homed in on him, and I saw tracers blaze from their cowlings as they immediately opened fire. Cursing, I honked my nose back toward them, regardless of the fact that, if they turned on me, I didn't have the speed to outrun them. But for the moment, they appeared to be fixated on their helpless prey.

I saw Staunton pull his .45 from his shoulder holster and pop off some shots, though surely ineffective. And then, in a sorry repeat of events, I was a mere five seconds from firing range when the enemy's bullets found their mark. His body thrashed wildly in his harness for a moment, and then his head slumped to his chest. Another five seconds passed—five, endless, futile seconds—and his body dropped into the clouds that would have otherwise saved him.

One of the Oscars did a fast, jaunty victory roll and began to climb out to my left. It was then that its pilot saw me, and only another second before his brain was splashed to the four winds by my six furious Brownings. It's a wonder I was able to even hit him, for by now, burning tears had reduced everything in my field of vision to clusters of sparkling crystal.

The other Oscar whipped around like a dog with a scalded hind end and latched onto my tail before I could even wipe my eyes. Again, tracers streaked after me, and this time, I didn't have anywhere near enough speed to escape. The Ki-43's initial acceleration was much faster than my Cat, and it would take more seconds than I had remaining to pull safely away from his guns.

Then, like a mirage before a dying man's eyes, a blue shape materialized above and in front of me, swooping in so fast that my brain didn't even register it as another Hellcat until it had already passed over me. I banked, whipped my head around, and saw six fiery, .50-caliber streams pumping from the leading edge of the Cat's wings. The Oscar immediately became a small, golden sun, spraying pieces of wreckage in all directions like blazing confetti. Kinney pulled up into a left chandelle, arced back toward me, and closed the distance to join on my right wing.

"Mr. Kinney, you magnificent little bastard," I said out loud. I could see him pressing his throat mike, but I pointed to my ears and shook my head to indicate my radio was out. Then I held up one finger, pointed at him, then straight ahead, signaling him to take the lead. He nodded to indicate he understood.

What a move, I thought. Getting in a killing shot at such an angle, at the speed he was going, was nothing short of miraculous. If I made it back to the barn after this ordeal, I fully intended to recommend Kinney for a Distinguished Flying Cross. Though I could not have known it at the time, assigning him to my wing had proven to be one of the wisest decisions I had ever made; certainly, it was the only reason I was still alive.

But as we cruised back toward our patrol zone in a lazy climb, bitter regret began to gnaw at my heart, nearly overwhelming me. I had ordered Collins's division to bear the brunt of the attack and two of his men had paid the price. Poor Jack Bartholomay had never known what hit him. But I couldn't help but believe that Ensign Archie Staunton had gone to his death feeling betrayed: first, I had missed shooting his attackers off his tail, which had forced him to bail; then, when the pair of Japs dove in to strafe his chute, I had been unable to either shoot them down or throw them off target long enough for him to drop into the clouds' safe embrace.

I hadn't known Staunton very well. He'd been a quiet, somewhat brooding young man, but made for amiable enough company. He'd come from Texas, if I remembered right, and wanted to fly commercially after the war was over—assuming we won it. I don't think he ever doubted that we would. Until the last few days, I had never doubted it either. Now it seemed that faith and hope and trust and all those virtuous beliefs we'd come out here with were simply little contrivances meant to bolster our nerves. The reality was that, in a week's time, our whole world had damned near gone to hell.

But I could not afford to bear a load of guilt out here; every one of us knew what could happen, and I above all knew that in the course of our tour men would lose their lives. My training dictated that I turn pain to power and use it against the enemy. If we were fighting only the Japanese, I think I could have managed it. But the knowledge that some terrible, unknown force awaited us at our home base was wearing me down, grinding my nerves to pulp. Never had the adage "caught between the devil and the deep blue sea" held such profound personal meaning for me.

By the time we reached what I assumed was 20,000 feet, my engine was rattling like a cracked snare drum, and my control yoke occasionally lurched in my grip like a struggling cat. Whether Old Grand-Dad was feeling the strain of combat as badly as I, or fatigue and nerves had simply distorted my perceptions, I couldn't tell. Over an hour of our scheduled patrol remained, though I knew that neither my plane nor my body could hold up to another encounter with the enemy. I had lost a quarter of my flight, and I didn't even know where the rest of it was—or whether any more planes had gone down after I had dove for my life. Under the circumstances, I could legitimately return to base, yet even now I could not bring myself to abandon the men who remained in my charge—not without collapsing into a pit of guilt so deep that I would never be able to emerge from it unbroken.

After a few minutes, Kinney rocked his wings to get my attention, then he tapped his headset and pointed to the northeast. Apparently he had made contact with the remaining Blue Devils, and he steered us on a course to meet them. Five minutes later, I saw four dark blue shapes cruising westward, one of which was trailing white smoke. As we closed the distance, I saw that it was Max Collins's Cat, oozing coolant from its cowling, which meant his engine might burn up long before he reached friendly shores.

Enough was enough. Wagging my wings, I slashed one hand across my throat and then pointed to the southwest, indicating that our patrol was over. We were doing no one any good out here now, for if we got into a fight, we could end up losing all our planes.

As we closed up our formation and turned back toward Conquest, I saw Collins smile and hold up three fingers. He then pointed to Willy Vickers and held up two fingers. And for the first time, it dawned on me that I was bringing home four kills. With Kinney's victory, that meant we had wiped out the entire enemy group.

Ten for two; it was an impressive morning's run. But that heartening little fact didn't stop my hands from shaking as we limped back home. And I doubted it would be much consolation to the families of Jack Bartholomay and Archie Staunton, whom I now owed letters of condolence. And I knew I had best write them before the supply gooney came and went later in the day.

Thursday, November 4, 1943
1210 hours
By God's grace, the six of us had landed safely beneath drizzling skies grayer than gunmetal. Barely managing to bypass Railroad Bill, who looked more ornery than a goaded rattlesnake, I made my way to my office and immediately sat down to write the three letters I owed to the families of my lost men. Each of them bore tearstains when I sealed them in their envelopes. Then I typed the morning's mission report, giving top marks to the deceased men and commending Ensign Kinney's valiant rescue of his commanding officer (who had expertly and ignominiously placed himself in harm's way).

I had just slipped the report into the appropriate folder and added it to the hefty pile in my "out" basket when Chuck Trimble came in, his face creased with several uncustomary worry lines.

"ComAirSols on the horn for you, Skipper. Something big."

"What timing."

"Also—the supply gooney is less than a half hour out. We'll have mail."

I pointed to my basket and sighed. "Bad outgoing mail, too." I groaned my way out of my chair and followed Trimble to the communications room, where I found two Marine PFCs on duty. They perfunctorily saluted, and the radioman handed me the headset and mike, asking if he should leave the room.

"No. I hope this won't take long." When I slipped on the headset and identified myself, I heard a few clicking noises and a hollow hiss as the scrambler kicked in. Then, the tinny voice of my immediate superior, Marine Colonel Oscar Brice, crackled over the earphones.

"Lieutenant Commander McLachlan. I understand you just came back with a big victory. Congratulations."

"Thank you, sir. It was expensive. I lost two good men."

"It's a hard thing," he said with a sympathetic sigh. "But according to Colonel Rooker, you've really distinguished yourself since you've been out there. One hell of a record. Now, we've got something in the works that you're going to be a part of. You're aware that Operation Cherryblossom has been successful to this point. But it has also been expensive—and it's very tenuous. We have information that the Japs are putting together a counterstrike from Rabaul. If they succeed, we're likely to get our asses bounced right off Bougainville."

"I see," I said, already getting an idea what he was about to say. I wasn't sure I cared to hear it.

Colonel Brice seemed to read my emotions over the radio and chuckled dryly. "It's all right. You're going to like it." Then he proceeded to outline the next day's mission in detail, never pausing for me to get in a word edgewise. When he finished, I wasn't sure if I wanted to laugh, cry, or crawl off and get very, very drunk—not so much for myself or the Blue Devils, but for the poor bastards that ComAirSols was about to send into the fiery furnace itself.

"Your ACIO will be receiving the finer points of the mission this afternoon by radioteletype," he said. "Your FDO will be the U.S.S. *Stark*, code name 'Sapphire.' Everything clear?"

"Yes, sir," I said. "Very clear."

"All right, then. By the way, Colonel Rooker tells me there's a possible problem with indigenous personnel on Conquest?"

My breath caught in my lungs. Under the circumstances, I wasn't entirely sure what I should say. "We believe it's possible, sir," I finally said. "We've had a couple of casualties."

"So I've heard. And I've made it quite clear to the Colonel that we have no resources whatsoever to devote to island security. Your men can handle any problem, I'm certain."

Colonel Brice's tone indicated the point was not debatable. "I'm sure we can, sir," I said halfheartedly.

"Good. I'll be counting on your group tomorrow. I suggest everyone get a good night's sleep tonight."

"We'll do our best, Colonel."

"I know you will. Once again, Lieutenant Commander, I salute your successes. You're doing a fine job."

"I appreciate it, sir."

Colonel Brice rang off, and I handed the headset and mike back to the Marine. Trimble was watching me from the door, and as we turned to head back to my office, he clapped me on the shoulder. "We have the easy part. You should be happy."

"Overjoyed."

"You'll be glad to know it's been quiet this morning."

"Good. The caves?"

"The opening has been resealed, we've doubled the guards, and our buddy Railroad Bill had an ingenious idea. He's rigged up a gun camera and battery so that if the seal is broken, it will start the camera going."

"That's some shit."

"You got it."

I had barely sat down at my desk when I heard excited voices outside, and I went to peer out my little window. From my limited view beyond the Quonset hut, I could see a few men hurrying down the jeep track toward the flight line.

"Supply gooney's here," Trimble said, cocking an ear to listen.

I nodded. The R4D—by way of Espiritu Santo, Henderson, and then Munda—would be bringing us additional fuel, machine oil, spare airplane parts, possibly fresh rations, and—most importantly—our mail. It would be the first batch for us since we'd embarked from the *Tarrytown*. I took a leather satchel from my lower desk drawer, took the neatly organized folders from my "out" box, and deposited them into the satchel.

"You wouldn't mind carrying this down for me, would you?" I asked, handing it to Trimble.

"Not at all." He took it and gave me a little smile. "Gonna stay up here and sulk?"

I reached into a desk drawer for one of the bottles of scotch Rooker had so generously offered me for the kills I'd made and held it up to show Trimble. "For the next ten minutes, I am off duty."

He smiled wanly. "Understood. See you later."

I watched Trimble walk off and took a couple of slugs from the bottle. No matter how many times you lost someone you knew in combat, the pain didn't go away. You steeled yourself, and you learned to accept it, but it still smoldered in your heart. If it didn't, you had no business being out here. If you didn't feel anymore, you were more dangerous to your own side than the enemy. A loose cannon.

I started to take another long swig, but then thought better of it and put the bottle away. And then I heard another commotion outside; at first I thought somebody must have received some exciting news from the mailbag. Then it occurred to me that they couldn't possibly have unloaded the mail yet, and these voices didn't sound particularly joyful. I dropped the bottle back into the drawer and stalked outside to see what was the matter.

The sight that greeted me nearly floored me: Rooker, Pearce, and a slim but rugged-looking Marine—Sergeant Jed Hawkes, the Marines' supply chief—were herding a disheveled, mud-covered figure toward the Quonset hut, half dragging, half shoving him forward, guns trained on his head. It was not one of our men.

"What's all this then?" I asked.

The gaze that met mine sent a thrill of genuine fear through my veins. The eyes beneath the broad, bony brow were blacker than oil, and I could not even see any white around the irises. Coarse, black, matted hair sprouted in awry tufts from an oversized, grotesquely misshapen head, and whiskers that looked like the spines of a cactus covered an insanely protruding, deeply cleft chin. The creature's skin was the color of burnt copper, mostly hairless but for a strip of black fur down the center of the bare chest. He wore only a leathery loincloth that looked like it might have been the skin of a shark or stingray. Most shocking were his hands, splayed out in front of him in the sand: the fingers were long and birdlike and ended, not in nails, but in long, razor-sharp claws the color of burnished steel. He was panting heavily through an open mouth, exposing two crooked rows of unnaturally pointed teeth.

"I found him hiding right over there, just at the perimeter," Sergeant Hawkes said, pointing to the treeline at the northeastern edge of the lagoon. "I think he was watching the gooney coming in."

As I studied the kneeling brute, there could be no mistaking the look of hatred in his eyes—and an absolute lack of fear, despite his being at the mercy of three men whose fuses were burning dangerously and conspicuously short.

"I don't suppose he understands us," I said. "But if we could communicate with him . . ."

"Be careful, Mr. McLachlan," Hawkes said, waving me back as I took a step forward. "He's strong—and faster than hell. I damn near had to shoot him to keep him from slashing my throat."

As if to illustrate Hawkes's point, the savage-looking figure sat back on his haunches, raised one hand and flattened it into a blade, the clawlike fingertips glistening ominously and pointing right at me. I had no doubt that a sudden blow with that living ax blade could prove lethal.

"I would venture to say this is one of our mysterious drummers," I said. "I wonder how many there are like him."

"He's the only one we found," Pearce said. "But I've got six men combing that area right now."

"Well, he's obviously not the only one on the island," Rooker said. "And they're getting brazen if they're coming right up to the edge of the base in daylight."

"The question is . . . what do we do with him," I said. "I sincerely doubt we're going to get much out of him by direct examination."

"Well, I'm not inclined to let him loose," Rooker said. "On the other hand, holding him here could start quite a row with his compadres, assuming they want him back. We keep him, we could end up with an honest-to-God war with whatever tribe he comes from."

"We already have a war," Pearce said, "after what they did to

Lester and Malloy."

"Assuming they're the ones who did it," Hawkes said.

Pearce scowled. "Of course they did it. They're the only ones who could have done it."

"Let's try something," I said, risking a step closer to the crouching figure. Pearce pressed his rifle barrel harder against the man's bony temple. I leaned forward and held out my hands to show they were empty and said in a loud, clear voice, "No weapon." I pointed to the guns trained on him, then at myself, and shook my head. "No weapon."

"I don't know what good that's gonna do, Drew," Rooker said.

"Well, like it or not, they were here before us," I said. "Maybe they think they're protecting their home. They don't understand that we never anticipated any contact with them."

"That's very charitable," Pearce said. "But it's a bit late for that."

"Maybe so," I said, still holding my hands out to the man. Somehow, I could not help but feel a measure of pity, albeit very slight, for this ugly, beastlike human now being handled like a rabid animal. "We don't mean any harm," I said to him in my most gentle voice.

The man growled low in his throat: a coarse, animalistic rumble that sounded more like it came from a caged tiger than a human being. But he looked straight at me with those onyx black eyes, still seething with anger and contempt, and in them I saw something more than sheer, primitive instinct. It was a gleam of intelligence, of cunning, a look indicating that, even if he could understand me, he would not listen. This was a being with a purpose—one that we could not possibly appreciate.

Still, I decided to press my attempt one step further. "Watch him carefully," I said, very softly. "I don't want to lose my hand."

"I'm not sure you're doing the right thing, Drew," Rooker whispered.

"I'm not either." I reached out with an open hand, very slowly, trying to keep my hand from trembling. I wasn't succeeding particularly well. But without hesitating, I gently clasped one bulging, muscular bicep, the way I might a friend's, just to assure him I didn't mean to hurt him. His skin was smooth and felt like hot, solid steel. He lifted his head and, surprisingly, gave me a thoughtful look that suggested he understood my intent. He muttered something low and incomprehensible in the back of his throat, and then he actually smiled, as if having come to some revelation. I took this as a good sign until—without warning—one clawed hand flashed up like a bolt of lightning aimed straight at my throat.

Only my quick reflexes spared me the blow, but I felt the rapid rush of air on my vulnerable skin. Then the solid whack of a rifle butt to the back of the brute's head slammed him to the ground. Hawkes pressed the misshapen skull into the sand with the wooden stock while Pearce thrust the muzzle of his M-1 into the back of the gnarled neck.

"Try that again, you fucking ape, and it's the last thing you ever do," he roared.

"It's no use, Drew," Rooker said. "Diplomacy is right out."

"Let's get him locked up somewhere," I said. "Maybe we can attempt a more reasonable approach after he's cooled off."

"Yeah, right," Rooker sighed. With a grimace, he stepped up to the prostrate figure and pressed his boot onto one of the mountainous shoulders, pinioning the man beneath his weight. Then he turned to Lieutenant Hawkes. "Go find some rope to tie this fellow up. And bring something to blindfold him with. He'll be less a threat if he can't see what he's doing."

"Yes, sir," Hawkes said with a nod, obviously reluctant to remove his weapon from the captive. But he finally turned and scurried off, leaving Rooker, Pearce, and me to tend the writhing beast on the ground.

"Drew, help me out," Rooker said. "This bastard's gonna wriggle right out of this."

I dropped one knee onto the small of the man's back and grabbed one of his thrashing arms with both of my hands. "Jesus, this mother's strong."

Just then, I heard the thudding footsteps of several approaching men, and I looked up to see Vickers, Rodriguez, Collins, and Woodruff hustling toward us, and just behind them, Doc McCall and a couple of more Marines.

"Jesus, Skipper, who—what—the hell is that?" Vickers exclaimed, his eyes brighter than a Hudson's headlights.

"My God, what a thing to find!" exclaimed Doc McCall as he stepped up to regard our captive specimen. The stocky, bespectacled man bent forward to study the figure, then got down on one knee and, to my surprise, began to gently stroke the man's shoulders. "Goodness gracious me."

"What, Doc?"

"His skin. Rub it one way, it's smooth. Rub it the other and it's rough, like sandpaper. Like a shark's skin."

"You telling us he ain't human?" Willy Vickers said, his expression indicating his disgust.

Noncommittally, McCall said, "Most unusual. Look at the hands. I've never seen anything like this." The brute jerked his head around to regard McCall with his oil-black eyes and growled like a threatened tiger. I tightened my hold on his arm. "I've never seen bone structure like this," McCall continued, unperturbed. "Protruding forehead and chin, large eyes, but sunken in protective cavities. Both hemispheres of the skull are disproportionately enlarged—like armor. One might say he is malformed, yet these features are not random aberrations. He is built for his environment, and he is a predator. See the teeth?

They indicate he's exclusively carnivorous."

"He's some kind of throwback?" Max Collins asked.

McCall shrugged. "I'd venture to say he's a product of a separate evolution than the rest of us. He appears primitive, but he is nothing like a Neanderthal or other early man. I would say he is actually quite advanced in his development."

"A fascinating analysis, Doc," Major Pearce said. "But I think we need to figure out what to do with this motherfucker before he kills someone."

As if he understood Pearce's words, the creature beneath me released a loud, grating bellow, and I felt the muscles in the arms tense, constrict, and then expand. To my shock, I found myself flying backward as if launched by a catapult, and my breath exploded from my lungs as I landed heavily on my back.

Dazed for a few seconds, I staggered back to my feet and prepared to launch myself at the rising beast-man, only to see Rooker tackle him—and then get tossed aside as easily as a small child. Then the creature was on his feet, rising to his full height. He was barely five feet tall, yet the ferocity of his appearance was truly striking to behold; the muscles of his arms looked more like body armor than flesh and blood, and his bronze legs rippled like coiled springs. His shaggy head swung back and forth several times, regarding his former captors with undisguised disdain. When his eyes fell on me, his thick lips spread in a wide grin, and in a deep, gravelly voice he said, *"Mi byong ki, ia eheyeh cho chiyo!"*

Just then, Sergeant Hawkes, carrying a coil of rope and a dirty cloth bag, appeared around the end of the Quonset hut. When he realized what was happening, he dropped his load, unshouldered his M-1, and swung it by the barrel, slamming the stock into the beast's ridged, rock-hard chest with a heavy thud. But the half-human, barely noticing the blow, spun around with surprising speed and swatted Hawkes with a wickedly fast backhand—and an eruption of blood sprayed from the sergeant's neck as he pitched backward onto the ground, one leg quivering spasmodically. His rifle whirled away into the underbrush.

"My God," I whispered, realizing that Hawkes's throat had been laid open by the extended, metallic claws. Doc McCall scampered to the fallen man, heedless of the growling figure a scant few feet away.

A shot rent the air, and the beast spun around, eyes widening in complete shock. He glanced down to see a hole the size of a nickel in his bare chest, just to the left of center. The lips twisted into an angry grimace, and the black eyes rolled up to regard Rooker, who was aiming his smoking M-1, preparing to fire again. But Pearce beat him to it, loosing three rapid shots, each of which struck their target just below the throat. This time, the creature spun around as if clubbed and fell heavily to the ground, his black blood quickly pooling in the sand beneath his head. The bronze limbs shook violently a few times, then went still.

"Fucking animal," Pearce whispered, his jaw trembling.

I hustled over to Hawkes, who was now lying motionless. Four pilots were gathered around him, trying to be helpful but mostly getting in Doc McCall's way. He waved them back, huffing, "Move it, please. Just stand back."

The older man laid one hand over the shocking gash in the Sergeant's throat, but blood oozed freely between his fingers and from beneath his palm. He leaned down and placed an ear on Hawkes's chest. After a moment, he drifted onto his backside, shook his head, and ran the back of his bloodstained hand over his sweaty forehead. "Hawkes is dead."

"So's this one," Pearce said, kneeling over the body of the killer. "Goddamn piece of shit." He spat on the ground next to the corpse.

For what seemed like hours, the jungle was frozen. Nary a

sound came from the shadowed foliage around us. Eventually, like a distant, incoming tide, we began to hear voices, and groups of men began to approach from all around the camp, at first cautiously, and then with increasing excitement and curiosity as they realized that death had again paid us a visit.

"All right," Colonel Rooker said at last. "I guess we'll bury this bastard—somewhere well away from base. I'd say let's throw the garbage in the marsh, but I wouldn't take the chance of going in there."

"Let me take care of it, Colonel," Pearce said. He gazed grimly at the corpse. "Afterward, I never want to see anything like him again."

"Begging your pardon," Doc McCall said. "But before we dispose of the body, I would like to examine it."

Giving McCall a sour frown, Pearce looked like he was going to protest. But then he said, "All right. You take it. Cut it into little pieces if you want to."

Seeing that a large number of pilots and Marine crew had gathered around the scene of carnage, Rooker raised a hand and said, "Gentlemen, listen up. These are my orders. From now on, there will be no attempt to capture or parley with these . . . people. They have proven themselves to be a deadly threat and beyond our ability to communicate with. Therefore, they are to be shot on sight. We will defend ourselves." Then he looked at me quizzically. "Do you agree, Drew?"

I gazed at the bronze, prostrate figure, and at the inky black blood that had seeped into the sand. "Yes," I said, with a halfhearted nod. "I agree."

I felt a comforting hand on my shoulder and turned to see Max Collins's brilliant blue eyes gazing warmly into mine, as if to remove any doubt that I was doing the right thing. But at this moment, there was no question in my mind. I had tried. I had tried to give the native man—or whatever he was—every benefit of the doubt, to make peace with him. *He* had been the one to refuse a gesture even he appeared to understand, and then went on to commit vicious murder.

We now had, beyond question, a war on two fronts.

Thursday, November 4, 1943
1900 hours

At chow time, I scarcely managed to choke down a bite—and not just because of Clarence's inability to wring flavor from our Navy-supplied rations. No one who had seen our late guest and the aftermath of his visit had much of an appetite. After the brutal violence of that afternoon, we looked forward to nightfall with marked apprehension, half-expecting that, for the first time, the mysterious jungle tribe might attempt to move against us en masse. Doc McCall had transported the body of the native to his sickbay—a small shack with a few tables and only the crudest implements for operating—and had set to work autopsying the creature. He had not emerged for over three hours.

Right at 1700 hours, the sound of drums came pounding through the jungle, distant but heavy with raw, chaotic power. They didn't last long—maybe five minutes or so—but during that time, I don't believe a single man on the base uttered a word or twitched a muscle. We had armed ourselves to the teeth, and to augment the barbed wire cordon around Tobacco Road and Marine City, Rooker's men had erected a barricade of sharpened bamboo staves, with more being added as quickly as they could be carved and planted. In areas where explosions posed little threat to our lives or real estate, Pearce had rigged a number of grenade traps, particularly in the area east of the operations hut, near the lagoon. This reinforcement of our perimeter happened so quickly that I barely realized its extent until I took a walk with Rook to inspect the line.

He noticed my surprise and chuckled. "At Cactus, we had

Japs at every door and window the whole time we were there. They'd punch through the line, we'd close it up, they'd punch again, and we'd shoot 'em up, sweep 'em out, and close it up all over again. In between, we'd actually get to work on the Wildcats. Hell of a way to earn your dollar."

"I should say." For my part, I had ordered a pair of F6Fs to be put on standby so that, if necessary, we could provide our own close air support. We could only do that in daylight, however. "We'll have flights up all day tomorrow. It would be lovely to get some sleep tonight."

"I'm going to have the maximum possible number of men up at a time, all night. We'll keep lights burning in potential hot spots, but we'll need hands close by to put them out if Washing Machine Charlie shows up." Rook gazed toward the deep jungle. "If these bastards are smart, that's when they'll hit us—when we're dark and already under attack."

"They must know every inch of this island. That goes a long way to making up for any lack of sophisticated weapons."

"I'd give a case of scotch to know how many of them there are—and more than that to know where they are. We've explored every nook and cranny of the cave, and except for that one opening, there's no other passage, not that's still accessible. Any others must have been closed off a hundred years ago or more—by natural means or otherwise."

"Any other nearby cave openings? Maybe even a whole different network?"

"None that we've been able to find."

"How's your claustrophobia?"

He chuckled grimly. "Acute."

I noticed his jaw working back and forth nervously, and I felt certain his thoughts—like mine—had turned to the subject of the *other* presence on Conquest. Intuition told me that none of our defenses would begin to deter it if it turned its wrath on us.

"Hey," he said, pausing as we walked along the jeep track back toward operations, his gaze locking on the summit of the mountain, barely visible through a narrow break in the tangled rain forest. "Listen."

As we stood there, I realized the jungle had taken on that damnable silence that inevitably indicated something was awry. Then my ears picked up a distant hammering sound that at first I thought came from maintenance. But then it was joined by a duller, pattering beat that assumed a rapid, rhythmic cadence, punctuated by apparently random crashes of what sounded like stone against metal. The sounds were coming from the northwest, near the apex of the ridge; then, a few moments later, another group of percussionists joined in from a point to the northeast, seemingly near the lagoon.

"Sounds like they're getting closer," I said.

"That's a signal, for sure."

I nodded. Then something moved at the corner of my eye, and I quickly shifted my gaze back to the mountain. "I saw something."

"What?"

The more I peered at the ridged, green and brown mass looming above us, the more frustration gnawed at me. Just as when I had reconnoitered the area on Tuesday afternoon, I could see nothing unusual when my eyes deliberately went looking. But as I started to turn toward Rook, I froze, for now—in the periphery of my left eye—*there it was.*

And only a second later, there it wasn't.

"Jesus, I saw it," I whispered, rubbing my eyes roughly as if to berate them. However, since I was trained to use my peripheral vision to its fullest, I decided to attempt a little experiment. First I concentrated on the mountainside where I thought the mysterious object must lie, then I rapidly and repeatedly shifted my gaze to the right. And each time I did, a dark stain seemed to materialize on the western edge of the mountain: a wavering, spidery shadow, suggesting a complex, organic structure. Yet it never remained stationary long enough for my eyes to register its full form.

"Yes," I said, my heart starting to pound anxiously. "There's something up there, all right."

"I don't see it," Rook said. "What are you talking about?"

I pointed to the spot on the mountainside. "Look over there for a few seconds. Then quickly glance to the right. See if you get something in your peripheral vision."

He stared long and hard at the mountain, then shifted his gaze to the point I had indicated. He did this several times, and finally his face lit up as if he had solved the riddle of the century. "By God, I do see it."

"Yeah? I was beginning to think I was losing my mind."

"Drew, if what we see really is up there, we damn near *ought* to be out of our minds."

The thing must have been hundreds of yards long. From a thick, cylindrical mass, numerous, curling arms sprouted like the long, undulating tendrils of a gigantic sea creature. But my impressions of the thing were so fleeting that I could not begin to describe it accurately. All I knew was that we were seeing—or almost seeing—something that absolutely should not exist.

The beating of the drums grew louder, stronger, becoming wilder and more frenzied. Their sound became a continuous thunder that built to a crescendo. Then the thing on the mountainside simply ceased to exist. No matter how many times I shifted my eyes, I could no longer detect any trace of it.

Then, the drums fell silent.

Rook and I exchanged glances, then stared in disbelief at the absolutely vacant mountainside. A second later, he voiced the very idea my brain was just beginning to formulate: "Those drums. You know, I do believe the bastards are talking to that thing."

"Yeah," I said. "And that can't be good."

Thursday, November 4, 1943
2045 hours

"He's human, more or less," Doc McCall said, then took a long slug from the bottle I had set out before him on my desk. When he replaced the bottle, it was empty. Doc, Rook, Pearce, Trimble, Comeaux, and Arsenault had all crowded into my office for a little skull session, and the scotch had become an unwitting casualty. The cigarette smoke was so thick my lungs were on the verge of rebelling. "Of course, with no better facilities than these," Doc said, "I can't do but so much. That fellow needs a full-blown pathology lab."

"The more human part is obvious," Rook said, scowling. "What about the less part?"

Doc shrugged. "All his internal organs appear normal enough. But the striated—voluntary—muscles are all overdeveloped, and not just from rigorous physical activity. Their basic constitution is uncannily dense. And his bones are like steel. I couldn't cut through the skull with a bone saw. Never seen anything like it."

"He's a walking weapon, then," Trimble said.

"Exactly. Also, as you saw, his blood is very thick and quite dark. Exceptionally elevated red count, highly oxygenated. But there's a cell in the blood that I've never seen before. I've not been able to determine its purpose. Under the microscope it appears quite black, with a blue or violet nucleus. This in itself would seem to place him in some category different than the rest of us."

"What about those teeth and claws of his?" Comeaux said. "Those are damn near nasty."

"At first I thought the teeth might have been filed to be sharp like that. The enamel on all of them is highly abraded. But that appears to be from gnawing on the bones of his prey. Their shape is natural. And the nails . . . well, unlike yours and mine, his are fused to the bone. In fact, his hands and feet appear more reptilian than human. And my guess that he is exclusively carnivorous appears to have been correct. The contents of his digestive tract are—to put it bluntly—quite disgusting."

"What do you mean by that?" Rook asked.

Doc's face darkened. "I found some pieces of undigested bone in his stomach. More specifically, human phalanges. Pieces of fingers."

"Jesus H. Christ!" Pearce exploded. "You mean to say he's a goddamn cannibal?"

"My guess is that they came from our dead men. Lester and Malloy."

"Butchering bastard," Comeaux growled. "Skipper, this is too much."

Arsenault simply nodded thoughtfully. "They must be destroyed."

Rook held up his hand. "Listen. Our guts are urging us to go hunt these motherfuckers down and annihilate them. But let me stress again, gentlemen, we do not have the manpower to spare, nor do we know their strength or where to find them. If we go out looking, ten to one we'll be on the losing end, regardless of our hardware advantage." He gave me a significant look. "And as you know, we have good reason to believe there is more out there than just these natives, something they are apparently on speaking terms with."

With that, everyone fell into silent contemplation. Even though they had no clue what Rook and I had glimpsed on the mountainside, each of them had heard its voice—itself a compelling deterrent to challenging its sovereignty.

Trimble finally said, "I know this may seem redundant, but I'll remind everyone that our primary goal is to keep our planes and pilots secure—especially for the next twenty-four hours, given the upcoming operation. As best as I can tell, the defensive measures we've taken are sound. Our duty now—in a worst case scenario—is to simply counter any offensive the island people might make."

Arsenault nodded. "Well said, Charles. I think it's safe to conclude that we're equipped to handle a frontal assault. It's those non-frontal assaults that are most worrisome." He shuddered noticeably. "Whoever or whatever hit our Marine friends surely took them unaware—and left no traces."

"Good point," Rook said. "One thing is certain. They will no longer have the same element of surprise on their side. Every man on base is going to be on the alert."

A knock on the door frame announced an unexpected arrival, which turned out to be José Rodriguez wearing a nervous frown. "What's up, José?" I asked.

"Señor Skipper, Colonel," he said, "there is something outside I think you will want to be seeing."

I scraped my chair back and rose from my desk. "What is it?"

"Out here. I think this is bad." We followed him out of my office and down toward the lagoon. As we stepped onto the white sand, now gray beneath the starlit sky, I saw several men gathered around an object that nearly caused me to retch. I could tell what it was long before we actually reached it.

It was the huge, mutilated head of the dead native, mounted on a bamboo pike—in the exact spot where the heads of Privates Lester and Malloy had previously been found.

"Who the fuck did this?" Rook roared. "Goddamn it, somebody had better speak up. Who did it?"

"I can't say. I don't know," Rodriguez said, twiddling his thumbs nervously.

"All right, who did this?" Rook said, casting his eyes over the gathered men. Most of them were Marines. None of them said a word. "So, nobody knows? You better hope you don't know."

"I did it," came a gruff voice from behind us. I turned to see a behemoth-like silhouette shambling across the sand toward us. "I did it, in case you got a problem."

It was Railroad Bill. He marched up to Colonel Rooker wearing a belligerent scowl. Rook's expression softened slightly. "Damn you, Bill, what's the meaning of this?"

"They were good men, the ones we lost," the chief said in an ominous whisper. "And I aim to fix these sons of bitches any way I can." He spat contemptuously at the head on the pike.

Doc McCall came huffing up to see what the commotion was about. Even in the dark, I could see his face turning purple. "Mr. Varn, you had no right to take that."

"Well, I do apologize," Bill growled. "But best as I can tell, you didn't have no more use for this thing. This will show those bastards we ain't taking their brand of murder."

"If I went messing around in your place, you'd break my arms," Doc said. "You better show the rest of us the same courtesy you expect."

"Bill," Rook said, "if any of them see this, it's only going to have them out for blood all the sooner."

"Bring 'em on. I'll tear their goddamn hearts out."

Rook hissed, "Bill, we're not savages. I will not have this."

"Take it down, Bill," I said as calmly as I could. "Let's just bury the damn thing and forget it."

"I ain't forgetting what this bastard did, no, sir," Bill said, giving me a threatening glare. "I'll put every one of their heads up, if that's what it takes. Just like you paint flags on your planes, I'll post their damn heads for everybody to see."

"That's enough," Rook said. "Look, I know what you're feeling. But we all have our jobs to do. We can't start fighting among

185

ourselves. I will not tolerate that. Not even from you."

I stepped up to Bill and said in an even voice, "Bill, how's Old Grand-Dad?"

"What?"

"Did you get Old Grand-Dad patched up? It was a bit of a mess when I brought it in."

"Mr. Mac, don't patronize me—"

"*Mister* Varn. I want to fucking know if you patched up Old Grand-Dad."

Bill eyed me angrily. "Yeah, Mr. Mac, I got it fixed up. New canopy, new clocks, patched the holes in the wings. She'll fly you tomorrow."

"Good. Now let's try to keep our focus where it's supposed to be, all right?"

He glared at me so hard I wondered if he might start swinging. Finally, he just said, "I hear you."

"All right, let's break it up," Rook said with a sigh. He pointed to two of his men. "Euliss, Burke, take this piece of garbage down and throw it in the jungle for all I care. Just get it out of here." He then turned back to Bill and laid a hand on his shoulder. "Come on. Let's go have a slug or two. We'll talk if you want to. I just can't have this kind of trouble in camp, you got me?"

Bill's blazing eyes finally softened slightly. "Colonel, I didn't mean you no trouble. But you gotta understand, I'm not gonna take this bullshit. I'm not going to."

"I don't blame you, Bill. We're going to figure out what to do. But let's work it by the book, all right?"

Rook seemed to be handling the near-berserk crew chief as well as could be expected. So I motioned to Trimble, Comeaux, and Arsenault and told them it was time to pack it in for the night. "We gotta get some sack time, no matter what," I said. "Briefing's at 0530 in the morning. There's going to be guards up all night, all over the camp. All we have to do is sleep."

"And good luck to you," Comeaux said. He glanced back at the crew chief. "I can't say as I blame the old boy. I might have done the same thing if it was one of us."

"Well, let's not dwell on it," I said with a sigh. "I understand it, but we can't let ourselves be suckered into losing our wits."

"Maybe, Skipper. But old Bill's got a point. They see that, they'll know we're not bullshitting either."

"I'm not worried about what they see or don't see. I personally do not want to goad them into a fight with us. We'll wipe them out."

"You're not bothered by that fact, are you, Athos?" Arsenault said, giving me a thoughtful look.

"Not in and of itself," I said, looking deep into the jungle as we walked toward Tobacco Road. "It's what might happen to us if we do."

Arsenault nodded his understanding and stopped walking. He peered into the unfathomable darkness and said, "I think that thing is out there right now. I think it knows everything we're doing and saying. I think it's just watching and waiting."

"What do you mean, 'it'?" Comeaux asked.

"Kinney's dinosaur, for lack of a better description," Arsenault said. "I don't know what's out there. It's not a dinosaur. But I wonder if it's not as old as one."

"You're as bad as he is," Comeaux grumbled, jerking a thumb in my direction.

"Cut the noise," I said, in no mood to listen to the two of them sparring.

As we continued on, I saw a figure just this side of our tent standing in the glow of a lantern, a rifle held at the ready. However, the idea was for the guards to stay out of the lights so that we could see the enemy if they encroached on our territory, not vice versa. After a few steps, I recognized our all-too-conspicuous sentry as Ensign Kinney.

"Hello there, young fellow, how are you?" Comeaux said, the jovial lilt in his voice barely masking his disdain.

"Good evening, sirs," Kinney said.

"What are you doing out here?" I asked. "You're not pulling duty now, are you?"

"Not officially, sir," he said. "But I'm not tired, so I thought I would join the watch."

"Well, that's fine," I said. "But you'd better get some shut-eye. You're on my wing in the morning."

"Yes, sir, I know that, sir. I guess I'll go on to bed directly."

"You got ammunition in that thing?" Comeaux asked.

"Yes, sir."

"Then don't point it at me."

"Sorry, Mr. Comeaux." Kinney swung the M-1 up and shouldered it, rather comically resembling a toy soldier. I appreciated his company when we were flying, but I didn't think I wanted him next to me holding a weapon.

"Hit the sack, Mr. Kinney," I said. "Chances are Washing Machine Charlie's going to drop by in a couple of hours. Might as well nab a few winks while we can. No sense in wasting minutes."

The redheaded lad looked crestfallen. "If you say so, sir."

"Yeah," Comeaux said and stamped his foot. "Get on now."

Kinney's eyes grew wide and he nodded nervously. "I'll say good night, sirs."

"Good night, Mr. Kinney."

The young man ambled off toward his own tent and the three of us slipped into ours. I had to admit, even with my nerves still jangling and adrenaline burning unabated in my system, my cot was beckoning me like a seductress. I had never felt so bone-tired in my life.

Arsenault lit our lantern and the first thing I did was make sure the floor and our beds were free of any crawlies. I took their absence as an encouraging sign and stripped off my shirt and boots. Then I saw the four envelopes on my cot that some thoughtful individual had apparently delivered to me during the afternoon. Two of them were from my parents; one was from an old buddy from the Naval Academy, now in Pensacola; and the last one was from my brother.

I felt a rush of excitement that crowded out all my thoughts of the darkness, the natives, the whole damned war. I hurriedly went through my usual evening ablutions and then settled into my cot to read my letters.

My folks were doing fine, they said, and hoped I was doing the same. There was little in the way of local news from back home. And their second letter was practically a repeat of the first. But to see my mother's elegant, flowing handwriting, and my dad's crabbed signature gave me a warm feeling that I had not known seemingly for ages. My friend Wayne Craft wrote that he was busier than hell teaching aviation cadets how to dive bomb, but he desperately wanted to fly combat missions rather than teach tyros how to do what he was not.

Finally, I opened my brother's letter, and as I began reading I nearly fell out of my cot. His first words to me were: "Drew— I've been transferred. Shore duty, stateside. Hallelujah. This is just what I've been wanting because—get ready—I'm getting married."

Jesus, I thought. I didn't see how Robert had been able to find time to even see a woman, much less get serious with one. He went on to say that he was going to be stationed at San Diego, which was our old teenage stomping ground. The girl's name was Monica Devlin, the daughter of a high-ranking admiral in the recently commissioned Seventh Fleet. They hadn't set a date yet, but he would be sure and let me know. He hoped when the time came I would be in a position to attend the nuptials.

"Good God, Robert," I whispered. Certainly, I felt pleased for him, but somehow, his news did more to dampen my spirits than elevate them. I often wished that I had someone waiting for me back home, but my commitment to the Navy allowed for little in the way of romance. Back in Pensacola, I had enjoyed something akin to a relationship with a lovely young lady named Joanna Westlake, but even though we had become reasonably close, we implicitly understood that, once I left for my assignment, neither of us could expect the other to come running after it was all over.

The simple reality was that a smart woman—and Joanna was smart—had no business committing her heart to a man who stood as much chance of coming home in a coffin as an airplane.

I dropped Robert's letter on the floor and heaved a deep sigh that both wished him and his bride-to-be all the best for the future and damned him for being the luckier of us. Then my eyelids collapsed. The last thing I heard before consciousness fled was some distant rumbling. I couldn't tell whether it was thunder or drums. And at that particular moment, I really didn't give a damn.

Thursday, November 4, 1943
2330 hours

I woke to the sound of Comeaux's breath grating like a buzzsaw and Arsenault rattling like a Pratt & Whitney with a bent propeller shaft. All my senses snapped to alert instantly, and I sat up quickly in my cot, trying to determine what had drawn me out of deep slumber.

There had been something in my dreams with me—something that came from *out there,* not manufactured by my own subconscious. Yes, of course: the faceless black man had been there, standing in the shadowed corner of a red-hued stone chamber, his two gigantic toad-like children nuzzling his hands and gazing at me with their black, bulbous eyes. From somewhere far away, I could hear the sound of shrill, chirping flutes and the muted, chaotic pounding of what sounded like drums—much like those we had heard coming out of the jungle. I could sense his hidden gaze falling appraisingly on me, and I felt chilled to my soul.

"I know you." His deep, resonant voice crawled across the space to invade my consciousness, bypassing my eardrums altogether. "Do you know who I am?"

"No," I replied, trying to get a look at his shadow-obscured face. "Who are you?"

His hands spread wide. "That will be for you to learn."

"What do you want?"

"To teach," came the voice.

"Teach what?"

"Power."

"Why?"

For a long moment, no response came. Then, with something like a humorous lilt, the voice said, "Because it is required."

Something seemed to change then, nothing tangible, just some sixth sense that screamed danger to me. Shadows now appeared to spread through the reddish chamber like creeping, inky fingers, gradually extinguishing the light.

"You have little time," the voice said. Then the light vanished, thrusting me into complete darkness, surrounded by the rising sound of insane flutes. That was when I awoke. Some remnant of rationality told me I was merely dreaming symbols, but my every instinct told me that they had been deliberately transmitted to my mind, and for a malevolent purpose.

By the thing we had half-glimpsed up on the mountainside.

I could interpret these dreams as nothing less than a

191

psychological attack, an effort to shatter or confound my defenses, to render me vulnerable to the unknown force out there. To my rational mind, such an attack seemed beyond belief. Yet to blithely cling to the idea that these images, these *intrusions,* were simply the result of my mind reacting to the stress of warfare was to deny an enemy no less genuine than the Japanese.

The night remained quiet, and neither of my tentmates so much as stirred in the darkness. But I had no sooner lain back down and tried to relax than the air-raid siren began to wail. Comeaux and Arsenault sat up, groaning and cursing, but none of us bothered to leave the sack. The siren whined for about a minute before burping back to silence, and a few minutes later, we heard the stuttering drone of the Betty's unsynchronized engines.

The bombs hit somewhere down near the beach to the southwest, far from any of our facilities. Apart from the guards, who were already up, I don't believe anyone bothered to drag himself out of bed—although I did reach for my .45, half-anticipating the announcement of an imminent attack by the brothers of the slaughtered jungle man. But none ever came.

Perhaps oddly, the most comforting thought accompanying me back into dreamland was that, tomorrow, I would return to fighting the very human Japanese, and the worst that could happen to me was merely the kind of death I had been trained to accept.

CHAPTER 8

Friday, November 5, 1943
0750 hours

I don't believe I had ever seen such a collection of weary, downcast faces in a ready room, not even during the Battle of the Coral Sea, when we were up against the Japanese at their peak and every man knew the chances of coming home safely were agonizingly slim. But at that time, we could sense a turning in the tide of war, and even if we were dog-tired and terrified of flying against the enemy, our spirits alone could keep us going. Here, some of the men bore dark, fatalistic shadows under their eyes. It wasn't right. So far, we had soundly thrashed the Japs for minimal losses on our side; by rights our momentum should be building. But all of us knew that something besides simple, hostile natives existed on the island. We had been deafened by its voluminous voice; we had witnessed the bestial appearance and disposition of its brutish subjects; we had heard their drums echoing from the jungle as they communed with it. For its own reasons, this thing was attempting to shatter our resolve.

Now more than ever I needed to ignite these men's spirits, to set an example that would restore their confidence.

"All right, gentlemen, listen up," I said, forcing as much zeal as I could muster into my voice. "Today, we will be taking part in a little operation that has been ordered by Admiral Halsey himself and will be overseen by Rear Admiral Sherman, commanding Task Force 38. During the past twenty-four hours, TF 38 has steamed to a point some fifty miles west of Buka Island, which puts it a little over two hundred miles south of Rabaul." I pointed to its approximate location on the map with my reed baton. "Beginning at 0900, the carriers *Saratoga* and *Princeton* will be launching a full-scale raid on Rabaul. For this operation, we will be flying CAPs over the task force, each lasting three hours, for the entire day. The combined Solomons-based fighting squadrons—ourselves included—will be code-named Task Force 33. Our job will be to repel any counterattacks the Japanese launch."

Fatigue vanished from the ready room like smoke in the wind. All eyes and ears concentrated solely on me. This was big. I glanced at my notes.

"Now. Intelligence reports that Rabaul's air strength will be at maximum. The 12th Air Fleet has been dispatched from Japan to augment Rabaul's 11th Air Fleet. Furthermore, complete air groups from two fleet carriers and one light carrier have been sent in to defend the region. They are currently dispersed between the five main airfields at Rabaul—Lakunai, Vunakanau, Tobera, Rapopo, and Keravat. We suspect that additional Imperial Japanese Army Air Force squadrons may have been called in since these reports were made."

I could hear a few nervous murmurs, but I had not yet finished the preliminaries. "Yesterday's recon indicates that a substantial surface fleet from Truk has joined up with the Rabaul fleet at Simpson Harbor, presumably for the purpose of crushing both Task Force 38 and the Cherryblossom amphibious forces. Admiral Sherman intends to stop this strike before it begins." I cleared my throat dramatically. "By now, you have probably guessed that the numbers are stacked against us—and Sherman's carriers may not survive a concentrated enemy counterattack. Task Force 33 is all that stands in the enemy's way.

"TF 33 will be flying CAPs over the carriers at various altitudes. The Fighting 39 is assigned to high cover, between twenty thousand and twenty-five thousand feet. Two full flights going this morning. You'll have no FDO contact because the fleet is maintaining absolute radio silence. That means you keep your eyes open. And no chatter. None.

"Now, you'll be using external tanks today. Before you go jumping into a fight, please remember to drop them—unless you enjoy flying a freight train. So, any questions?"

"Hey, Skipper," Dusty Woodruff called, his face a little gray. "Are we going to get sent to Rabaul too?"

"It's not in the immediate forecast," I said. "But never rule out a rough day's work."

Kinney raised a hand. "Mr. McLachlan, with all that air-power at Rabaul, do you think the enemy will hit Conquest?"

I shook my head. "Doubtful, Mr. Kinney. But again, we can't rule out anything. We can only interpret so much from recon reports."

Colonel Rooker came forward with a little wave, and I gave him my place at the podium. "I would say the Japs are far less likely to worry about us than the carriers that are beating at their front door," he said. "Their forces will be committed to holding Bougainville. To waste any of them on a minor base like Conquest would be foolish."

"Then I'd say we'd better be on the lookout for trouble," Ho-agie said. He got a few laughs and a thump on the head from José Rodriguez, seated behind him.

"All right, let's get moving," I said. "We're on station at 0900."

As we made our way out of the ready room, Rook stepped up beside me and asked, "You all right, Drew?"

I nodded. "Just a little tired. You look a bit washed out yourself."

"Bad night."

I stopped. "Any dreams?"

He gave me a reluctant nod. "Hellish dreams. I'll have to tell you about them later."

I gave him a thoughtful glance. "I might have had the same ones."

"It wouldn't surprise me," he said with a sigh. "Well, take care up there. We need you back here safe and sound."

"Mind the store. I don't want to come home to trouble."

"If there's any trouble, we'll be the ones causing it," he said with a little laugh, his bravado a pale shade of what it had been only a few days ago.

I slid into the driver's seat of the first jeep and was joined by Vickers, Rodriguez, and Wickliffe. I shoved the vehicle into gear, and off we lurched down the muddy track toward the flight line. The hefty Tank Wickliffe looked like he hadn't gotten an hour's sleep and I noticed he was anxiously watching the shadows beneath the trees as we drove.

"You all right, Mr. Wickliffe?"

He nodded. "I'm all right. Restless night."

Rodriguez agreed. "I barely get back into sleep after that damn washing machine come over."

"We're all wound up," I said. "But I don't have to tell you to be alert up there today."

"No shit, Skipper," Rodriguez said, a hair too belligerently. I gave him a sharp look, and he bowed his head in token apology. A few harsh words of rebuke nearly rolled off my tongue, but then I decided to say nothing. Tired men could be cranky. No sense in making anyone crankier.

The roar of impatiently idling engines grew louder as we rolled toward the flight line. When I pulled up next to Old

Grand-Dad, I noted that the number of gray patches on the wings and fuselage had multiplied considerably over the last couple of days.

"You people are gonna run me out of bandages," came the gruff voice of Railroad Bill. He emerged from behind my Hellcat, looking about fifty percent his usual, crusty self. "Save your beer today, Mr. Mac. My boys have had enough at your expense."

"I'll do my best, Bill."

"I expect no less."

I gave him a long look in the eye, as Sergeant Shaw came over to help me with my chute. "Take care today, Bill. We're going to get through this."

His eyes betrayed a rare glimmer of humility. "I know we will, Mr. Mac. You be careful."

"I will."

Once my chute straps were securely fastened, I climbed up to my cockpit and settled in the seat, feeling as if I were finally in my element. In a few moments, I would be airborne, the one feeling in the world that absolutely nothing could surpass. I gave my clocks a quick once-over, satisfying myself that all was in order.

When I received the signal to roll, I nudged the throttle and began taxiing across the apron to the runway. A few moments later, I was roaring down the metal-matted surface, then lifting into the air. The rush of wind into the open cockpit was intoxicating. Old Grand-Dad felt a bit sluggish, though; the extra fuel tank attached to the bottom of the fuselage added a few hundred pounds of weight to the plane. I managed the yoke gingerly as I made my turn to head out over the ocean.

As we formed up at 5,000 feet, southeast of the island, I happened to glance back toward the mountain. And I saw it. Just for a fleeting second, on the green, southern slope, the massive, dark stain with long, spindly appendages flashed in and out of existence, as if to affirm that it was still there, watching and waiting. I wondered if, at this moment, the drums in the jungle were going great guns.

Clouds surrounded us for most of the commute, but by 0850, only the thinnest haze obscured the distant horizon. Soon I could see several tiny white streaks in the deep blue field ahead: the wakes of Task Force 38's ships, which had turned their bows northeast, into the wind.

The task force consisted of the carriers U.S.S. *Saratoga* (CV-3) and U.S.S. *Princeton* (CVL-23), two light cruisers, and nine destroyers. As we drew nearer, I could see the carrier decks loaded with aircraft, and while I watched, a navy blue Grumman F6F-3 Hellcat soared off the deck of the *Saratoga*. The carriers would be launching their entire complements for the mission to Rabaul: a total of fifty-two Hellcats, twenty-two SBD dive-bombers, and twenty-three TBF Avenger bombers. The scene below was an awesome display of our naval muscle; yet, compared to the enemy force waiting at Rabaul, this impressive gathering might amount to little more than a swarm of mosquitoes against a vast net. A cold lump rose in my throat at the thought of so many of our pilots flying straight to almost certain doom.

Flying high at 25,000 feet, I led my planes east for several miles and then swung northward, putting us in optimal position to intercept a direct attack from Rabaul. The remaining squadrons would surround the task force, creating a defensive screen against approaches from virtually any direction. Still, if the enemy dispatched even a modest percentage of their air power against us, we could be overwhelmed. But I refused to entertain the possibility of failure.

After an hour, the milky white mist had curdled into thick clumps, obscuring the wakes of the ships below. By now, the leading edge of the attack force would be showing on Rabaul's radar screens, and chances were, even at this moment, the enemy would be scrambling to get their defenders into the air. For all we knew, they might have already launched a raid on our carriers. Our one advantage was that the Japs could not have an accurate picture of our aerial defenses.

My formation remained tight, and as ordered, we kept strict radio silence. As the hours of our patrol dragged on uneventfully, my backside began to ache for *something* to relieve the drudgery.

The break came a few minutes later. I saw it to the northwest: a single, slim silhouette at 20,000 feet, heading away from us on a perpendicular course. The pilot had seen us and was running: no doubt a Jap scout plane looking for the task force. If he found it, he would radio his compadres, whom I guessed would be combing an area somewhere nearby. We needed to put this bastard down.

My division dumped its drop tanks and dove to pursue. With our altitude advantage, I thought we would be able to catch up to the Jap readily, yet the lone plane somehow managed to stay well ahead of us. After five full minutes of the chase, I had the bad feeling that the scout was a decoy, meant to draw us away from our patrol zone.

After another minute, however, I realized we were slowly but surely closing the gap. And our quarry was not a Zeke or Oscar, but a sleek, silver-gray fighter with a long, graceful snout housing a water-cooled, inline engine: a Kawasaki Ki-61 Hien, or "Tony"—the first of its type I had actually witnessed in the air. Once the Nip realized he could not outrun us, he began to sideslip to the right, gradually angling toward the north. Chances were, he was going to lead us right into a nest of waiting enemy.

With my anger heating up, I jumped to war emergency power

to wring the last bit of horsepower out of my engine. The Tony driver realized his imminent danger and threw his plane into a hard right turn, hoping to veer inside of us and reverse course. The Ki-61 was considerably faster than either the Zero or Oscar, and no slouch at maneuvering. As it zoomed past my right wing, I honked my nose around and fired off a wild lead shot. I missed, but by now, the Jap was near panicking. He broke into a wild, high-G barrel roll that made him an impossible target but cost him some vital speed. Now, Comeaux's division was closing in on his left, while Collins, Penrow, Kinney, and I split into high and low sections to his right. The Tony had no escape.

Comeaux fired a burst across its path; I didn't see any tracers making contact, but the Jap threw his plane into a violent skid that actually caused his wings to ripple. The tail of his plane slewed around in an impossible reversal, and he came roaring back, directly toward Comeaux's wingman, Mike Dillon. The Tony's guns cut loose, and I saw bright white and yellow sparks splashing off the nose of Dillon's Cat. Something large and crucial blew out from the engine—a cylinder head, I think—and rocketed into space. A thick gout of black smoke exploded from the cowling.

"Jesus," came Dillon's voice. "I'm hit, I'm hit bad."

"Get your nose down and head south," I said. "Try to glide her down."

"Working on it."

I couldn't pay Dillon any further mind at the moment, for the Tony was veering back toward Kinney and me at a steep climb. Collins and Penrow went left to flank him, but they would not be in time to stop him from making a firing run on us. Then, without warning, Kinney swerved right and nosed up, exposing his Cat's belly to the Tony's sights. The Jap could hardly avoid taking advantage of the golden opportunity; his guns flashed, and Kinney's Hellcat shuddered as 12.7mm bullets and 20mm cannon shells hammered his wings and fuselage. But now, the Tony was beginning to falter as its airspeed dropped in the climb. Its nose slipped earthward right in front of my guns, and I opened fire, my .50 calibers finding the sweet spot at the root of the damaged wing, sending it flying like a jet-propelled whirlybird. The wrecked Ki-61 went into a violent tumble earthward, streaming black, white, and gray smoke.

The pilot, whose wild, vicious attacks had struck me as worthy of a valiant samurai, apparently had less desire to join his ancestors than many of his brothers. I saw his canopy pop open, and with amazing adroitness, he climbed out of the plummeting wreckage, leaped into the air, and ripped open his parachute. The white silk flower blossomed a thousand feet below me and began drifting toward the safety of a thick cumulus mass that smothered the ocean.

Then, in a move that was contrary to everything instilled in us as fighting men, Comeaux and his division went into slow, spiraling dives, lined up on the dangling figure, and opened fire with their .50 calibers. As if in a daze, I found that I had also pushed over and was following them down to set up an attack on the hapless pilot. One or more of the preceding strafing runs had been partially successful, for the whole upper part of his body was a mangled, bloody mass. He still clung to life, however, for I saw him writhing and kicking in his harnesses, obviously in mortal pain.

As I cut my speed and turned my nose toward him, I realized that in five seconds, he would disappear in the clouds below—and visions of Archie Staunton's final plight began reeling through my mind. Though this Jap might not have been one of the murderers, to my mind he was no different than his barbarian kindred. As if separated from my own body, I watched myself wait until I was only 200 yards from the dangling figure and then cut loose with all six .50s. The body jerked and spun like a dervish, and a portion of the Jap's head simply vanished under the onslaught of my bullets. Then his straps came apart and his body slipped away, falling toward the clouds below until they swallowed it. The empty chute began to whirl erratically without the weight of the body to stabilize it.

"That's for Archie Staunton, you piece of shit," I breathed.

Then I heard Ensign Kinney's soft voice come over the radio, "Mr. McLachlan, I'm afraid my plane's shot up. Ailerons are a mess."

Glancing around in search of my wingman, I saw him nearly a half mile behind me, flying straight and level, fortunately leaving no smoke trail.

"Mr. Dillon, are you still there?"

I waited several seconds for a response, and heard nothing. "Red Two, do you copy?"

Then, Comeaux said in a low, flat voice, "He's gone, Athos. He blew up."

My heart sank like a rock in quicksand. My blood cold, all I could do was mutter, "Oh, Jesus." Then, hardly daring to hope, I asked, "Mr. Kinney, do you have control?"

"For the moment."

"Head for the barn. I'll cover you. Porthos, take the lead."

"Roger, Athos, good luck."

Heart lodged in my throat, I turned southwest, tucking in close to Kinney's bullet-riddled plane. If we ran into trouble now, we were as good as dead. Worse, our squadron was being slowly whittled down to the point of seriously compromising our effectiveness; no replacement pilots or planes had yet been scheduled for us.

We had already used the radio, but I kept my mouth shut all the way back, even though I ached to give Ensign Kinney a thorough tongue-lashing for having needlessly placed himself in jeopardy. It certainly wasn't like him to make a foolhardy—much less suicidal—move in an airplane.

When the dark hulk of Conquest Island materialized in the distant haze, I felt an equal measure of relief and renewed anxiety. Life on the home front had hardly proven to be a respite from the rigors of combat. I had that terrible feeling of wanting to jump right out of my skin, and my nerves jangled like discordant wind chimes. I hoped Colonel Rooker still had plenty of scotch, for by now I had made up my mind to shamelessly anesthetize myself. At the moment, I probably could have sucked down a whole bottle and barely felt it.

For the first time in my career, I had committed cold-blooded murder. I had killed men in combat, yes. But I had never, with malice aforethought, butchered a helpless victim before.

True, the Jap was dying before I shot him. But it was my bullets that finished him. Yes, he would have killed me, given the chance; hell, he had already tried. And he had killed Mike Dillon. Furthermore, had he survived, he would likely end up back in the air, ready, willing, and able to bring down yet more of our men. I had all the justification I needed for doing what I had done.

But nothing in my life had ever felt so wrong.

As I descended toward the runway—in front of Kinney, in case he crashed—for a second I heard a horrible, low, sonorous voice speaking in my head.

"You are learning."

Friday, November 5, 1943
1730 hours
"What the hell were you doing, lamebrain?" I roared, as soon as Ensign Kinney climbed down from his cockpit. "Trying to get yourself killed?"

Kinney's pale face turned to white gauze. He pulled off his

flight helmet quickly, so that sprigs of red hair stood out ludicrously from his narrow skull; his trembling fingers throttled his helmet. "Mr. McLachlan, I—"

"Do you have any idea what Railroad Bill could do to you for this?" I was hardly joking. The giant crew chief was already on his way over, and his face was beet red. I stepped protectively in front of Kinney in case the Marine attempted to deck the young man.

"Mr. McLachlan, my guns were jammed. I couldn't shoot."

"What?"

The little man lowered his eyes. "That Jap was lining up on you. I made myself a target to draw his fire."

"Your guns were jammed?"

"Yes, sir."

"Why didn't you say so?"

"No time. It was too late."

"Jesus H. Christ." Here, long after the fact, I realized that Ensign Elmer Kinney had once again saved my life. He had simply been performing his duty the only way he knew how. I had failed to recognize his maneuver simply because it would not have occurred to me to do the same thing.

Thoroughly deflated, I lowered my head and put a reluctant hand on Kinney's shoulder. "I'm sorry. I didn't realize."

"It's all right, I understand."

"No, it's not all right."

Just then, Railroad Bill lumbered up in front of me and peered over my shoulder at Ensign Kinney. "I oughta take this one out of your hide, little fellow. You shoulda taken your chances with the Japs."

"Cool it, Bill," I said. "Mr. Kinney already took all the chances any man ever ought to."

Bill's eyes narrowed. "How's that?"

"He put himself in harm's way to save his commanding officer."

"That for real, young man?"

"Yes, Sergeant," Kinney said meekly.

"Mr. Varn," I said. "This man is an officer in the United States Navy. Let's conduct ourselves appropriately in his presence."

Railroad Bill's eyes turned suspicious, flicking back and forth from mine to Kinney's. "You're serious, right?"

"Very."

He scratched his head and shrugged. "Well, all right. So what happened up there?"

"We lost a man," I said woodenly. "Ensign Mike Dillon is dead."

"I see." The crew chief's voice was a whisper now. "Well, I'm sorry to hear that."

"Thank you."

"I mean it, sir." Railroad Bill turned to look at Kinney's Hellcat, which looked like it had been riddled with buckshot at close range. "Well, I guess there's a job to be done. Might as well forego the beer. I don't reckon we need any more just now."

"Everything all right here?"

He gave me a tentative nod. "More or less. Colonel Rooker, well, he's on edge, you might say. Thinks it's too quiet today."

"Right," I said with a sigh. "Well, carry on. See what you can do with that airplane."

"Yes, sir, I will."

As Kinney and I began walking toward the parked jeeps at the edge of the apron, Bill called to me, "So, Mr. Mac. Did you at least knock down some Japs?"

I paused, then shook my head. "None that I would claim,

Bill. None that I would claim."

Friday, November 5, 1943
1925 hours

"Okay, gentlemen, we've got the latest official numbers," Rook said as he walked into the ready room, where Trimble, Comeaux, Pearce, Doc McCall, and I were doing damage to full tumblers of scotch. I was on my third, at least one shot ahead of the pack. I handed a waiting glass to Rook, and he took a healthy slug while glancing at the sheet of notepaper in his hand. After a deep gasp to cool the obvious burn, he said, "Okay, we lost five bombers and five fighters over Rabaul—a total of fifteen men either killed or missing. Unfortunately, even if any of them survived, chances are no one will ever see them again. However . . . this is what we did to the enemy. For air kills, twenty-eight confirmed, nineteen probables, and seventeen damaged. And this afternoon, B-24s from New Guinea hit them again, but we don't have their stats yet. What this means, gentlemen, is that the Japs' Rabaul fleet is for all practical purposes drydocked, and their air forces are crippled. As near as we can tell, Sherman's gotten away clean. The task force is well out of the danger zone by now."

An audible, collective sigh rose from our group, and some of us were actually smiling.

"Kee-rist," Comeaux said. "That means we whipped their asses against all odds. What do you make of that?"

I was feeling comfortably mellow and this news bolstered my sagging spirits several notches. I had thanked God many times over for bringing the rest of my pilots home without incident. As it turned out, shortly after Kinney and I had departed, they had linked up with six Hellcats from VF-12, so they had never been as vulnerable as I had feared. For the rest of the day, none of the patrolling squadrons had made any further contacts.

"That was a hell of a day's work," Pearce said, his stern features warmed by the glow of alcohol and genuine pleasure at the news from ComAirSols. "Busting up Rabaul may be the biggest thing we've done since taking Cactus."

"That'll sure ease the pressure at Torokina," Trimble said. "Without air and sea support, the Jap ground forces will be driven out soon enough."

"We'll probably be called on for close support," I said, not sure whether I liked the idea. "That means brushing up on our strafing skills."

"I know who I'd like to practice on," Comeaux said, downing a serious slug of scotch. "If we could find them."

I nodded, my mood darkening a degree. My glass was empty, and I was on the verge of refilling it when an almost-forgotten sliver of common sense pricked my brain: one more drink and I would be one unhappy pilot the next morning. I settled for a cigarette instead. Noticing that Comeaux's gaze had fallen longingly on the bottle, I tossed him a smoke as well. "We'll be better off if we don't," I said.

"The voice of wisdom," Doc McCall said, putting his glass aside, looking more than customarily tipsy. "But this is such good medicine."

Rook chuckled. "Don't get used to it. There isn't that much left."

"Colonel, you have a crisis," Comeaux said.

"Don't remind me."

I had just crushed out my cigarette and was about to light another when I heard the clatter of footsteps just outside the door. A second later Arsenault appeared, out of breath and pale-faced. "Athos," he said, "something's up at the caves."

"What is it?" Rook said, shooting to his feet.

"The seal's been broken. And at least one casualty."

"Jesus," I groaned. "Come on, let's go."

We made tracks toward the cave entrance without pausing to acknowledge any of the questions the curious pilots and crew fired at us. By the time we reached the dark mouth, we had an entourage of a dozen or so men, and more coming as word began to spread. A number of Marines huddled just inside the opening, leaning over a fallen man. The setting sun cast an ominous, bloody hue over the tableau.

Corporal Pete Gruber—one of the jeep maintenance crew, if I remembered right—stepped up to Colonel Rooker. "It's Private Jurado, sir. He was watching the entrance."

"What happened to him?"

Gruber shook his head uncertainly, his face ashen. "There was nothing there, then . . . something. We heard a crash—the concrete shattering. Jurado went to look, and then he went down."

"You were inside the cave?" I asked.

"Yes, sir, back by the fuel drums. Me and Scott, er, Private Kaplan."

"Which one is Kaplan?"

"That's me, sir," said a tall, muscular man of about twenty-five, with close-cropped auburn hair and small, gray-blue eyes. He was one of the few clean-shaven men remaining in camp. Now his complexion looked like white paraffin.

"You see anything?"

"Just what Private Gruber said, sir. We heard this noise, Jurado went down the passage a ways, then got cut down. But there was nothing there. He just fell, and he was like . . . that." He stepped aside and pointed to the body lying prostrate on its back behind him.

The body had no head. Black blood was not only pooled around the figure, but splashed on the walls all around the entrance. It looked like the head had been twisted and then ripped right from the neck.

"He didn't even have time to scream," Gruber whispered.

Doc McCall dropped to his knees next to the body. Blood seeped into the fabric of his trousers, but he ignored it. He gently rolled the body to one side and examined its back. "Looks like something grabbed him first, spun him around, and then tore the head off. There are deep lacerations below the shoulders."

The smell of death was overpowering in this confined space, and my stomach lurched at the odor and sight of the carnage. I turned away and took several deep, steadying breaths, which only halfway worked; then, seeing Private Gruber a few feet away, I asked him to lend me his flashlight. Taking it, I played its beam over the uneven stone floor and cautiously made my way past a number of fuel drums, into the deep alcove. Sure enough, all that remained of the concrete seal was thousands of tiny fragments—just like the first one. Stepping through the rubble and dust, I aimed the flashlight beam into the tiny shaft, but it illuminated only bare stone walls. Surely, even the smallest of the beast-like natives could never have made his way through such a narrow passage.

But somehow, something powerful enough to brutally murder a man had passed through it.

Glancing down, I noticed an electrical wire coiled near my foot; following it with my light, my eyes fell on Railroad Bill's gun camera in a dark corner several feet to my left. The camera had been mounted on a large rock, braced by two smaller ones, with a 12-volt battery tucked next to it; both were covered with dust but appeared intact. Bill had apparently rigged a breaker to the battery so that pulling the trip wire would activate the camera. He had also strung several 100-watt bulbs to illuminate the dark end of the alcove, but all were now broken. Ordinarily, when mounted in the wing of a fighter, the camera ran for only a few seconds at a time, whenever the guns fired; therefore, the device held no more than five minutes' worth of film. But that would be more than enough if this rig had actually worked.

I heard the shuffle of footsteps behind me and turned to see Rook and Pearce coming into the low passage, each warily scanning the sloping walls and ceiling. The Colonel looked as if he expected the mountain to collapse on his head.

"Is it intact?" Rook asked, pointing to the camera, his voice low and wavering.

I nodded. "Looks like it. We should get this developed right away."

He lifted the camera as if it were a live grenade and then handed it to Pearce. "Get this to the darkroom at once," he said. "Have Private Southworth do his best and fastest work with it."

Pearce nodded. "I'll set up the projector."

"Good," I said. "Maybe we'll get a clue from this."

"We'll know soon enough."

Pearce hurried off, and I started back toward the entrance, my insides frozen in knots. I expected Rook to be at my heels, but when I looked around, I saw him crouched in front of the tiny opening, peering intently into its depths.

"You see something?"

He shook his head. "No. I guess not."

"You all right?"

"Yeah, just a little shaky," he said. "It's this place. I guess we'll have to start making arrangements to move the fuel. What a job that's going to be."

"Let's worry about that later, shall we?"

He nodded and finally turned away from the opening, mopping his forehead with a handkerchief. In the dim light that filtered from behind me, his face looked like an oriental death mask. "I have to get out of here," he whispered and began walking stiffly back toward the entrance.

A litter had been brought from the sickbay, and two crewmen were moving the body onto it under Doc McCall's guidance. As I approached them, the thick, sour smell of blood almost made me gag. "I'm heading back to operations," I told Rook.

"Wait," he said. "For all the good it'll do, I'd recommend none of us goes anywhere alone. Gruber, walk with Mr. McLachlan, will you? I'll catch up to you later for debriefing."

Private Gruber nodded an acknowledgment and fell in beside me, a decade's worth of creases etched into his otherwise cherubic face. As we walked the path toward the Quonset hut, I listened to our footsteps squishing in the soft earth and to the terrible, harsh silence of dark rain forest that ought to be teeming with life.

"Mr. Gruber, you say you saw nothing in there?"

He shook his head. "Not a thing. Well . . ." For a moment he looked doubtful.

"What?"

"Maybe a shadow. Or something. Then the lights were smashed."

I nodded and patted the .45 in my holster. It didn't offer much comfort. Fortunately, we had a relatively short walk to the hut. All the while, my feet wanted to break into a run and keep going far, far away from here. But there was nowhere to go. Not out here.

The jungle, in its silence, seemed to be laughing.

Friday, November 5, 1943
2105 hours

Our 16mm projector was hardly a deluxe piece of equipment, just an old, simple machine that—on a good day—ran the film you put into it without chewing it up. Major Pearce had set it up in the center of the ready room, aimed at a collapsible, silver-tinted screen in front of the chalkboard where I ordinarily gave my briefings. Private Rod Southworth had hurriedly processed the gun camera film and was now fitting the reel onto the projector's spindle arm. Rook stood at the outside door clutching his .45 in one hand, his eyes constantly peering out into the darkness; Comeaux was leaning back in his chair, one ear pressed expectantly to the nearby window. The hairs on my arms and the back of my neck prickled as if lightning were about to strike.

For the first time since I had known him, Jasper Arsenault appeared ill at ease.

"Okay, it's ready," Private Southworth said. "Somebody wanna hit the lights?"

Rook's hand moved to the switch without a moment's hesitation. When the room went pitch-black, my heart jumped in unexpected shock. But a second later, the projector whirred to life, and a brilliant white rectangle appeared on the screen, replaced a moment later by the film leader counting down from five to zero.

Gun camera films had no sound. When a blurry image of the cave wall appeared before us, dimly lit by the string of 100-watt bulbs that crisscrossed the ceiling, only the grinding and clicking of the projector motor accompanied it. But in the center of the screen, a white, circular mass—the concrete plug in the shaft opening—seemed to be twisting and pulsating like something alive. Then, with a silent crash, it toppled to the floor and shattered, as if pulverized by a giant, invisible hammer. A thick cloud of dust erupted from the rubble and rolled toward the camera, momentarily obscuring the view; then, as the cloud slowly dissipated, I could see the exposed black opening, from which a few wispy tongues of dust or smoke lapped at the stone walls.

Then an elongated shadow crept into view to the left of the screen: Private Jurado stepping into the alcove to investigate the disturbance. Gradually, the picture became distorted, as if we were watching through a fish-eye lens. The roughly circular opening turned oblong, and the ridges on the walls seemed to stretch as if the stone had changed to elastic. Something—another shadow—briefly darkened the screen, and then a whirling, black cyclone whipped past the camera's eye, lasting little more than a second.

The lights in the cave flared brilliantly and died. The screen darkened, and the projector whirred noisily as blank film cranked past the projection lamp. After a moment, Private Southworth shut off the power. The whole event had lasted less than fifteen seconds.

"Well, that's it," Southworth said. "There's nothing more on the film."

"Show it again," Rook said. "That machine doesn't run at a slower speed, does it?"

"No, sir. I'm afraid not."

He nodded, frowning in frustration. "I want to have another look at that last second or two."

Southworth rewound the film and started it again. As the picture of the cave reappeared, I leaned forward and focused intently on its features, scanning the field by quadrants as I might search for fighters in a clear blue sky. Again, the concrete plug toppled and was smashed to dust by an unseen force. The shadow on the left slid into view, and the picture became distorted. Then the spinning, black cyclone rushed in and out of view. The light bulbs flared a final time, and everything went dark.

"Can you freeze the picture on that thing?" Rook asked.

"It'll melt the film."

"Back it up and run it one more time. There's something there—right at the end."

"Yes, sir."

Southworth reset the film for a third time, and we watched it again in total silence, terribly aware that we were seeing something that simply should not exist. As the sequence drew to its conclusion, Rook said, "Screw the film. Freeze on that shape at the end."

With the black cyclone whirling across the screen, Southworth hit the stop button but left the projection lamp burning. For a few seconds, we studied the image, but then a brown stain materialized on one side of the frame and quickly spread like a pool of bubbling ink. Southworth shut the lamp off immediately, but I knew that its intense heat had ruined at least an inch or more of film.

However, in the additional few seconds the pause had afforded us, I had seen, in the center of that inky, funnel-shaped mass, a tall, spindly silhouette draped in some kind of billowing fabric, with wiry arms spread at its sides at awry angles. The image was blurry but unmistakable—and the expressions on the faces of everyone in the room indicated they had all seen it.

"It was there, wasn't it?" I said. "You saw it?"

Rook nodded. "The figure you've seen in your dreams."

"Yes."

"Spinning like a goddamn dervish," Chuck Trimble said. "It came right out of the opening."

Arsenault nodded. "But moving faster than the eye could actually see."

"Incredible," Pearce huffed. "Absolutely in-fucking-credible."

"That's what killed our men?" Doc McCall said, his face a leering mask of disbelief. "Some kind of phantom?"

"One that strikes like lightning," Rook said softly. "And leaves no footprints."

"But it's impossible."

"You saw it for yourself."

"We all saw it," I said. "That's the same figure that I've

dreamed about. And I think I've seen it at other times."

"That's what you shot at the other day, isn't it?" Arsenault said.

"Yes."

"That's not all," Rook said. "Both Commander McLachlan and I have seen some kind of . . . shape . . . up on the mountain. It's not clear to the naked eye, but there is a *presence* up there at times. I believe that it—and the thing in this film—may be one and the same."

"What makes you say that?" Pearce asked.

"Just a theory. One that I think Mr. McLachlan shares with me." I nodded tentatively, wondering just how much Rook had figured out, or thought he had. "I believe that what we're seeing is a mask, of sorts, for something altogether different."

"Intriguing concept," Arsenault said. "But where do you suppose such a thing would come from?"

"Outer space," Pearce suggested.

"Somewhere *between* the spaces we know," Rook said, his eyes far away. "Something with no regard for the laws of conventional physics."

"Such an idea is not without precedent," Trimble said. "Albert Einstein, among others, has proposed that, on a quantum level, certain objects can move from one place to another without physically existing in the space it traverses. Of course, I'm no physicist. But it's plain that this thing has properties we can't begin to understand."

"The question is—how do we fight it?" Comeaux said. "Or can we?"

"The key to winning a fight is to know your enemy, to anticipate his moves," I said. "Gentlemen, we don't know this enemy. But it knows us."

I noticed Arsenault had cocked his head, and a moment later, he rose and went to the nearest window. "Drums," he said.

"The drums have started."

Every man in the room held his breath, and in the silence, I heard the low, muted thrumming of distant percussion. If, as we believed, the natives communicated with the entity using their drums, I would make book that the thing was somewhere nearby, perhaps watching us. Even listening to us.

A few of the men had come prepared with M-1 carbines; I had only my holstered .45. But Rook disappeared into his office and came out a few moments later carrying two rifles, one of which he handed to me, along with a couple of extra ammo clips. Then, on a spontaneous impulse, we all began filing out the door into the night, where the sound of the drums playing point and counterpoint pounded through the jungle with greater resonance and clarity, rising and falling with the cadence of incomprehensible speech. Several lanterns wove through the darkness down at Tobacco Road, and voices speaking in hushed, tentative tones rose from nearby. By now, everyone knew that the drums portended anything but a peaceful night on Conquest Island.

A couple of men came trotting up the path from Marine City, calling for Colonel Rooker. "Sir," cried one of them, a PFC named Hodges, "there's torches up on the mountain. Lots of them!"

From where we stood, the nearest trees concealed the summit of the looming mountain, but as we began to move toward the lagoon, I could make out a line of individual twinkling flames in the jungle above us—certainly no less than a hundred. As I watched, the lights began slowly moving in unison down the slope like a giant, slithering glowworm, flickering in and out of view as they passed among the trees. As if to punctuate the air of danger closing in on us, the drums began to beat louder, more frantically. They, too, seemed to be getting nearer.

"Get everyone to their defensive positions," Rook said to

Major Pearce. "The far side of the trail to the cave will be our first line of defense—just inside the barbed wire. Have Gruber pull a truck into the cave entrance to block it. I don't want any of these bastards getting to the fuel if we can avoid it. Hodges, what's your job?"

"Defending the ammo dump, sir!"

"All right, get to it."

"Yes, sir!"

I knew that Rook had been plotting defense for the base in our absence each day; his experience during the dark days on Guadalcanal might yet prove more valuable than any of us could have realized. By now I was already hustling toward Tobacco Road with Comeaux and Arsenault in tow, and several of the pilots were on their way to meet me. Max Collins and Hank Hubbard each toted a heavy canvas satchel of grenades they had taken from the armory—whether with or without approval from Rook's quartermaster, I didn't care to know.

"I think we're about in for it, Skipper," Collins said. "We figured we'd get these distributed to our guys."

"All right. Our most vulnerable flank will be down by maintenance. There's no barbed wire or grenade traps down there. Also—Rook's going to have some men down at the flight line but they'll be spread thin. Porthos, take your guys down to the Cats and give the crew a hand."

"Roger that, Athos," he said, his ordinarily jovial face now taut and severe.

"Aramis," I said, "get your guys to the ammo dump with Railroad Bill. That could be a hot spot."

"Indeed," he said with a curt nod and immediately turned to muster his men. Several of the pilots were now grabbing grenades from the satchels and clipping them to their web belts. I saw Elmer Kinney, José Rodriguez, and Willy Vickers coming from Tobacco Road, each carrying a rifle. In all our time training together, I had hardly expected to be overseeing a ground defense of our airbase.

"Okay," I said, "we'll form a line this side of the track, to protect the Marines' left flank. We'll be close to the cave entrance, so be alert. The last thing we want is natives with torches in there. If that fuel blows, it'll finish off everything and everyone on the island." There were spirited affirmations from the men, but all the faces around me were grim and apprehensive. The flickers of torchlight in the trees indicated that the approaching horde had reached the base of the ridge, some 300 yards from our position. They were moving amazingly quickly through the thick, tangled growth.

As we rushed toward the cave, I could hear the grinding of gears as Corporal Gruber maneuvered a tow truck into the opening, which would hinder access if not totally block it. He shut the engine off and then came hustling down the path; some thirty yards to our right, he dropped into the foliage, just this side of the barbed wire perimeter. In the solid darkness we could not see Rook's men, but I could hear frantic voices whispering back and forth.

I wondered: Would the attackers be armed? How many altogether? Would several groups make a multi-pronged attack from different directions? Did they actually intend to fight us to the death, or could they have another, unforeseen reason for approaching us this way? In a fighter plane, my every action was virtually automatic, my tactics and movements practiced and assured. Like all servicemen, I had been introduced to ground combat maneuvers in basic training, but since then, all my efforts had been to refine my aerial combat skills. In this, an entirely different environment, with unknown variables, I was just a tyro.

Our superior firepower, and the combat experience of the Marine unit, would almost assuredly spell doom for the islanders. But that might be our very undoing, I thought. The natives and the unknown entity shared a special bond. They revered it. Perhaps they saw it as some kind of guardian.

I had no time to ponder the point. We had almost reached the cave, so I turned my group to the left of the track, where we dug in behind a barrier of tightly spaced trees, partially camouflaged by thick clusters of orchids and ferns. Perhaps automatically, my men had formed around me the same way they would in the air: Kinney to my left, Vickers and Rodriguez to my right, and Collins, Penrow, Hedgman, and Hubbard behind them. The Marines, in front of us and to our right, would get the first crack at the attackers; our job would be to cut down any that managed to get past them or that made their way as far as the cave entrance.

I lifted my M-1, chambered the first round, and flicked off the safety, taking aim at the pitch-black jungle in preparation to fire. The leading torches were now about a hundred yards away, and I could intermittently make out a number of dark silhouettes moving in the light as they leaped and hopped like huge, grotesque insects through the undergrowth. I knew Rook's men would not shoot until the attackers were too close to miss. My group would fire only after the Marines opened the engagement.

I suddenly felt something attach itself to my left hand—something light, but with sharp, barbed appendages—and I realized a critter had come out of the undergrowth to walk on me. Trying unsuccessfully to withhold the involuntary gasp of panic, I shook the thing off my hand, which in turn caused my right index finger to tighten on the trigger of the M-1. Only by a miracle did I avoid squeezing off an accidental round. I had rid myself of the unknown beast, but I wondered if we might have settled into a nest of them—the terror of which, for a moment, exceeded all fear of the approaching islanders. I barely forced myself to remain stationary, certain that if another such animal should tread on me, my next reaction might not be so controlled.

I could now hear a low swishing sound alternating with a rising *thud-thud-thud* in the darkness, which I identified as the sound of onrushing feet. A literal explosion of torches lit the night less than a hundred yards away, all bobbing and swirling like huge fireflies, some trailing streamers of orange sparks. A deep, vibrato chorus of voices crept ahead of them—a low chant, I realized, that sounded something like *"Eega ganai mi, eega ganai mi,"* repeating over and over and growing steadily louder. The drums reached a crescendo, still distant but horrifically loud, as if somehow amplified. I expected to hear the Marines' opening shots at any moment.

To my left, two torchbearers broke through the trees, and I swung my carbine around to draw a bead on them. In the firelight, I could see that these islanders resembled our original visitor in every detail: large, bulbous heads with protruding foreheads and chins, and long, almost pointed ears; thick, stocky torsos that rippled with muscles, resembling bronze armor more than human flesh; sculpted arms and legs that bulged with formidable power; and talons that belonged not to men but to birds of prey. Apart from the torches, the brutish figures did not appear to be carrying any weapons.

I expected this pair to run straight into the all-but-invisible strands of barbed wire strung along the edge of the track, but at the last second, as if sensing the lethal barrier, both drew up short. Surely, I thought, they could not actually see it in the darkness. But sure enough, they began skirting the wire, moving to our right—straight toward Rook's concealed Marines.

The first gunshots sounded like cannon fire, and the muzzle flashes lit the night like brilliant white flares. The two islanders were both picked up and swept backward as if kicked by a huge, invisible boot; both landed heavily on their backs with limbs askew. Then the M-1s turned toward the approaching body of flame-limned shadows and opened fire in earnest.

My ears screamed in protest at the deafening blasts of semi-automatic rifle fire, and in the white, strobing flashes, I saw several shadowy figures twisting and falling, their torches whirling into the trees like pieces of blazing shrapnel. Twenty yards away, a dark, twisted-looking silhouette hurtled headlong into the barbed wire barrier and unleashed a sickening, agonized scream like the cry of a wounded cougar; the figure writhed and thrashed frantically in an attempt to free itself until a rifle at point-blank range silenced him with its own deafening noise.

Now, the trees were alight with torches moving wildly to and fro, and I could see countless grotesque shadows pressing doggedly forward. Rising from their midst, the chant *"eega ganai mi . . . eega ganai mi"* thrummed louder and louder in rhythm with the feverishly pounding drums. The Marines unleashed a coordinated volley into the trees, and torches went spinning into the air as .30-caliber bullets ripped into their bearers. Then a small, dark object flew out of the foliage at the far side of the track, and three seconds later, with a deafening boom, the grenade illuminated the night with fire, sending tree limbs, underbrush, and native bodies flying into the air like randomly hurled garbage.

The chanting voices were becoming less and less unified as the gunfire broke the natives' charge, but if anything, our resistance seemed to have incited the attackers to even greater fury. The chant became a piercing, collective howl, so ferocious and animalistic that I could scarcely believe it came from the throats of men. Thus convinced that these brutes shared little in common with us, I felt no remorse whatsoever when I emptied my clip directly into the face of one who was attempting to wriggle through the barbed wire. The bullets slammed him onto his back, leaving his legs tangled awkwardly in the spiked metal strands. In that moment, I felt a strange giddiness, a thrilling charge of passion—more intense than any I had known even in aerial combat—that I can only describe as bloodlust.

Several more shadowy figures, sans torches, were moving furtively to the left now, in the direction of the cave entrance. Exhilarated by a raging sense of power, I slammed a new clip into the magazine and squeezed the trigger several times in succession; a pair of inharmonious screams rang out as my bullets struck home.

To my left, I could see Ensign Kinney's pale face contorted in an expression of sheer horror, but when a black silhouette materialized this side of the barbed wire barrier and began loping toward us, he promptly raised his rifle and fired. Either the bullet missed or the onrushing creature simply ignored it. Kinney fired again, this time squeezing off a half-dozen rapid shots. The advancing figure now keeled over with a hoarse grunt and lay still.

"Jesus," the young man whispered. "What the hell are they?"

A number of shouting voices rose in the distance—behind us—and gunfire erupted from the direction of the maintenance shed. *Jesus!* Another group of natives must have come down from the ridge to the northwest—without torches. What if this frontal assault were merely a feint, I thought, meant to divert our attention while other, perhaps larger groups attacked simultaneously? If so, the enemy's numbers would have to be vast indeed.

Although the beast-men were proving hard to kill, our bullets had finally begun to take a toll on them. The number of torches in the jungle had diminished considerably, and several motionless bodies hung in the barbed wire like filthy, discarded rags. Rook's guns raged on, however, and a couple of more grenades flew over the wire, their blasts hurling flaming pieces of unidentifiable debris into the undergrowth.

My clip was empty. I yanked it from the magazine and was about to drive home its replacement when a broad, simian silhouette appeared directly in front of me, outlined by roiling columns of flame. The creature released a banshee scream, his eyes blazing like headlights. Then his hand slashed downward like a battle ax, drawing a shrill cry of surprise and pain from Willy Vickers, who toppled backward, clutching his throat. José Rodriguez immediately raised his rifle and smashed its butt into the brute's bony cheek—a blow powerful enough to have dropped the hardiest man, but which failed to so much as faze this one. Now, in desperation, I wrenched my .45 from its holster and drove the muzzle into the native's muscle-armored chest. I squeezed the trigger once . . . twice . . . three times.

As if time had frozen, the beast-man's eyes rolled to meet mine, first alight with unspeakable fury, then glazed with what seemed to be the realization of a long-anticipated death. One shaking, talon-like hand slowly lifted and grasped my right forearm, then went limp as his life's essence gushed from the spigot-like wounds in his chest. For a long moment, his gaze met mine, exhibiting the same cruel, cunning look I had seen in the eyes of that first native we had been forced to kill, then his lips spread in a parody of a smile, exposing jagged yellow teeth now stained with blood. Then the eyes rolled up in their sockets and the body toppled at my feet.

With his death, I snapped out of my daze. Behind me, I heard Vickers moaning and choking as he rolled in agony on the ground. Rodriguez dropped to his knees and tried to get his hands over the grievous neck wound to help staunch the flow of blood. Max Collins and Jimmy Penrow came hustling toward me and, before I could even issue the order, grabbed the native's arms and legs and dragged the body into the trees behind us, getting it out of our way. Farther down the line, Hoagie Hedgman and Hank Hubbard were firing on targets that I couldn't see.

"Oh, God," Vickers whispered in a choked voice. "Get me out of here. Please get me out of here."

"Hold on, amigo," Rodriguez said gently. "I will get you to the help." He turned to me with dark, worried eyes. "Señor Skipper, I take him to Doc."

I gave Vickers a quick glance and realized that he might live if he received medical attention quickly. "You're on your own, José. Be careful—there may be more of them down there."

He nodded grimly. I helped him drag Vickers to his feet and draped one of his arms around Rodriguez's shoulders. "Willy, use your other hand and put pressure on that wound. You've got to stop the bleeding."

Vickers nodded painfully but managed to comply. Then Rodriguez began half-carrying, half-dragging his injured section leader into the darkness toward the camp. I only hoped that they could find Doc McCall without being ambushed. There was no telling what might be happening elsewhere.

"Mr. McLachlan," Kinney whispered, "I think there's more of them, to the left."

I couldn't see anything at first, for most of the nearest torches had been extinguished. But as my eyes roved the shadows, I detected a subtle movement just on the other side of the track. I raised my rifle and fired, and a hoarse grunt confirmed I had hit my target.

Then, to my left, something came barreling through the brush and leaped toward Kinney and me, loosing a howl that seemed to shake the earth. I raised my rifle but a terrific force knocked me backward, sending my carbine flying into the darkness. An iron claw encircled my throat, drawing blood and crushing my windpipe. Another strong hand gripped my waist, lifting me off the ground. Overcome by sheer panic, I could only thrash my arms in a vain attempt to unbalance my attacker.

I thought I heard someone calling my name, and several shots rang out. But the pressure on my throat only increased, and I could no longer see the glow of torches in the darkness. Somehow, though, my questing hand brushed the sheath on my web belt, and I managed to grasp the handle of my bowie knife. Desperate now, I jabbed the blade recklessly toward my own throat, hoping to stab the hand cutting off my air. The knife met resistance, and I thrust it forward with all my strength, but the claws still pressed mercilessly into my flesh.

Then, somehow, a hand abruptly snatched the knife from my grasp. A moment later, the pressure on my throat subsided, and I tumbled to the ground, landing heavily on my back. For several moments my lungs struggled painfully for air, until I gradually began to feel revitalized. Then, from out of the darkness, a bony, iron hand landed on my shoulder. I expected to be grabbed again, but now the hand was limp, and something wet and warm began pouring over my back.

"Skipper!" I recognized the voice as Max Collins's.

I finally gathered the strength to prop myself on my elbows, and with blurry, tear-laden eyes, I saw the hideous face of the islander a few inches from mine, eyes rolled upward in death.

His throat had been cut.

A pair of strong hands grabbed me under my arms and hoisted me to my feet, then held me to keep me from collapsing again. I saw Max Collins's sea-blue eyes shining at me in the darkness. "Take some deep breaths, Skipper. You'll be all right."

I raised a hand to my throat, rubbing the tender, now-bruised flesh. "What the hell?"

Then I saw Ensign Elmer Kinney standing in front of me, holding my bowie knife. Its blade was dripping with blood.

"Mr. Kinney?"

The young redhead nodded. "Are you all right, sir?"

I found myself whispering, "Mr. Kinney, you magnificent little bastard."

"I'm sorry?" he asked uncertainly.

I looked around, realizing the gunfire was now sporadic, most of it distant. Rook's Marines had risen from their defensive positions and were driving a number of surviving natives in the direction of the lagoon and—

A huge explosion ripped through the night a hundred yards to our right, and I heard a few shrill cries of agony, then several gunshots. A second explosion erupted a few seconds later.

The grenade traps. Rook had turned the remnants of the charge right to where he wanted them.

Looking back at my young wingman, I could only grin foolishly at him. "Mr. Kinney, you have saved my life yet again. There's only one thing left to do."

"Sir?"

I laid one weary hand on his shoulder and gave it a grateful squeeze. "Mr. Kinney, I dub thee d'Artagnan."

Friday, November 5, 1943
2208 hours

The gunfire had dwindled and fallen silent not long after Rook's defenders had broken the islanders' charge and routed the remainder into the grenade traps. Apparently, only a small number of natives had managed to work their way northward to attempt a direct assault on our facilities; as far as we knew, all of them were now dead.

A small contingent of Rook's Marines remained posted this side of the barbed wire, but most of his force, as well as my men, had regrouped in front of the operations hut to assess our situation. One Marine—Corporal Pete Gruber—had suffered a broken arm when one of the natives, before being killed, drove through the defensive fire and attacked him. Apart from Willy

Vickers, the Blue Devils suffered no casualties; Comeaux's men, down at the flight line, never so much as glimpsed a single islander. José Rodriguez had successfully borne Vickers to sick-bay, and, thanks to Doc McCall's quick and efficient efforts, the young man was probably going to live. He would, however, have to be flown to Espiritu Santo for more comprehensive medical care at the earliest possibility. Rook had already called for an emergency transport, which would arrive at dawn.

Good news—but it also meant that I would be short yet another pilot.

We had beaten back what must surely have been the natives' sole possible attempt to overpower us. But at the moment, none of us felt even remotely safe. They had proven they could move quickly and stealthily in the darkness, and those who remained might now be more determined than ever to rid the island of those they regarded as trespassers, now their mortal enemies. A wounded beast was always the most dangerous.

And so it was that, as we accounted for ourselves at the operations hut, a commotion erupted a short distance into the jungle, and a few moments later, I heard a gunshot and a screech of agony that could only have come from the throat of an islander. Now carrying flashlights, Rook and I hurried up the track to where two Marines appeared to be kicking at a fallen figure, obviously not yet dead. As our lights fell on the native, we saw that he was thrashing and snarling at his attackers, a freely bleeding bullet wound in his abdomen having rendered him incapable of rising to his feet. As we approached, the men stopped kicking him, though with obvious reluctance.

I eyed the beast warily, finding myself eerily captivated by the pair of bright, cunning eyes that glared from beneath a grotesquely misshapen, protruding ridge of bone. His expression was one of expectation—or recognition. Like his brethren, his eyes intimated a profound, secret knowledge, a dark wisdom that so far exceeded our intellectual capacity that, in comparison, we were little more than contemptible, ignorant interlopers.

"What the fuck are you looking at?" Rook whispered to the creature, and his tone immediately sparked a surge of adrenaline through my body, as if his ire were contagious. And then, to my surprise, his booted foot lashed out, striking the fallen man across the jaw. A low grunt escaped the native's lips, but his eyes continued to glare at us, unshaken by the blow.

As if simple reflexes had taken over my will, I felt my own leg muscles contracting, and with all my strength, I kicked the native in the face, feeling a gratifying crunch as leather met bone. Then, without a word, the two Marines each placed a solid kick to the man's bleeding abdomen, and he released a screech loud enough to shock me back to my senses—just in time to see Rook draw his .45 from its holster and aim it at the native's head.

"We did nothing to your people," Rook said, kneeling so that his eyes could meet the native's. His voice had a cold, calculated tone I had never heard before. "We bore you no malice. We took nothing that belonged to you." He pressed the cold muzzle of the gun against the bony temple. The native obviously understood what the lethal instrument could do, for his eyes turned away from Rook's and took on a faraway gaze, as if he knew death was imminent and he intended to embrace it.

I thought Rook was simply going to pull the trigger. But then he leaned close to the native's ear and whispered, "What is it you speak to in the jungle? Is it your god?"

As if he understood, the native rolled his eyes to meet Rook's, and his thick lips spread in that venomous, inexplicable smile I had seen before. And I knew then and there that, somehow, these people did understand *us*, even if not our language.

I knelt next to Rook and heard myself say, "Speak, you devil."

The dark man turned his smile on me and, in a gruff whisper, said, *"Eeyah, baung chiyo mi . . . eeyah, baung chiyo shaggat . . . eeyah, baung chiyo no gogo ganai."*

I could barely suppress a shiver. "He answered," I said to Rook. "It's in his own language, but by God, he answered the question."

Rook nodded, then said to the native, "Tell us what that means. Tell us!"

Like a striking viper, a hot, taloned hand shot forth and grabbed my forearm, and I instinctively drew away, but the grip was only firm, not murderous. The native's eyes had glazed over, and his breathing was becoming shallow. His lips then began to form words—weakly and awkwardly—that for one fleeting, impossible moment, I swore sounded like English.

"The old one lives . . ."

Then a final breath hissed from the islander's lips, and his eyes went dim. The four of us remained frozen around the body, unsure whether we could any longer trust our senses. The dead man's words could not possibly have been in English, yet we each wore shocked, incredulous expressions.

"Rook?" I said, gazing at his shadowed features. "Did you hear it?"

"He simply said something in his own language. We misheard him."

I nodded, only half-convinced. Then, again feeling as if I were outside my body, watching a stranger go through the motions, my hand dropped to my belt and drew the bowie knife with which Ensign Kinney had earlier saved my life. Clutching the haft firmly, I knelt and pressed the blade into the flesh of the dead man's throat, just beneath the bulbous jaw, cutting deeply through the sinews, sending a torrent of still-warm blood over my hand. I felt the same rush of excitement as when I had gunned down our attackers—but now my heart and soul were wholly dedicated to sawing through dead flesh and bone. I felt utterly dissociated from everything I knew myself to be, free of all restraint, of discipline, of anything that bridled my own inner beast. The bloodlust that had earlier brushed me with its tantalizing fingers now held me in an unbreakable grip.

When the knife blade crunched against the cervical vertebrae, with all my strength I could not push it through, so with my other hand I spread the ruined tissue of the throat, my fingers seeking the join of the two vertebrae. When I found it, I put all my weight behind the knife, and it passed through the spinal cord, completely severing the head from the body. Grasping the head by its wiry hair, I rose to my feet and held my trophy up for the men around me to view. At this point, I don't know if I expected their approval, their rebuke, simple revulsion . . . or anything. But no one had tried to stop me. No one had said a word in the minute or so it had taken me to perform the grisly task. The air was silent and solemn, and I felt three pairs of eyes watching me intently, their gaze bereft of judgment or condemnation. Blood ran freely from the severed vessels and down my arm toward my shoulder.

Giving the head a last look, I drew my arm back and hurled the thing into the trees with all my strength, listening with satisfaction to the dull *thud-crunch-thud* as it hit the ground and bounced several times, well out of my sight. I swallowed hard and took a deep breath, feeling for a moment as if I had somehow sold my soul to the devil.

I vaguely heard footsteps approaching and turned to see Arsenault, Comeaux, Pearce, and Trimble coming up the track with guns at the ready, apparently concerned about our prolonged absence. Gradually, I think I must have begun to return to myself, for the blood on my hands finally struck me as being *wrong*, and my stomach quivered as the men approached, not with horror at the deed I had committed, but in fear of their reaction to it.

"I don't know why I did that," I said softly. "I'm sorry."

"Are you all right, Athos?" Comeaux asked, a little too calmly, his eyes studying the headless body.

I nodded, half uncertainly. "I think so."

Rook looked into the night for several moments. "Doc said he thought these natives were not primitive, but specially evolved. I believe he was right, in a way. I think they must have lived with whatever is on this island for so long that they have been changed by it—physically and otherwise. Perhaps even they were once 'civilized.' "

"What you're saying, Colonel Rooker," Trimble said, "is that if we remain here we will eventually become like them."

Rook shrugged. "We may have even had a head start on them, men like us. Look how quickly we've been affected."

Comeaux's broad face was a clenched fist as he turned to gaze into the black jungle. "Somehow that thing must be destroyed."

"Listen to me," Rook said. "We are soldiers, not butchers. No one must ever speak of this." He turned to his two men and pointed to the body. "Get rid of that thing."

"Yes, sir."

As we began walking back toward the Quonset hut, I fell in next to Rook, remaining silent for several long moments. Finally I said, "He spoke to us in English."

"It did sound like it, didn't it?"

"Just as if he pulled it right out of our own brains."

"If it was English, wouldn't it be more likely that he simply mimicked words he had heard?"

"You don't believe that any more than I do."

He shrugged his shoulders.

"I think that thing out there is somehow getting into our minds," I said. "And these natives . . . they're attuned to it."

"You really believe that?"

"I don't know what else to believe."

We both fell silent, bewildered, frightened, overwhelmed. Still, when we had gathered back at the hut, we put on our most stolid faces and, with an almost tangible air of effort, battened down our emotions in preparation for the tasks that still loomed before us. Rook assigned a squad of men to scour the camp and haul any native corpses to the lagoon, where they would be burned. Any bodies lying beyond the perimeter would remain there, at least till daylight—assuming the remaining islanders did not collect them under cover of darkness. The rest of us would alternate watches through the night; no one would be getting much sleep. Yet, like it or not, the Fighting 39 still had a mission scheduled for tomorrow morning, and come hell or high water, we were going to fly it.

The cleanup detail had just moved out, with Colonel Rooker himself leading them, when a Marine appeared at the door of the hut and called, "Commander McLachlan, ComAirSols is calling."

I followed the radioman to the radio room, where he handed me the headset and motioned for me to have a seat at the console. "McLachlan here," I said into the mouthpiece, once I had settled myself in the chair.

"Lieutenant Commander," came the distant, tinny voice of Colonel Oscar Brice. "I received a message from Colonel Rooker there's been trouble out there. An emergency R4D is set to arrive there at dawn. What's up?"

"A short time ago, we were attacked by a large number of islanders. We suffered only minor casualties, but there was serious fighting."

"What about the other side?"

"Significant casualties, though I can't give you an estimate yet."

"Are your facilities secure?"

My hesitation must have telegraphed my misgivings to Colonel Brice. "You all right, Commander McLachlan?" he asked.

"Yes, sir, I'm all right. But I would say the security of the base is in question."

"Can you elaborate on that?"

I had never lied to a superior officer, nor did I intend to now. Yet I could hardly expound on the thing (the "old one"?) that existed in the jungle—or on the events that had followed the skirmish. An icy lump formed in my stomach as Colonel Brice waited for my answer. "Colonel, the number and strength of the islanders are unknown to us," I said at last. "But we have reason to believe there are more of them, and they are extremely well concealed. My opinion is that the risk of sabotage is high. And we may be subject to additional . . . offensive action."

"Where is Colonel Rooker?"

"Taking stock of our situation and formulating an estimate of enemy casualties, sir."

"Have him call me first thing in the morning. What about your squadron?"

"Secure, for the moment. But given the losses we've suffered in combat, pilots and planes are starting to run thin, sir."

"Noted, Commander McLachlan. I may be able to work on replacement planes and pilots for you in a few days. That's the best I can offer just now."

"Understood, sir."

"Are you and your men fit to fly tomorrow?"

"Yes, sir."

"Good. I'm confident that, between you and Colonel Rooker, you'll have the situation well in hand." There was a long pause, and I wasn't sure whether Colonel Brice might be gearing up to chew me out. I knew him to be a man who abided no bullshit, and I realized that, if I were on his end of the line, I might consider the vagaries of such a report as mine suspect. But, finally, in what sounded like a gentle tone, he said, "Commander McLachlan, I wish I could give you more assurance. My hands are tied, though, as Conquest Island is not considered top priority by the higher brass. I'll do as much as I can for you, all right?"

"Yes, sir. It's appreciated."

"You have another big mission coming up in a couple of days, and I want you to be ready for it. Do the best you can, Lieutenant Commander. There's a lot at stake out here for all of us."

"I understand, sir."

"All right. Be sure and give my message to Colonel Rooker. I'll be talking to you in a day or so."

"Very well, sir."

I signed off, heaving a sigh that was anything but relieved. I had said everything I could and should have to Colonel Brice, and I welcomed his candor; however, as for our situation on Conquest, nothing was even close to being resolved. After what I had seen and heard tonight—and what I had done—how would I be able to face my peers—or myself—ever again?

I had just stepped back outside when I heard a distant, stuttering drone, somewhere to the northeast. It took several moments to realize the sound came from the engines of an approaching Betty bomber.

Washing Machine Charlie.

I lackadaisically walked toward the lagoon, where I saw Rooker and several of his men dragging a few bodies to a pile not far from the water's edge. Comeaux and Arsenault were there as well—their clothes stained with blood—and they casually turned their heads to watch the sky as the plane drew nearer. Our one concession to the enemy's approach was to turn off our flashlights.

When the eggs fell, none of us bothered to so much as duck or even cover our ears. A stick of 500-kilogram bombs hit the beach a half mile from the base, sending up a beautiful plume of flame and smoke that did nothing more than set the branches of several palm trees on fire and upset a few night birds. We watched the flames lick at the darkness for several minutes until they went out.

Washing Machine Charlie finally made his exit to the southwest, chased by sharp, ringing peals of laughter that spontaneously rose from all over the worn, battle-weary airbase—even from my own shamed, tortured throat.

CHAPTER 9

Saturday, November 6, 1943
0320 hours

My eyes opened to a veil of complete darkness, and for many long moments I had no idea whether I was awake or dreaming. My senses told me that I was lying in my cot, for I could hear the gentle patter of rain on the roof of the tent, and, only a few feet away, the rhythmic hisses and groans from my tentmates' throats. Somehow, though, my surroundings seemed unfamiliar and menacing, as if the prosaic sounds to which I was accustomed masked something just beyond the edge of my hearing. I could feel the light, cotton bedsheet wrapped around me, and the coarse, webbed mosquito netting draped over me from the head of the cot. I slipped my hand underneath the netting and reached for my gun on the nightstand behind my head. But when my fingers touched the cool metal, I hardly felt any reassurance.

Something outside was moving.

The rain whispered and pattered through the jungle, but a deep, repetitive undertone insinuated that something of great size was passing among the trees not far from my tent—and coming closer every second. My muscles froze, and even though my heart had begun to race, I could not have escaped my bed if it were on fire. I felt like an insect facing the hovering fangs of a huge spider as it positioned itself to strike.

The sound of movement stopped, but I knew that the unseen

entity remained just beyond the wall of canvas. I imagined that the thing could even hear my heartbeat, which now clanged so loudly it could not possibly fail to betray me.

Then I became aware that my tentmates and I were no longer alone inside the tent. Slowly turning my head, my eyes fell upon a tall silhouette, blacker than the surrounding blackness, standing only a few feet away from me, in all respects featureless, yet immediately identifiable as the dreaded, cloaked figure of my past dreams and visions—the thing that had *almost* appeared on the gun camera film. It seemed to be studying me with its unseen eyes, and after a time, I sensed that it was slowly moving nearer. I automatically attempted to shrink from it, yet my muscles remained paralyzed; only my lungs responded, by quickening my breathing. I tried to lift the gun from the nightstand, but to no avail; I knew from experience that, even if I could fire it, bullets would have no effect on this alien visitor.

The stranger did not speak—not even in its voice that was not quite a voice. Yet words or thoughts, transmitted through the space between us, formed in my brain as a soft whisper.

"Soon I shall give you a gift."

"What gift?" I asked.

"The gift of power."

"We wish nothing from you."

"But it is what you desire, is it not? What is power but freedom from restraint? From guilt?"

The tones in my head seemed hypnotic, relaxing, as if to dull my throbbing sense of imminent peril. The black silhouette had moved very close to me now, and I felt the air growing uncannily cold. Now it seemed as if a deadly viper were closing in on me, its supple, rhythmic swaying merely a ruse to persuade me that I was in no actual danger. But the abrupt revelation of my own vulnerability broke my trance-like state, and I jerked upright in my cot, my hand finally able to move and grasp my .45.

Now believing I was fully awake for the first time, I expected the silhouette to vanish. Yet, for several seconds, it remained, like the afterimage following a blinding flash of light. Then, I perceived that it was leaning forward and over me, and for a scant millisecond, I saw something where its face should have been:

A rounded, black globe, featureless but for a pair of hair-thin, slightly luminous slits that, for a brief moment, offered a glimpse of the truth that hid within: a seething, barely contained inferno that raged as violently as the heart of the sun, a furnace fueled by some dark, unknown force. I felt myself cringing, realizing that I faced the sum-total of all human insanity, somehow bottled up inside this spectral, black vessel.

Inside that thing lay power. Depraved, twisted—and communicable—power.

Its power had been revealed to us, intimately, earlier in the night as we had massacred the islanders. Its madness was our madness. In our fury, we had all but destroyed them, those misshapen creatures that served or idolized the dark being in their own nameless fashion.

We had done only what we had had to do.

"To the victor goes the spoils. In return for my gift, you will share the spoils."

I sat upright in a cold sweat, completely alone in the tent with Comeaux and Arsenault, who seemed to be sleeping peacefully. But outside, the rain had stopped, and the jungle was utterly silent. The insects and night birds had again hidden themselves as something else passed through their domain—this time moving away from our camp.

For a few fleeting seconds, from somewhere far, far away, I thought I heard the cacophonous strains of madly piping flutes.

Then the night again turned totally, maddeningly silent, and, in the aftermath of the dark revelations seemingly couched in a nightmare, I could only lie shivering beneath my covers as if I were nestled in ice water.

Saturday, November 6, 1943
0700 hours

No blaring strains of reveille jarred us from sleep just after sunup; instead, the men on the morning watch came to our tents and quietly roused us, intent on keeping noise in camp to a minimum. Outside, I found a clear, brightening sky and a fresh, salty ocean breeze; to my gradually awakening senses, the prosaic beauty of the morning suggested that the violent horrors of the previous night had been merely a vivid nightmare, and the nightmare only a meaningless illusion. Arsenault and Comeaux dragged themselves from their cots, grumbling with their usual disdain for the hour, neither showing a trace of discomfiture or distress. As they shambled out of the tent and made their way to the head, I found myself trying very hard to believe that our world had somehow returned to normal—such as normal could be in the Pacific theater of combat.

As I gazed at the sparkling tropical dawn, I summoned all my inner resources to drive away any lingering fear from the previous night; I needed to devote all my energy to the tasks that lay in store for us in the upcoming hours and days. My orders for today, which had arrived shortly after my conversation with Colonel Brice, were to lead a flight to Bougainville and hit ground targets near Bonis and Buka. My prediction that we would be flying strike missions had been quickly borne out.

I went through my morning ablutions and got dressed feeling a bit dopey from fatigue, but otherwise more like myself than I would have dared hope only a few hours before. The aroma of frying bacon and eggs wafted from the direction of the mess tent, almost tantalizing, even if their flavor might fail to tempt the palate. I wasn't hungry, however, and decided to skip breakfast. Then, as I started walking toward the operations hut, I heard the distant thrum of engines to the southeast. Making my way past the trees that sheltered Tobacco Road, I saw a distant flash of silver in the sky and realized that it was the R4D coming to haul Willy Vickers back to Espiritu Santo. I trusted he had made it through the night and would make a full recovery at the rear area medical facility.

Looking to my right, toward the maintenance area, where the sickbay was located, I saw two Marines, accompanied by Doc McCall, loading a litter bearing Willy Vickers onto the back of a jeep. He had lost a dangerous amount of blood, and I worried that his attacker's talons might have infected him with God knew what kind of microscopic horrors.

"Hey, Commander McLachlan," came a deep voice to my left. I turned to see a fatigued-looking Major Pearce walking toward me, his forehead bearing a fresh, jagged laceration, apparently from the previous night's battle. "You all right this morning?"

"Tolerable," I said. "You hurt?"

He shrugged. "Nothing serious. I gather your man's going to be okay there."

"I hope so."

"You seen Colonel Rooker this morning?"

"No. I just got up a few minutes ago."

"Me too. He's not over in operations, and he's not in his tent."

A little alarm bell went off in my head, but I forced myself to ignore it, for there were plenty of places the Colonel could be; my nerves were still on edge, regardless of the improvement of my mood. "Down at maintenance, maybe," I suggested.

"Maybe," Pearce said. "Anyway, here's news. The native bodies beyond the perimeter are all gone. They must have been collected during the night. So there's still a fair number of them out there."

"Nobody on the watch saw or heard anything?"

"Not a thing. The bastards are all but invisible."

"Somehow I'm not surprised."

Pearce eyed me with an unusually critical gaze. "I'm sure they hate us for what we've done."

"We didn't start it, Major."

"This is their home. We weren't exactly invited."

"I'm surprised to hear you taking their side."

"I'm not taking their side. But now we've killed a substantial number of them . . . I can't help but expect reprisals."

"We've reduced their strength considerably. They've surely learned that we have superior weapons. I don't think they're in a position to do us any more harm."

"That," Pearce said with a visible shudder, "is exactly what worries me."

I nodded reluctantly, for his meaning was clear. Even if the dark being had appeared to no one but me, I was far from the sole object of its influence. As Rook said, our minds had been touched, but to me, that fact could hardly assuage the burden of guilt. The war with the Japanese had already put our emotions, our self-control, our fundamental beliefs regarding life and death to the ultimate test; the thing on this island, for reasons of its own, was simply exploiting our vulnerabilities.

What is power but freedom from restraint? From guilt?

"You say something, Commander?"

I shook my head. "No. Nothing. See if you can hunt down the Colonel. We have a briefing in fifteen minutes."

Pearce nodded, his eyes still strangely cold. "Commander."

A bit disconcerted by Pearce's unusual mood, I walked to my office, relieved to see several off-duty mechanics standing guard near the barbed wire perimeter. The loud cackling and chirping of the jungle birds and insects reassured me that, at the moment, no undesirable neighbors were lurking nearby. I found Chuck Trimble sitting on the little wooden step in front of my hut, flipping through a folder of the day's notes. His graying hair looked as if it had gone two shades lighter since yesterday.

"Morning, Skipper," he said. "Got our latest recon reports. Looks like the Japs have managed to get a number of transports into Matchin Bay and have dispatched at least one infantry division to Torokina. We're supposed to hit them in transit."

"That could be a tall order if they're beneath the cover of the jungle."

"Well, there's only one road for them to use, and it's relatively easy to spot from the air." He showed me a small chart he had drawn up with the appropriate areas marked. "Based on these reports, it's a simple matter to calculate where the column will be. I'll get you there, all right. All you have to do is shoot 'em up. And with Bonis and Buka neutralized, it's unlikely they'll have any air support."

"It would be nice if we had a few 500-pounders to drop on their heads." I glanced toward the jungle. "And maybe for out here as well."

Trimble chuckled mirthlessly. "Requisition them. Maybe it'll actually go through."

"Maybe even in time for the next war."

I heard footsteps approaching and turned to see Arsenault, Comeaux, and José Rodriguez coming around the corner of the Quonset hut. Rodriguez looked grim.

"Willy Vickers is away," Comeaux said. "He should survive, as long as he didn't get infected by any dread diseases."

"Good," I said. "Mr. Rodriguez, I'm going to give you the number three slot and put Dusty Woodruff on your wing. You don't object to that, do you?"

"No, señor Skipper, not at all."

A few voices drifted around the corner as the pilots began filing toward the hut for the mission briefing. Trimble stood up and dusted off his trousers with one hand, tucking his folder under one arm. "Well, I guess we can get this show on the road. I'll have—"

Trimble's voice trailed away, and he cocked his head. I heard the sound at the same time as he, as did the other men with us: the drone of engines, rapidly approaching at low altitude.

The sharp, distinctive drone of Japanese engines.

Fighters.

"Zekes!" Arsenault cried, scurrying toward the clearing at the front of the hut. The rest of us followed him at a sprint, eyes darting upward to peer through the limbs of the nearest palm trees. For several moments I saw nothing, but the engine sound was growing louder every second. Then a movement at the corner of my eye drew my gaze to two forest-green shapes hurtling over the treetops less than a thousand feet overhead; they must have cruised in under radar, I thought. A few Marines went racing at breakneck speed in the direction of the lagoon, as if competing with each other to get to the ack guns first. Glancing back, I saw the two Zekes swinging into a low, tight bank, just short of the ridge—no doubt to make a run on our Hellcats, which would be lined up on the apron in preparation for the morning's mission.

"Son of a bitch!" I growled to Comeaux. "General quarters!"

He nodded, pulled his bosun's whistle from his shirt, and blew a sharp, warbling burst. Several pilots who were just entering the Quonset hut quickly reversed direction and began running toward the lagoon and the gun emplacements there. I heard the engine of a jeep start up and saw Hoagie Hedgman behind the wheel of the nearest one, waving for men to join him.

"The planes are all gassed up," Hoagie called to me. "Let's go up after 'em!"

"Belay that," I called back. "You'll never make it off the ground. Get down to the line and start shooting with whatever you've got!"

Hoagie's face fell, but he nodded his acknowledgment. Under the circumstances, any plane on the runway was worse than a sitting duck.

I leaped into the driver's seat of a second jeep, cranked it, and shoved it into gear before Arsenault, Comeaux, and Rodriguez had even settled themselves inside. Hoagie's vehicle, loaded to capacity with Cox, Hubbard, Willis, and Woodruff, lurched into motion in front of me. I had just started moving when I felt the jeep rock, and I looked around to see Smitty Hensley's bulky figure land in the back of the jeep, smashing the much smaller Lieutenant Rodriguez into one corner.

"Morning, Skipper," Hensley said, his eyes bright with excitement. "Who opened the door for the goddamn Japs?"

"Where the hell they come from?" Rodriguez asked. "Surely not all the way from Rabaul!"

"They must be, unless there's a carrier somewhere out here," Arsenault said. "Scouting us out, I'm sure."

"With permission to attack, too!"

"They Jap army or navy?"

"Can't tell," I said. I could not see the Zekes at the moment, but the harsh whine of their engines rose above the gruff chugging of the jeep motor. Then, to my dismay, I heard the staccato crackle of machine gun fire that I knew was not ours: the Zekes opening fire on our planes.

"I'm going to take this out of their goddamn yellow hides," Comeaux growled, rising to half-stand in the passenger seat, craning his neck to get a view of the beach beyond the trees to our left. I heard a deep thud and saw an orange flash down by the beach, followed by a billowing mushroom of thick black smoke.

"Christ, they hit something," Hensley called out.

"Get off my foot, amigo," Rodriguez snapped.

"Sorry."

We broke into the clear in time to see both Zekes zoom skyward near the southeastern end of the runway, then bank again to head back toward the Hellcats. Now I could hear machine gun fire from the field, and tracers began arcing toward the attackers, but none came very close. The Zekes remained just beyond the range of the .50 calibers.

About halfway down the flight line, one of the F6Fs was burning.

"Jesus," I whispered, still half-stunned by the surprise attack. We had been so preoccupied by our enemies on the island that we had neither foreseen nor prepared ourselves for an attack by anything other than the all-but-inept Washing Machine Charlie. The last thing we would have expected was a single pair of fighters to fly a long distance just to strafe the base.

Behind us, a deeper, slower thudding commenced: the 20mm, pumping shells at the marauders. I could see bright orange tracers hurtling toward the green fighters, none making hits but coming close enough to prompt the Jap pilots to zoom out over the ocean before making another run on our fighters.

I stomped on the brakes just short of the apron, where several ground crewmen were scurrying toward the burning Hellcat with fire extinguishers in hand. There were two .50-caliber guns mounted behind sandbags off to my right, vacant and waiting for gunners. I took off running toward them with Comeaux in tow.

"Ammo boxes should be under netting behind the sandbags," I said. "Let's get 'em going."

The two Zeros swung back inland to the south, barely crest-ing the lower slope of the mountain as they made their turns, aiming their noses at our flight line. I had just leaped into the sandbag-girdled machine-gun emplacement when I saw one of the Zekes veer toward the mountain's summit, wagging its wings from side to side as if the pilot were attempting to view something below.

Now curious, I watched the second Zeke follow the first, also rolling its wings oddly up and down, its pilot evidently searching for something among the trees on the lower slope of the mountain. The first Jap turned slowly back toward us, but did not appear to be preparing for another strafing run. He had cut his speed significantly, and I now began to have a strange feeling about what was happening up there.

Suddenly, both Zekes turned away from the mountain and began roaring toward our flight line—not to attack, but as if to escape something pursuing them. I watched the leader push his nose down until he was zooming over the beach straight toward me, below treetop level. Comeaux had broken out the box of .50-caliber ammo and was feeding a belt into the Browning, but too late to get a bead on the fighters. The first Zeke roared overhead, and I involuntarily ducked. Then, at the corner of my eye, a bright orange and gold flash lit the sky, and I swiveled around in time to see a mass of burning debris hurtle through the air and fall amid the trees at the base of the mountain, sending up huge splashes of earth, flame, and smoke. It took a couple of seconds for the thunderous boom to reach my ears, and half of forever for me to realize that the trailing Zeke had just exploded.

My jaw dropped. None of our gunners could have shot that plane down. The leading Jap had apparently seen his partner go down in flames; rattled, he wove indecisively, then veered southward to fly out to sea. He lowered his nose and poured on the power, now apparently hell-bent on beating a hasty retreat from whatever had destroyed his wingman. But then I saw tracers rising from the lagoon, and a plume of black smoke erupted from the Zeke's engine cowling. The plane veered wildly back toward the lagoon, barely under the pilot's control.

The fighter was losing altitude rapidly, and it had little to spare in the first place. The pilot tried to bank back toward the flight line—obviously to go out in a suicidal blaze of glory—but he didn't have enough energy to make the turn. He wobbled over the blue water at less than fifty feet, his prop windmilling, then the plane fluttered like a wounded moth and dropped straight down. With a huge splash of white foam, it smashed into the water on its belly, barely a hundred yards off the beach.

From where I stood, I could see the Zero sinking rapidly, but a second later, the canopy flew open and the pilot appeared, struggling to escape before being dragged under. He managed to break free of his harnesses and scramble out of the cockpit just as water began pouring over the sides. Then it was all over for the airplane; its tail bobbed up and down like the tip of a fishing float and then slid quickly beneath the waves, leaving a spreading pool of slick black oil on the surface of the water.

It was just before the plane vanished that I noticed the one distinguishing feature that explained its presence here at Conquest Island.

I grabbed Comeaux by the arm and said, "Drive back up and tell Colonel Rooker we've got a Jap survivor just off the beach. If he's not there, tell Major Pearce. Let's fish this one out."

"Roger, Athos," Comeaux said, never taking his eyes off the distant struggling figure. He hurried to the jeep, started it, and roared off, tires spitting mud and sand. Out in the water, the pilot jerked his head back and forth frantically, obviously uncertain whether to swim toward shore or end it all before we could capture him. The Marines had a motorized launch for picking up pilots who had been forced to ditch near the island, though I doubt anyone had foreseen using it to retrieve one of the enemy.

Rodriguez was staring at the black column of smoke rising out of the jungle. "What the hell knocked that one down?" Rodriguez asked. "It wasn't our guns."

I glanced back at the mountain and—for a brief moment—thought I saw a shimmering heat-haze on the edge near the summit.

I shook my head and turned my attention back to the downed pilot. He was treading water in place, though the current seemed to be carrying him slowly toward us. He knew we were watching him, and I half-suspected he would try to drown himself before allowing us to take him alive. Several pilots had gathered at the water's edge, and I practically had to grab Rodriguez to keep him from swimming out after the Jap.

"Keep your shorts on, José. He's not going anywhere, except maybe three times under."

"He should die, but not like that," Rodriguez said with a spiteful hiss. "What else we going to do with him?"

"Maybe get some information out of him. You see what that plane looked like?"

"A Zeke."

"With a tailhook. It came from a carrier."

Rodriguez's eyes widened. "They're going to attack us!"

"They're getting desperate now," I said, never taking my eyes from the struggling figure beyond the breakers. "They stand a better chance with us than with the Torokina forces. This could be their last ditch effort to save face in the theater."

Arsenault came up behind me, having heard my last remarks. "You might be right, Athos. But I don't think anyone here speaks Japanese. Getting anything out of that character's going to be like drawing blood from a stone."

"You know a few words, don't you?"

" 'Hello,' 'goodbye,' and 'can you direct me to the cat-house?' "

"We'll have to make do with that." Just then, far to my left, I saw the small launch jetting out from the lagoon with two men inside it. As they drew up near the Jap, one of them motioned frantically at the floating figure while the other trained his rifle on him. The pilot obviously was not inclined to allow himself to be captured, and his head slipped beneath the water. For a moment, I thought the first Marine was going to dive in after him—an unwise move under the circumstances—but then the pilot came up again, waving his arms in panic. The Marine knelt in the launch and held out a beckoning hand to the floundering man.

A full minute of indecision passed, and the Jap went under one more time. Apparently disliking the prospect of drowning more than he anticipated, he finally paddled toward the boat and accepted the Marine's proffered hand. The second Marine kept his rifle at the ready as his partner deftly hauled the smaller figure into the launch. Then, once they had the pilot securely in their custody, they turned the boat back toward the lagoon.

"Let's go," I said to Arsenault. "I hope Colonel Rooker has shown up by now." We climbed into the jeep Hoagie had driven down, leaving his group to trudge back up to operations on foot. I drove at breakneck speed up the track and deposited the jeep back at the hut. I saw Comeaux on the path to the lagoon, but when he noticed us, he stopped and waited.

"They beat me to it," he said. "Pearce already had the launch set to go."

"Colonel Rooker here?"

Comeaux shook his head. "Not as far as I know."

"Damn it. Well, come on," I said, leading the way toward the lagoon, where I could see the launch coming in with its new passenger. Pearce and several other Marines were waiting on the beach with their guns drawn. As the small boat putt-putted up to the shore, the muzzles of several more guns trained themselves on the Jap pilot, who clasped his hands above his head, eyes darting apprehensively at his hostile-looking captors. Pearce waded out and grabbed him by one arm, ordering him to get out of the boat. Whether the Jap understood English, I'm not certain, but Pearce's command was unmistakable. The pilot—who looked no older than his early twenties—climbed out on wobbling legs, and then, to my surprise, pointed toward the mountain and spouted a rapid string of Japanese in a high-pitched voice. His eyes gleamed with obvious terror.

"Let's take him to operations," Pearce said. "Maybe we can get something useful out of him."

"What the hell are we going to do with a P.O.W.?" Comeaux asked. "We've got no place for him."

"What do you suggest we do?" Pearce asked. "Kill him?"

For a second, Comeaux's eyes lit up with an uncharacteristic spark, but then he shook his head. "No, of course not." Then, in a lower voice, he said, "Not unless he tries anything stupid."

We walked back up to the Quonset hut, surrounding the prisoner like vultures. Pearce dragged the man inside and sat him down in one of the chairs at the front of the ready room.

"What's your name?" he asked.

The Japanese glared at him, his almond-shaped eyes radiating both defiance and dread, but he did not speak. Finally, Pearce leaned down into the pilot's face.

"Tell me your name," he hissed.

The pilot swallowed hard and then set his jaw firmly, indicating that, despite his fear, he would not cooperate with his captors. Then he raised his eyes to regard a new arrival, and the rest of us turned to see Colonel Rooker stepping into the room, his eyes narrowing at the sight of the Japanese prisoner.

"So, we did manage to get one of them," he said in a low

voice. "Excellent."

"Colonel," Pearce said with a curt nod. "Glad to see you."

"Where were you, Rook?" I asked. "We've been looking all over for you."

"At the cave," he said with a distracted air, his eyes focused intently on the pilot. "Considering what to do about moving our fuel. However, I see now that that is the last thing we actually want to do."

"Perhaps," I said, looking at him curiously. It was hard to feature the claustrophobic Colonel spending the morning in the dangerous confines of the cavern. "I trust there were guards there with you."

"Yes."

I nodded, vaguely troubled by Rook's distant, terse manner. I pointed to the Jap. "Well, we've got him, but it's going to be difficult getting any information out of him."

"Let us see," he said. He motioned for Pearce to step aside and then leaned down to look into the pilot's eyes. "Tell me your name," he growled. Then he repeated the question—but this time in apparently lucid Japanese. *"Na wa nanto iu?"*

The pilot's look of surprise was no less profound than our own. If Rook spoke Japanese, it was news to me.

Slowly, the pilot said, *"Kaigun Shousa Yoshizawa Noboru."*

"Shousa. He's a Lieutenant Commander," Rook said. "Well, *Shousa* Yoshizawa Noboru, you're a poor excuse for a pilot."

My eyes darted between the Colonel and the enemy pilot. "I didn't know you could speak Japanese, Rook."

"I picked up a little at Cactus," he said, not looking at me. To the pilot, he said, *"Dono fune no monoda?* What ship are you from?"

The man called Yoshizawa blinked uncertainly. Rook repeated the question, this time leaning close to the prisoner's face. Yoshizawa looked into Rook's eyes and visibly quailed, as if he saw something terrifying in them. He stammered, *"Ku . . . kuubo Shinkaku de aru."*

"He's from the carrier *Shinkaku*," Rook said, his face alight with satisfaction. He stepped over to the chalkboard and drew a crude circle surrounded by wavy lines, which I realized represented Conquest Island. Then he faced the pilot, motioned expansively to our surroundings, and pointed to his drawing of the island. Then he bent to face Yoshizawa again.

"Show me where your fleet is."

The pilot shook his head. Now Rook grasped the man's shoulder, pulled him out of his chair, and dragged him roughly to the chalkboard. The rest of us simply watched in abject surprise.

"Show me! *Fune no ichi o kaizujo de shimeshitemiyo!*"

Any remaining defiance melted, and he nervously pointed to the upper right corner of the chalkboard. *"Kokoyori gohyaku kiro hokkusai ni itta tokoro da."*

"Four hundred kilometers northeast," Rook said. "That's about three hundred miles, which would put it roughly . . . here." He tapped the designated spot on the board. "And what is the composition of your fleet? *Kisama no buntai, shozoku no gunkan no kazu wa?*"

With a trembling hand Yoshizawa pointed to the chalkboard again. *"Kuchikukan yonseki, junyoukan niseki to, kuubo isseki."*

"Four destroyers, two heavy cruisers, one carrier," Rook translated. His voice coarsened and he said, "And aircraft. How many aircraft? *Sentouki no kazu wa?*"

"Sentouki ga sanjukki to bakugekki ga juugoki."

"Thirty fighters, fifteen dive-bombers. *Shutsugeki yotei wa?* When do they plan to attack us? *Itsu-itsu?*"

Yoshizawa now looked as if he were going to collapse in terror before Rook's glaring eyes. *"Asatte to omou,"* he whispered.

Now Rook's face beamed with satisfaction, his eyes bright

with the distinctive gleam of bloodlust I had seen the night before, when he faced the native we had killed. "The day after tomorrow, he thinks. He's not privy to command decisions, of course."

I gave the frightened pilot a long, appraising stare. He looked too young for such a high rank, I thought. Was the enemy so desperate for pilots they were now making lieutenant commanders out of children?

"He's lying," Pearce said. "Why would they send two planes to attack us more than a day prior to an offensive?"

"They wouldn't expect to lose both of them—or for us to gain any information from one of their pilots," Rook said. "They probably intend to set us off-balance with a few harassment raids, lay off, then hit us hard. These two were sent to gauge our strength and inflict whatever damage they might."

"When their pilots don't return, they'll be the ones off-balance," Comeaux said.

"They still won't believe we know anything," Rook said, staring coldly at Yoshizawa. "Their pilots are trained not to be taken alive, much less reveal any information to the enemy."

"Yet we have a live one and he's talked—such as it is," I said, again gazing at Rook thoughtfully, feeling an inexplicable apprehension in my gut. "I wonder how you were able to pry information from him so easily."

Yoshizawa now looked at me with a look of pleading and said, "*Aitsu ga ore o korosouto shiteiru wakedana. Kono shima niwa, omae no shiranai koto ga aru. Ano otoku wa shitte iru.*" Rattling off several more strings of incomprehensible words, he again pointed toward the mountain.

"What did he say?" I asked.

Rook shook his head. "I'm afraid I couldn't catch much of it."

I had no real reason to doubt him, but I somehow felt he was being less than candid. But then I glanced at my watch and realized we were late for our takeoff; the enemy attack had at least succeeded in buying their ground troops on Bougainville more time. "We're twenty minutes overdue. I'd better inform ComAirSols of our situation," I said, realizing Colonel Brice was not going to like what I had to report.

But Pearce spoke up, "Already done, Commander. Your orders for the morning are rescinded. Colonel Brice will be calling you later."

Now more surprised than ever, I gave Pearce a hard stare. "Well, thank you for letting me know," I said sharply.

"There wasn't an opportunity earlier," he said defensively. "We are rather preoccupied here."

I nodded, half apologetically. At least I had been spared the ordeal of having to report the disturbing news to the boss myself.

Yoshizawa now looked at me again with an expression of humility, his eyes pleading. Again he said something in a quavering voice. This time he pointed to Rook.

I shook my head. "I don't understand. Rook?"

He shrugged. "He said he is glad he did not die in the crash. We saved him."

"Is that it?"

"Best I can make out," Rook said. But again his eyes hinted that he might be withholding something.

"So what do we do with him?" Pearce asked. "We don't exactly have a stockade."

"We'll put him in a tent, under guard, until we can get him shipped out to Espiritu," Rook said. "We can't call another gooney in here under the circumstances, so we'll just have to sit on him until whatever happens happens. Agreed, Drew?" He narrowed his eyes at me.

"It's about all we can do," I said and then turned to

Comeaux. "Okay, let's get the squad together. We're going to see what we can do with the information this fellow's given us."

Comeaux nodded and went off to muster the pilots. Now that ComAirSols had canceled our scheduled mission, I could, at my discretion, organize one befitting our current circumstances. I left the Quonset hut and found Arsenault and Trimble waiting outside. "Aramis, get down to maintenance and have Railroad Bill's crew hang drop tanks on twelve Cats. We need 'em fast. And get an account of whatever damage those bastards caused."

"So we're going up?"

I nodded grimly and looked out to sea. "Yeah. We've got an appointment to keep." Then I turned to regard the shadowed, forbidding mountainside that overlooked our base and wondered if we were at this very moment being watched. I noticed that Trimble's eyes, too, were on the mountain, and his face wore a thoughtful expression that made me wonder if he had not also been party to certain ominous and cryptic revelations in the dark, early hours of morning.

Saturday, November 6, 1943
1230 hours

By late morning, I had three divisions patrolling an area 150 miles north-northeast of Conquest, in the direction that *Shosa* Yoshizawa had indicated his fleet would be. I took us no farther, however, to avoid being picked up on their radar. By now the enemy would have realized the first pair of pilots wasn't coming back; if the fleet was as close as Yoshizawa had said, they might decide to launch a full-scale attack sooner than he'd indicated. I wanted to be ready for them when they came.

My guess was that the *Shinkaku* had been dispatched to locate and destroy Admiral Sherman's retreating task force before it could reach safety. Having failed its primary objective, the *Shinkaku,* already far from its home base, had been ordered to strike the nearest strategic target—Conquest Island.

The Zekes had destroyed two Cats and shot up a third almost beyond repair. By hitting us early with just a single pair of fighters, they had effectively knocked us out of participating in the raids at Bougainville—and driven home the fact that we could no longer operate in the area with impunity. However, they would never expect any of their pilots to have divulged such crucial information about what they had in store for us. The question now was: how could we use that knowledge to our advantage? The enemy had the numbers and the firepower. We had no ordnance that could sink a carrier, much less its escort of heavily armed warships. I had reported our situation to ComAirSols and been given the standard order to hold our position. As expected, no resources could be diverted from Operation Cherryblossom to assist us.

My deepest concern at the moment, though, was with Colonel Rooker. He had changed in the last twenty-four hours, and I didn't think I liked it. More and more, his eyes seemed to be taking on that cold, cunning gleam I had seen during our bloody clash with the islanders. And, somehow, the fact that he spoke at least marginally intelligible Japanese seemed almost too coincidental to me. Yet he had questioned the Japanese pilot and received cogent answers—itself a dubious fact, since prying a name from even the rawest recruit in the Imperial Japanese Navy might be considered a minor miracle.

After three hours, having spotted no sign of any enemy, I led the group back to Conquest and put down, figuring on sending up another patrol in less than an hour. For the first time in recent memory, Railroad Bill saw us land without any damaged planes. But we were bringing home no kills, and we had seen nothing to either confirm or refute Yoshizawa's claims.

The base seemed extraordinarily quiet on this early afternoon.

Dark clouds crawled along the southeastern horizon, but the sun blazed brilliantly overhead. I could hear no activity coming from maintenance, and few mechanics or pilots were in evidence outside their tents. When I reached the operations hut, I saw no sign of either Rook or Pearce, although a Marine guard stood at his post this side of the barbed wire perimeter.

"Everything okay?" I asked him.

"All clear, sir."

"Where's Colonel Rooker?"

"I'm afraid I couldn't say, sir."

Nodding, I turned my eyes to the dark, brooding slope of the mountain, half expecting the all-but-invisible specter to be lying there in wait. To my relief, the mountainside appeared vacant. But I had no sooner turned away than, as if on cue, the jungle fell totally, deathly silent.

I turned around slowly, back toward the mountain, anticipating the thudding sound of distant drums. But none came. Had the surviving islanders gone into hiding? Having failed in their attempt to vanquish us, were they now fearful of their dark god's anger? Something tickled my ears, and after a moment, I detected a low sound rising in the distance: a mournful, if menacing, inhuman moan; a parody of wind rushing through the trees. The sound went on for a full minute before slowly dying away, leaving me again in total, eerie silence.

Jesus, I thought, realizing that the sound had come from the direction of the mountain. The hairs on the back of my neck rose and prickled my skin. I recalled Rook's assertion that the unknown horror might have come from dimensions unknown to us, not outer space but *other* space. This remote island, barely noticed by civilized eyes for perhaps thousands of years, must somehow be the middle ground between our world and that of the black horror. And the cave served as the passageway from one to the other.

257

Bucking my every instinct for self-preservation, I took off at a run toward the cave entrance. Earlier, Rook had gone there under the pretext of evaluating the logistics of moving the fuel. Plausible-sounding, yes. But I didn't buy it.

Something told me I might find him there again.

As I penetrated the shadows of the towering trees, from the direction of Tobacco Road I heard a sudden, sharp noise: a yelp of surprise or pain, quickly stifled; whether human or not I couldn't say. I turned from the path and went tearing through a tangle of brush and creepers, blithely disregarding the less than congenial wildlife I might encounter within. But it was a spidery tree branch that materialized from the shadows above and grasped my throat, throwing me off balance. I dropped to my knees and fought myself free of it, but one of its questing fingers snagged the back of my shirt and ripped it open from collar to belt. With a curse, I shrugged off my aggressor and rose to my feet, but that brief hesitation afforded me a glimpse of a figure some fifty yards to my right—near the last few tents on Tobacco Road. At first, I didn't recognize him, then I realized it was the face of Major Pearce, painted with crimson.

"Major!"

Instead of answering me, Pearce ducked quickly out of sight, and his footsteps went thudding away toward Marine City. I leaped onto the path and galloped after him. At the end of Tobacco Road, a dense row of palm trees grew like a bulwark dividing the sections of the camp, and I had to slow down to thread my way through them; for a brief instant I glimpsed a distant figure running past the Marines' tents. I shouted, "Major Pearce!" but immediately wished I had kept quiet, for my voice echoed eerily amid the trees, accentuating the awry stillness of the atmosphere.

Marine City appeared desolate. A few tent flaps hung open, revealing only vacant quarters. To my left, I could see the huts and revetments of the maintenance area, also empty except for a couple of damaged Hellcats parked for repair. Somehow, I appeared to be the sole human being at this end of the base. Pearce, it seemed, had managed to elude me.

I slowed to a stop and propped my arm against the trunk of a tall palm, panting hard to catch my breath. When my breathing began to slow, I finally heard the first sound of life in the jungle since the unearthly silence had fallen: the buzzing of many flies. I turned slowly to the right, and my gorge rose. A few feet away, lying in a cluster of blood-spattered orchids, was a human head, severed at the neck. The hair was inky black, the face smooth and bronze.

It was *Shousa* Noboru Yoshizawa.

Pearce, I thought. *He must have gone mad.*

But if he was mad, what about everyone else? Could they all have snapped while my flight had been patrolling for the enemy? Where were they?

I thought I had an idea.

Clutching my gun, I turned back the way I had come, until I found a spot where the brush was thin; I left the path and made my way through the trees until I reached the track that led to the cave, coming out at the very spot where we had made our stand against the islanders. Several blackened, skeletal trees stood as grim memorials to the conflagration, and shreds of red-stained cloth littered the ground like grotesque, fallen leaves. A twisted strip of something pink and black dangled obscenely from a strand of barbed wire, and again I heard the buzzing of many flies. Here the air still smelled of blood and cordite. Anxious to leave this ghastly site behind, I pressed on.

Ahead lay the cave. I could see it now: the gaping, black wound in the side of the mountain, its edges overhung by sagging palm trees. The urge to turn and flee was strong, but at the same time, a compulsion to enter the gaping, mysterious mouth almost overwhelmed me. I was being drawn here, it seemed, by some willful force, guiding and directing me from afar. If I continued on this course, I wondered, would I forfeit control of my body and mind? The prospect horrified me.

"*Soon I shall give you a gift.*"

The words rang in my memory like an alarm bell. But I could no more alter my course than I could have restored the Japanese pilot to life; my legs moved automatically, bearing me straight toward the opening in the rock from which I now detected a low humming sound. This was not the voice of the specter, however, but a low, musical droning that issued from the throats of men.

Leading with my gun, I stepped into the opening, and a chill fell over me like a cold, damp blanket, extinguishing the warmth of daylight. No lights were burning inside, but a number of vague, shadowy shapes moved subtly in the pitch darkness, and with a tremor of apprehension I realized that my silhouette against the backlit entrance exposed me fully to those within, so I stepped into the deep shadows.

As my eyes adjusted to the darkness, I made out a number of figures standing in the great chamber, all facing the alcove we had unsuccessfully attempted to seal. Virtually the entire complement of VMF-264 appeared to have gathered here; with them, I saw Rick Bellero, Danny Grogan, Hoagie Hedgeman, and Tank Wickliffe, all of whom had remained on the ground during our morning patrol. None of them paid me any mind; all their attention was focused on the deep recess in the rock. All were humming softly, their voices blending in rich, harmonious tones that seemed to flow with no pauses for breath.

"Hello, Drew," came a soft voice to my left. I turned to see a tall silhouette moving slowly toward me, and I realized that it was Rook. I could not make out his features in the darkness, only his faintly gleaming eyes that appraised me coolly. "I was almost thinking you wouldn't come. But it's right that you're here."

"What the hell's going on?" I whispered.

"We were so wrong. No one here has any reason to fear."

"How can I believe that?"

"It has offered us its gift. Do you remember?"

"I heard something like that—in a bad dream."

"Not a dream; a revelation." His eyes shifted toward the others. "You see everyone here? They have heard it and answered its call. You're here. It has called you, too."

"Rook, we talked about it ourselves. These dreams were hellish things. It—and those islanders that worship it—killed a number of our men. How can you say there is nothing to fear?"

"We were mistaken. Drew, the islanders . . . they were never its worshipers. They were its *jailers.*"

My jaw dropped as an icy blade stabbed the back of my neck. "What?"

Rook's voice took on a faraway quality. "It comes from a place eons distant. Its name—as close as we can place it—is Viran Ghurak. Once it was a king among its own kind. But others desired its power and conspired against it. Eventually, its enemies gathered together and overthrew it, and banished it to this very place. They set guardians against it, both to prevent it ever escaping and to destroy anyone who attempted to set it free."

"The islanders."

"They have been here for thousands of years, holding Ghurak prisoner. In past centuries, natives from other islands came here, but Ghurak's guards destroyed them all. Eventually, outsiders stopped coming altogether, and except for these wardens, Conquest has been deserted ever since—until we arrived and roused them again."

"So they attacked because they wanted to prevent *us* from

freeing this thing?"

"Yes. As Doc McCall himself said, they were specifically designed as killing machines. But their progenitors never foresaw the development of weapons such as ours on this planet. They arrived when the earth was young, and humans were no more than semi-mindless apes. To those long-dead usurpers, we would be as incomprehensible as they to us. But when we came to Conquest, Ghurak saw its opportunity. Through us it has overcome its repressors. Only a few of them are left, and they can no longer contain it."

"Where are they?"

"In the forest. We never found them because, until they awaken, they simply become one with their environment. Then they spring from the earth itself. Truly a marvelous form of life, in their own way. Remember when the islander spoke to us in English? Given time, they would begin to absorb our thoughts, and then they would be able to comprehend us—and defeat us. But Viran Ghurak has seen to it that they were not given the time. It merely wishes to be free and return to its original home."

My knees felt as if they were about to buckle. "So, it used us. It's killed our men and driven us to the brink of insanity."

"It simply ensured that we would destroy the creatures that threatened both it and us. And we have done so. Our minds are susceptible to its influence, whereas the islanders are not. It did what it had to do. But in return it has promised to reward us with great power."

"What power?"

"The power to bring it forth. And to take our own high places as it assumes its rightful role as king."

"King of what?"

"Realms beyond anything we can imagine. Many worlds. Galaxies. Including ours."

I drew in a deep breath, and my lungs nearly burst. "How do you know these things?" I whispered.

His shadowy hand rose and touched his temple. "It speaks to us . . . here. How do you think I was able to communicate with that Jap? It can draw what it needs and then feed it back to another. Imagine an alliance with such power! You yourself have heard its voice, but you do not open your mind to listen. When you do, the fear leaves you. And you come to see the truth."

Several pairs of pale eyes in the darkness had turned to regard me, though the humming did not waver. "Rook, this is crazy. At best, you've been misled."

"You naturally fear what you can't understand—and deny its validity. Simply listen to its voice, Drew. It will explain everything to you. And with the knowledge will come understanding."

I recalled the increasingly cunning looks I had seen in Rook's eyes—and I remembered the cold, calculating way I myself had decapitated the dead islander after the battle. "I understand that this thing drives us with its own will. I've felt it. I feel it now. But you've allowed your mind to be influenced, twisted. These things it has 'opened our eyes to'—they're terrible, vile things. It drives us against our own natures."

"You're quite wrong about that. It does not force us to do anything. It simply breaks down our inhibitions. You're thinking about the islander you mutilated. You consider it immoral only because of an unnatural, learned discipline." Again he tapped his temple. "We are being freed from those bonds. Freed to *power*. What is power but freedom from restraint? From guilt?"

I shuddered at those words, remembering where I had heard them before. "Our discipline is as much a part of us as our basest nature, Rook."

"A part of who we *were*. Now we are transcendent. Tell me you didn't feel the power flowing in your body when you

263

decapitated that creature. That was not wrong, Drew. It was a simply a release of everything you've been forced to hold back. Restraining such a fundamental part of ourselves . . . *that* is unnatural."

"That discipline is all that allows us to live together."

"Then what are we fighting this war for, Drew? Do you believe it's not about power? We're fighting to stop the Japanese, who seek to control their own destiny, by all available means. But power can't be eliminated; it's only transferred. If we win, then not only are we the more powerful, we gain all that had belonged to the loser." He sighed as if he were trying to explain the complexities of the universe to a fidgeting child. "Please, Drew. I understand your difficulty in believing. I resisted the truth to the last. But now I know better, I could never go back."

There was an urgency in his voice now that conveyed imminent danger. He took a small step toward me. I raised my pistol in a shaking hand, but he ignored it; as yet, I could hardly bring myself to shoot him. To deflect him, I asked, "What is the meaning of all this? What are you trying to do?"

He nodded thoughtfully. "Remember the islanders' drumming? We believed they were communicating with Viran Ghurak. But that was not exactly the case. They were using sound waves to drive it back. These images we have seen—the figure on the mountain, the cloaked man—they are only projections of the true being imprisoned beneath this mountain. Until now, the surface of this island has been as far as its reach extends." He pointed to the unseen alcove. "But this cave, this conduit, leads directly to its earthly prison. Our chorus—the vibrations—will finally free it. You see, just as Ghurak is not a being of matter as we know it, the walls that contain it are not entirely physical. Every prison has guards; we have removed them. All that remains is to shatter the last wall that separates it from our world."

"And then?"

He shrugged. "And then those of us who have accepted the new reality will receive our reward. Stay here, Drew. It's not too late for you."

I saw his eyes glaring at me. "No, Rook. You're wrong. It's not too late for *you*. Come with me out of this place."

"It *is* too late to go back, Drew." He turned again toward the alcove and lifted a hand. "See? You see?"

Something at the corner of my eye moved. Almost against my will, I turned and saw a fluttering shadow, blacker than black, like a huge, onyx moth. Heavy, crushing terror fell upon me as the swirling figure emerged into the open, gradually assuming color and shape. As if illuminated from within, crimson, wing-like robes materialized around the spinning form, and as the figure slowed to a stop, a pair of long black arms spread wide in a gesture of greeting. As always, its face—if it had one—was nothing more than a pitch-black hole in space, now and again lit by a pair of pale, greenish slivers that seemed to glare mockingly at me. For a moment, I almost believed I was back in my tent and dreaming, for so many times, this thing had appeared to me when my mental and emotional defenses were at their most vulnerable. But this was no dream, no vision, and even fully awake I felt no less vulnerable. The being called Viran Ghurak—or its avatar—drifted toward the center of the chamber, and the humming voices became a loud, wailing siren.

"It's time," Rook whispered.

"I think," came a sharp voice from behind me, "that will be enough of that."

I spun around and saw two figures coming down the entry-way, dimly illuminated by the distant sunlight from outside. They held rifles at the ready, their shocked faces locked on the strange being that had emerged from the aperture.

"What the hell is that?" Arsenault whispered, poising his gun to fire. Comeaux held up one hand.

"Are you all right, Athos?" he called.

"Yeah," I said, backing away from Rook, toward Comeaux and Arsenault. But the moment I moved, a spike of pain blazed down my spine, freezing me in my tracks. Blood thundered in my ears, and the musical humming rose to an incredible volume, painfully and unnaturally amplified.

"It calls you, Drew," Rook said. "Accept it, and the pain will leave you."

"Only a liar uses pain to sway another to its purpose," I said, struggling to keep from dropping to my knees. "No truth can be served by coercion."

"It can if it is to save you from a worse fate," Rook said, his gaze earnest.

I knew now that he was beyond the reach of logic or the appeal of a friend. Gritting my teeth against the white-hot pain arcing down my back and through my limbs, I backed slowly toward Comeaux, who trained his rifle on Rook. "Colonel, we're getting the hell out of here," he said. "You can come or don't, but if you try to stop us, I'll shoot you where you stand."

"I will not try to stop you," Rook said with an air of sadness. "I'm sorry, Drew."

"Me too, Rook."

The green slits in the abyss brightened briefly and then turned away with an air of finality, as if dismissing a traitor who had refused a final reprieve. The voices in the chamber now rose and roared into a swirling cyclone, no longer sounding human, but bestial. At the edge of my hearing, a distant, windy voice seemed to be struggling to rise above the cacophony, forming unintelligible words; I deliberately shut my mind to it, for the prospect of comprehending its strange but alluring call filled me with cold dread. Comeaux held his rifle in one hand and grasped my arm with his other. I felt a gentle pressure as we began to back toward the entrance.

At the corner of my eye, I saw Arsenault moving slowly but deliberately toward the right-hand wall of the cavern, keeping his rifle aimed directly at the wavering, crimson-robed figure. At the last moment, I realized what he was doing. A second later, a blaze of light flared in the chamber as the overhead bulbs came on, and finally the roaring in my ears began to diminish, becoming once again a chorus of vibrating, humming notes intoned by the seemingly mesmerized men.

In the light, the robed figure vanished—or dissolved, it seemed—and in its place I saw a semi-transparent, charcoal-tinted tendril that writhed and twisted angrily, slashing back and forth in the air like a gigantic, spitting snake. The long, smoky arm extended across the cavern floor and disappeared into the alcove that concealed the small tunnel. I realized now that the image of the cloaked man was merely the tip of some monstrously long appendage that had wriggled up the tiny passage from untold depths below the mountain. The figure had merely been a phantom, an image painted on the canvas of my mind by a shrewd alien hand.

The pain in my body fled like a ghost from the light. "Get out," I growled to Arsenault and Comeaux. "Come on, let's go. Let's go."

We flew through the passage into the blinding daylight. Arsenault let out a gasp, and shielded his eyes with his hand. But none of us looked back as we fled down the track toward operations, chased by the sound of rising, rushing wind. I didn't realize until we reached the Quonset hut that my own gun dangled from my numb, rigid fingers.

"Holy shit," Comeaux intoned. "That was the thing on the film, wasn't it? Did you see what it really was? Holy shit. Holy shit."

"What was going on in there?" Arsenault asked, lowering his

hand and squinting at me. "That looked like most of the damned Marines."

"And some of ours, too," Comeaux said softly.

"What are we going to do? We can't stay here."

"I don't know what we're going to do," I said, propping an arm against the side of the Quonset hut, barely able to support myself on my wobbly legs. I nodded in the direction we had come. "Whatever's going to happen, it's going to be soon."

I heard a growl coming from the track that led to the flight line, and a movement caught my attention. For a second, I had the impression we were going to be attacked by some giant, roaring beast, then I realized that a jeep was tearing up the road at breakneck speed, its tires spitting dirt and coral. I lifted my gun, fearing we were about to be assaulted by someone controlled by the thing in the cave. Then I saw that the driver was Railroad Bill.

The jeep screeched to a stop in front of me, and the big crew chief jumped out with surprising quickness, his arms flailing wildly at the sky.

"What the freaking hell is going on up here? All morning, people coming and going, but nobody talking. Have you people got no goddamn clue?"

I could only give Bill a quizzical look. When he realized I truly didn't have a clue what he was talking about, he shook his head and spat on the ground. "Mr. McLachlan, we're about to be trounced by one hell of a mess of Jap planes."

Now worse than overwhelmed, all I could do was gawk dumbly at him for several seconds.

"Where's the goddamn air-raid alarm? Who's minding the radar? What the hell is going on?" Bill's beet-red face turned from Arsenault to Comeaux to me. "Christ, you're all whiter than a bunch of bleached sheep."

"Bill," I said as calmly as I could. "There's a lot more wrong here than incoming Japs."

He glanced toward the cave track and cocked an ear. "What the hell's that noise? Where's it coming from?"

I started to answer, but my words were cut off by a harsh, rapidly deepening drone that rolled out of the sky like mechanized thunder. The faint chorus of voices from the cave dwindled beneath the heavy roar of airplane engines, and a fast-moving shadow blocked out the sun directly over our heads. Another shadow passed, and then another.

When I looked up, I saw a score of Japanese Zeros soaring over us at 2,000 feet. Behind them flew a dozen Kates with 100-kilogram bombs hanging from their undercarriages. They zoomed out of sight beyond the trees, but the sounds of their engines rose in pitch. They were swinging around to begin their attack.

My feet refused to move, but a few seconds later, I heard a screaming whine and looked up to see a low-flying Zeke explode into view just above the trees, its wingtips flashing. The deafening clatter and clang of bullets smashing into the metal siding of the Quonset hut finally drew us from our dazes.

"Good Christ!" Arsenault cried. "The sky is falling. Athos, tell us what we're going to do."

I looked briefly at him, and then at Comeaux. "What we're going to do is fly. Let's go, gentlemen. This is the Blue Devils' final fight."

Saturday, November 6, 1943
1425 hours

We piled into Railroad Bill's jeep and went tearing toward our parked planes, some of which had already been started by the sparse remaining flight crew. Along the way, we passed several other pilots racing on foot toward the flight line, and halfway there, another jeep full of Blue Devils appeared on my tail, with

José Rodriguez at the wheel. I saw Ensign Kinney hoofing it alongside the track, and as we passed him, Comeaux reached out, grabbed his arm, and deftly pulled him into the jeep, depositing him ungently in the back.

"We're being attacked, sir," Kinney said matter-of-factly, his face an indignant mask.

"So I gather." Then I said bluntly, "Look, I don't know if we'll even make it off the ground, but we have to try. We're in a bad situation that's gotten worse."

"Roger that, Skipper," Comeaux said weakly, craning his neck to peer at the flight line ahead. "Jesus, they're strafing the field."

In the mirror, I saw Arsenault with bowed head, eyes closed, and lips moving in a silent prayer. It was the first time I had ever actually seen him pray.

"Bill, are those planes refueled?"

"Some of them," he replied. "Maybe seven or eight. I've been shorthanded."

"We'll have to make do."

I slammed the jeep to a stop in front of Old Grand-Dad. The men clambered out and began running, and, behind me, Rodriguez's vehicle screeched to a halt, hurling his passengers onto the deck. I saw Penrow, Cox, and Hart scramble to their feet and sprint toward their planes. Directly overhead, a wedge of three Zeros arced across the sky not a hundred feet up, and as they came out of their turn, they cut loose on the nearest Hellcats. I heard a metallic clanging as the bullets smashed home, and a plume of smoke rose from one of the planes a hundred yards down the line. I was now swearing a blue streak under my breath, and as I clambered up on the wing of my Cat, above the rumbling engines, I heard a few additional emphatic curses.

I had just thrown a leg into the cockpit when I felt a hot wind across my face and chest, and I was blown backward into the air; I landed heavily on the wing, and threw one arm out to grasp its leading edge just in time to keep from tumbling to the ground. Only then did I hear the deafening, bone-jarring *boom* and register the huge blast of flame and smoke before me. A bomb had exploded beyond the flight line, in the direction of the runway—a good 200 yards away, but with sufficient force to knock just about everyone on the hard-packed earth off their feet.

I groaned and pulled myself upright again. I knew the chances of getting a plane airborne were somewhere between slim and none. But between the horror in the cave and the raiders in the sky, I decided that, in my last living moments, I would rather confront the latter. That enemy, at least, I recognized and understood.

Thankfully, I had stowed my chute and life vest in the seat; I tugged them on, fastened the chute straps as quickly as I could, and slid into the cockpit. I had no flight helmet, so I just grabbed the radio headset and slipped it over my ears. I saw a ground crewman—Sergeant Shaw—running up to my plane, punching the air with his fist, swinging it in a circle, and then pointing toward the runway to let me know that my plane was fully fueled and ready to go. Small comfort, I thought; when the inevitable bombs fell again, at least the explosion would probably vaporize me instantly.

I maintained the presence of mind to thoroughly check my clocks, as I would before any routine flight. Satisfied, I set the fuel mix to full rich and thrust the throttle forward, which sent my plane bouncing onto the apron. I barreled along straight ahead, with Kinney and Comeaux rolling out just behind me. Just before I reached the runway, I pressed the left brake to make the turn onto the matting, and sudden vertigo seized me as the plane swung into a too-fast turn, the left wheel coming up off the ground and hanging there. The plane jittered for a moment, unable to decide if it was going to flip into a fatal ground loop. At last, the wheel came down again, and I shoved the throttle forward, happy just to have come this far alive.

Old Grand-Dad raced down the runway, and no enemy appeared within my field of vision. But just as my wheels lifted off the ground, I turned to look behind me and wished I hadn't.

Two silver and green buzzards were closing on me so fast and so low I thought they were going to crash into me. Golden tracers began zipping past my canopy, and I heard the clatter of bullets on my wings. Old Grand-Dad shuddered just above the runway, and I thought for sure I was going to plummet. But then the two Zeros roared right past me, too fast to get a solid bead on me. In seconds, they would recover and come around again. I was at this moment more vulnerable than if I had been sitting in the middle of the runway wearing a big target.

I frantically pulled up my landing gear and went into a hard right turn, out over the water, hoping the Zekes were still too fast to pull in on my six. But when I looked up, I saw one of them go over the top of a loop and start to dive right on top of me. His guns flashed, and I saw tracers falling around me like glittering rain.

A bullet smashed through my canopy and hit the metal plate just behind my head. I pulled the stick as hard right as I dared and kicked left rudder. I was only going 150 miles per hour; my wings began to wobble as I side-slipped through the right-hand turn. But the maneuver threw off the Zeke's aim. He zoomed past again, no doubt frustrated at being foiled twice. I couldn't see his wingman; I could only assume he had looped over and was coming up behind me again, unseen.

The tracers I expected did not come, so I took the opportunity to level out over the ocean and start gaining speed. Turning to look back at the field, I could see at least a half-dozen zooming fighters and dive-bombers strafing the operations area, and several more were hitting maintenance. A huge ball of flame erupted from the main hangar, and for a bizarre moment, I hoped that all of the mechanics were in the cave.

A moment later, Comeaux pulled up on my right wing; I signaled him to make a gentle, climbing right turn. If we could grab some altitude without being attacked, we might be able to engage the enemy as more than sitting ducks. Glancing back, I saw two more Hellcats coming to form on me—Arsenault and Kinney.

I led this makeshift but very welcome division in a wide arc back toward the runway, where several more Hellcats were taking off in rapid succession. But then, I felt a chill of horror as I saw three Kates appear over the runway, dive, and release their bombs. Helpless and furious, I watched as the bombs exploded just in front of one of the accelerating Cats, sending it whirling into the air and over the apron, where it smashed to earth in a ball of flames. I didn't know who was in it, but the pilots were starting to chatter over the radio. Somebody called, "Oh shit, that was José!"

"Skipper, where are you?" came Rufus Cox's voice.

"Feet wet, heading toward those Kates," I called back, setting my sights on the nearest of the bombers. "Mr. Kinney, stick tight. We'll take the leader. Porthos, you and Aramis target the other two."

"Roger that."

Livid with rage and sadness over Rodriguez's death, I roared in after the slower Kates, holding my fire until I was close enough to see the face of the rear gunner as he began popping off rounds at me. Not a one came close. I pressed the trigger and felt the plane shake as my guns rattled off their streams of tracers. The converging bullets ripped into the fuselage just aft of the cockpit, and the whole tail assembly broke away and went tumbling earthward. The gunner leaped into space as the foresection of the bomber plummeted, and I saw his chute spew from his pack. But he didn't have nearly enough altitude to bail; his writhing body slammed onto the sandy beach and shattered, and his half-open chute drifted slowly down over him. The pilot rode the wreckage down to its fiery end.

The feeling that spread through my entire body at the death of my enemy would have delighted Viran Ghurak.

"Athos, watch it!" came Arsenault's voice. "Zekes in at eight o'clock high!"

No sooner had he warned me than a hail of tracers flashed past my canopy. A loud *clang-thunk* nearly popped my eardrums, and my plane lurched as if a giant hand had grabbed it in midair. I saw pieces of blue metal spinning into space, and the stick became a bucking beast that refused to be tamed. I pulled the throttle back and desperately twisted my trim tabs, hoping to level out before I went into a deadly spin. I managed to hold the wobbling plane steady, but I knew that the killing blow hung right over my head. All I could do was wait for it to fall.

A Zeke appeared off my left wing—apparently the one that had shot me—but instead of weaving back to fire at me again, the pilot flew straight and level, apparently looking back at something over his left shoulder.

"Jesus God almighty," I heard someone say over my headset. A second later, the radio became a cacophony of near-hysterical chatter.

"What the hell is that?"

"Oh, my God!"

"Turn away, Penrow. Turn now!"

I cranked my head around to see if I could locate what was causing the commotion, but at the moment, the only unusual thing I saw was a Japanese Zero flying slow and steady in the middle of a life-or-death battle. Taking advantage of the moment, I lowered my nose and carefully pushed my plane down under him, out of his field of vision. My controls no longer appreciated being handled, and when I throttled up again, the engine torque nearly dragged me into a nasty spin. I had apparently lost a good section of my rudder and probably an elevator.

I would be lucky to survive the next few minutes. Even if I wasn't attacked again, I might not be able to keep my stricken fighter under control.

"Jesus," came Arsenault's voice. "Skipper, you're clear. But just keep going. Don't try to turn, whatever you do."

"What is it? What's going on?" I demanded.

"Listen to Aramis," Comeaux said. "Just keep flying."

Muttering a curse, I nudged the stick to the left, pressing hard on the left rudder pedal, which resisted angrily. My left wing dipped, but didn't pull me over. Now when I looked back, I caught a glimpse of what I thought was a huge column of smoke rising from the island. It was only when I managed another few degrees of turn that I was able to see clearly what had upset the men and cost a Japanese fighter pilot a ridiculously easy kill.

Above the mountain, a pillar of dark haze climbed into the sky, its pinnacle far higher than any of the airplanes. It had a vaguely human form, with a tall, narrow torso and spindly arms, which extended from its sides and wavered in the air as if to aid its balance. Atop it, a huge, bulbous sphere was forming even as I watched, and like the avatar I had witnessed so many times on the island, this monstrous thing exuded cognizance, an awareness of everything and everyone about it, down to the slightest man. At its feet, a huge mass of smoky tendrils swirled and writhed like great serpents, spreading through the jungle and reaching all the way into the burning operations center. The edges of the giant silhouette flashed with crimson fire, giving it the appearance of a black figure wearing a brilliant red cloak.

Slowly but inexorably, Viran Ghurak was clawing its way into this world. In my mind I could hear the wailing of voices in the cave as their insane chorale mounted toward a crescendo.

A trio of Kates came bearing down on the giant figure—to press an attack, I realized. Their guns flashed, and one of them, which still carried its payload, lowered its nose to make a low-level bombing run. It sailed over the treetops at high speed, and just when it looked as if it might collide with the shadowy shape, it released its egg and veered away quickly. A second later a huge, golden blossom of flame erupted at the thing's base, and tongues of fire lapped up its sides as if it were coated in oil.

If the thing were moving from its distant, unknown realm into our physical world, I wondered, might it not be subject to the natural laws that governed the existence of every living thing on our planet? I watched with a tiny but rising glimmer of hope as black smoke from the blast rolled up and around the vast figure—which for a moment seemed to waver and flicker, as if on the verge of collapse.

But it did not fall. As the smoke from the explosion cleared, the living tower shimmered briefly and then stabilized, shrugging off the impact the way a man would dismiss the slap of a child's hand.

But it *had* been affected. And when I saw two vics of Zeros swing around to make a frontal attack of their own, I found myself urging them on and wishing them success.

But the Zeros' tracers sprayed into the black mist without apparent result. One of the vics banked away at high speed, but the leader of the second pulled his nose up, apparently in an attempt to fire at what he took to be a more vulnerable segment of the giant body: its head. His wingmen followed his lead, but the leviathan rose higher than they could climb. They loosed a few futile shots and then fell away, recovering quickly and banking into a retreat where they could gain some altitude.

Sharp pilots, I thought, realizing that facing them in combat would be a challenge at the best of times.

Just then, one of the giant black arms lashed out with shocking speed, curling directly into the Zeros' flight path. Too late, the leader realized his predicament and tried to roll out, but the lashing tendril swept through the formation like a whip, scattering the planes like toys. All three fighters came apart, and the pieces went whirling to earth like glittering confetti.

My stomach went cold. As I was witnessing this spectacle, my plane had been gradually turning toward the giant, all but beyond my control. I pulled the yoke to the right and stomped the right rudder pedal—too hard, for my right wing dipped and nearly pulled the plane into a deadly spin. I somehow got the plane level, but I was still on a collision course with the towering horror. Sweat began to trickle into my eyes, for I had little hope of avoiding the same fate as the now-dead Japanese pilots.

"Athos," came Arsenault's voice. "You need to bank right."

"Working on it," I growled. "You guys break off, don't stay with me."

"Just turn your damn plane."

I heard Jimmy Penrow's voice on the radio. "Okay, we're making a firing run. Cox, take left, Albanese, take right. Stick tight."

At the corner of my left eye, I saw a blur of blue, and I turned to see Penrow's three Hellcats banking hard toward the shape. They were fast and climbing, and it looked like Jimmy also meant to target the head. But the figure seemed to have grown even taller in the last minute or so, and the Cats didn't have enough speed. Still, they pressed their attacks, and as they closed in, their guns unleashed simultaneous streams of tracers that arced up and into the cloud of shadow. They fell far short of their marks. Like the Zekes, they fell away dangerously close to the rising figure, and I caught a blur of motion as the bulbous head tilted down as if to gaze at them in amusement.

The great arm again swept across the sky; Albanese and Cox, who had come in slightly lower than Penrow, dropped their noses and pulled out of harm's way with a split second to spare. But Jimmy's plane disappeared in a fiery flash as the shadowy appendage sped through space like a black tidal wave. After the arm passed, not even a piece of wreckage remained to flutter back to earth; the Hellcat and its pilot were vaporized.

"Jesus God almighty," came Comeaux's voice.

Now another group of Japanese came roaring in, firing madly at the thing. A few blue planes appeared among them, and there were no exchanges of bullets between friend and foe. There was only human against invader, and I saw a Cat—Hensley's, I thought—with two Zekes covering his wing. They soared in firing, their tracers hitting their marks but without effect.

Moments later, they too were swept from the sky without a trace.

I was manipulating the stick and rudder pedals as gingerly as I could, and Old Grand-Dad was finally responding enough to pull me away from a head-on collision with the monumental giant—which seemed to be gradually losing its hazy contours and becoming more solid. I perceived now that it was gazing directly at me, and an icy blade of terror penetrated my chest. Yet from Viran Ghurak, it was not a sense of anger or hate I detected, more of disappointment, as if it regretted what it must do since I had declined to pledge myself to its service. But power belonged to *it*, and I had no doubt that it would reach out and smite me with no more concern than it had when it destroyed those anonymous Japanese pilots—men who had given their lives for what they saw as the greater good, regardless of their previous intentions.

If Viran Ghurak bore sheer power against its enemies, its attackers bore against it the better part of valor.

Far to my left, I saw a black arm—easily a half mile long—

swing out and break up a formation of Zeros. Two of them disintegrated; one burst into flame but did not explode. I watched it arc downward, trailing black smoke, toward the base of the mountain and the writhing tendrils at the monster's feet; a second later, the Zero disappeared in the jungle and exploded. And then I saw a strange sight: like the flickering image on a movie screen when the film slips from the projector sprockets, the huge silhouette seemed to flash in and out of existence, there one second, gone the next.

After a few moments, the giant figure reappeared, again only semisolid, as it had appeared when I first saw it. And in that moment, I think I understood what had happened. Our attacks were all wrong.

"The cave," I called on my radio. "There's still people in there generating sound waves. That explosion interrupted them. We have to target the cave."

"Athos," came Comeaux's quiet voice. "Regardless of what's happened, those are still our men in there. They're Americans."

"Maybe," I said. "But they're no longer our friends. They're not the people we knew."

"Are you sure about that?"

I shook my head to myself, remembering my final confrontation with Rook. He was misguided, obviously influenced by the power of an alien force beyond anyone's comprehension. But he had been rational. He had not been a complete stranger to me.

"No," I whispered. But then I remembered Major Pearce, his face painted with blood, the mad gleam in his eyes. He had savagely killed our prisoner in cold blood. "But it's the only way to stop it. Someone has to do it."

The towering figure had completely re-formed, and it seemed to bristle with malevolent energy, now infuriated by the hurtful blow against it. I saw its massive, globular head roll in my direction. And as if it had identified its one true enemy, its arm began to reach for my plane. I was no longer heading directly toward it, but I could not escape its long grasp.

"Athos, look out!" Arsenault cried.

I desperately pushed the stick forward, no longer caring how damaged my plane might be. My Cat bucked and groaned in protest, and all my strength barely forced the nose to go down. The wind began to roar past the canopy as my speed increased, and a weird, piping shriek reached my ears. When I glanced up, I saw a huge, onrushing wave, like a solid wall of pitch-black smoke. In seconds, I would be swept into oblivion, and there appeared to be no way to stop it.

"Push over, Skipper," came Ensign Kinney's thin voice. "You can do it, just push hard over."

Something in the young man's voice gave me a surge of confidence, and I shoved the yoke forward as hard as I could. As if something had snapped, the stick unfroze, the nose went down, and my controls seemed to at least partially respond again. My elevators had not been destroyed but jammed by an obstruction, which now had worked itself free.

When I looked back up, I saw the giant arm passing high above my head. I was clear!

But then I heard a roar and a crackling sound in my headset. Arsenault and Comeaux simultaneously cried out in shock, and I saw something blue flash past my right wing.

"I'm hit," came Kinney's calm voice. "I'm going in."

"Mr. Kinney, pull out," I replied, my voice cracking against my will. "Try to get it back under control."

"Missing half a wing," he said. "Engine's burning. No way I can bail."

I rolled my Cat to the right; it still wobbled precariously, but I was no longer in danger of going into a sudden spin. Kinney's blazing Hellcat was arcing toward the island, trailing sparks, smoke, and debris. Indeed, he was way too fast and low to bail.

"It's been an honor, Skipper," Kinney said. "Thank you for having me in your squadron."

Somehow, Kinney was keeping his plane from plummeting straight down. He maneuvered as best he could toward the airfield, descending all the while. Then, when he was over the runway, no higher than a thousand feet, he aimed his plane toward the base of the mountain.

"Skipper," said Comeaux. "Get away from the island. For God's sake, let's get out of here."

"Yeah," I said, kicking my Cat around to the left, heading east. "Everyone back out of here, right now."

"Roger that, Skipper," came Albanese's voice, followed by a couple of more anonymous acknowledgments.

I looked around once and saw the monstrous arm sweeping back across the sky in my direction again, now a long way off, but still a potential threat. I lowered the nose, poured on the throttle, and soared out to sea, keeping my head turned toward the island. My view was distorted through the curved Plexiglas behind me, and I completely lost sight of Kinney's rushing plane.

But a second later, I saw a brilliant gold flare spreading past both sides of my canopy, and I banked left to get a better view.

Kinney's fatally damaged aircraft had driven right into the hidden cave entrance and torched off 10,000 gallons of 100-octane avgas. The blast was blinding, and I had to shield my eyes; I barely missed ramming Comeaux, who had also turned to gaze at the scene of unbelievable destruction. The spreading ball of orange flame consumed two Japanese Kates that were still buzzing near the foot of the towering giant.

"Only Kinney could have known precisely where to hit," Comeaux said softly. "He did what he had to do."

"God bless his soul," Arsenault added.

"You magnificent little bastard," I said. "D'Artagnan."

As I watched the roiling fireball spread toward the heavens, I heard a distant, muffled *vroom-doom,* gradually rising and diminishing, finally drowned by the roar of my engine. But huge billows of flame and smoke seemed to pump endlessly from the mountainside, engulfing the monstrous black shape that now flickered and flashed like a broken film image.

"He did it," I said. "He's won."

A huge column of black smoke climbed slowly into the sky, eventually dwarfing even the fading silhouette of Viran Ghurak. A thick black pall spread over the jungle and beach, expanding farther and farther until I could no longer see the runway. Trees were burning all over the island, and the mountain itself resembled an erupting volcano. But as the pillar of smoke began to thin and spread westward on the afternoon winds, I saw very clearly that the colossal figure that had dominated the sky no longer existed.

Gone. Vanquished. If not dead, then condemned again to its eons-old prison.

But at such cost: the lives of so many of our friends—or men who had once been our friends. Driven by impulses not of their own making, they had pledged their allegiance to something from another world, a thing that must have promised them more than they could have dreamed in this life. I chose to believe that they had been deluded, and could not be held responsible for their actions. I remembered the terrible power that had gotten inside my head; if I had not been away from the island when it exerted its most potent influence, perhaps I, too, would have been among them.

I dared to turn my plane back toward the island, for I knew that we still had friends at the airfield, Chuck Trimble and Railroad Bill among them. The idea of losing them broke my heart. But as I closed in at less than a thousand feet, it became plain soon enough that no one could have survived. The entire

base was a mass of raging flames, and wreckage from maintenance was strewn all over the runway. Between the Japanese attack and the explosion of the fuel depot, the whole southeastern
end of the island had become an inferno. Confirming my fears,
I saw a few burned and broken bodies lying on the beach at the
water's edge; no doubt, they had tried to escape to the safety of
the water, but had been caught by the blasts. Mercifully, I could
not recognize any of them from this altitude.

I still had to fight to control my plane, for the rudder was still
shot, and I did not dare get any closer to the island. As it was,
the air was thick with smoke, and visibility was getting worse
and worse.

"What do we do now?" came Comeaux's voice. "We can't
land here."

I looked at my fuel gauge. I still had half the auxiliary tanks
and most of the main. "Those with fuel can head for Munda.
Everyone check in, please."

I got a count of eight: Arsenault, Comeaux, Albanese, Cox,
Hart, Hubbard, Willis, and Woodruff. Hank Hubbard and Tubby
Willis were flying planes that had not been refueled prior to
takeoff; they probably only had a few minutes' flying time
remaining.

"Just call for a dumbo for us," Hubbard said. "We'll settle for
ditching."

"Tubby?"

"Agreed, Skipper."

"All right, then. We head for Munda. I'll get on the horn for
a dumbo. When you go down, I'll call in the coordinates."

It was a solemn and silent group that turned eastward from
the burning island. But a few seconds later, Rufus Cox let out a
holler. "Skipper, we have another survivor."

I looked left and saw a straggling Hellcat trying to close in
our formation. It was Max Collins, and I saw him pointing at

his headset to indicate his radio was out. So I was going home with nine.

But we were in for another surprise only moments later. Not far behind Collins's plane, I saw another dark shape approaching—slowly, as if to join up with us. I could tell immediately it was not one of our F6Fs.

"Bogey at seven o'clock," Comeaux said, late for once with his observation.

"Got it," I said. "He doesn't appear to be attacking. Hold formation."

Slowly, the new plane gained on us, maintaining a wide buffer zone to my left. But as it drew nearer, I saw that it was indeed a Japanese Zero. As the pilot cautiously guided his fighter closer to my left wing, I realized it was the same one that had shot me up during the battle.

Anger flared like a grenade in my gut, and I nearly forgot the critical damage to my plane, coming dangerously close to initiating an attack. I checked myself in time, and I gave the Japanese pilot a long, hard stare.

His eyes met mine, and his hand rose in a salute; he flew alongside me for what seemed like hours while I regarded him silently. Finally, I brought myself to return the gesture. Thus released, he nodded grimly at me, then snapped into an instantaneous bank to the left and soared out of sight, to rejoin whatever might be left of his own squadron. I watched the Zeke shrink rapidly in the distance and finally disappear against the smoky backdrop on the horizon.

I found myself *almost* hoping that he and his surviving comrades made it safely back to the *Shinkaku*, which would be waiting for them somewhere north of the now-dead Conquest Island. For now, our differences seemed trite, indeed irrelevant. Together, his countrymen and mine had faced a common enemy and emerged far from unscathed, but by all accounts victorious.

Perhaps when the impact of the extraordinary events of this day had faded in memory, as the impact of even the greatest events will, we would meet in combat another day.

Ten minutes later, Tubby Willis's engine sputtered and died, its fuel spent. Comeaux, Arsenault, and I followed him down in his long glide. He opted to put the Cat down in the ocean rather than bail, which he did successfully. The F6F skimmed over the surface of the azure water, then dropped in with a huge splash of foam. Willis popped his canopy, scrambled out onto the wing, and inflated his tiny, one-man life raft; he was safely in it when we left him. I called into ComAirSols at Munda and gave his approximate coordinates; happily, I was told that there was a rescue sub thirty miles to the north, which could speed to Willis's position within a couple of hours. I warned them that there might soon be another downed pilot in close proximity.

Sure enough, not five minutes later, Hank Hubbard's Cat gave up the ghost and started down. But it had taken some damage during the Japanese attack, and Hank opted to bail rather than glide to a water landing. I saw his chute open and he drifted slowly down to the water. When he waved at us from his life raft, we climbed again to 5,000 feet and continued on our way to New Georgia, still a half-hour distant.

Behind us, the sun had begun its long descent toward the western horizon. Even from here, many miles away, a thin black plume and a dark haze remained visible in the cobalt sky, and I could scarcely keep myself from looking back every few minutes, half expecting to discover something poised to snatch us from the sky before we could reach the relative safety of the Munda airbase. Finally, though, when I glanced back, only clear sky and empty ocean met my searching gaze. Soon I picked up chatter on the radio from the operations at Munda, a prosaic if oftentimes urgent vocalization of the ongoing struggle we faced in the Pacific theater. Such a small thing, it seemed, after the threat that just a few men, both American and Japanese, had confronted and overcome.

Operation Cherryblossom was still going on to the northwest, and the New Georgia forces remained a fundamental element in the overall strategy. I announced our arrival so that we would not find ourselves intercepted by a group of antsy fighter pilots, and we were given clearance to land immediately. As we descended toward the field, a flight of Marine Corsairs passed us to the north, climbing to their cruising altitude, and off to the south, a division of USAAF P-38s was circling to set up a landing approach just behind us. In a way, I found all this hub-bub and activity comforting, for it assured me that even here, so far across the ocean from our homes, the long arm of what we termed "civilization," with all its connotations, good and evil, still reached.

But less than 200 miles to the west, unknown to the good people swarming in the air and on the ground ahead of us, at a bleak, obscure spot of land rising from the ocean, it ended.

I led my flight down to the runway and touched down just as a light spring rain began to fall on the field. Munda Point, not unlike Conquest, had at one time been a forward field, barely separated from the wilds of the New Georgia jungle. Now, with the Japanese having been routed, it was a bustling hub for the Allied air forces, and soon, I knew, it would be considered a rear staging area as our northward push took us to Torokina and beyond.

As I taxied off the metal-matted runway onto the earthen apron, I could see before me a cluster of makeshift barracks, a tall control tower, and a Quonset hut, which I assumed was the operations center. A number of plane captains stood ready to assist the pilots and secure the airplanes, and one of them directed me to steer into a slot next to a group of Corsairs; once I had parked, he clambered up on the left wing and gave me a cheerful thumbs-up.

Once I had slid the canopy back, I found myself so weak and washed out I could not even rise from my seat. The young man helped me unfasten my harnesses and then offered me his hand; I gratefully accepted it, and with a soft groan I hauled my brittle bones out of the cockpit.

"Rough time of it, eh, sir?" the young man said.

I nodded. "Lost a lot of friends today, son."

His face turned somber. "I understand, sir. It's some war."

I looked into his youthful, brash, but naïve eyes. "You don't know the half of it."

I carefully lowered myself to the earth and propped myself against the side of Old Grand-Dad until my knees felt that they could support my weight. For the first time, I was able to look over the damage to my Hellcat, and the extent of it thoroughly shocked me.

The entire rear section of the fuselage was riddled with bullet holes—apparently from the Zeke's 7.7mm machine guns. If he had hit me with his cannon, I would have been blown from the sky. But when I looked at my tail section, I nearly swooned. The upper half of the rudder had been shot away, and the lower portion was barely hanging on. Fragments of it were still lodged between the elevators and foresections of the horizontal stabilizers; apparently, a larger piece had completely jammed the elevators until my efforts at the controls finally worked it loose. But both elevators were half-shredded, and I knew that nothing short of a miracle had kept me airborne.

I owed my life to God and the Grumman Ironworks—the perennial claim of just about any Hellcat driver.

"Hey, Athos," came a low, weary voice, and I turned to see Comeaux and Arsenault shuffling toward me on weary legs. To my dismay, Arsenault's forehead was bleeding severely; he had ripped off his shirtsleeve and wrapped it around his head, but a thin trickle of blood still ran down one temple.

"I'm all right," he said with a weak smile. "Got sideswiped by a small bit of ammunition that lost its way."

"He did more damage to it than it did to him," Comeaux said, the shadow of a smile on his face.

Arsenault gave me a long, thoughtful look. "You all right, Drew?"

I think it was the first time he had ever used my given name. After a few moments, I said, "I reckon I am."

For an endless time, none of us could say a word. We merely shared long, soul-searching looks, which could only be understood by comrades who had lived through an extraordinary, life-affirming ordeal.

None of the base personnel approached us. I think they recognized our need for a few moments of uninterrupted sharing. And I don't think any of them would have begrudged us a few tears, although not a one of us wept. None of us was willing to open the floodgates, for letting out the pain allowed in the horror.

Finally, with our arms around each other, we began to walk slowly toward the operations hut. Once, I glanced back toward the ocean and saw that, in the west, the clouds had converged into a ghastly black column with a bulbous crown, backlit by crimson rays from the late afternoon sun. A quick mental calculation placed the image directly in line with Conquest Island.

When I turned away from the sight, I did not look back again. Beneath that cloud there were too many friends. I could not handle the reminder, for I knew I would be seeing their faces— and the faceless thing that had destroyed them—for a long, long time to come.

POSTSCRIPT

My final, official report of VF-39's departure from Conquest Island states that on Saturday, November 6, 1943, a large force of fighters and bombers from the Imperial Japanese Navy carrier *Shinkaku* attacked our field. Due to a technical problem, the base radar never detected the intruders; therefore our fighters failed to intercept them. The extreme number of American casualties, both in the air and on the ground, was attributed to the effectiveness of the enemy attack overall, and the catastrophic explosion of our concealed fuel depot, most likely caused by an errant but (for the enemy) fortuitously placed bomb.

My recommendations for Air Medals for several of the men, and the Distinguished Flying Cross for Ensign Elmer Kinney, to be awarded posthumously, were all accepted without question. I was not surprised to learn, however, that VF-39 would not be reconstituted and redeployed—in spite of the squadron having set one of the most impressive records of air-to-air kills in the theater. The surviving pilots were transferred to other active squadrons, and I accepted an assignment as flight instructor, stateside, at Pensacola Naval Air Station.

As for the events in the closing months of 1943, I have satisfied myself by committing them to paper and leaving them there. I often wonder what actually became of that eldritch horror on the island—and where it originated in the first place. Had it actually been destroyed? Or merely banished, to again lie in wait for individuals who might be manipulated and coerced into bringing it fully from its nether world into our own. If our good Colonel Rooker's words were true—and I had no doubt that they came directly from the source—then the future that was averted when Ensign Elmer Kinney destroyed the human beings who sought its freedom would have proven dire indeed.

And now, in light of the discoveries made shortly after our evacuation of Conquest Island, I am even less certain of Viran Ghurak's fate than when we retreated from that blazing inferno, after the towering horror had vanished for the final time.

We abandoned Conquest on the afternoon of Saturday, November 6. At dawn on Sunday, November 7, a flight of PBY Catalinas, escorted by Marine Corsairs, flew to the island in hopes of finding survivors. To the shock of all, the entire island had vanished from the surface of the earth.

All that remained at the location was a steaming, bubbling ocean, and a large amount of floating debris. The rescue planes discovered no life rafts or other vessels by which any survivors might have escaped to safety. Thus I am assured that the only Americans who left Conquest Island after the Japanese commenced their attack were the ones who flew out with me.

In the years since the cessation of hostilities between the United States and Japan, no Japanese source that I am aware of has ever mentioned the events of that day. A few combat reports retained by the Japanese government and private individuals make mention of a successful raid by forces from the *Shinkaku;* none make reference to any unusual circumstances.

In light of the new discovery, the official report concerning VF-39 was amended to indicate that the fuel depot explosion might have been a result of unforeseen volcanic activity. This theory also explains the island's cataclysmic destruction and has been officially logged as if it were fact.

My guess—my hope—is that the actual truth will never be discovered.

But I will never forget what I know to exist beyond the shaky reality that we human beings believe ourselves to be firmly in control of. I fervently hope that, to the end of my days, this comfortable illusion, however marred by war, human frailty, and endless suffering, is never shattered.

Davis "Porthos" Comeaux, after a six-month assignment as flight instructor at Los Alamitos Naval Air Station, was transferred to the elite VF-20 aboard the U.S.S. *Enterprise,* where he scored four more kills in aerial combat. However, on December 14, 1944, while flying with Lieutenant Alex Vraciu over Leyte Gulf, he was shot down by Japanese antiaircraft fire. His body was never recovered, although years later his dogtags were sent home by unidentified Filipinos. Sadly, I only had the opportunity to see him once before his untimely demise, and even then, not one word about our experiences on Conquest passed between us. During my military career, I allowed few people to get very close to me; in wartime, friendship is a dangerous investment. But with Comeaux I took that risk, and despite his absence, I consider it one of the best risks I ever took. I will always miss him.

Jasper "Aramis" Arsenault, after a long rotation to administrative duty at Pearl Harbor, also served another combat tour, this one with VF-30 aboard the U.S.S. *Belleau Wood,* where he scored six more kills—five of them in a single mission, on June 22, 1945, in the Battle of Okinawa. Just before the end of the war, he was promoted to the rank of Commander. After the war, Arsenault settled in Las Vegas and became an ordained minister. He retired to a small town in the Pacific Northwest after breaking the bank at the El Rancho Casino in 1959. Since our respective retirements, he has visited me on those occasions when he has a hankering to travel. As with Comeaux, he has never broached with me the subject of Conquest Island. And in these, his twilight years, he absolutely hates to fly.

ABOUT THE AUTHOR

Stephen Mark Rainey is author of the novels *The Lebo Coven, Balak,* and *Dark Shadows: Dreams of the Dark* (with Elizabeth Massie); three short story collections; and over eighty published works of short fiction, which may be found in magazines and anthologies such as *Cemetery Dance, The Best of Cemetery Dance, The Book of Dark Wisdom, Strange Tales, October Dreams, Miskatonic University, Robert Bloch's Psychos, The New Lovecraft Circle,* and many others. For ten years, he edited *Deathrealm* magazine, and in 2004, he compiled an anthology of reprinted stories, titled *Deathrealms,* for Delirium Books. He has also edited the anthologies *Song of Cthulhu* for Chaosium and *Evermore* (with James Robert Smith) for Arkham House. Mark lives in Greensboro, North Carolina, with his wife Peggy and three critters of the feline persuasion. Visit Mark on the Web at http://home.triad.rr.com/smrainey.